SWORD OF DELIVERANCE

Curt & Jana,

Faith is a risky business, but then again so is fear.

Grace & Peace

11-18-16

SWORD
OF
DELIVERANCE

DOUGLAS J TAWLKS

MOVEMENT PRESS
CALIFORNIA

Sword of Deliverance
By Douglas J. Tawlks
Copyright © 2016

The Defenders of the Breach Series
Book 1   Defenders of the Breach
Book 2   Sword of Deliverance
Book 3   Coming Soon!

History and Background
For more information about names of characters, roles and history depicted in Sword of Deliverance and Defenders of the Breach, go to...

www.defendersofthebreach.com

All rights reserved solely by the author. The author guarantees all contents are original and do not infringe upon the legal rights of any other person or work. No part of this book may be reproduced in any form without the permission of the author. The views expressed in this book are not necessarily those of the publisher.

First Edition August 2016
Published By Movement Press, California
ISBN 978-1-4951-3509-5

PRINTED IN THE UNITED STATES OF AMERICA

DEDICATION

I dedicate this book to the memory of my stepfather, Allan G. Tawlks, the man we called "Dad." He was a man who deeply loved my mother, my siblings, and me. His life was a great example of a heart willing to take the risks required to live the adventures life has to offer. He was not afraid to go after the things he loved, and we were fortunate enough to be on that list. I thank the Ancient of Days for allowing us to share life and family with him. I miss you, Dad, and look forward to sharing my books with you when I see you in heaven.

ACKNOWLEDGEMENTS

There are so many people to thank for their support in this project. Unless you have written a book, you have no idea the sacrifices that have to be made. No great accomplishments are made without a team. First I thank Shari, my wife, who in countless ways is the strength and foundation of who I am. I love you, Babe. I also thank my daughter Krysta for her dedication to this project as an editor and her keen insight into writing fiction. My sons Kyle and Jarrod also have my gratitude for their support and excellent suggestions to the story line.

Thank you to my strategic marketing guru Bralynn Newby of Message Mosaic who is a wiz when it comes to building a brand. To Rose Campodonico for her excellent cover designs and to Annette Anderson for her gifted work in content editing. Finally, heartfelt gratitude is offered to all the Defenders fans for their love of the characters, the stories and the messages in these books.

PROLOGUE

With great effort and the help of his two aids, Graybeard finally reached the top of the stone steps leading to the tomb of the kings of Talinor. He paused to catch his breath before entering the chamber. When the door creaked open, the smell of stale air and dust assaulted their senses. The younger of the two aids coughed, then he sneezed and quickly covered his face with his robe. He then took hold of Graybeard's arm to help him into the chamber. The second aid held two torches to push back the darkness in the room. The old Prophet shuffled across the floor to stand before the memorial altar of Kem Felnar, the first king of Talinor. The tomb was modest by kingly standards. Several layers of dust covered the wooden box that sat on top of the stone table in front of the altar. Only the prophets and those they chose to accompany them were allowed in these sacred rooms. Graybeard had not been in this place since the burial of Kem Felnar. That seemed like several lifetimes ago.

He reached for the box to brush away the layers of grime on the top. A golden eagle was at the center embedded in the wood. Below it, written in the elfin tongue, were the words: All honor be given to the Ancient of Days. Light comes to darkness and darkness cannot overcome it.

Graybeard paused before continuing the task he had come to accomplish, which was to open the box and retrieve its contents. As he ran his fingers over the eagle, he began to tremble. Memories flashed from the past, beginning with the early days of the reign of Kem Felnar until the current reign of King Shandon. When he came to more recent times, he paused to picture the battle of Talinor from two years ago.

He felt a twinge of shame as he remembered how weak he had been in the days leading up to that battle. The whole kingdom had all but lost its faith in the Ancient of Days, and he felt he was chiefly responsible. His own leadership and faith had been weak.

Although he was weak, others had been strong. The young cupbearer, Cyle, had led the Gap Warriors back to Talinor to fight in the void against the shadow wraiths. Through his journey, Cyle had discovered that he was a Gap Warrior. He thought of Lena, the Intercessor, who in the face of impossible odds never seemed to lose faith. In the end, Talinor defeated the massive Boogaran horde and the shadow wraiths. While the Gap Warriors fought the spirits of darkness, the dwarves, elves and the Talinor warriors fought against flesh and steel.

It is never one standing alone that brings the victory, thought the Prophet. It is the many united in faith against the enemy. They had all played a part in defending the Breach.

Graybeard breathed in deeply and grabbed the latch on the box with his gnarled hands. He fought against the searing pain in his joints as he worked to pry open the lid. One of his assistants reached to help him. "Stop," he warned. "Only a prophet is allowed to open this vessel."

The hinges creaked as he pushed it open to reveal its contents. On a bed of dark blue velvet lay the sword of Kem Felnar. He reached down to pick it up, and as he did, he almost fell backward to the ground. His aids steadied his faltering frame.

He knew his time in this world was coming to an end. Not only was his health failing him, his mission in this world would soon be accomplished. There was one more thing he needed to do before he left this life. Sadness welled inside at the thought of an ending of an era. He looked up at the altar before him and prayed softly, "To whom shall I deliver the sword?" Then he paused to listen for a response. His question was met with silence.

SWORD OF DELIVERANCE

Defenders Of The Breach Saga

CHAPTER 1

The fluttering of wings disrupted the comfort of dreamless sleep. Piercing light exploded into blue sky as a majestic eagle soared high overhead, carried along by the thermal winds between billowing thunderheads.

Startled by the images in his mind, he awoke from his temporary refuge of sleep; eyes swollen, pressing to open as the enveloping cold came back with a relentless reminder that he was not in that place of beauty he once called home. Disappointment flooded as he realized he was not in Talinor, that far away land where he grew up thriving in its freedom and beauty. A wet prison cell deep within a dank dungeon was his existence, where even his dreams could not save him from its taunting. Each new day brought unspeakable despair, tearing away at the corners of his fragile faith. Damp and dank, the cold stone beneath him that had become his bed was the first thing to assault his senses, quickly followed by the smell of that horrid stench caused by the remains of human waste. In the beginning, the smell had caused him to wretch almost daily, making it hard to keep what little food he ate in his stomach. It was just one of the things that he had grown accustomed to behind these prison walls.

Gerrid pulled his weak frame up to face an empty cell and, like every other day, he reluctantly began to pray, mostly out of habit formed of devotion to his faith, which now hung by a fragile thread like the scabs on his body. For two years and seventy-five days, he had been in this wretched hole, and each day seemed to grow longer than the last one. Then he remembered that before he prayed, he needed to perform his morning ritual of exploring his own body for signs of infection or teeth marks on his skin from the rats that would visit him during the night scavenging for nourishment. Their chewing on his flesh would usually awaken him, but sometimes he would sleep through it, especially when he had returned exhausted from the torture chambers. The little varmints were getting more aggressive lately, coming in the light of day. He hated them but couldn't blame them. They were hungry just like he was, and sometimes they were the only company he had for days.

Gerrid's body was a pale image of what it once was, having lost over fifty pounds. His strength was virtually non-existent. Living on the slop they called food provided little nourishment. Recently, he had briefly seen a reflection of himself in a window while walking to his torture session. He didn't recognize himself, and it wasn't until the next day that he realized it was his own image in the reflection. Something about the eyes looked familiar… Nothing else.

His prayers seemed to grow shorter and shorter as the days grew longer. It was difficult to reconcile his condition with his faith. He had been challenged in this dark place to the point of utter ruin. How could his God let this happen? He was convinced that he had come to this land for all the right reasons. It was all so clear at one time. He had received a vision similar to the one in his dreams. The great eagle had crossed the sea to Abbodar, and it was there that he believed he was to go. And he did. Full of faith and promise, he left behind so much of who he was to fulfill a mission he believed in, only to end up here in this light-forsaken realm. He had come here to this country to share the message of hope, the message of the One Faith, but it was much darker here than he had ever anticipated, it was a country with ancient roots in the darkest of magic and a history of ritual sacrifice.

Two years ago when the soldiers came and arrested him, he was leading a small community of believers at the edge of the city. Not long after Gerrid came to Abbodar, he discovered a small group of followers committed to the One Faith, living in obscurity. There were several religious sects in Abbodar, but there was only one religion recognized by the Abbodar governing rulers. It was called Terashom, named after their ancient gods of fortune and pleasure. Any religious sects outside of Terashom were free of persecution as long as they had incorporated Terashom into their own belief systems, but not the small group of forty adults and several children that Gerrid had discovered when he first arrived in this kingdom. The group quickly embraced him as their leader, and he offered them hope in a time of persecution. Arresting Gerrid was another way of punishing the group that had been labeled the Dissenters. Commoners and the ruling officials treated them as outcasts and made it difficult for them to live peacefully within the city limits. After Gerrid's arrest, most of the small band of the believers scattered without his leadership and left for more remote regions of the kingdom, seeking to escape further persecution in Abbodar.

Gerrid rose slowly from the damp stones beneath him, attempting to minimize the piercing pain in his side. Due to the torture he endured at the hands of his enemies, he was forced to learn different ways of breathing to minimize the pain they inflicted. Torture had become a regular part of his life since being imprisoned, and he often wondered why they didn't just send him to the arena to have him sacrificed to the Terashom gods or let him battle against one of the arena warriors. Over two years of imprisonment had taken its toll on him, draining him of his strength. He knew he would die if he were given the chance to fight, but he was a warrior. Death was something that warriors accepted, so he prayed that some day he would have the chance to battle for his life even if it meant certain death.

They had stopped asking him questions during his torture sessions. Now they just inflicted pain, and they appeared to enjoy hurting him. For some dark reason they found pleasure in his torment. In the beginning they would ask him questions about the Dissenters and about his faith, but he gave them nothing.

He would rather go to the arena to fight and face death there than wither away to nothing and die a victim's death while his strength wasted away. Even though had he walked away from the life of a warrior where he once served as the chief commander of the Talinor military, he believed he still had enough fight in him for one last battle. The thought of dying a passive death sickened him and deeply offended his warrior sense of nobility.

A few small cracks filtered light from above, bringing in precious little fresh air, while the smell of urine and feces canceled out any hope of enjoying it. What possible purpose could there be in this imprisonment? The doubt tore at him and he tried desperately to hold onto his faith. He did at first, but with the passing of time and the suffering he had to endure in the torture chambers, he felt that he was losing grip on hope. It was still there, as weak as it was, barely hanging by a thread. Even though he thought of turning away from that faith, he knew he would not, because there was no other place he could take his heart. He had walked away from his faith once before, as did most of his fellow countrymen. Talinor had slowly fallen from the great One Faith that it had been founded on. It was during the second war against the Boogarans, when the Gap Warriors had returned to Talinor, that he reclaimed his lost faith. He had witnessed the power of the One Faith, and it was enough to bring his heart back to what he once believed in. And it came back like a firestorm seizing every part of his life, so real and alive within him. Gerrid fought to keep the flame burning inside, but his memories of Talinor seemed like a distant tale, no longer real to him. And where had his faith led him, but to this dark place of hopelessness and despair where he could only wait, as he always did, for the passing of another desolate day.

Saltwater spray mixed with the sea wind and gently caressed Lena's face. Standing at the bow of the little ship, she looked out over the mild ocean swells as the horizon slowly brightened with the approach of a new day. This small space at the front of the bow had become her war zone, a place of intercession. Before the light of each day she made her way to this place where she would intercede. It was what she knew and what made her feel the most alive. Sea gulls fluttered overhead, and below a school of dolphins frolicked in the frothing wake of the Talon as she sliced her way through the crystal waters of the Sea of Baddaris.

Lena could not remember the last time she had ventured this far away from the walled city of Talinor. She loved her home, and at her age she was content to spend her days there interceding. Her king, Shandon, was dying and soon a new king would be chosen. She regretted not being there to witness it. A cloud of sadness pushed inward as the fear of never returning to her homeland gripped her heart. She had no way of knowing the validity of the impressions that haunted her thoughts of not returning, but she had a strong notion she would not see her beloved Talinor again. That brought a sense of fear and grief that she had not felt in a long time.

Lena's thoughts drew her back to what had brought her to this place as she recalled the day her dear friend Graybeard the prophet came to her late one night. She had been out walking the streets of Talinor, as was her custom, interceding for her kingdom. It was an unseasonably windy evening when she felt a presence that startled her. Quickly, she looked up to see someone approaching her from a distance. Out of the darkness a figure emerged, moving slowly in her direction. The moment she realized it was Graybeard, a pang of fear vibrated through her spirit. A late night visit by the prophet could only mean something was wrong. Lena held herself in check, not wanting to jump to any conclusions.

"What is it?" she asked softly.

"What, no words of greeting for an old friend?"

"My apologies Graybeard. It's just that I know you have not been well lately, so this visit must be more than a hungering for freshly baked bread."

"Well, now that you mention it, would you have any on hand?" Graybeard coughed at the end of his sentence.

"I'm sorry my friend, not tonight. Jef came by earlier, and as you know he can eat a battalion's share of rations. I regret that I have nothing to offer you. Please don't keep me in suspense. I know you are here for a reason, and I'm sure it's not warm bread."

"Of course. My apologies. I have grown quite fond of your

bread, as have so many others. You can't blame me for trying."

Lena just stared at the prophet. She loved feeding her friends, but now all she wanted was to hear what the old prophet had to say.

"I am dying," said the prophet with a hint of pleasure in his voice. "The time of transition has come."

Lena didn't have to ask what he meant by transition. She understood the progression of things. Graybeard was speaking of passing on his mantle of prophecy to another for the next generation.

"Surely you are not here to give it to me?" asked Lena suspiciously.

Lena interrupted, "but what can I do, but pray?"

"There is a journey involved, and I want you to accompany me. I dare not go without an Intercessor. I would like Jef to come with us as well. As you know, two are always better than one."

"What kind of a journey and how far?" asked Lena defensively. "I haven't traveled in ages. Look at me. How can I take on such an assignment?"

Graybeard ignored her last question. "It is time for me to bring the prophetic mantle to the next generation prophet. I don't know who that is. All I know is that we must travel west across the Sea of Baddaris to the lands beyond. That is all I have for now. I know not who is to receive the mantle, but as you know matters such as these will bring resistance from dark realms and there will surely be intense battle over this."

"West across the sea to the lands beyond. Are there any there who follow the One Faith?" asked Lena.

"Of that I am unsure. What I do know is that we must leave at daybreak."

"Daybreak. How can this be? How can I possibly—how can we possibly be ready?"

"King Shandon has prepared a ship for us and a crew. I have already spoken to your friend Jef, and he is prepared to join us. The time is now Lena. The darkness is already gathering against us." Lena stood stunned to silence by the prophet's words. Too old, she thought, Too old for this.

Before she could speak Graybeard offered, "There is one more thing. I am bringing the sword."

Lena stumbled back, "No." It was all she could manage to say as she found herself gasping for air. She knew the prophet was referring to the sword of Kem Felnar, the founding king of Talinor and the first and last war prophet to carry the weapon. The sword, also referred to as the sword of deliverance, had not been carried since the time of his reign. It had lain in the vault of the kings under Talinor guard since his death. This could only mean one thing. A time of great conflict was coming. Grief overwhelmed her. She had seen enough war and bloodshed to last for a lifetime. Lena had hoped and prayed that she could finish her life out in peace, walking and praying in the streets of Talinor. That hope was quickly fading.

"Lena." A familiar voice pulled her back from her thoughts. It was Jef, her friend and self-appointed protector. "You were lost in thought."

"Hi Jef. How did you sleep last night?"

"You know I don't like the open water. It was a difficult night for me, but I managed. Like most foot soldiers, I prefer the feel of solid ground beneath my feet."

"A few more days and we will make land. Then you can catch up on your sleep, dear Jef."

"What are your prayers telling you Lena? I've seen the restlessness in you of late."

Lena paused looking up at the sea before answering, she felt the wind as it blew the hood off of her head. Jef could see a sadness in her eyes that was not uncommon to Intercessors. "It is difficult to put into words Jef. All I know is that we are headed into darkness unlike any I have ever known, and the thought of it brings a heaviness to my heart that oppresses me."

"How can I help, Lena? It is difficult for me to see you this way."

"You are a good friend, Jef, and I thank you for your concern. You can join me in intercession and bear the load with me. It is the weight of it that calls me here daily to intercede. Surely you must feel it too?"

"I do. I think it has more to do with my sleepless nights than the sway of the ship."

"Then let us intercede together and share in the battle that lays before us."

The passing of days lost all significance to Gerrid as the setting and rising of the sun was something he had not seen since coming here. New sores appeared on his body, reminding him that he was still alive. Life in this prison cell had become so mundane, so numbing, that he found himself touching the walls just to make sure it was all still real. A movement of the cell door startled him as it screeched open on its rusty hinges to reveal one of the guards.

"It's time," said the guard.

Gerrid thought he detected a hint of sadness in his voice. He cringed knowing exactly what that meant. It was time for another torture session. The guard led him down the familiar hall toward the chambers where they would work their dark magic on him. It was painful but not as much as it had been in the beginning. Using the dark arts to inflict pain was a common practice in Abbodar, but his torturers would complain because the effects of the magic often fell short of their expectations when they used it to torture his broken body. They were relentless and it seemed as if they were trying to break him. It all seemed pointless to Gerrid. There were questions at first when it all started two years ago. Mostly about the believers he met with. What was his role? What were their intentions? Now they seemed to be testing him to see if they could break him with the magic. When the magic failed to break him they resorted to physical torture, and it was this one thing that kept Gerrid hanging on to his almost forgotten faith. The fact that the dark magic could not break him was just enough to stir up a defiance in him that seemed to sustain the small amount of hope he had left.

As they walked down the cold damp hallways and past the other prisoners, a familiar voice spoke through bars to him as he staggered by. "Hold strong, friend. Hold strong." Gerrid didn't know the man's name and he was unable to see him, but for the last year the man had been there with the words of encouragement each time he passed. On Gerrid's return to his cell the man would say, "Another day. Another day to live my friend."

The familiar stench of human waste and the sounds of men groaning greeted Gerrid as he entered the chamber. Robed priests moved about the room attending to their duties with their acolytes following closely. Several candles casting a dim glow off the gray walls provided the only light in the room. Many souls had been tortured, and he was just another in a long line of victims. The infliction of pain wasn't always about extracting information out of prisoners, although that was the case for most. It was also about experimentation. The king's son Vanus frequented the chambers, primarily because he was fascinated by all forms of magic—especially its use as a method of torture. Some believed he was obsessed with the black arts, and the chambers provided him with a kind of laboratory to experiment on prisoners. The atrolis was a talisman of the dark power and the primary instrument deployed for torture. It was comprised of a small staff with a red stone affixed to its end. When applied to the flesh of a man or woman, it could bring not only physical pain, but also a wretched kind of soul torture that would leave most of its victims writhing in unspeakable agony. For some, it ended in death. It was rumored that the Maggrids, the chief priests of Terashom, had been assigned to the task of developing the atrolis's powers through researching the black arts, conjuring and other unknown rituals they practiced in darkness.

Soul torture administered through the atrolis was a relatively new form of magic that, when applied, penetrated the defenses of denial that shielded the heart from its own depravity.

The priests who developed the instrument did not know that this would be the end result of their conjuring. Once they discovered its capacity, they continued to use it if for no other reason than to exercise its power over its victims, driven by a sadistic pleasure to torture. It stripped away the veil of self-denial and revealed the raw depth of shame and evil that the heart tended to bury away in the subconscious in an attempt to escape the torturous shame of deeds done in darkness. Once the defenses were gone, the victim was left with no hope of redemption, only the overwhelming weight of condemnation. Many died, but those who survived its wrath returned from their sessions drooling and muttering unintelligibly, never to recover.

Gerrid would never forget the first time the torturers touched him with the atrolis. He was strapped to a post by the arms and feet when they placed the device against his chest. The searing pain shot through him. A fierce burning sensation penetrated through the muscle down to the bone as dizziness swept over him, and a wave of nausea welled up in his stomach until he vomited all over himself. But that was just the beginning. The physical pain alone was enough to break most men, and for many it ended in death.

What came next was a level of emotional agony that he could have never imagined. Gerrid lost all sense of his surroundings as the fire that coursed through him erupted into a dark revealing. Later he would call it the unveiling of his deepest shame. The evil in his own heart was uncovered, leaving him without the restraint of denial and the rationalization that most used to avoid that evil. After years of self-deception, all that he was and had been came crashing in on him. For the first time in his life he was seeing himself as he truly was. Every dark and unspoken deed he had ever committed or imagined crawled up out of the hole of his soul and taunted him with the truth of how utterly despicable and degenerate he was. In that deepest and darkest realm of his being, the voices of doom and condemnation cried out to him from beyond the fog and mist. Demons appeared in blurred images taunting him—their voices screaming at him that he was condemned and that there was no one that could rescue him from his own depravity. It had suddenly dawned on Gerrid that this was the place he had heard so much about, that place where evil resided in untold numbers and unmeasured power. This was the void and the atrolis had brought him to its very threshold, threatening to leave him there with no hope of redemption.

It was during this first torture session with the atrolis when it happened. Vanus, the king's son, watched with great pleasure on Gerrid's suffering. For Vanus, it brought him the greatest pleasure to torment the stronger prisoners. So many of them were weak of body and conviction. He had watched as the atrolis brought the weaker ones quickly to unspoken ruin and left them lying on the ground in a pathetic heap of insanity covered in their own urine and muttering unintelligible words as foamy saliva frothed from their mouths. This brought Vanus great pleasure, but nothing like the pleasure it brought him to break a stronger man like Gerrid, a man he knew to be a person of virtue and faith. Vanus viewed Gerrid's faith as a form of magic, and he obsessed about defeating it.

Vanus wouldn't admit it to himself, but he feared the good ones, the strong ones. In fact, he despised them, and he viewed Gerrid as one of them. Not only did Gerrid have a deep conviction of faith, he had also been a great warrior at one time, a leader of warriors, but Vanus knew that he had since left that life behind to live a simpler life and serve among his own followers. The thought that any man would surrender power and position to choose the life of a servant disturbed Vanus deeply. If he could break Gerrid, then in some twisted way Vanus could prove to himself that this mysterious faith, and the ones who followed it, was a farce, and that his own system of faith was more powerful.

Vanus looked on with great interest and anticipation that first time the atrolis was used to torture Gerrid. His hopes were high that this would finally be the time of his demise. When touched with the talisman that first time, Gerrid writhed in unspeakable physical pain that seemed to penetrate every area of his being. When it reached the level where he thought he could stand no more, it began to fade, and his body went limp. The moment between the pain and what came next was too brief. He was quickly overtaken with unspeakable shame and hopelessness. He felt himself cowering from the scowling phantoms of the dark void as they closed in to taunt him.

The last of Gerrid's courage melted away into self-loathing as the demons called out to him the sins of his past while implanting pictures in his mind of the deeds he had done and the lives he had scarred by his actions. The despair and shame assaulted him to the brink of insanity when suddenly he saw a stirring in the void around him. Shadowed figures appeared from the mist. Blurred to his vision and barely discernible, he could see them shrouded in the swirling fog as they encircled him in ghostly movements. The mysterious beings appeared carrying weapons as they stood with their backs to him, encircling him in defensive formation, facing the demons and holding them at bay. Then a sound like thunder and the rush of a mighty wind blew through the wretched fog of condemnation and shame. At first Gerrid thought it was another assault coming at him so in desperation he forced the only prayerful words he could utter from his lips, "Help me." It felt like his words reverberated through the void. He thought he heard demons in the distance screaming in pain, but he was sure it was just his imagination.

A familiar screech echoed from high above, and then a flutter of giant wings rustled about him, covering him with a fresh wind. He knew that familiar sound, and it brought even more shame to him. It represented a kind of purity and nobility that did not belong in the presence of his utter depravity, and he felt the urge to cower and flee. The sound of blades and cries of death surrounded his fallen form. Through the covering wings, Gerrid could see warriors battling as blades and arrows struck the attacking demons with deadly force. A peace beyond comprehension flooded his being, and a thought borne on the wings of clarity pierced his heart. You belong to me. Nothing will befall you without my permission. Suddenly, a commotion to his left and a crashing sound disrupted his brief respite of peace. A powerful shadow wraith, covered in scales and wielding a double edged sword, broke through the barrier of defending warriors. The demon's blade arced out with deadly ambition slicing within an inch of Gerrid's throat. Then another blade, fast and sure, sliced into the attacking wraith, sending a fountain of sparks outward. The dark creature howled in pain before it faded backward into the void.

The defending warrior that had dispatched the demon, turned to charge back toward the battle. He paused, looked back at Gerrid, and spoke, "My apologies, good knight. Some of them prove to be a little more difficult than others."

"Bixby," a voice shouted through the clamor, and then a young elf girl appeared holding two sparkling swords and a flute strapped to her back. With the fire of battle in her eyes, she fought for breath. "Come with me now. We need your sword. There are six of them pressing through on the other side."

Bixby smiled at Gerrid, and he suddenly recognized the two Gap Warriors from the Battle of Talinor. They disappeared behind the covering of the surrounding wings and were gone.

When Gerrid woke up he lay sprawled out on the floor face down, and when he opened his eyes, the first thing he saw was the disappointing gaze of Vanus who was hoping for a complete breaking of his prisoner. But what the king's son saw he would never forget—Gerrid's eyes looking up at him as he lay shaking and gasping for air and struggling to regain his senses. When Vanus saw the look in Gerrid's eyes, he felt rage stirring inside, and at the same time, disarmed. There was no anger, no bitterness in his eyes. This once great warrior and commander of the Talinor armies who had withered to skin and bones fearlessly looked into Vanus's eyes. No prisoner had ever done that after the atrolis had been applied. Somewhere in those eyes that met his, Vanus thought he detected mercy, and it offended him. He wanted to turn away because mercy was something that was both alien and threatening to him personally. It was not something he sought or gave to others. Vanus found that he felt intimidated by it all. As the feelings increased, he had to exert great effort to wrest his own eyes away from Gerrid's gaze before he was able to walk slowly from the torture chamber into the outer hall. The Maggrid priest administering the torture looked on in confusion at what had just happened, but this was not the end of it for Vanus. There would be many more torture sessions for Gerrid to endure because now the king's son was even more determined than ever to break the former leader of the Remnant. He told himself that it was the last time he would look this prisoner in the eyes, but in the days ahead, no matter how hard he tried, he could not forget the disquieting mercy in that gaze. How could he have possibly known that it was the look of forgiveness?

CHAPTER 2

When the knife sliced across the guard's throat, his body fell toward a rack of weapons that would create far too much noise and alert the others. The killer, cloaked in darkness, was void of emotion as hands struggled to direct the limp form away from the rack and toward the earth for a softer landing. Success. The dead guard crumpled into a lifeless heap. His killer then wrestled him into a wedge in the wall where he would not easily be discovered.

There was no moon this night, and the sky was covered with dark clouds. Mist had already invaded the streets of Abbodar, creating the perfect scenario for an assassin to come and go undetected. The king's quarters were well guarded on most nights, but tonight was different. Tonight he was being honored by his own emissaries for the successful siege of Caragis, a small kingdom to the south. A seemingly worthless piece of land except for the fact that its location was strategic for trade, Caragis just happened to be in part of Abbodar's plans for total domination. It was once a peaceful kingdom, but now it was a kingdom under siege. That night most of the guards had been re-positioned to serve at the ceremony, leaving the royal quarters with limited protection.

This would be easy, thought the killer. Scale the tower and wait in hiding until the king returns to his room, and then take his life after he has fallen asleep. There would be no hesitation and no second thoughts over the spilling of his blood. This assassin's heart was as dark as the night sky that surrounded it, and like most assassins, emotion just got in the way when it came to killing. This was an assignment like so many assignments before it. Death would come to the victim after he slept, and life would not return with the morning dawn.

Two more guards were dispatched with ease, then dragged into the garbage heap just outside the kitchen. No one would find them until their bodies began to stink of death. So far it had been fairly routine, and scaling the rock walls was not a problem either. The rocks protruded just enough to provide finger and foot holds adequate for a skilled climber to make the vertical climb three levels to the king's quarters. Now, it was just a matter of waiting inside the room until the monarch fell asleep. Once the king was eliminated, there would still be the benefit of the cover of night, making it easier to sneak past the guards, across the rooftops—beyond the walls of the palace and into the massive city where it would be simple enough to blend in. For now, it was a waiting game. Time would pass slowly until just moments before the kill, and then time would stop completely, if only for a moment. It always did the moments before a life was about to be terminated.

Vanus resisted his father's order to release prisoners, but he knew it was necessary due to over—crowding caused by an influx of the latest prisoners of war. He had tried to talk his father, the king, into building more cells and increasing the guard, but the king had other concerns related to the current military campaigns being waged by Abbodar. Building a bigger prison was not one of them. Now that they had taken siege of Caragis, they needed to make room for the newer prisoners of war. Every couple of months during times of war there was a releasing that took place and this time Vanus had decided to include Gerrid in the release. The prisoner was an uncomfortable reminder to the king's son of his inability to break him with the Atrolis. He could have held him and sent him to the arena at the celebration of Terashom, but he was too weak to fight and though he had not broken his spirit, he had broken him physically. Vanus doubted that the prisoner would ever recover from his current condition caused by two years of prison and intense torture. He had wasted away to a shell of the man he once was.

Gerrid heard the shuffling of boots before the cell door creaked open. The guard looked in and simply said, "come with me."

Gerrid followed him and several other prisoners down the dark and musty hallways for several feet before the guard took a direction unfamiliar to him. They walked through what appeared to be catacombs that reminded Gerrid of where the Remnant had once gathered in the past in secrecy to worship. He was almost exhausted to the point of not being able to take another step when they stopped and the guards struggled against two massive doors. He could hear the grinding of metal hinges as they slowly creaked open. A flood of light washed over the group of squinting prisoners who held their heads away from the piercing pain of the streaming sunlight that flooded the dark room. The guards forcefully pushed them outside, like cattle being led to slaughter. At least two hundred of them, tattered and torn shuffled through the doors, some barely able to walk, including Gerrid. One prisoner grabbed hold of his shoulder to assist him. He looked familiar. It was the man in the halls who had encouraged him on those days he was headed to the torture rooms. Out of breath from the walk from his cell, he would not have made it on his own. Once the last prisoner had been pushed out into the open streets, the metal hinges moaned once more as the guards closed the massive doors, slamming them shut.

Silence. For a few moments they all stared at one another and at the massive door. One bewildered prisoner walked over to it and with all the strength he could manage, knocked on it crying out, "Let us back in, please. Let us in." Then he fell to his knees sobbing.

Gerrid looked and saw in the distance the bustling city beyond the palace walls and wondered if he should look for his friends, the followers of the One Faith. It had been over two years since he had been with them. He knew that the tide of opinion had long ago turned against them. Their ways were detested in this land of shadows. Abbodar's ruling class preached tolerance of different faiths and belief systems, but for some reason they were unable to accept this one group.

A faint thought occurred to Gerrid that he should move out of the sun before it burned his skin, which hadn't been exposed to its rays in over two years. He made his way to a cluttered alleyway where the buildings cast enough shade for cover. As he leaned against the cool walls, he started to drop to a seated position, and then he heard a loud angry voice. "Away! Away with you." It was a shopkeeper holding a broom threatening to strike him with it. "We don't want your kind here. Leave now or I will call an officer."

Gerrid struggled to his feet; pain and nausea threatened to overtake him. He gathered his balance and headed down the alleyway, away from the main street until he could walk no further. Lying down next to a pile of garbage, the smell almost unbearable. He didn't have the strength to care as his head grew heavy, and darkness closed in about him. He faded into sleep.

When he awoke, it was nighttime. There were still a few people ambling up and down the window lit streets, but for the most part it was quiet. The smell of rancid garbage assaulted him afresh as a door opened, and someone dropped a fresh batch of trash onto the garbage heap nearby. The former prisoner shuffled over to inspect it. There was some stale bread and a few apple cores. He devoured them, and to his surprise they filled his mouth with flavor. He hadn't had fruit since he had been locked up. He suddenly felt a desire to bathe, and thought if he could just find some water he would not only wash himself, he could try to clean the rags that covered his thin body. He had no idea where to go but he knew he wanted to get as far away from the prison as he could, so he started walking.

The night air was refreshing on his skin and a welcomed stranger after spending countless hours in a stifling cell cut off from fresh air. The sound of a dog barking in the distance was abruptly interrupted by the familiar blare of palace horns. That meant something was wrong. Gerrid had heard that sound several times over the past two years when someone had tried to escape or when the palace guard needed to be summoned for some kind of emergency. A dreadful question formed in his mind. What if they were sending the guard out to hunt down the released prisoners? It was not beyond reason to think that Vanus or Drok Relnik would give such a sadistic order. The punishment for escape was always instant death upon capture.

Shouts and the pounding of running feet grew louder, echoing off of the stone buildings, and suddenly they were upon Gerrid before he could discern what was happening. Dust rose from the ground, and as the soldiers ran past him, he heard the commander barking orders to his men about an attempt on the king's life. At the end of the alley they were dispatched in different directions with orders to search for the assassin, and within seconds they had disappeared into the darkness of the streets.

After stumbling along through empty alleyways, driven by the desire to get as far away from the palace as possible, the glow of the morning dawn shone on the horizon. Gerrid collapsed to his knees in exhaustion for the second time when a group of young men approached him. He could tell by the way they carried themselves that they were looking for trouble. There were three of them talking loudly and teasing one another. Then they noticed him kneeling hunched over on the ground and breathing heavily.

"Look here", taunted the tallest one, "gutter filth."

They shifted their course of direction and walked toward Gerrid, but he was too weary to care.

"He reeks of prison rot," said one.

"I heard they just released a whole lot of them to the streets. That's all we need is more garbage to clutter the roadways. It's hard enough to get around as it is," said another hatefully.

One of the men grabbed a pail of garbage from a nearby pile and walked toward Gerrid, lifted it over his head and dumped the contents out on top of him. The smell of it brought a wretched stench to his nose while they continued to laugh and taunt. "You are nothing but garbage," sneered the tall one. "Lift him to his feet."

"But he smells," protested the short stocky one.

"I said lift him!" yelled the tall one a second time. He was obviously the leader. The other two jumped at his command raising Gerrid to his feet. He was barely able to stand without the aid of the other two. The tall one grabbed a piece of rotting cabbage and shoved it into Gerrid's mouth. He spat it out, and pieces of it landed on the tall one's leggings. Instantly he was enraged and struck Gerrid in the rib cage causing him to hunch over. "Hold him up," shouted their leader.

"Let me hit him," pleaded one of them. "I want a turn."

"When I am done." The tall one struck him across the face. The others laughed.

Gerrid hardly felt it.

"It's my turn," pleaded the stocky one. "Give me a shot at it."

"When I am done," growled the leader, raising his hand to bring another blow. Gerrid braced himself for another strike. Something caught his eye, past his attackers in the shadows beyond, a slight movement. Then came a shuffling and a thud as the tall one buckled to the ground, revealing a cloaked figure standing where he once stood. The two holding Gerrid released him. Long knives flashed from beneath their cloaks as a glint of light sparkled across one of the blades. The tall one quickly recovered to join them.

The three attackers hesitated as the cloaked one spoke from the shadows in a haunting whisper. "Will this be the night you cross over to the other side?"

"There is one of you and three of us," said the tall one.

"Soon there will be only me," replied the shadowed figure.

The tall one lunged first with his blade held high, but he was not fast enough to protect himself. A gut-wrenching moan followed the thrust that would end his life. He fell to his knees, holding his stomach frozen, and then he fell, slamming into the ground. The other two stepped backward, glanced at one another briefly, and then they turned and ran into the fading darkness.

Gerrid was on the ground, his body aching from the beating. The stranger stood silently for a moment and without a word, turned to walk away. Through ragged breaths, Gerrid managed to say, "Thank you for your kindness."

The stranger, halted in stride, turned to look back from the shadows. Gerrid looked up at the dark figure before him, and their eyes briefly met. The ground beneath him started to spin. Gerrid fought to maintain his consciousness, but it was no use. The world around him faded into the darkness.

CHAPTER 3

When the wind blew through the streets of Abbodar, it brought with it showers of dust and anything else that wasn't tied down. The people of this land called them the howls because they sounded like a pack of wolves howling at the moon. The howls were heard before the wind arrived and, like a siren, they served as a warning to find safe cover. Superstition held that the deadly winds were a signal of the wrath of the gods of Terashom. Abbodar was a kingdom ruled by magic and myth, therefore omens were taken seriously and sacrifices were made to appease the gods when they became hostile.

In Abbodar, if you were part of the commoner class, the howls brought with them an additional horror beyond being swept away to death. Children, adults and even the elderly could become the victims of sacrifice. Terashom, the religion of Abbodar required the blood of humans. To sacrifice an animal would be considered an insult. Only humans were considered acceptable, and the Dissenters, followers of the One Faith, were the ones often chosen to suffer this fate. Those who opposed Terashom were considered prize sacrifices, so when the howls came, the Dissenters fled the winds and the possibility of death by sacrifice. Sacrifices were carried out either at the temple or in the arena. Death in the arena could be by fire or by the blade. Arena sacrifices not only appeased Terashom's gods, they also appeased its followers. It was a long-standing tradition in the annual arena games to offer sacrifices prior to combat.

This day the winds howled with a fury, as if screaming out for the blood of commoners to be sacrificed. After the last gusts of dust had died down, the streets of Abbodar stood in a ghostly silence until the alleys and byways slowly began to fill with merchants and residents scouring to collect their possessions that had been strewn about. Stray animals had to be rounded up and brought back to their owners, but commoners were nowhere to be seen. This was the time of their hiding. Bounties were offered for their capture, so citizens and soldiers alike would be looking to collect them. The commoners would stay hidden until enough of them had been rounded up and taken to the temple priests who would decide their fate. Once the rounding up was over, the commoners would begin to appear in public again until the next time the howls came to haunt them.

Gerrid awoke to a throbbing headache. A single candle cast shadows on the walls where animal hides hung from wooden beams above. Unable at first to remember the events that led up to this point, he looked around and noticed he was lying on a cot and saw someone standing in the shadows just beyond the light of the candle flame. Then he remembered the last thing before he passed out—the assault by the street thugs and the rescue by the stranger.

"Where am I?"

"You are safe," came a soft whisper.

"How did I get here?"

"The howls came, so I brought you to this place," said the voice.

Gerrid leaned forward to try to see the person standing in the shadows. He sensed it was a woman by the sound of her voice. "What happened to the one who rescued me?"

The shadowed person paused before answering. "You are welcome to rest here until you regain your strength. The people who own this place will allow it until you are stronger."

"And you. What will you do?"

"That does not concern you."

"I believe you were the one who saved me. Thank you."

Silence. From within the shadows the stranger looked at the pathetic form lying on the bed. Dirty and still smelling of prison rot. The odor that filled the room was unbearable.

"What is your name?" asked Gerrid.

"Bryann," came the answer after some hesitation.

"Thank you, Bryann."

Bryann did not respond. She wanted nothing to do with this one, and yet she was still standing there talking to him. Why had she stopped to help one such as this? She had other things that needed to be tended to, and this situation had just slowed her progress. She felt it was a sign of weakness helping this man, and the thought if it annoyed her. She wondered what strange magic was confusing her judgment. Something had happened on the streets that night. She felt that some inexplicable force had drawn her to that place, and it aggravated her still that she had allowed this to happen. She had violated her personal code when she stopped to help someone, especially a man.

"I need to go. I have business to take care of."

"It's not safe out there as long as they are looking for sacrifices," warned Gerrid. He wanted to see the face of the one who had saved him.

Bryann snapped back, "I don't need you to caution me. I know how to take care of myself."

"Of course you do. My apologies."

Bryann avoided looking into his eyes. She had made that mistake the other night. She recalled how she was ready to leave him on the street, but just before he fainted she looked him in the eyes, and something pierced right through her. When she turned to walk away from the lifeless form on the ground, the sound of the howls could be heard in the distance. She tried to walk away, but she couldn't. She cursed herself under her breath because she wanted to leave him there. She had no time for this. What did it matter to her what might happen to this man? She resented the feeling of concern she was having. It was alien to her, but had she known what to call it, she would have known that it was mercy. It was an emotion that she considered to be a sign of weakness.

Without another word Bryann turned and walked out the door. Gerrid realized he still hadn't seen the face of his rescuer. He grew drowsy, lay back on the bed and fell quickly into a deep sleep.

Vanus paced the floor nervously as Drok Relnik stood quietly watching the king's son move back and forth. The warlock was growing weary of Vanus's seemingly endless rant about the assassination attempt on his father. Relnik knew his concern had little to do with genuine love for his father for whom he had little affection. Their relationship was more a matter of state and politics rather than the love of a father and son. It had more to do with fear for Vanus than anything. If someone could come that close to killing his father, then they could get to him too.

"Who would be foolish enough to send an assassin into the heart of Abbodar to kill the monarch of the most powerful kingdom known to man?" raged Vanus, not really expecting an answer.

"Your father has made many enemies through the conquering of kingdoms. It should not surprise you that many would pay well for his death. But your father lives, and he will go on to reign as he always has."

The warlock knew that his words had little effect, so he waited quietly for the king's son to empty himself of his rage. He had learned long ago that it was no good trying to talk to Vanus when he was like this. The king's son was easily distracted from reason by emotional extremes and impulsive notions. Given the time, he would eventually calm down and return to some manner of clarity.

Finally, after several more rants, Vanus pressed the warlock again as if he would have a different response. "An assassin makes his way into the king's chambers past several guards and lies in wait for hours undetected. If it had not been for the second chambermaid alerting us, the king would have been slain. And if the howls had not kicked up, we would not have lost the assassin's tracks. Tell me, warlock, what magic is at work here?"

"This was not the work of magic. It was merely bad luck on our part."

"Luck," spewed Vanus. "How is it that a kingdom so rich with the power of magic could lose out to the chance of bad luck?"

"Someday, Vanus, we will control even the wind." Relnik walked over to the window and crossed his arms as he looked at the sprawling city. "Be patient my friend, our magic grows stronger, but there is still much to be learned on our part."

"Patience for me is like an ill-fitting suit of armor. It only causes me discomfort." Vanus looked at the warlock and huffed, "What evidence have we gathered to aid us in tracking this assassin?"

"There has been no evidence found yet."

"The assassin failed in his assignment. Surely he's left evidence."

"If he had, I would have told you," offered the warlock. "They are still investigating. Something will turn up."

Vanus didn't feel safe knowing an assassin was able to penetrate their security. Had his father been murdered, he would have become king and the next target. He knew that his day to rule Abbodar would come soon enough, but for now he was more interested in pursuing magic. Though his father was an aging monarch, he was still very much in control of his own destiny as his lust for power and control of other lands continued to increase. Vanus was in no hurry to take on the weight of managing the demands of an ever-expanding kingdom the size of Abbodar.

Drok Relnik had other concerns pressing him. He had spies keeping a close eye on developments in the kingdom of Talinor and its allies, the dwarves and the elves. They were the last known allied kingdoms to honor the One Faith, and Talinor was central to those alliances. Relnik could still taste the bitterness of the failed attempt by the Boogaran nation to conquer Talinor two years ago.

The warlock had tried and failed to convince the king of Abbodar to make Talinor part of his plans to expand his kingdom, but the emperor was focused on his latest campaign to conquer Boogara. The Boogaran military had been depleted in the battle at Talinor, and with them still recovering from their losses, Emperor Krim meant to take advantage before they had time to rebuild any further.

Relnik had witnessed first hand what Talinor was capable of when they had defeated the Boogarans in battle by successfully defending their own homeland against overwhelming odds. A kingdom as small and seemingly insignificant as Talinor should not have survived against the strength of the military might of Boogara. Boogara had the advantage from the outset of the campaign, both in numbers and through their alliance with the shadow wraiths. With Talinor having turned away from its faith as a nation, and an ailing monarch who had done the same, it seemed like the perfect scenario for victory. But it was not enough to bring the Boogarans the victory they sought.

On two different occasions twenty years apart, Boogara had attacked Talinor. In the second engagement the Tals had foolishly agreed to make alliances with the dark magic through the Zarish Priests. Victory was almost in hand for Boogara, but in the end, the Tals found their return to the One Faith played a key role in their victory. Drok Relnik reeled at the thought of how close they had come to conquering the Tals only to come up short—due, in no small part, to the effort of the Intercessor Lena and the Gap Warriors. Relnik was no fool, and as much as he hated to admit it, the Intercessor had a powerful magic of her own. While he could not completely understand it, he knew that it was her magic that aided in defeating the Boogarans in battle.

The warlock believed that he who controlled the magic had the most power. His interest in controlling kingdoms and riches was fueled by his lust for the power that magic gave him. A kingdom like Abbodar had the might to control the natural order of politics and people, yet they saw value in a warlock like Relnik, whose alliance with the shadow wraiths gave him access to their power.

Emperor Krim recognized the importance of the magic that Relnik had access to. But what he prized most was the warlock's knowledge of the strengths and weaknesses of the Boogaran military that he had gained during his time in Boogara when they attacked Talinor. Now that Caragis had been defeated, Abbodar would move on to conquer Boogara. The timing was perfect because Boogara was still weak and recovering from its loss to Talinor.

CHAPTER 4

When Gerrid awoke, he heard shuffling in the corner of the room. A woman stood with her back to him pouring something into a bowl. She must have heard him stir because she turned to look at him as he sat up in bed. She was middle aged with blond shoulder length hair, slightly grayed. When she turned to look at him, a smile formed on her face. "Hello, my friend," the woman spoke in a kind voice. "My name is Pamela. I own this place."

"Thank you for your kindness, Pamela," said Gerrid as he struggled to sit up. He groaned against the pain that lanced through his ribs from the beating he took the other night. "How long have I been out?"

"It's been three days." She handed him a cup of warm tea. "Here, dink this. There are herbs in it that will help you heal."

Gerrid took the cup and drank it deeply. The taste was bittersweet and somewhat familiar. "Tell me, Pamela. How is it I ended up in this home?"

"Bryann brought you here because I am the only person she trusts in the city, and she knew I would help you."

"And where is Bryann now?"

"I am not sure. She doesn't tell me her business. She left a few days ago, but I am confident she will return. She owes me a favor and I intend to collect on it."

"But why would you show me this kindness? You don't know me. I am a prisoner."

Pamela corrected, "You were a prisoner, and you are right. I have never met you, but I do know of you. I know that you once led the people some call the Dissenters…"

"You speak of the followers of the One Faith. You know of them?"

"Yes, I have friends who live among them." Pamela's tone reflected a subtle sadness.

Gerrid was wide awake now and eager to know more. "I

need to find them."

"Yes, you do, and they need you to find them," said Pamela. "Much has happened since you have been gone. They have a new leader now and shortly after you were imprisoned most of them fled the city to escape the sacrifices and the arena."

"Please, Pamela. Where have they gone?"

"A few are scattered throughout the city, but most have fled to the mountain regions to escape the annual Terashom festival. That's all you need to know for now. It is better at present if some things are left unsaid. For now you need to rest, and in a few days you will be stronger and ready to travel. When that time comes, Bryann will guide you to where they are in hiding…" Pamela paused, "…at least I am hoping she will. She can be stubborn, that one. Please," Pamela changed the subject, "I have prepared a meal for you. You need to eat now so you can regain your strength. You are going to need it to make this journey."

She turned quickly and disappeared through the door, closing it behind her, and left Gerrid alone with his thoughts.

The front door to Pamela's home opened and closed as Bryann, who was out of breath, quickly stepped into the house. Her eyes darted about the room.

"I don't know where you have been, and I don't want to know, but promise me you aren't bringing any trouble to this place," warned Pamela as she moved pots and pans about her kitchen.

Bryann was an independent spirit and accustomed to doing things on her own, but when it came to her Aunt Pamela, she felt a small measure of intimidation. Bryann's mother was Pamela's sister, and she died when Bryann was thirteen. Soon after that, her father left to fight in the military, and Bryann hadn't seen him since. After her father's absence, Bryann was sent to live with her Aunt Pamela. Their relationship was full of conflict because both of them were similarly strong willed. At seventeen she left her aunt's full of anger and bitterness over the loss of her mother and a father who had abandoned her. That was ten years ago, and she had not seen her aunt until the other night when she had showed up on her doorstep with Gerrid.

"Why do you assume the worst of me?" countered Bryann. "It's been ten years and still you push."

"Dear Bryann, you and I will always be like two wild cats meeting on a narrow trail, but one thing you must always know is that I love you." Pamela thought she saw a slight smile on the lips of her niece but couldn't tell for sure. "Please come. We need to talk."

Bryann sat down at the small table where her aunt was seated. "I fear to have this conversation with you. For some reason I think we are about to argue another matter."

"You may be right, dear niece, but as with all other arguments, we will survive this one. I do not believe that you're coming here after all these years is a coincidence. There is destiny in this reunion, and I don't want to miss it."

"Please don't start that again. I haven't seen you in ten years, and you still speak of destiny as if there is some greater purpose in life beyond survival and suffering. How is it after all you have lost, with so little gained in your life, that you still hold on to these empty fantasies?"

"You know little of what this life has given me girl and don't assume that you can understand the heart of one who follows the One Faith. This life has been hard, but I have made my choice, and I have no regrets. I wake up everyday and give thanks for the breath of life that flows through me. When you have lived as long as I, then you can lecture me on the meaning of life."

"I still don't understand this foolish faith of yours. What has it ever brought you that you can speak of? You still live in squalor and have barely enough food to feed yourself. And now something tells me that you are about to ask me to support your faith at some level. You know where I stand, and you know I don't want anything to do with it."

Pamela pushed back, unmoved by her niece's rant. "Then why are you here? You picked up a stranger on the streets and brought him to me. You and I both know that is against your natural way of doing things."

Bryann bristled at the question, but she wasn't about to let on. She wasn't about to tell her aunt that she was dealing with some trouble of her own and needed to get out of Abbodar as soon as it was safe. Something had compelled her to bring Gerrid here, but she didn't have to understand it, and she wasn't about to believe it had anything to do with destiny of faith. "What is it, Aunt? What would you have me do? You might as well speak your mind. You always do anyway," Bryann fired back in defense. She really didn't want to hear it, but she knew she was going to. She sensed that her debt was about to be called in.

"I'm dying." Pamela's words cut through the room and stilled the tension between them. Silence hung in the air as Bryann's eyes widened with concern.

In the deepest corners of Bryann's heart, pain threatened to rise to the surface, but she would not allow it to free itself from that inner prison where she kept such emotions locked away. "What are you saying?" She asked softly.

"I'm dying of a sickness that I, nor anyone else really understands, but I do know that it's going to kill me. However, I still have some time left," said Pamela as if it was of no concern to her. "Not to worry. Everybody dies eventually. Besides, I'll get to escape all this sorrow and suffering you keep reminding me of that I have had to put up with all these years."

Bryann was silent. She didn't know what to say.

"Well, dear niece, I guess there is a first for everything. You have nothing to say. That's okay by me. Nothing can be said in light of such news?"

"What do you want from me?" asked Bryann softly. "Whatever it is, I will do it. You were good to me when you took me in. I owe you that much."

"You owe me nothing child and never speak of it again. I do need a favor from you, but let your decision be by your own choice, not by obligation."

SWORD OF DELIVERANCE

"Tell me of this favor so I can decide."

"I need you to take Gerrid to the Remnant."

"The Remnant?" Bryann appeared confused.

"The remaining clan of the followers of the One Faith. The dissenters. Gerrid needs to rejoin them, and you are the only one I know who can help him get there."

"Where is this Remnant to be found?"

"The last I heard they were hiding somewhere in the Hebron Forest."

"That's a big forest."

"You will find them. I have no doubt," said Pamela.

"And how is it I will find them? Will your destiny guide me?" said Bryann sarcastically.

"Destiny is always a factor, but I know you well enough to know that you will find a way. You may be the daughter of my sister, but you and I share a common trait. We are both stubborn, and sometimes that stubbornness serves us well as long as we don't allow it to cloud our way."

This time Bryann's smile in response to her aunt's words was unhindered. It had been years since Pamela had seen that smile and how it lit up the girl's face. Bryann knew it was a compliment, and one she appreciated. Her stubbornness was one of the few things that Bryann liked about herself.

CHAPTER 5

As Gerrid awoke, he saw movement in his room. Light from a crack in the window curtains provided just enough illumination for him to see that someone was in the room with him. As his eyes adjusted, he recognized that it was Pamela holding something for him to eat.

"You are awake. How do you feel, Gerrid?"

He had to think about it for a moment while he cleared his head and reached over to feel his ribs. "I am better, Thank you for asking."

Pamela handed him a plate of bread with fruit and cheese. "It isn't much, but it will help to bring much needed strength." Gerrid ate it quietly as his host watched him in silence. He savored the cheese and fruit with each bite and had to make an effort not to eat it too quickly. The juice kept running down his chin, and he would quickly wipe it off with the back of his hand. It had been over two years since he had tasted anything like it, and he was relishing every bite.

"My niece has agreed to take you to your people," offered Pamela. "I think you will find she is a capable guide."

Gerrid finished chewing the food in his mouth and then said, "I'm surprised she agreed to that."

"Well, she can be stubborn. I will grant you that, but once she commits, she will see it through."

"I owe you a debt of gratitude for your kindness. I don't know that I can repay you, but I am willing if I can."

"Well you can start by taking a bath," said Pamela with a hint of sarcasm in her voice and a smile on her face.

"Of course. I can't imagine how I must smell to you."

"And after that, you can find the Followers and return to the place of leadership you once held."

"I am not interested in returning to that role. I am going home to Talinor, and before I leave I need to see my friend Dallien. I'm sure he will want to come with me. He was with the followers when I went to prison. Besides, I believe the followers have a new leader now. What did you say his name was?" asked Gerrid.

"I didn't say." Pamela seemed a little uneasy at the question. "His name is Kevis."

"Yes, I know him well. He is a zealous one and was always at odds with me. It was no secret that he wanted to be in charge. I guess he got what he wanted."

"I know little of the politics of leadership," mused Pamela, "but I do know one thing; the followers need you to lead them."

"And why do you say this Pamela? You don't even know me."

"I know of you and what you stood for. These are difficult times for the Remnant, and if they are to survive, they will need someone like you to lead them."

"And what is someone like me?"

Pamela paused as if to measure her next words. "You have led men into battle. You are a proven leader. I know that about you. Kevis does not know what he is doing. I fear he will take us to our end. So many have scattered under his guidance. I know in my heart that this is not good."

"As you said, these are difficult times. Maybe the scattering of the followers was meant to be."

"Maybe," agreed Pamela, "but I know in my heart that it is time for us to come back together. I don't know exactly why, but my dreams have been telling me so. Not long after you left the followers of the One Faith, I joined them. I was looking for something to give more meaning to my life. The One Faith did that for me. Before the time of the scattering, when I was with them, I heard the stories of how you led the troops in the battle at Talinor. How you overcame impossible odds and went on to victory."

"Please, Pamela." Gerrid objected. "I had such a small part in all of that."

"A significant part, nonetheless. I have heard the stories for years told around our campfires to our children. They were glorious stories of magical soldiers called the Gap Warriors. They returned to Talinor after twenty years to stand against the dark magic. There was one who helped them, the Intercessor known as Lena. She interceded as the Gap Warriors defended the breach against the demons of the void." Pamela's passion intensified as her voice filled the room. "You must be here for a reason, Gerrid. All this way you have come from Talinor to lead us. I believe that your time as leader of the Remnant is not yet finished."

"Why do you call them the Remnant?"

"They are all that is left of us, and I believe they will not survive without you."

"I don't know, Pamela," Gerrid shifted uneasily and began to pace. "So much has changed in two years. I've been in a deep pit of darkness that has drained me in so many ways; both physically and my faith. I fear I have little left in me to lead anyone." Gerrid's head dropped and Pamela could feel his shame.

Pamela shot up from her seat. "We have all been in a pit, some darker than others. Abbodar is an unbearable pit where the dark magic has free reign here. I have witnessed the sacrifices of the innocent and faithful until I thought I could bear it no more. I am not willing to give up my hopes to such evil." Pamela stepped closer and hovered near enough that he could see the vein swelling above her eye. "One thing I knew the minute I looked into your eyes is that you will lead my people. You are the only one who can lead them."

Gerrid was startled by the intensity of Pamela's challenge, and for one brief moment he felt a distant stirring inside and thought that her words might hold some measure of truth. "We shall see what destiny holds for us, Pamela. My heart is as weary as my body. It's difficult for me to think clearly."

A smile crossed Pamela's face. She was getting through to him. She was sure of it. "Tell me, my friend, did you know the Intercessor, Lena? Are the stories true? Did she really enter the temple at the battle of Talinor and destroy the idol with the same staff she used when she was a Gap Warrior?"

Gerrid smiled, "She did. And how is it you know of such things?"

"I once heard a traveling minstrel sing a song that told the story. You never know with minstrels if you can depend on the truthfulness of their songs, but somehow I knew it was true." Pamela smiled and paused to gather her thoughts. "I would like to meet her before I leave this world. I would love to travel to Talinor one day to walk the streets and intercede with her. It is my dream. Maybe she would teach me the way of intercession." Pamela took the empty plate from Gerrid. "Oh how we could use such a force in this dark place."

"I believe it would take an army the likes of her to bring light to a kingdom such as Abbodar," said Gerrid pensively. "I fear there are so few Intercessors left in the world."

"Maybe there are more than we think. It is a big world. Who knows. Maybe they are out there somewhere." Pamela smiled as she moved toward the door. "I have prepared a bath for you. Tomorrow at first light, you and Bryann will leave for Hebron Forest. Normally it is a two-day journey, but in your weakened, condition it will take longer."

Pamela left Gerrid alone with his thoughts. He did not want to make this journey to find the Remnant, at least not for the reasons that Pamela wanted. He just wanted to go home. He was, for the most part, unmoved by most of what Pamela had said, but he was not going to argue with her any further. Even so, he would go to the Remnant because he would not leave without seeing his friend Dallien and give him a chance to go with him back to Talinor.

Drok Relnik entered his private chamber where he prayed to the dark spirits in whom he had long ago placed his trust. The room he often retreated to for times like this had a table standing in the center with lit candles, and in the corner was a fireplace that provided most of the light for the room. He preferred the darkness to the light, and so did those he worshiped and prayed to. Today he hoped for a visitation, but he knew that in order to ensure such an event, blood would need to be spilled.

The warlock felt a tinge of uneasiness as he thought of the release of the former Talinor Commander from prison. He doubted Gerrid was any real threat in his condition, but he could not be sure. As long as he was still following the One Faith, there was always a possibility he could cause trouble. Then there were the Dissenters. Most of them had been scattered due to persecution. Some perished as sacrifices in the arena, but they could not be ruled out completely as a threat. until the last of them had been destroyed. That would no longer be a problem once they were tracked down and brought to the arena games to be sacrificed.

In the corner of the room sat a young elf girl trembling with terror in her eyes. Her hands and feet bound by ropes and her mouth gagged to stifle any unwanted screams. Near her was a blood soaked slab, and next to the slab was the ceremonial bowl used to catch the blood spilled during sacrifices. On top of the slab lay the instrument of death, a ceremonial dagger crafted from Obsidian.

Relnik's black robes floated along the ground as he moved silently toward the cowering figure in the corner. He relished this opportunity to sacrifice an elf on the altar of Gizshra, the shadow wraith. Elves were highly valued for sacrifice and understandably hard to come by in these lands for that very reason. They were mystical creatures of light and known for holding a deep devotion to the One Faith. Relnik anticipated that this sacrifice would earn him a visitation from either the dark spirit of Gizshra or one of his workers. As he picked up the girl to place her on the slab he could feel her trembling form beneath his grip. He did not hesitate to look into her trembling eyes. What he saw in them gave him a twisted sense of elation. His steady hand gripped the dagger and he began to cut the bindings on her wrists and feet. A tear trickled from the corner of her eye and landed on the blood soaked slab beneath her. Relnik could hear her desperately praying through frightened whimpers.

"Silence," he screeched through a harsh whisper. He loathed the sound of prayers offered to the Ancient of Days.

A knock sounded at the door, and when Jef opened it, he was greeted by one of the seamen. "Lena wishes to see you, sir."

Jef gathered his things and made his way to the bow of the small ship where he found Lena hunched over groaning in great pain.

SWORD OF DELIVERANCE

"Are you okay Lena?" yelled Jef above the wind as he ran to her aid.

"I'm fine, Jef," said Lena through labored breath. "We need to intercede," Lena groaned as the words left her lips.

"Do you know what it is?"

"Darkness…great Darkness and death. That's all I know."

Jef knelt down next to Lena, and a sudden rush of intense fear swept over him.

"Pray against it, Jef. Don't let the fear distract you. Pray against it. Reject it."

Together they knelt on the wind blown bow and interceded. Hours passed and when they sensed they could finish, they rose from their knees and in the distance they could see land.

Relnik held the dagger above his head gripped tightly in both hands and began his incantations. "To the supreme one I bring this sacrifice of innocence. May you receive the blood shed for you through this offering."

The elf girl's eyes grew wide as she stared up at the blade hovering above her body.

Pounding, the door crashed open and a priest rushed into the room. "Fire," he said out of breath. "Fire! Someone has set fire to the temple pyre."

"Why bother me with this?" raged the warlock. "Surely, you can handle it."

"My apologies, master. We fear there is danger afoot with the recent assassination attempt on the king, so the temple guards insisted I find you."

"So be it," Grumbled Relnik under his breath as he bound the elf girl to the post, and then he turned and followed the priest out the door, cursing under his breath as he slammed it behind him.

Something scratched and rattled at the window of the sacrifice chamber. It jolted and then creaked open, and a familiar face poked his head into the room. Packer. Relief washed over the

37

elf girl as he leapt into the room and quickly produced a small dagger from his waist. He quickly cut the girl from her bonds and then removed the gag from her mouth.

"Packer," She cried. "How did you…"

"Shh… Quickly we have to go. We don't have time."

Her rescuer led her to the window ledge where a rope was tied and waiting for them to descend. It was dark outside, and in the distance they could hear the commotion caused by the fire. The girl smiled and kissed her friend on the cheek. He blushed and looked irritated at the same time. Then he motioned to her, and they both disappeared over the edge.

CHAPTER 6

Bryann was having second thoughts about fulfilling her aunt's request to assist Gerrid on this journey. Not only was this a disruption in her own plans, but she always tried to avoid the role of looking after people. She knew he would still be weak, and that was a burden she resented taking on because she loathed weakness in people. Gerrid had been in the room sleeping almost the whole time he had been at her aunt's home, and she had not seen him since the first morning after their arrival. The plan was to leave early the next day, and no matter how hard she tried she could not talk herself out of it. She owed her aunt, so she would repay her, and then she could move on. Pamela had been busy all day gathering supplies to take with them. Breads, cheeses and dried meats, along with bedding and extra clothing, were in short supply, but what she could gather would have to do.

The bedroom door opened, and Gerrid stepped into the main living area. Appearing slightly disoriented, he noticed Bryann stuffing supplies into a small backpack. When she turned to look at him, it was the first time he had a good look at her. The first thing he noticed were her doe shaped eyes. They were beautiful. She was beautiful. She glanced at him briefly and then turned back to her packing as if she didn't notice him. He thought he sensed anger behind those eyes.

Gerrid just stared at her, not sure what to say as he could sense the tension in her. He knew she did not want to accompany him on this journey. Pamela entered the room just in time to interrupt the cold silence. "So, I see you two are getting acquainted. Good, because you are going to be spending some time together."

Bryann bristled slightly and rose to her feet. "We leave at first light, so if you have anything that needs to be packed, now is the time to do it."

Then she realized that he had nothing in terms of personal possessions. How could he? He had just gotten out of prison. Gerrid smiled at the comment and held out his empty hands.

"I packed extra clothes for you, Gerrid. I'm not certain how they'll fit," said Pamela.

"I'm sure they will be fine, thank you."

"How are you feeling?" asked Pamela as she handed him a cup of hot tea.

"I'm feeling stronger. I will be ready to go by morning. One more night's rest will help."

Knock. Knock.

The three turned to each other as Pamela whispered, "Who could that be this late at night?" The others shrugged.

Knock. Knock. This time it came a little louder.

Pamela motioned for Gerrid to go to the back room. "Who is it?" she whispered through the door.

A muffled response came quickly. She opened the door and waved them in to the room.

"Packer, are you okay?" asked Pamela, sounding motherly in her tone. She recognized the elf girl but couldn't remember her name.

Packer quickly explained what had happened, gasping

to catch his breath as he recounted the rescue of Sera. Then he added, "They are looking for us. The warlock is desperate to spill elf's blood on his altar. We have to get out of the city. I have to get Sera to the forest where she will be safe."

Pamela looked at Bryann.

"No, I am not going to take them with us. I have enough to deal with having to take care of him." She nodded toward Gerrid, stinging him with her words. He resented the weakness in his body and that he needed someone to protect him. It was made worse knowing Bryann despised being responsible for his safety.

"Packer can help you Bryann." Pamela pleaded.

Bryann bristled and stepped backward to protest.

"He knows every back alley between here and the edge of the city. Trust me. He will be an asset to you. He's lived on the streets of Abbodar all his life." Bryann sized up the skinny little boy with the bushy head of hair dressed in street rags. She didn't want this. She wanted it to be over and it was just starting.

"To the edge of the city. That's it, and then you are all on your own."

"You should leave tonight then, under cover of darkness. It will be more difficult if you wait until tomorrow."

"Tonight it is then," said Gerrid, breaking his silence.

Bryann shot him a cold glance as if to silence him, then she returned to gathering their gear. "You two will have to help carry the supplies. Our friend here is not yet strong enough to share in the burden. And you," she pointed at Sera, "cover those ears unless you want everyone looking to collect a bounty tracking us down."

The elf girl smiled back at Bryann and it caught her off guard. A frown would have been expected in response to her harsh tone.

"Then it is settled," said Pamela. "You will leave tonight."

Pamela ran to the storeroom to gather extra supplies to accommodate Packer and Sera. When it was time to leave, Pamela pulled Bryann aside to say goodbye. "Be careful, Bree. I know you are in some kind of trouble. I could tell it the minute you arrived here with Gerrid. I recognize that look in your eyes from when you were younger. I trust it will not get in the way of what you need to do here."

Bryann looked at her aunt with those empty eyes that Pamela was all too familiar with. She just shrugged as she picked up her two short swords and concealed them within the pack she planned to carry.

"I love you, child," said Pamela softly.

Bryann wouldn't look her in the eyes. "Don't worry about me. I know how to take care of myself."

"That you do, my niece, but I shall pray for your safe passage nonetheless."

Bryann ignored the comment, and as the others turned to leave, Gerrid thanked Pamela once again for all she had done. Bryann stopped short of the door, paused briefly as if she wanted to say something, then turned and hugged her aunt. Pamela smiled and held her tightly.

Then they were gone into the night.

CHAPTER 7

The Talon had landed in the harbor of a small fishing village called Fair Winds. The streets were buzzing with shop owners out front calling for customers, and the local fishmongers were packing the latest catch from the boats in the harbor. Jef had left the ship upon arrival and returned by midday with enough horses for them to make the trip. Although they were overpriced and undernourished, it was the best he could find on short notice. Eight in all would make the journey inland: Lena, Graybeard, his assistant Pell and Jef with the four Tal warriors Rafe, Lebo,

Grib and Fenly. Jef had pressed Lena to consider taking more soldiers, but the Intercessor had insisted that a smaller number would draw less attention, and besides, there was no real security in the numbers.

The aging Prophet remained unclear about the details of their final destination, but that did not concern him as long as he knew what direction to head. Lena put her complete trust in Graybeard in these matters, but Jef was not as confident in the old prophet as she was. He had conveyed his fears to her several times because he had noticed that Graybeard was losing his memory and appeared disoriented on several occasions.

"He is old," Lena would say. "He may forget some of the past but he doesn't forget what is revealed to him, and when the time is right, he will know what we all need to know."

"And what is it that he will know Lena?" Jef would ask.

"When the time is right, he will know where to go and how to find the one this sword belongs to."

After staying one night in Fair Winds collecting supplies and getting their land legs back, they spent all of the next day traveling inland. When the day's journey came to an end, Lena was exhausted. The traveling and riding horseback would take some getting used to. The small band of travelers broke to camp in a small clearing of giant pine trees near a fresh spring. The area was heavily wooded, and the forest undergrowth was thick with ferns and briar, but the trail they traveled had been clear and easy to navigate with the horses.

Rafe and Lebo finished building a fire while Grib and Fenly tended to the horses and supplies. Once they finished, they prepared and ate a warm meal of boiled jerky and potatoes. Then they gathered at the fire. Graybeard had eaten very little and insisted on retreating to his tent. His voice was weak, and he looked exhausted from the day's journey. Lena felt the weariness of a long day in her aged bones, but she enjoyed the warmth of the evening fire and felt torn between remaining close to the flames and going to bed. Grib and Fenly took positions on each side of the camp to take the first watch of the night.

"How is it you can be at peace, my Lady, not knowing our final destination?" asked Lebo looking across the flickering flames.

"Everyday is a journey of unknowing. We just think we control our coming and going, and that is where we are wrong. Does a man know for sure that when he rises in the morning to go about the day's work that he will not be interrupted by life?" Lena paused and stared into the flaring embers and smiled before continuing. "The great illusion is that we have any control at all. To put faith in such illusions is for the foolish and those marred by life's darker moments."

"I guess I am one of the foolish ones who struggles to have faith. I find it a challenge in times like these," said Lebo anxiously. "I don't like not knowing the exact nature of this quest. Help me. What is the secret to faith?"

"There is no secret to faith, but there may be a measure of mystery to it, and it is the mystery that so often intimidates us and causes us to fear. We believe that if we could control the outcome of things, we will find the security we seek. Security is mostly a superstition that carries an empty promise of safety. If the point of power is merely controlling others, or securing happiness, then we have missed the true purpose of power."

"And what is that?" asked Rafe, the quieter of the two.

"True power is the ability to discover the path we are meant to travel and then to boldly walk that path wherever it may lead us. If power is about gaining safety, then we lose one of the greatest benefits of faith."

"And what is that, my Lady?"

"Adventure."

Adventure?" said Rafe. "I still do not understand."

"Without faith there can be no adventure." Said Lena with a smile returning to her face. "When we attempt to control our own destinies, we remove the possibility of risk. Our attempt to control life is driven by fear, but trusting in what you believe in the most drives faith. As for me, I believe in following the One Faith. I not only believe in it, but I put my trust in the Ancient of Days who gives my heart the fire and desire to risk all by placing my trust in His ways. I would not be on a journey such as this one if I did not have faith."

"I believe in the Ancient of Days," said Rafe. "I just don't know if I trust Him the way you do. I've always known about the One Faith, but to trust the way you speak of is a mystery to me. It seems reckless to me to put your faith in any system of belief that can not be proven"

"Ah, but that is part of what makes it an adventure," said Jef adding to the discussion. "Faith is not a guarantee of safety or predictability. It is not a fire you can control by putting rocks around it." Jef pointed to the campfire. "No, it is a fire you must dance upon with all your might, and when the dance is finished, you will find that you have been consumed by that fire. You may be unrecognizable because faith has a way of changing us to the core of who we are."

Rafe and Lebo stared at the campfire in silence, taking time to mull over Jef's words.

"Think of the quest we are on now," Jef continued. "To some it may seem reckless to follow a path that is unclear, led by an invisible guide with no guarantee of outcome. Now that is what I call adventure. If it is security you seek, then journeys taken away from a place of predictability and comfort will only confuse you."

Lena looked at Jef. "Our security is not found in the things we can see or touch. It is found in our faith in the Ancient of Days who leads us by his Spirit Wind."

"Spirit Wind," Lebo repeated the word slowly and then took a long deep breath before exhaling the air from his lungs. "I know so little about the Spirit Wind. When I hear talk of it, I grow uneasy."

Lena smiled. "Maybe your uneasiness is because you have not yet truly surrendered to the ways of the faith you claim to follow. Many say they are followers, but in truth they are not. Until you are willing surrender to the Spirit Wind, your belief will be incomplete and fear will have free reign in you. As long as fear reigns inside, we walk in partial ignorance of the true knowledge of the One Faith."

"I prefer to use my reasoning," said Lebo. "And I have found reason enough to follow the One Faith. Is that not enough?"

"Maybe for your head," said Jef, "but then you are left depending on reason to lead you in times like these. If we had been using reason alone, we would not have left Talinor on this quest."

"It is the Spirit Wind that guides us here," said Lena. "We are not going to divorce reason from the Spirit's leading because both are necessary. Without the Spirit, there is no true faith. Without faith, there is no real adventure."

"I'm beginning to like the sound of it," said Lebo, his voice rising with a tinge of passion. "I remember the attack against Talinor by the Boogaran Horde. I was too young at the time to fight in that campaign, but I remember it well. I recall thinking that we were all going to die, and somehow against all reason we prevailed in the end."

"I believe you are beginning to see the bigger picture, young Lebo," said Jef.

"And now it seems that instead of the darkness coming to us, we are heading toward the darkness," put in Rafe. "Does the faith you speak of put us in harm's way?"

"What you say is true," answered Jef. "There is danger and a darkness that awaits us. Light cannot prevail against the darkness without a terrible battle. Some who follow the One Faith believe that we should live on the defensive and remain behind the safety of stone fortresses instead of advancing against the darkness, but we have a different view. There are times when we have to push back the darkness, and the only way to do that is to attack it."

Shivers raced down Rafe's spine as he took in the words of the veteran Talinor warrior. "How can we fight darkness?" asked

Rafe cautiously. "We are but men with weapons of flesh and blood. We are not like the Intercessors or the Gap Warriors who fight with their powerful weapons. How can we possibly stand in the day of battle against the magic of the dark side?"

"Everyone of us has been given what we need to make our stand against whatever darkness comes against us," challenged Jef. "Not all of us are meant to enter the void to battle dark spirits and not all of us are impassioned by the call to intercede. Some of us, like you, Lebo, and others are equipped to defend with weapons fashioned by hands to fight against flesh and blood. It takes warfare at every level to defeat the dark magic."

"Let the siege at Talinor always be a reminder of this truth," said Lena. "The Gap Warriors and the Intercessors could not have won without the Tal warriors who battled against the Boogaran Horde. Each has a role in the battle against whatever the darkness sends against us. Evil comes in many forms, and your part in fighting it is no less important than ours."

"But who will fight the dark magic if it comes in the form of a shadow wraith or some other spirit?" asked Rafe anxiously. "There are no Gap Warriors with us on this quest that I can see."

"That is a good question, young warrior," said Lena. "There is no doubt that we will face strong opposition from the dark ones on this quest, and I assure you if that is the case, there will be Gap Warriors to aid us in the fight."

"And why is the prophet on this journey?" asked Lebo. "It seems to me that he has little life left in him."

"Graybeard seeks to pass on his mantle of prophecy before he passes from this life. The heir of his mantle has yet to be revealed to him." Lena's voice softened. "Whomever receives the mantle will also receive the legendary sword of Kem Felnar. Some call it the Sword of Deliverance. This is the first time the sword has left its resting place in Talinor for generations. I fear we are headed into a time of great upheaval. I worry that Talinor may be in danger, but I cannot be certain."

"The hour is late," said Jef. "We will need our strength for the journey, and tomorrow morning will come quickly."

Lena lay in bed trying to sleep, but her heart would not rest after the conversation at the campfire. She knew Gap Warriors would be joining them at some point, and she hoped it would be sooner than later. She knew how vulnerable they were without them. Her times of intercession had told her so. The darkness that lay ahead of them was different than what she had prayed against in the past. She did not quite understand it, but she did not want to underestimate its scope and power.

As the Lena slowly faded into a restless sleep, the last thoughts on her mind were of her grandson, Cyle. She had not seen him since he left Talinor over two years ago after discovering that he was a Gap Warrior. She ached to see him again in this lifetime, and she fell asleep praying that he would be one of the Gap Warriors sent to aid her in this battle.

CHAPTER 8

This day arrived once a year with great dread and overwhelming sadness. It was the memory that brought back the greatest heartache of Gafney's life, so he did his best to numb the ache inside. This was the day he had lost the woman he was to marry. He had loved her beyond what he could have ever imagined. The grief was undeniably the greatest of his life. He had suffered great physical wounds in battle, but nothing compared to the pain he felt at the loss of his one true love. For one day each year, on the anniversary of her death, he would revisit that shadowed valley of torment where the memory of her death would haunt him. And on that same day he would also visit the nearest pub to find drink to aid him in his journey.

When he first entered the tavern on the edge of the small

fishing village of Palladrim, the smell almost repelled him to the point of leaving. Pipe smoke filled the dimly lit room, and the odor of stale fish mixed with days-old sweat that clung to the bodies of tired old fisherman assaulted his senses, but he pushed through it. After a few pints of ale, the smell, along with the rest of the world, began to fade away into a foggy haze, but the drinking could not quench her memory. It only dulled the pain. The more he drank, the more he remembered moments shared with his lost love. It was a bittersweet reunion of sorts; for brief moments he could smell the fragrance of her skin or hear the pleasant tone of her voice, but memory was a tricky thing when mixed with strong drink. A pleasant image of love shared would emerge, and then it would fade as quickly as it had appeared, only to be replaced by unspeakable sorrow and gut wrenching pain. Back and forth he would go for the rest of the night, willing to suffer through the pain of what was lost in order to have the sweetness of what he had before she was gone.

Two weeks ago he had been fighting in a Gap battle where his assignment, along with three other Gap Warriors, was to protect the elf prince of Krellander who had been sent by his father to recover an ancient and sacred scroll that belonged to the elves. After completing that assignment, Gafney was summoned through his dreams to cross the Sea of Baddaris and travel eastward to lands unfamiliar to him. In the dreams he saw the great eagle flying across the sea, and as he flew, other smaller eagles joined and followed him. When he woke up that morning, he headed toward the kingdom known as Abbodar. Now he would wait until things were made clearer to him. Such was the life of a Gap Warrior, and he understood that.

He ordered another pint from the barkeep as the walls around him began to fade in and out. His powerful hands clung tightly to the fresh goblet as if someone would take it from him. One more, he thought, and then he would go to the edge of town and sleep for the night near the river. But he had thought that it was his last one each time he ordered another drink. One more kept turning into one more.

Something moved across the table from where he sat. A young man pulled up a chair and sat down. Gafney made no effort to hide the frown that crossed his face when he grumbled under his breath. This young man was as an interruption to his annual ritual, but he soon forgot his irritation as the boy, with great excitement and eyes wide, began to tell the Gap Warrior of his plans to marry his sweetheart, Addie, a week from the day. Gafney found himself fighting through the haze of the drink to hear the boy's story as he recalled how he fell in love with a fisherman's daughter. He would have sent the young man away because this day was a day reserved for Gafney to spend alone with his memories. Something about the boy's story reminded him so of his own, and without realizing it, he found himself fighting through the fog to capture every word.

The young man's name was Drew. He was a hunter and his father was a farmer. He spoke cautiously of how he had grown up here under the shadow and the tyranny of Abbodar. Their village had been subject to paying impossible taxes and suffered greatly under the punishment that came when they were unable to pay them. Most of what they harvested from the sea and their farms would go to supporting the soldiers and after that, there was little left over to live on.

Drew spoke of how he had been able to avoid being taken by the military to fight in one of their campaigns. His tone grew somber as he reflected upon the times he watched helplessly as the soldiers came unannounced to his village. Addie's family had not been so lucky. On one occasion when they came to town, Addie's sister did not make it to safety in time. One of the soldiers wanted to take her with him. Her parents tried to intervene; they were killed in the streets while the rest of the villagers looked on in horror. Over the years, if they were not careful enough, the young girls would be taken from their families. The laws of the land allowed it. Those in power had the right. It was not uncommon for soldiers to take young girls from the village to serve their needs, only to be found a few days later lying dead beside the road after they grew tired of their company. Such was the fate of Addie's sister.

Gafney saw the fear in the young man's eyes growing so he tried to move the conversation in a different direction. "We could talk for days of life's injustices," he said through slurred words, "but for now tell me more of your sweetheart. It brings me a glimmer of joy on this, of all days, when I need it most."

The two of them continued to talk late into the night. Gafney told the young hunter the story of his lost love, and when he came to the end of it, he grew silent and sat staring at the empty goblet on the table for several minutes until it became obvious to Drew that his new friend was fighting to stay awake. The young hunter offered him a place to stay the night in his family barn, but Gafney insisted he sleep by the river under the stars. With no small effort Drew helped his new friend stumble his way to the river's edge where he was camped. Gafney was quickly fading so Drew did his best to lay him gently on the ground, and then he covered him with a blanket. By the time Drew placed a pack under Gafney's head, he had fallen into a deep sleep.

CHAPTER 9

It was mid morning the next day when Drew walked back into town with a stringer full of rabbits and squirrels to show for his morning spent in the woods. As he headed for the market square to see what price he could get for his bounty, he sensed a presence and glanced up to see Addie walking toward him. The first thing that caught his eye was the sun shining off of her blond hair and the curve of her slight build. She smiled at him first, and then they both smiled at one another as young lovers often do.

Her walk quickly turned into a run that ended when she leapt into his arms, and with a small squeal of delight, she kicked her heals up off the ground.

"My brave hunter is back from the hunt," said Addie giggling with joy, she squeezed Drew's neck and kissed him on the cheek several times.

Drew didn't respond immediately as he was always a little embarrassed by Addie's expressions of affection when displayed in public. His face flushed, and he knew it and wished it wouldn't do that, but Addie seemed to gather some pleasure from it.

"Are you so easily embarrassed by the affection of your future wife?"

"Perhaps my future wife should show some restraint when in public. We wouldn't want to give the townspeople the wrong impression now would we?"

"And what impression would that be? The impression that you are deeply in love with me?"

Drew couldn't help noticing how infectious Addie's smile was and the way her long blond hair danced about her shoulders when she laughed.

"The only one who needs to know that is you. The rest of the world is but a mist to me when I'm with you."

"Good. Then you won't mind if I kiss you again." Addie kissed him on the lips, and then she pulled back with that look in her eyes that reminded Drew why he loved her so much.

The smile on Addie's face faded when she felt a gentle tremor vibrate beneath her feet. They both looked toward the edge of village and saw a plume of dust rising in the distance that quickly gave way to riders on horseback as they passed through the haze into view.

"Soldiers," said a woman to warn the surrounding crowd. Several families began to retreat behind the shops for safety. Why had there not been a warning from the watchman? Drew's heart pounded. He grabbed Addie by the arm. "This way. You must hide."

They ran toward a side street, and once out of sight, they headed toward the forest. Drew could feel the fear in Addie as his own heart pounded. He scanned ahead between the buildings. "We will be safe once we reach the forest."

Movement ahead. A rider on horseback appeared near the forest edge. He kicked his mount, and in no time he was upon the two. Dust sprayed around his mount when he came to an abrupt halt in front of them. The dust settled enough for them to see the malevolent smile on his pock marked face.

"And where is it you two think you are going in such a hurry?"

"We have work to tend to sir." Drew hated that his voice sounded small and full of fear.

The soldier looked at Addie with desire in his eyes. "Well then, before you leave, my captain may have need of your services. Now turn and go back the way you came."

Panic threatened as Drew glanced about to see what his options for escape might be. This was the worst thing that could have happened to them. He imagined every dark scenario this situation could lead to for Addie if he could not find a way out of it.

The soldier reached for his sword to threaten. "Move now."

Drew and Addie quickly turned to walk back toward the crowd that was gathering on the main street of the village. Their eyes darted in every direction to find an escape route, but it was too late. Soldiers on all sides surrounded them. They were already taking supplies from the shops and street vendors. One middle-aged lady was pleading with one of the soldiers to leave some food for her children while she clung to a bag of potatoes. He wrenched it away from her, and she fell to the ground.

Soldiers were seen in every direction, some standing, others on horseback. Telsar, the commander in charge, sat atop a powerful black horse wearing black armor of stiff leather with metal greaves and a buckler on his right shoulder. He was a huge man with a red beard braided to a point and slightly overweight with powerful forearms. He motioned to one of his men who responded by walking over to address of the crowd. He went to pull a young girl from among them who was trying to hide behind her mother near the back of the crowd. It was Addie's friend Mara. When the man grabbed her arm she began to scream and grab for her mother. The girl's parents pleaded for mercy, but their cries fell on deaf ears. The soldier commanded the distraught girl to keep silent, but she only cried louder. He hit her on the cheek with the back of his fist, sending her in a heap to the ground. Her cries quickly turned to whimpers. Then two of his comrades jerked her up by the arms and led her away with her feet dragging. The mother started to run after the girl, but the father held her back, and after fighting to free his grip, she gave up and fell sobbing in his arms.

"If there is no one to champion this girl, then it is decided," said the commander. "She will serve the needs of the empire."

The crowd was stunned to silence except for the sound of a weeping mother; no one stepped forward to fight for her. It was Abbodar's law that anyone could champion on behalf of another in order to overrule a sentencing or a decree made by a representative of the realm. If someone was willing, they could fight the soldier who claimed the girl. If the challenger emerged victorious, the girl could stay in the village. It had been a long time since anyone had championed one of the village girls. Most of the young village men had already been taken to fight in battle, leaving mostly widows and elderly men who wouldn't stand a chance of defeating an Abbodar warrior.

Telsar, the lead commander, turned his gaze to scan the crowd until they fell upon Addie who was standing at the back trying to hide behind Drew. An almost imperceptible smile crossed his lips, but Drew caught it instantly, and it sent an explosion of fear roaring through him. He squeezed Addie's hand and felt her shuddering beneath his grip. They were surrounded with no way of escape. The commander prodded his horse to cross the open ground between them until he was almost upon them. The surrounding crowd did not move as he halted his mount and smiled through stained teeth looking down at Addie who was still trying to become invisible behind Drew.

"And how is it that we have missed this one?" said Telsar.

Silence hung in the air until Drew offered a quivering response that was barely heard through his panicked breathing. "Please sir, we are engaged to be married." He heard his own words coming out of his mouth, and he hated how small and powerless he sounded. Everything was crumbling around him, and there was nothing he could do about it.

"Ah, very well then, young man. Since you are planning to marry, then no doubt you will be the one to champion her." Telsar looked at his men who were laughing and then at the crowd. "I welcome the challenge. It has been a long time since our last one."

Whispers floated through the crowd and Drew felt like someone had punched him in the gut and the wind had been sucked out of his lungs, but he knew what he would do. He knew what he had to do. Against impossible odds, he would fight this fight, and he would most likely not survive it. Better to die once trying to save the one he loved than die a thousand deaths losing her to such an awful fate.

"Well, what will it be? Will you champion your bride to be, or will you slink back into whatever hole you crawled out of?"

Defiance welled inside, and Drew released his grip on Addie's hand, he looked her in the eyes where the sparkle that had been there moments ago had faded into fear, but before he could speak she pleaded with him.

"No, please, you will surely die. I will go and you can live."

Addie pulled free of Drew's grip, and with terror in her eyes, moved to surrender herself to the dark fates, but Drew would not allow it. He grabbed her arm forcefully and pulled her close to him.

"Please, Addie," He knew how stubborn she could be. "It is not your decision to make. It is mine and I have made it."

"This is foolishness, my love. You will die, and I will be left to this unspeakable fate." She grabbed his face in her hands and pulled him close. "Please let me go now, and we will end this day with a hope of being united in the future. Somehow, some way we can be together again."

Drew desperately wanted to believe that there was hope in her words, but he knew he could not release her to such a darkness and live with himself. There was always a possibility that he could win. No matter how small, he had to cling to that hope.

"I have made up my mind, my love." Drew pulled Addie close, kissed her forehead, then he whispered in her ear, "I will always love you."

The young hunter wrested free of Addie's grip and turned to face the commander to accept the challenge to champion her freedom. Before he could speak, the commander laughed and taunted, "So we have a champion after all. I didn't think you were man enough to face me, but now I see that I have underestimated the blindness of young love."

The crowd shuffled back as Drew stepped slowly toward the middle of the town square to stand before his challenger. He hated how small he felt in the face of this powerful man, and to add to his desperation, he could hear Addie crying in the distance. He was about to speak when suddenly a powerful grip ceased his arm, and he heard a familiar voice from behind him. "I accept the challenge. I will champion the girl."

Drew turned to see a calm grin on Gafney's face. He started to protest, but his burly friend held up his hand. "Let me take care of this lad. You go down to the river where my camp is and bring me my weapons pack."

Drew hesitated for a moment.

"Now go and move quickly. I'm going to need them."

"And who are you that you should champion this girl?" demanded the commander as his mount shifted restlessly beneath him, stirring up dust.

"I am her protector." As Gafney spoke the words he thought he noted some unease in the commander's bearing.

"Well then, so be it. But if I am to fight the girl's protector, then you shall fight mine."

The Abbodar commander turned to signal his men, causing the crowd of villagers to move backward. A Grunting and snorting sound could be heard coming from beyond where the troops stood. The sounds intensified as the massive head of a beast appeared. The soldiers quickly parted to make way for the thing to pass into the clearing.

"Meet my protector." The commander smiled as he imagined what would happen next. The creature wore a metal collar around its neck, and a chain for a leash was held by one of the soldiers.

The beast was covered in patches of coarse fur and a lizard-like hide that held it all together. Its massive arms ended in clawed paws that scraped the dust on the ground as it walked. Two of the soldiers appeared carrying a battleaxe that took both of them to lift it to the beast who took it in his clawed hand, raised both his arms with the axe in one hand, and roared with glee as if he could taste the blood that was about to be spilled. It towered over Gafney standing at least nine feet tall. A gargenmall that can manipulate a weapon. How can that be? Thought Gafney.

"You can use any weapon you like," said the commander, smiling. "Also, if you lose this contest, the girl goes with me and the boy goes to the battle front."

There came a second stirring from among the troops as five scavenger hounds held by chains appeared from among them.

"And one more thing," said the commander. "I will loose the scavs on this village if you do not survive this contest."

Gafney seemed to ignore what the soldier had said and looked about to see if Drew had returned yet with his weapons. The commander wondered if Gafney had even heard his words. No single man had ever defeated one of these monsters created of magic and flesh. He had seen many try in the arena, but the power of these creatures was far too strong for mere flesh and blood. The darkest part of his soul relished the thought of releasing the scavs to feed on the villagers; they had produced little in recent months to supply his troops, so they would not be missed.

The crowd parted, and Drew appeared out of breath with Gafney's weapons bag slung over his shoulder. The Gap Warrior held out his hand to receive it, and then he turned to the commander and lifted his battleaxe from the bag and said, "I hope you are not too fond of this creature."

As the Gap Warrior gripped the handle of his weapon, the commander thought he saw a flicker of light dance beneath the big man's fingers. He quickly dismissed it, assuming it was just the sun reflecting off the blade.

Commander Telsar's soldiers had not seen blood for sometime. His command had been in Abbodar recruiting new warriors for the distant conflicts, and when they could gather enough of them, he would be released to return to the battle lines. To Telsar, these villagers were of no value unless they could provide a sufficient amount of supplies for his troops. He had, on more than one occasion, loosed scavengers on a village when they failed to meet his expectations. He had also done it to send a message. Today it would be to send a message. Don't defy a commander of Abbodar. The laws of the arena extended throughout the kingdom, and those laws allowed citizens of Abbodar to champion another in a battle to the death. The victor would decide the fate of the one championed. In a warrior culture, many disputes were settled at the edge of a blade. It was very rare that a villager championed a challenge, and Telsar wanted to make sure that it stayed that way. Abbodar ruled by inflicting fear and terror through power, and Telsar would have it no other way.

"Let's get on with it," said Gafney, shifting back and forth, spinning the axe in his hand.

Telsar signaled, and the creature raised its crudely honed axe and howled a cry that shook the ground. Gafney assumed battle position, and he could feel his axe, Demon Slayer, vibrating beneath his grip. Supernatural energy pumped through him and his blade, causing his heart to race as fear and courage merged. These emotions were no stranger to this Gap Warrior; they were his call to battle.

    The beast attacked first in a lumbering charge that Quickly closed the space between them. The onlookers pressed backward, but Gafney stood his ground. If the enemy you face is bigger and decides to charge first, it's always better to hold your position. Use his momentum and power against him. Sparks danced upon the axe blade in his hand, sending a rush of energy bolting through him.

    The soldiers cheered and the children in the crowd ran for cover. The beast bore down on Gafney in a rush, and with both of its paws, swung its axe in a vertical motion downward toward his head. Gafney took two steps to his left and rolled forward in one fluid motion, and with his axe gripped in both hands, he sliced it across the thigh of the beast and it screamed in rage as blood and sparks exploded from the wound.

    "What manner of magic is this?" said Telsar to his second in command who offered only a shrug in response to the query. "How dare a commoner use magic without it being permitted?"

    The beast lumbered to its right, growled and swung its blade a second time at the smaller man. Gafney blocked it with his own weapon and a small spray of sparks erupted when they connected. The force of the giant axe sent a stunning jolt that knocked Gafney to the ground half dazed. He shook his head and quickly regained his focus. Can't do that again. The creature growled, bearing his dripping maw full of yellow teeth and sent another angry strike aimed at Gafney's midsection. But the Gap Warrior rolled to his right and the giant axe shattered the ground, sending dust spraying. He knew the opening would come if he was patient enough, and when it did, Gafney seized the moment and charged straight at the beast as if he would attack it head on. At the last minute he ducked down beneath a slashing claw, sliding between its legs to his feet on the backside of the monster. In one fluid motion that merged a deathly blend of quickness and raw power, the Gap Warrior sprang to his feet behind the beast and hammered his blade, demon slayer, into the lower back of his foe.

Sparks erupted, and the creature could be heard shrieking in pain throughout the village and into the surrounding woods. Gafney ran up its backside before it could react and drove his blade for one final strike into the back of the thing's head. It went silent, arched forward and toppled to the ground dead. Gafney was still standing on its back, the whole place was briefly silent, even the soldiers. Then the villagers exploded in cheers. Addie jumped up and down, latching her arms around Drew and screeched in joy.

"Enough," cried an angry Telsar, bringing the crowd to silent submission.

Rage gripped the Abbodar warrior as a flood of shame threatened to drown him. He had been openly defied in front of these pathetic village commoners, and now he wanted blood.

"The use of magic without sanction of our high priests is a violation of law." Telsar stepped toward the Gap Warrior. "Therefore, your victory is meaningless, and your actions have brought judgment upon this village."

Terror erupted throughout the crowd as they scattered in every direction. Some ran for the cover of buildings and others toward the forest. Snarling could be heard from the ranks of the soldiers, as if the scavenger hounds knew what the commander was about to do next. Telsar raised his hand, sending a signal to his men. They quickly responded by releasing a pack of the scavs on the fleeing crowd. Horrifying screams filled the village when they realized what was happening. The creatures bolted in every direction seeking flesh to devour. Then Telsar released his men.

One scav bore down on a small boy who was fleeing toward the nearest building, but the child was not fast enough to outrun the swifter creature as it quickly closed the gap between the two of them. The beast sprang at the child baring its fangs—tasting the blood before its final strike But it would be denied as Gafney arrived at the same time with rage flaring in his eyes. He severed the beast's head with one swing of his blade, grabbed the boy and carried him to safety.

Too many to fight, I can't help them. He glanced up to see

Drew sprinting with a bow and in full stride the hunter pulled an arrow from the quiver on his back, released the shaft, and it found its mark in an Abbodar warrior's chest, knocking him backward off his horse. Warriors and scavs chased down the fleeing villagers who offered no resistance. I hate scavs. Gafney charged one of the beasts lashing at it with deadly force, but to his surprise it suddenly backed away from him as if waiting for something. Then he saw why. At least five of the demonic hounds circled and closed in on his position. Sparks danced along the blade of his axe. Gafney's heart pounded in his chest as the hopeless reality of his plight sank in. What now? The Gap Warrior spun in a circle trying to keep all of them in his view, they continued to close in on him slowly, methodically. An arrow from Drew's bow pierced the neck of the one nearest to him. The hound winced and swatted it away with its paw.

    Not willing to wait any longer to become scav meat, Gafney charged at one of the demon beasts, and to his surprise, it startled backward just enough to leave a small opening. Gafney bolted past the startled scav, clubbing it aside with the end of his axe, and he flew past in a blur. The others turned in hot pursuit. He knew he could not outrun them and that they would catch him soon enough, but he was out of options. With a little luck, if he could make it into one of the buildings, he might be able to hold them off. Their visceral snarls closed in from behind until they seemed to completely surround him. I'm going to make it. Just a little more, and I'll be there. Thud. The paws of one of them slam against his backside sending him chest first, pounding him into the dirt. Twisting to his back he desperately tried to find room to swing his blade in defense, but there was little room. He pulled a long knife from his belt and shoved it into the gut of the one on top of him. Something clamped onto his leg. Pain lanced through him as he felt the teeth digging in. He lashed out with the knife in his hand while his axe lay at his side in the dirt. Another bite fastened on his shoulder. Dizziness threatened—he was starting to fade.

Flashes exploded around him as the scavs howled and released their grip. The one on top of him fell to the ground dead with smoke rising from its hide. Through the fog in his head and the dust swirling about, Gafney could see a lone figure attacking and spinning in fluid motions bearing down on the creatures. With great effort he rose against the pain in his leg and shoulder. Gripping his axe in his good hand he launched it toward the closest scav drawing sparks and blood.

The surviving scavs retreated in the direction of a less powerful prey. Gafney saw his rescuer standing over one of the slain creatures looking in his direction. The wounded Gap Warrior thought he looked familiar, and he knew he must be a warrior of the Gap, but he could not recognize him.

Then the stranger spoke, "This isn't the first time I've had to get you out of a bind, old man."

Gafney shuffled toward him, peering through dust-filled eyes, trying to recognize the man the voice belonged to. When he was close enough to him, he grabbed the man's shoulder and pulled himself upward to look him in the eyes.

"Cyle?" questioned Gafney through ragged breaths. "You've picked up some skills since I saw you last."

The wounded Gap Warrior's eyes rolled back in his head. The chaos continued all around. Cyle quickly surveyed the area. Then he realized he was struggling to hold the larger Gafney upright.

A soldier flew in from behind Cyle—a bolt hit the attacker in the center of his chest. His feet dragged forward, and then he fell lifeless to the ground.

"He's losing blood," yelled Cyle's friend, Choppa, as he restrung his crossbow. "We have to get him out of here, or he won't make it."

"We need to take him to the boat—over there." Cyle motioned to a horse that had been abandoned by a fallen warrior. "Help me get him on its back, and you can take him to the boat. I'll join you as soon as I can."

Several villagers lay lifeless and some near death. Their bodies scattered along the road and next to buildings. Others had been fortunate enough to reach the safety of the forest. Drew had never killed a man before this day, but in the last few minutes he had slain three with his bow. They were easy marks compared to the smaller game he was used to hunting, but already the images of the men he had shot haunted his thoughts. Each time he played it in his mind, he felt sick to his stomach and wanted to vomit. Suddenly, it dawned on him that he needed to tell his parents what was happening. He grabbed Addie by the arm, and they ran toward his family's farm to warn them. When they reached the edge of town, Drew looked back and saw smoke rising to the sky. His heart sank when he realized they were burning the place down.

The two of them ran through a field of corn and then crossed an empty field that came to a stream bordering one side of his family's farm. After they waded through the cold water, they stopped to take cover at a stand of trees within view of his home. Drew's heart raced as his eyes scanned the property, looking for signs of any soldiers.

"Wait here," whispered Drew, pointing to stand behind a tree.

"I'm going with you," pleaded Addie.

Drew put his finger to her mouth to silence her. "No, it's not safe. Something is not right. Let me check it out first."

The doors of the house opened, and two soldiers exited. One had hold of his mother, almost dragging her as she stumbled trying to keep her feet. Fear struck, and without thinking, the young hunter bolted toward them. His right hand had already strung an arrow, and in full stride, he pulled it back to full force and released it. The wind swirled about the shaft as it found its mark in the neck of the man walking in front. Drew reached back for another arrow as he ran forward at a full sprint. His hand flailed for an arrow, but the quiver was empty. The remaining warrior pulled a blade and plunged it into his mother's back. Drew's heart stopped. She fell limply at the man's feet.

An explosion of rage erupted in the young hunter as he ran toward his fallen mother. Two more warriors stepped out from inside the house with swords drawn. Drew came to an abrupt halt leaving several paces between him and the three soldiers.

"Why?" yelled Drew through tears, fighting to fill his lungs with air and maintain a strong front.

"You defied an Abbodar commander," one of them spoke coldly. "Now you and your girl will pay the price for it."

The soldier motioned in the direction where Drew had left Addie at the tree line. He heard her scream and saw another soldier appear holding her against her will. She struggled to get free of his grip; Drew turned and ran in her direction and he was almost to her when he caught sight of something moving in the shadows of the trees nearby. First there was a blur of motion and then a thud. A wooden staff came crashing down on the head of Addies's captor dropping him to the ground, and where he once stood, Cyle appeared.

"This way," Cyle motioned. "Gafney sent me. It's okay. I'm with him."

Drew embraced Addie and hesitated, looking back toward the house where the three soldiers were moving in their direction. "I can't. I have to help my parents."

"Your parents are gone. There's nothing you can do now except save yourself and your girl."

Drew looked back at the house again and saw the approaching soldiers. He felt like his insides were being ripped out. He looked to Addie and saw the terror in her eyes, and he realized that he had to leave. He had no choice if he was going to protect her, so he took her hand and ran with Cyle toward the stream in the direction of the village with the soldiers in close pursuit. They could hear the soldiers from behind them barking out orders to give chase.

"Where are we going?" asked Drew.

"To the docks. We have a boat."

By the time the three of them broke clear of the cornfield, they had widened the distance between them and their pursuers.

There was a thick haze of black smoke from the burning of the village, and Cyle could hear the voices of soldiers in the distance calling out to one another through the smoke, but there were no villagers to be seen. As they neared the river's edge, the smoke cleared, and Cyle could see Choppa waving to him from the edge of the docks.

To their left, four Abbodar warriors broke clear of the smoke and moved to cut them off. From behind, the three who had been pursuing them were closing in.

"Keep running," cried Cyle. "Help is on the way."

Smoke swirled over the end of the docks, and Choppa disappeared into the haze.

"Go to the end of the dock, and you will see a boat waiting there." Cyle pointed. "Now! Before it's too late."

Drew knew he could do nothing but run. His arrows were spent, and if he stopped to fight, he would leave Addie exposed. Cyle turned toward the attackers to make a stand.

"What about you?" asked Drew. "There are too many of them."

"I told you. Help is on the way."

Drew looked back at the approaching warriors, not wanting to leave the young man with the staff behind to face them alone. Then he felt a tug on his arm. It was Addie looking up at him with pleading eyes.

Reluctantly, he took her hand and pulled her toward the dock when suddenly, through the haze, they saw two stout figures running toward the one with the staff. What are dwarves doing here? wondered Drew. They both had long shaggy hair and scraggly beards and carried battleaxes. One of them wore a patch over his left eye. As the two ran by, they yelled an unfamiliar battle cry, and then the sound of metal on metal rang in the air.

Choppa appeared, calling and motioning them in his direction, "Quick! Help me with the lines." He reached down and started unrolling the ropes wrapped around the moorings.

Once Addie and Drew finished pulling ropes, they jumped

on board while Choppa held the last line, watching nervously in the direction of the two dwarves and the staff warrior. They heard the cries of soldiers and the sound of feet pounding on the peer right before they saw Cyle and the two dwarves running toward them with a band of Abbodar warriors chasing close behind. The two dwarves piled onto the bow with Cyle right behind them. He launched himself from the dock with his staff and landed on both feet on deck.

The one-eyed dwarf grabbed a pole and pushed them away from the dock while yelling at the other dwarf. "The sail. Hoist the sail Bernard."

"Of course I will hoist the sail, cousin," said Bernard with irritation under his breath. "What does he think I'm going to do? Stop and fish?"

Soldiers cursed as they watching helplessly at the end of the dock. The wind caught the sails of the old fishing boat and pulled it sluggishly toward the middle of the river. Then it seemed to pick up speed as it headed down stream. Drew and Addie clung to one another as they watched their village fade from view with tears forming in their eyes. They feared it was the last time they would see their home.

CHAPTER 10

Gerrid and his company had traveled through the night under the cover of darkness in order to protect the elf girl. The going was slow because the former prisoner had to stop several times when he grew fatigued. Each time they stopped, Bryann would become anxious and push to keep them going. Abbodar was not a city one would want to be caught outside at night. Packer was a street hound, and like most of his kind, he lived in what they called a pack. A pack was a gang of hounds that ran a section of the city that they controlled at night. Packs often fought one another trying to gain more territory. Some packs were less hostile than others, and on two occasions Packer knew the pack leader and was able to barter passage by trading something from his backpack.

Gerrid was glad to be leaving Abbodar, and the closer they came to the edge of the city, the lighter he felt. He had lived under the tyranny of darkness for too long and he was ready to finally leave it behind. Not much had changed since he entered prison two years ago. The warrior class continued to live in extreme prosperity while most of the city lived in squalor. The priests and the elite warriors lived in the finest houses and enjoyed a lifestyle that rivaled royalty. Their children attended the most prestigious schools where they were trained in the art of weaponry and indoctrinated into the military culture.

Abbodar was unique because the combat arena and the temple of worship were viewed as places of worship. They both represented the pinnacle of what their culture stood for. In the temple the Maggrid Priests led the worship of their gods, and most sacrifices were done only in the company of the priests. In the arena, the gods worshiped were the most powerful of the warrior class, and sacrifices sanctioned by the Maggrids were done in the arena for all to see.

All of those that were part of the warrior class wore a small star-shaped tattoo on their left temple next to their eye. Each additional star represented a victory in the arena. The ones with the most stars, reflecting the most kills in the arena, were afforded the highest level of social power and respect in the kingdom. Many became commanders in the army while others ruled whole regions of the realm as magistrates.

For centuries the Maggrid priests of the Terashom faith had served in the duties of temple worship and as advisers to the king. This gave them great power and influence. As the warrior class of Abbodar increased in power and gained positions of influence, the Maggrid priests saw this as a threat to their own status, so among them arose a new class of warrior priests.

Through a ritual of sacrifice, these new Maggrid warriors opened themselves to the dark magic by inviting the spirits of the void to invade their physical beings. The new warrior class became known as the Ravens.

There were two classes of Ravens - Black and Red. The Red Ravens were the more powerful and exclusive of the two. If a Black Raven went undefeated after twenty battles in the arena against foes picked by the Maggrid priests, they would earn the rank of Red Raven. Once the Red Ravens came to dominate the arena games, their reputation grew throughout several kingdoms, which brought the finest warriors from faraway lands to battle against them. No Red Raven had ever been defeated in arena combat due to their supreme fighting skills which had been honed in them since birth. They also possessed empowerment that came from the dark spirits of the void that infested them.

The Ravens represented the might of Abbodar's warrior class, and the citizens idolized them as their greatest heroes. Their primary role was to protect the king, guard the Temple of Terashom and carry out any assignments that suited the interests of the kingdom.

Gerrid recalled the day the Red Ravens came to arrest him. They had gathered in a barn of one of the faithful where over one hundred worshipers of the One Faith met to hear his teaching. He had just finished telling them of the first time he had seen the great bird on the day of victory when Talinor defeated the Boogaran horde. The clouds had parted, and as the light streamed through, a giant eagle burst into the blue, screeching a terrifying sound that penetrated him to his core.

"For the first time in almost twenty years, the people of Talinor began to sing," he told them. "Not only had we been set free from Boogara, we had been freed from ourselves and our empty life of faithlessness."

The doors of the barn suddenly burst open as soldiers

entered, led by two of the Red Ravens. Gerrid's friend Dallien and five others wanted to fight them, but he would not allow it, knowing that they would have perished instantly. He convinced them to hold back, and then he willingly surrendered himself to the soldiers.

At the time of Gerrid's imprisonment, the followers of the One Faith had been growing rapidly under his leadership. Drok Relnik had convinced Vanus that Gerrid should be taken into captivity before the dissenters grew any larger. The warlock had only been in Abbodar for a short time, but his mastery of the dark magic impressed Vanus, and Relnik had been part of the Boogaran nation. This made him valuable to the king who was already planning to invade their kingdom. In short, the warlock's value had brought him into their inner circle where he became a trusted adviser to both of them.

"Gerrid." Packer's voice brought him back from his thoughts. He had been scouting possible routes to exit the city. "There are two main roads we can take, but both are being patrolled by soldiers looking for Sera and the assassin."

"Well then, I guess we'll have to find another way out. Sera would never make it past the inspection post."

"There is another way," he advised. "We can travel north of the last road and leave through the corn fields. They haven't harvested yet, so if we keep our heads down, we should be okay."

Bryann stood quietly by as Packer offered his assessment. He had brought them this far without incident, and his knowledge of the city was greater than hers, so she was willing to trust his judgment. She hadn't said much since they left her aunt's home, and Gerrid found that he was feeling a little uneasy with her dark and distant mood. He had tried to talk to her to get her to open up, but each time he was met with resistance. She had little to say and had made it clear that she just wanted to get him to his destination, and then she would be moving on.

"That sounds like a good plan to me Packer. What do you think, Bryann?" asked Gerrid, trying to draw her into the conversation.

"Whatever you think is fine with me." Bryann shrugged. Then added, "My only concern is what happens when we get beyond the fields. We will be in the open and there are mostly rolling hills with only a few rocks and trees for cover." Bryann lowered her voice so the sleeping Sera could not hear her. "If we didn't have the elf girl, we wouldn't have to worry about all this."

"She stays with us," Packer fired back loud enough to cause Sera to stir in her sleep.

"Of course she does," said Gerrid, shooting a stern glance at Bryann.

"Listen, I promised my aunt to get you to Hebron Forest. If the girl becomes a problem, I say we leave her behind."

"That's not going to happen," Gerrid replied. "I owe my life to the elves. If they had not joined us in our battle, Talinor would have fallen to Boogara." Gerrid leaned toward Bryann. "You're welcome to leave any time you like, but she stays with us."

The fire in Gerrid's eyes took Bryann off guard. Until now he had said very little, and she too had been quiet, mostly keeping her thoughts to herself while seething over her obligation to fulfill this quest for her aunt. She resented being stuck with this so-called holy man and his weak body that was slowing them all down. She hated weak things, and to her, his faith was nothing but a crutch for the weak and helpless. She would be happy when this whole thing was over and she could move on.

"As I promised my aunt, I'll see you to the forest. After that you are all on your own," said Bryann as she turned to walk away.

Gerrid struggled with Bryann's disposition, but he was willing to put up with it because he knew her fighting skills might be needed at some point. She had an edge to her, and he saw the walls she had erected around herself as a challenge. As long as she was with them, he would keep trying to get past her shell, even though he knew that it would irritate her. He found some pleasure in that.

"It's settled then. We wait until dark, and then we leave.

That will give us the night for cover when we clear the fields at the base of the hills." Gerrid glanced over at the sleeping Sera. "And I will sleep now. I suggest you all try to do the same. We will be traveling through most of the night."

The stone wind shelter they had settled in for the day was like one of many that had been built throughout Abbodar to protect against the howls. As Gerrid moved to the corner of the shelter to sleep, he felt annoyed with his lack of energy and how drained he was from all the walking. Sleep did little to energize him, but he welcomed the break it gave him from the exhaustion, and he found that when he closed his eyes, the next thing he remembered was waking up.

Packer settled down next to Sera while Bryann paced restlessly outside the shelter until she settled into keeping watch.

Gerrid looked at Packer fading quickly to sleep next to Sera and realized that he liked the street hound and admired his strong sense of survival and street smarts. In the short time they had traveled together, Packer was always collecting things and stuffing them in his pack or one of the numerous pouches hanging from his shoulders. He was constantly stopping to make trades with any stranger on the street that would stop long enough to discuss a deal. He would lag behind, working with someone to make a trade. Often they would lose sight of him, and then he would re-appear running to catch back up to them, excited about his latest barter.

Packer had told Gerrid that the other street hounds used to call him the rat until one day his friend Runner was attacked by a scav, and the only reason that he survived his wounds was because Packer had the medicine in one of his pouches that saved Runner's life. After that they started calling him Packer, and he was proud to bear a name given him because of an act of kindness he had performed.

Abbodar was a harsh society where the ravages of war and lives lost in the arena left many children homeless. Some ended up being prostituted by the streetcorner pimps, and others became slaves in the homes of the rich, but some were able to

SWORD OF DELIVERANCE

escape those fates and managed to join a pack of street hounds where they lived in the back alleys and streets of Abbodar.

Street packs, became the new families to the orphaned children. Every pack had a section of the city they considered their own turf. Travelers in the city had to pass through the different pack territories. Travel by day was not a problem because the packs were mostly active at night. It was Packer who led them through the city avoiding the more hostile packs.

Gerrid attempted to sleep, but his thoughts would not settle into cooperating with his sore muscles and weary bones. Doubt continued to tear at the frayed edges of his faith. Pamela had pressed him to go to the forest to regain leadership of the followers, and he had agreed primarily because he was too tired and weak at the time to resist her passionate challenge. He thought of his homeland, Talinor, and the freedom he once enjoyed there that he had taken for granted. It was a beautiful land that he felt deeply connected to, and best of all, it was his land, the place of his birth. When he was in prison he had often dreamed of the day he could return there and walk back through the gates of the walled city. Some days it was that dream that was the only thing that got him through the day.

You have lost what faith you had, said the voices in his mind. You have nothing left to offer the followers. The thoughts pressed in upon him. The voices felt hostile and alien, but he found that he was agreeing with them; and when he did, he felt a deep restlessness in his soul. He could not see the shadow fairies that carried the messages to his mind. They were invisible to him, sent from the darkness of the void—fluttering about at the edges of his conscience, shaming and taunting him to doubt who he was and what he once stood for.

How can you put your faith in the One who left you to rot in that place? One of the fairies whispered softly as it fluttered about his head. Gerrid agreed with its offerings, half asleep by now. The fairies pressed harder with Gerrid's agreement and repeated the thought, only this time it was slightly different. How can I put my faith in the One who left me to rot in that place? This time the thought seemed less of an intrusion and more familiar, as if it was his own. It was the last thought on his mind as he faded into a restless sleep. *How can I put my faith in the One who left me to rot in that place?*

The haze of exhaustion was slow in releasing its iron grip on Gerrid, he fought his way through the fog of sleep until he came to awareness. It seemed as though he had only been out for a few minutes. Staring wide-eyed inches from his face was the elf girl, Sera, and behind her was a bushy-headed Packer.

"Time to go," the elf girl whispered softly, grinning from ear to ear. She remained motionless as Packer rushed to gather his remaining pouches.

Bryann shot the look of impatience that was becoming all too familiar to him. He gathered his belongings into his bag, and Packer offered him a piece of bread and a half eaten apple. Gerrid looked suspiciously at bites on the apple, and Packer nodded toward Sera as if to blame her for its condition.

Packer led the way and Bryann followed. After passing through several narrow alleyways littered with garbage that caused an unbearable stench, they arrived at the edge of the city where a cornfield sprawled out before them. On the other side they could see the moonlit foothills that lie at the base of the mountains.

"Bundle her up and make sure those pointy ears are hidden," snapped Bryann. "There's still a lot of light with the full moon and we can't be too careful."

Sera hooded her head and the four of them set out across the open field. For the first time Gerrid felt as though some of his strength was returning, but he knew he still had a long way to go before he would regain the weight he once carried.

The corn in the field still hung from the stalks and Packer kept stopping to pull the cobs and stuff them into one of his bags.

When they came to the end of the field, they started up the gentle slope of the foothills, and Gerrid looked back at the vast city of Abbodar silhouetted against a canopy of stars. He felt an emptiness inside as he took it all in. For some reason he found himself searching his heart to regain the passion he once had for this place when he first came here. He had once forsaken all, left his homeland to travel here to bring the message of the One Faith, but there was nothing of that passion left in him. He felt only emptiness as he struggled to recall the feelings he once had for this dark and foreboding place. A deep sadness set in when he realized that the fire of his mission here had been swallowed up by the consuming power of this evil land. He had arrived here with great faith and vision to bring the story of his One Faith to any that would receive it, but so few had been open to it and the ones who had received the message were mostly beggars and commoners who ended up fleeing in fear to the hills for their own survival.

Anger stirred inside at the thought of the followers fleeing the city—Gerrid pushed it back. How could he blame them for running to the mountains? He was doing the same thing. Running. All he wanted to do was live free. If the followers had not left the city, most of them would have ended up dead in the arena and their children sacrificed in the temples.

The shadow fairies appeared suddenly, fluttering about his head, their tiny wings flashing blue sprays of light as they hovered near his ears. This place swallows the light, and the light cannot overcome it, they whispered softly in unison. It's true, agreed Gerrid in his thoughts.

The darkness is too great. It was a mistake to come here in the first place, the voices whispered again.

"It was a mistake coming here," said Gerrid softly to himself, thinking no one had heard him.

"It was not a mistake," the voice broke into Gerrid's thoughts.

It was Sera staring up at him with her Elfin eyes filled with tears. He suddenly felt the deep sorrow they carried within them, but he did not know what it was about or why he felt it so deeply.

"Your journey is not yet finished and the path before you

continues. What you think is behind you, is not behind you. Give faith a chance to finish the work it began in you and in this place," whispered Sera holding her ground in front of Gerrid. "And one more thing. You must take hold of what is before you. It is yours and yours alone to grasp."

The gentle strength of her spirit began to draw him in, but the shadow voices would not back down. She doesn't know what you've been through. She's too young to understand.

She doesn't know what I've been through, thought Gerrid, agreeing with the voices in his mind.

Then, as if she was reading his mind, Sera said, "You must choose the voice you will follow. No one can do that for you. The shadow voices do not bring truth. They only bring deception."

Her words were bewildering, but before he could ask her to explain, Bryann hissed at them. "We are wasting time here. We need to go and get clear of the city before we lose the dark."

Gerrid ruffled against Bryann's request, but he knew she was right. He turned to ascend the hill, and the voices whispered again. She is only a child. What can she possibly know of such things? Gerrid thought. She is only a child. What can she possibly know of such things? The shadow fairies flitted about, singing and celebrating the fruit that their newly planted seeds were producing in Gerrid's mind.

CHAPTER 11

Drok Relnik was still agonizing over his lost opportunity to sacrifice the elf girl at the altar of Terashom. The fact that there had been no success in tracking her down intensified his distress. Getting to sacrifice an elf child was rare, and the loss would not soon be forgotten. When his scouts brought him news of rumors spreading near the coast of a ship landing in Fair Winds flying the flag of an eagle on its mast, he flew into a rage and started cursing and hurling pottery vases against the wall of his chambers. To add to his consternation, they also told him of an incident in Pallarim where an axe-wielding warrior had killed a gargenmall single-handedly with the use of magic, and in retaliation, the soldiers had burned the whole village to the ground. The axe warrior had escaped with two dwarves and another warrior who handled a magic staff.

He screamed at the scouts when they first reported the news, "Why would Gap Warriors be coming anywhere near Abbodar?" The scouts had no idea who Gap Warriors were, and therefore, had no response to his rant which only increased the warlock's rage. His men watched anxiously as Relnik seethed, pacing back and forth across the chamber floors. They could only passively listen to the sound of his boots crunching noisily on broken pottery shards until he stopped suddenly and gave them orders to dispatch two groups of three Black Ravens with instructions to kill anyone matching the descriptions they had been given.

The warlock enjoyed a position within the hierarchy of the kingdom that allowed him to command the Maggrid Warriors to carry out his bidding. This was the first time he gave orders to the Ravens and chose not to inform Vanus of his plans.

Cyle stood on deck of the Sea Horse carefully scanning the shoreline in search of any pursuing soldiers. Energy from the battle coursed through him as he fidgeted with his staff, spinning it in the air over his head in circular motions. He knew it would take a few hours before he could settle that after-battle energy to a more peaceful calm. So far he had seen nothing to concern him.

Bernard and Ginzer were the proud captains of the Sea Horse, a rundown fishing vessel whose sails seemed tattered to the point that they might rend to pieces at any moment. He was surprised the sails had sustained them on their journey across the sea. The smell of stale fish melded with the boat's creaking deck planks. Cyle tried to ignore the odor, but he did find that the river breezes which floated across the vessel helped to dissipate the smell and provide brief moments of relief. Keeping watch gave him something to occupy his mind; it took the edge off the restless energy that drove his constant need to stay in motion.

He reflected on his life since leaving the kingdom of Talinor almost two years ago. Cyle had grown up in the walled city across the sea, and since leaving there two years ago, he had not been able to return. Life as a Gap Warrior had kept him busy, taking him to other lands and cultures where he fought in several gap battles, defending the breach. His last battle had taken him into the void to battle a horde of demons that were attempting to cross over and wreak havoc among a caravan of elves who were traveling from the Elvin kingdom of Krellander to sing in a worship festival held by the Highlanders. They were known as the Cantors of Krellander and renowned for their majestic singing of the high praises of the Ancient of Days. Due to seeds of pride and bitterness bringing discord among the singers, a breach opened in the void. This allowed the dark ones to cross over and disrupt their worship in song. They were spending more time fighting one another rather than doing what they were called to do, sing the high praises of the Ancient of Days.

Once Cyle finished his assignment in the Highlands, he and his friend, Choppa, who had been traveling with him since he had left home two years ago, wanted to visit nearby Talinor. They were almost to the walled city when Mellidar, Cyle's Guardian, disrupted their journey with another assignment redirecting them to cross the sea of Baddaris to the lands of Abbodar.

Both were unhappy about the change of plans. Both wanted to return home, but Cyle's frustration was mostly because Mellidar's directive meant that he would not be able to see his grandmother for the first time in almost two years. He had tried to reason with Mellidar, hoping the Guardian would grant him just a few more days to make the trip, but he was unwavering. Since that moment, there had grown a seed of discord between the two of them.

Mellidar continued Cyle's instruction in Gap warfare for the two years following Talinor and the great battle with Boogara. Recently the Guardian's training regimen had intensified with more frequent visits and longer sessions that sometimes lasted until late into the night.

In the beginning of Cyle's training before he knew he was called to be a Gap Warrior, Mellidar would appear to him in his dreams. At first, Cyle thought they were nothing more than dreams until they became as real as if he was awake. It was in his dream state that he learned how to fight using the weapon chosen for him, a simple staff given to him to battle shadow wraiths and other dark creatures of the void. Then one morning he woke up to find a staff lying by his side. He often recalled the first time he attempted to fight with the staff. He was amazed to discover that the skills he had learned in his dreams had transferred into the real world.

Since that time, Cyle had engaged in several Gap battles, fighting demons on both sides of the void. He preferred the battles fought here in this world when the demons crossed over to the sphere of flesh. He would never get used to the chaos of the void and the hideous beings that oppressed him every time he entered there to battle.

Faced with the task of crossing the Sea of Baddaris, he and Choppa went to the seaport city of Velarga, just three days walk from Talinor. Their plan was to hire a ship for the crossing, so Choppa went to the docks to find a sailing vessel for passage. He returned with the old dwarves, Ginzer and Bernard. Seeing the one-eyed Ginzer and his cousin Bernard was a welcome sight to Cyle after the letdown of not being able to go to Talinor. He had built a strong bond with the two dwarves who had fought side by side at the front lines in the battle of Talinor. When the battle had ended, they retired their axes, took up fishing, and purchased a rundown fishing vessel that barely qualified as a small ship. The two insisted that the Seahorse was a hearty vessel and strong enough to make the journey to cross Baddaris. After two years of fishing the waters up and down the coastal region, they had grown restless for new adventure and had insisted on providing their ship for transport. Cyle and Choppa were happy to reconnect with their old friends from Talinor and had hoped the two could give them some updates on how things were in their homeland, but Ginzer and Bernard had not been back to Talinor since the victory over Boogara.

"We need medicine or your friend will die." Drew's voice brought Cyle back to the moment. "His wounds are badly infected, and he runs a fever."

Cyle nodded at the hunter and headed toward the room where Gafney was being cared for. When they entered the small cabin, they found Choppa and Addie trying with little success to give him a drink of water. Most of it spilled down the side of his mouth. Blood soaked bandages clung to the sweat-covered skin of Gafney who was unconscious and moaning in pain. Both arms and one leg had been wrapped to slow the bleeding. Addie dabbed his forehead with a wet cloth and looked up, her eyes filled with concern.

"He grows weaker by the moment and I fear for his life. Please, isn't there something we can do?"

"I already spoke with Ginzer and Bernard, and they have no medicine to help us," said Choppa as he dipped another rag in a bowl of fresh water and handed it to Addie to wipe Gafney's brow.

"What about the Buntoc?" asked Addie as she looked to Drew with pleading eyes. "They have strong medicine and they would help you."

"Who are the Buntoc?" asked Cyle.

"They are a nomadic tribe of warriors that live in the high mountain regions, and she is right, they would probably have what we need to help him. They are experts in the natural herbs that can be found in the wilderness."

"That settles it then. We leave right away," said Cyle. "How long will it take to get to them?"

"It's hard to say," offered Drew. "They are constantly moving about because they want to avoid being found by the military. They are a strong people and have refused to come under the rule of Abbador."

"How is it you know them, Drew?" asked Cyle.

"I met the chief's son on one of my recent hunting trips. We have hunted wild boar together many times. I believe he will do what he can to help us."

"Choppa," Cyle nodded at his friend, "let Ginzer know that we need to land this thing, and see if Bernard can pack some supplies for the three of us."

Choppa nodded and headed for the galley.

Addie reached out for Drew's hand and pulled him to her. "Please be careful. They will be looking for us."

"We will be fine, my love. We'll back here in two days." Drew pulled Addie close to kiss her on her forehead. Addie smiled and buried her head in his chest.

"Two days," said Cyle. "That may be too long. Look at him, his fever worries me."

Gafney's body jerked. Then he grunted and said, "I'm not dead yet, boy. I'll be fine. I might even do some fishing while you are gone." Then he fell back to his bed and passed out.

Bernard entered the room with a cup in his hand and a scowl on his face. "Why didn't someone tell me of the fever?" The dwarf shuffled over to Gafney, lifted his head and proceeded to pour the contents of the cup into his mouth while some of it drizzled out the sides. He choked most of it down.

"This won't fix it, but it will cut the fever. It will have to do for now," barked Bernard, and then he headed for the door mumbling under his breath something about not ever being told anything. He stopped at the door and growled, "What's everyone waiting for? Your supplies are ready. Collect them and be on your way."

Drew led Cyle and Choppa at a brisk pace, and after two hours had passed, the path began to grow steeper. The Gelderine was a densely wooded region filled with thick ferns and moss hanging from tree limbs and fallen branches. Beams of light broke through the overhead canopy lighting up patches of the forest floor.

"Did you say they were a nomadic tribe?" asked Cyle just after crossing through an open meadow and re-entering the tree line.

"How will we find them if they are always on the move?"

"We won't," answered Drew, surveying the area. "They will find us. They probably already know we are here."

"What? You mean, they might be watching us?" said Choppa nervously. "They don't eat people, do they?"

"Only when it's a full moon," responded Drew, trying to sound serious.

Choppa glanced up to study the sky, and Cyle Laughed under his breath.

"I'm hungry," said Choppa.

"Of course you are," said Cyle. "We can take a short break so you can eat. I don't want to have to carry you if you end up fainting on the trail for lack of food. Why don't you see what Bernard packed you to eat?"

"I already ate it."

"You what?"

"I was hungry."

"When did you have a chance to eat your food?" asked Cyle, sounding a little irritated. "Never mind. Don't answer that."

Cyle reached into his pack and tossed Choppa a food wrap. His friend's eyes lit up as he tore it open to search its contents.

Drew sat down on a log to search his own pack and asked, "How do you two know each other?"

Cyle and Choppa hesitated, looked at each other as if waiting to see who would answer, then Choppa responded, "It seems as if we've always known each other."

"And where do you come from?"

"Our homeland is called Talinor," answered Cyle. "Have you heard of it?"

"I can't say that I have. I have spent most of my life here in this region of the country. I haven't even been to the city of Abbodar, but I have traveled close to its border in search of game. I have no desire to go to such a place. My home has always been the village of Pallarim and the wilderness where I hunt." The hunter paused, staring sadly at the apple in his hand. Then he continued, "Now I fear Pallarim is no more."

"I am sorry we could not save your parents…"

"It is not your fault. You did what you could," said Drew.

"And it is not your fault either, Drew," said Cyle firmly. "You would have lost your life trying to save theirs. You need to think about you and Addie now. That's what they would have wanted."

Drew changed the subject as tears welled up. "So what brings the two of you here to these lands?"

"It's hard to explain," answered Cyle. "Partly because we don't know for sure yet. Our purpose here has not yet been revealed."

"I don't understand. You have come to this land and you don't know why you are here?"

"You could say we are on a quest, but the details have not been revealed to us yet."

"And when will you know the details?"

"What do you believe in Drew? What do you put your faith in?"

"My people believe in the land and its resources. We are supposed to believe in Terashom, but we refused that form of faith long ago. It is a darkness my people want nothing to do with."

"So you recognize that it is a force and that it is real?" asked Cyle.

"I have no doubt that there is a force behind Terashom. A

very dark force."

"We are people of faith, too," said Cyle, "and it is our choice to follow that faith that brings us here."

Drew looked slightly worried.

"Do not fear our faith, Drew. It is not your enemy. Our faith always stands against the dark magic you speak of and in the force behind Terashom."

"I saw magic in the axe when Gafney fought the beast." Drew paused and took a deep breath. "Did you know the use of magic is forbidden by the Emperor unless it has been approved by the Maggrid?"

"Who are the Maggrid?" asked Choppa.

"They are the temple priests who propagate the Terashom faith and serve the Emperor. The Maggrid are the ones who created the beast Gafney battled. But there is a group to be feared even more than the Maggrid priests."

"And who is that?" asked Cyle.

"They are called the Ravens, a sect of Maggrid warriors that rose out of the Maggrid order. Some say that they are infested with spirits from the void."

"I've never heard of such a thing." said Cyle. "But if the spirits of the void can infest other creatures, like the gargenmalls and scavs, then I guess they could infest men."

Drew stood and slowly scanned the forest. "Something watches us."

Choppa jumped up.

"Easy. Don't make any sudden moves," cautioned Drew.

The forest shadows seemed to shift around them as their surroundings grew darker and deathly silent. The three men stood motionless, waiting to see what would happen next. Then a beam of light broke from above and lit the area, revealing an ocean of spears surrounding them. Cyle gripped his staff in front of him, and Drew grabbed his arm to hold him back.

"Don't move," cautioned Drew.

Choppa froze, shadows shifted, the forest went silent. A

chill traveled down his spine, and then a sea of men appeared painted in green, wearing only leather loincloths about their waists and a vest of colorful beads on their chest. They wore on their heads hats that looked like a small basket with two to three small feathers attached to them.

"Chenda fey," shouted a voice. "Chenda fey."

A section of the green men separated, and a powerful looking man holding a bow, wearing a band of feathers around his neck and a vest of reeds over his chest stepped through the opening.

The green warrior stared silently at the three of them through fierce eyes as his face remained expressionless until a subtle upturn at the corner of his mouth appeared to form. "Drew, friend of the Buntoc." Then the man held up his hand, and the surrounding spearmen pulled back their weapons.

"Nolan." Drew stepped toward the leader as they clasped forearms to welcome one another. "We have come seeking your help."

Drew explained their need for medicine to help their friend who had been injured when he had slain the great beast using a magic axe. He told Nolan how these he had brought with them opposed the dark magic of the Maggrid and had defied the orders of the Emperor by using their own magic to battle the creature.

Nolan studied Cyle and Choppa with suspicious eyes. "Friend Drew, if what you say is true, then we will do what we can to help them." Nolan looked at the staff in Cyle's hand and asked. "What do they call you, man with the staff?"

"I am called Cyle."

Nolan furrowed his brow and asked, "What tribe do you come from?"

"I am from the Gap Warrior tribe."

Nolan's brow lifted. "Gap Warrior."

He looked at one of the tribesman standing next to him and spoke to him in their native language. After a brief exchange

Nolan turned back to the three and he noticed the eagle on Cyle's staff and the one hanging from the chain about his neck.

"My people have heard stories of a fierce tribe called the eagle warriors. It is said they fight demons with magic weapons and that these weapons are powerful enough to defeat the magic of Terashom."

"There is some truth in what you speak, but I do believe that any weapon is useless without a warrior who has the skill and the faith to wield it," said Cyle.

"All men have faith in something. Are you saying that the eagle warriors have faith in their weapons?" asked Nolan.

"The eagle warriors are men and women just like you, but the weapons they fight with are not of the realm of flesh and blood. They have a power that finds its source in the One Faith."

"Then you have heard of these warriors."

"I have," said Cyle.

"I believe you are an eagle warrior, Cyle."

Cyle smiled and did not respond.

Nolan returned the smile. "I want to know more about this kind of faith." The warrior pointed toward the forest. "Come and we will help your friend who needs medicine."

"Thank you, Nolan of the Buntoc," said Cyle. "We must move with haste. He is very sick."

CHAPTER 12

Gerrid felt his strength slowly returning to his body. Travel was less demanding, and his muscles were slowly beginning to harden. It had been a long time since he had felt this kind of energy, but he knew that he still had a long way to go before he was the man he used to be. He had struggled to find his wind and keep up with the others when climbing the hills, and it was obvious that it irritated Bryann to have to wait for him. She would stand at the top of the trail waiting impatiently with her hands on her hips and a scowl on her brow. Then when Gerrid reached her spot, she would turn and walk on without waiting for him to rest.

Bryann treated everyone with the same cold indifference, rarely speaking unless spoken to first. For some reason, Gerrid found himself trying to break through the walls she had erected to keep him out. He would ask her questions to pass the time on the trail, but she was not interested in talking about herself, where she lived, or her opinion on any matter. Bryann would ruffle at his questions and was always short and to the point when she did answer. Gerrid could feel her displeasure increase each time he questioned her, and it made him want to try all the harder to break through her protective shell.

Bryann had proven she was adept at fighting when she rescued him back in the city. She showed an impressive display of quickness and mastery of the blade that left him wondering where she had learned to fight so skillfully. He had seen in her an almost imperceptible rage that boiled beneath the surface when she unleashed it on those men who attacked him. He wondered what story from her hidden past nurtured that rage within her. He tried to push back the questions that plagued his thoughts, but it was no use. He wanted to know the answers.

Gerrid, Bryann, Packer and Sera arrived at the city of Karn two days after leaving Abbodar. Karn was a thriving city, teaming with trade and travelers passing through on their way to the arena Festival in Abbodar. Packer quickly found them lodging upstairs above the Brown Bear Inn near the center of the city where the streets were crowded and noisy with local activity. Bryann had suggested taking two days to rest and restore their supplies for the next leg of their journey. Gerrid welcomed the rest. The last two days had taken a toll on his strength.

Karn was under the rule of Abbodar and in many ways just as dark as its mother city. An oppressive spirit hung over the city that could be seen in the coldness between people in the streets and the forlorn looks on their faces. The streets were filthy, and many of the people appeared and smelled as if they hadn't bathed in weeks. Gerrid noticed that they rarely gave one another eye contact when passing each other or transacting business. Soldiers walked through the marketplace, taking from the shop owners and street vendors whatever pleased them without offering payment. They often harassed the commoners by physically shoving and verbally assaulting them if one accidentally stepped in their path.

The day they arrived in Karn, a crowd had gathered in the middle of the city square to watch a middle-aged man who had been bound by his hands to a single post. Two soldiers whipped the man as he screamed each time the leather straps lashed his back. The crowd watched in silence as the soldiers finished the whipping and left him lifelessly hanging from the post. No one bothered to take him down. He died later that day still hanging from the pole. Someone said that he was caught stealing a melon from one of the street vendors.

The Brown Bear was a noisy place with a busy tavern downstairs that kept travelers and city dwellers well fed and full of drink. Their room was small but adequate, although it had a musty smell that lingered even when the windows were opened to bring in the fresh air.

After their first night at the Brown Bear, Packer fumbled through the door at midmorning with bags of supplies spilling onto the ground. The street hound scrambled unsuccessfully to maintain control over the contents. Sera rushed to help him minimize his calamity, trying as best as she could to stuff them back into their containers. Bryann rolled her eyes with annoyance and then began pacing back and forth, stopping repeatedly to look out the window.

"I have to get out of here," she said with irritation in her voice. "I need some air or I'm going to crack."

"I think you should wait until dark before you go out,"

cautioned Gerrid.

"I agree," said Packer. "There's a lot of tension in the streets right now. I don't like it—no, not one bit."

"Well, I don't need either of you telling me what I should or shouldn't do," huffed Bryann, accompanied by another roll of the eyes. "I'm well aware of the conditions out there, and I know how to take care of myself without you all trying to watch over me."

Bryann nervously gathered her overcoat and flung it over her back in an attempt to cover her two swords. Then she tightened the straps on her leather leggings and started for the door.

Gerrid stood before speaking, knowing full well he would be resisted, but now, with his strength returning from the night's rest, he found the energy to speak up. "You could be putting us at risk by going out. Why not wait until dark? Then tomorrow we will be out of here."

"Like I said, I'll be fine," glared Bryann.

"It's not you I'm worried about," countered Gerrid. "I just have an uneasy feeling about you going out right now and the attention it might bring back to us."

Bryann moved to within a few inches of Gerrid's face and placed her hands on her hips, a gesture he was growing accustomed to when he saw defiance rising in her.

"It isn't your job to protect me. It's my job to protect you," spouted Bryann as her tone intensified. "I don't have to like it, and I don't. I'm here to fulfill a promise to my aunt, and I don't need you telling me what to do." She was now face to face with Gerrid looking into his eyes and doing her best to back him down. He wanted to smile at her, but he knew it would be a mistake to do so. Never smile at an angry woman when she was in the middle of her tirade. That's never a good idea. He looked her in the eyes, and it wasn't the first time he noticed how beautiful they were even when she was mad. A slight smile lifted from the corner of his lips, and he knew the minute it did that he would regret it. He stiffened and waited for the backlash. To his surprise, she hesitated for just a moment before speaking, and the look on her face was both angry and mysterious at the same time. There was something behind those doe-shaped eyes that puzzled him. With her standing this close he could feel the sadness behind the exasperation, but it was only there for the briefest of time, and then the anger took over again.

Bryann stepped backward and for a brief moment Gerrid thought that she was going to back down, but he was wrong.

"Like I said," she stated softly, but the intensity still remained, "I am going out." Then she turned, unlatched the door and slammed it behind her.

Gerrid stared at the closed door for a moment wondering if she was gone never to return.

"She'll be back," said Sera, as if she was reading his mind. "I think she likes you."

"Well, she has a strange way of showing it, if you ask me," said Packer.

"What would you know of such things?" asked Sera playfully. "You are just a boy, and what can a boy know about the matters of a woman's heart?"

"And you are but a girl."

"A girl I am. At least you know that," giggled Sera. "Now I am in the mood to dance."

"No," pleaded Packer. "Please don't."

Sera jumped up and began to twirl around the room in leaping spins and jumps, her black hair bouncing with every movement. She enjoyed it all the more knowing that Packer was uncomfortable with her dancing. Gerrid sat, quietly amused with the whole thing.

"Oh no, not again." Packer moaned the words as if he was in deep pain as he rolled on the floor.

"We elves love to dance," Sera smiled as she twirled about with her tiny feet, spinning and jumping even higher. "Almost as much as we love to sing."

"No please don't," Packer moaned again as if it tortured him beyond his ability to bear it. "Please don't start singing. Please."

"From a distant land he comes,
carried on eagles wings.
A warrior who lost the song
his heart no longer sings.
Day will turn to night,
and night will turn to day.
The light will call him home
and he will find his way.
A weapon forged within the fires
in a time of long ago.
And when he holds it in his hands,
its power he will come to know.
Freedom reigns within the light;
there is no other way.
Freedom reigns within the light,
where he will lead the way."

When Sera finished her song, she looked at them and smiled. Then the air about them grew mysteriously still. Packer had ceased his protesting and sat, full of emotions that he could not begin to understand, and he appeared to be speechless. Gerrid felt like the wind had been squeezed out of his lungs, and for some reason he felt like he wanted to cry. He thought of the elves, and one thing that always stood out in his mind was the depth of their faith and the suffering they often endured because of it. They would not last long in a place like this. Sera needed protection, and Gerrid felt a strong sense of responsibility for her safety, and he knew that Packer carried the same burden.

Several hours had passed since Bryann had left them, and Gerrid was growing restless with her absence. "I'm going to see if I can find Bryann," said Gerrid. "Something is not right. I can't explain it, but the uneasiness I'm feeling won't go away." Gerrid gathered up his overcoat and headed for the door. "The two of you should stay here until I get back."

"Wait," Packer rustled through his pack pulling out a small hunting knife and held it up to Gerrid. "You don't have a weapon. Take this with you."

Gerrid stared at it for a brief moment before responding. "I'll be fine. You keep it. You might need it. I'll be back before dark if I don't find her by then."

When Gerrid stepped onto the street, a warm wind carrying the smell of roasting meat on the outdoor pits hit him. His stomach complained, and he realized he hadn't eaten anything substantial for the better part of the day. He remembered he had some fruit and a block of cheese in his pocket. He pulled it out and bit into an apple as he surveyed the street. The apple was sour and a bit dry, but the cheese was delicious and had just the right amount of bitterness. Along with the food vendors that littered the streets, there were soothsayers on every corner selling fortunes and the small graven idols of Terashom.

It was impossible to walk more than a few feet without someone beckoning him to sample wares or purchase a telling. At first he didn't notice the voice calling to him above all the street noise, but she finally caught his ear. He turned and saw the woman pointing at him and calling him over to her booth.

"I have a bit of telling for you, young man," she spoke through a whisper. "Come, I will tell you what you seek to know."

Gerrid tried to walk on, but something drew him in her direction. She wore several colorful scarves around her neck and was younger than most in her line of work.

"For a small price, I will give you a telling," she offered a second time as she smiled, revealing a gold tooth on her upper row.

"I am a man with no means to pay you, and besides I have no interest in your divining."

"Then why have you stopped at my table?" The teller floated one of her scarves across Gerrid's shoulder. "Perhaps the gods have brought you to me for a blessing of prosperity?"

"Perhaps your gods have made a mistake bringing someone like me who cannot pay for your services."

"Surely you have something of value to trade," she whispered sweetly.

"As I said, I have nothing, and I think you have nothing for me."

"Ah, but you do have something of value." The teller took his hand into hers and he pulled back unsuccessfully to free it from her grip. "You guard a great treasure."

Gerrid jerked his hand away from hers as if it had stung him. "I will be on my way. I told you I have no need of a telling."

"Maybe not, young traveler, but I have need of what you guard."

"I don't know what you mean," Gerrid knew she was talking about Sera.

"Thank you. You have been most helpful."

Gerrid's heart pounded as he turned away and started up the street, confusion and a nagging sense of dread closed in. How did she know about Sera? As the question pulled at his thoughts, he stopped suddenly, and the feelings of unease intensified until he could suppress them no longer. Gerrid walked a little farther down the street until his anxiety overwhelmed him, and he turned and ran back toward the Black Bear. As he drew closer to his destination, his anxiety increased. When he reached the door to their room behind the inn, it suddenly broke open, and Packer came running out with panic filled eyes.

"They have taken her. I stepped out for just a few short moments and when I got back, she was gone," shouted Packer, fighting to breathe.

"With me. Quickly," ordered Gerrid as he headed for the alleyway across the street.

"It was just a few minutes to get some water. I don't understand what happened."

"Don't worry about it, we will find her," assured Gerrid as he ran. "Did you see anything, anything at all?"

"No, nothing. I was inside the tavern, and when I got

back…"

"Then we will check the alley. That's where I would go to steel away."

Gerrid ran and Packer followed close behind. Both of them fought through the busy street, bumping into people who cursed at them until the crowd finally thinned. Gerrid remembered the soothsayer, and somehow he knew she had something to do with this. The sun was setting, and they were quickly losing light. Shortness of breath and loss of energy was already setting in, but the former prisoner pressed on against it. For the first time since prison, he felt desperate to have his old strength back. He thought he might be needing it.

Bryann strolled back to the Inn at a leisurely pace and while part of her resisted going back, she pushed the urge aside for the sake of the promise made to her aunt. Three men appeared from behind a corner to her left. They looked to be in a hurry. Then she saw what she almost missed. It was Sera, and she was being held in the arms of one of them with his hand over her mouth. She was not fighting or resisting her captors, but Bryann could see the fear in her eyes. They suddenly changed their direction, turned and headed toward her.

Bryann pulled the two short swords from the sheaths on her back and steadied herself for a confrontation. The tall, bald one with the feathered earring spoke, "Step aside little girl, and you won't get hurt."

In the center of the tall one's forehead was a circular tattoo, and in his right hand he held a saber. Sera looked on with terror in her eyes.

Bryann could see that these men were fighters and that they held the odds at three to one, but she was not going to back down. It just wasn't in her, and besides—she didn't like being called a little girl. Maybe she would only have to fight two of them since the other one would have to restrain Sera to keep her from running away.

She felt a stirring behind her, but she was too late, and

she cursed herself under her breath for making such a foolish mistake. Something crashed against the back of her head—bright lights flashed behind her eyes, and she found herself lunging forward with the ground beneath her spinning out of control. She felt the swirling in her head that came before blacking out, and somehow she was able to hold on to consciousness.

Focus. Don't lose it. Her own thoughts cried out to warn her.

She was looking at the ground fighting to clear her head when she heard something pound into the back of the one holding Sera. He stumbled off balance just enough to give Gerrid a chance to gain purchase of the sword tied to his waist. Then the former prisoner pounded the faltering man in the side of the head with the hilt, sending him to the ground unconscious. On the way down, he released his grip on Sera, and Gerrid thought he saw the elf girl smile as she slipped away to freedom.

Bryann watched in stunned disbelief at what happened next.

Gerrid launched a vicious attack on the three remaining men with the force and skill of a seasoned warrior; his blade struck out against the tall one as a look of confusion and fear swept over the man's face. Metal clashed with metal, and the sound of ringing blades echoed off of the nearby rock walls. Another attacked from the right, thinking he would gain the advantage on the left handed Gerrid. Mistake. At the very last second, Gerrid shifted his weight, tossed the blade to his right hand and stepped to the side, blocking the incoming strike, then countered with a sweep that sliced across the man's chest. The attacker wailed, grabbed at the wound, then stumbled to his knees. The tall one noticed Gerrid fighting to catch his breath and sprang at him to seize the advantage. In the separation that came before death or life, Gerrid calmed his spirit like he had been trained to do as a soldier long ago. He recognized the death look in the eyes of his enemy that he had seen in others countless times before. After countering the oncoming blows, he responded with equal intensity, but his strength was waning, so he stepped back to regain his breath.

His attacker shrieked at the remaining man to help him

finish it. "Now, you idiot. Can't you see he tires?"

Bryann was slowly rising to one knee, still fighting against the fog in her head. The two attackers were on Gerrid, driving him backward toward the wall. With his lungs burning and muscles fading fast, he knew he was running out of time. Something whizzed through the air and crashed into the head of the one closest to him. The man's head jerked and he was unconscious before he hit the ground. Packer stood several paces away fitting another rock into the sling he was holding. The one left standing began shuffling backward, realizing the odds had turned against him. He glanced nervously to his right and his left, spun around and fled into the fading light of the nearest alley.

"Bounty hunters," said Gerrid through labored breathing, and before he could speak another word, Bryann was upon him spewing out rage.

"How is it a holy man fights with the skill of a deadly warrior?"

Gerrid looked confused, still trying to catch his breath.

"What else have you hidden from me?" she said, pressing him now face to face.

"Perhaps if you hadn't spent all your time sulking around and been so busy avoiding conversation, I would have told you something about my past." Gerrid could feel the intensity rising in his voice.

"Don't make this about me," countered Bryann. "You intentionally deceived me, and you know it."

"Deceived you. Why would I deceive you?" shouted Gerrid. Now he was yelling.

"I don't know. You tell me." Bryann's hands were back on her hips.

Gerrid leaned in even closer now, staring straight into those eyes that held a mysterious mix of intense fear and incredible beauty. "You aren't exactly an open book either. I know only that you have an aunt and that you are as mean as an alley cat."

"You are still avoiding my question." Bryann's voice

softened slightly. "How is it you, a holy man, can fight like a trained killer?"

Gerrid brushed the dust from his clothes before answering. "First off, I never claimed to be a holy man, and if you had taken the time to have one decent conversation with me before now, I would have told you that I used to be a soldier before I came to this land. I haven't held a sword in over two years, and I found no joy in holding one today." He glanced over at the dead man he had slain laying a few steps away. Then he looked down at the blood stained sword in his hand. Unmistakable sadness marked his face as he released his grip on the blade. It rattled to silence when it hit the cobbled street beneath his feet.

Bryann spun in a huff and walked toward Packer and Sera mumbling something under her breath. Gerrid looked on still confused by the whole ordeal. "By the way, you are welcome."

She stopped suddenly, turned and fired back, "For what?"

"Saving your life."

"I was doing fine without your help," barked Bryann.

"Of course you were. I could see that. What was I thinking?"

"We don't have time for this. We need to go back to the inn and gather our gear. Others will come for the girl," glared Bryann. "I say we move quickly and get out of town while it is still dark."

During their walk back to the inn, Bryann remained cold and silent, lost to a whirlwind of thoughts. What was happening here? She had always been careful not to let others get close, especially men who were anything like her father. He too was a military commander, and she cringed at the memory of him. Where was this anger coming from? What was it about this man that she would care anything about him or his past? The thought that she had hoped to trust him frightened her. She would not allow herself to feel anything when it came to a man, and she was not about to start now. She wanted to run, but she couldn't. She owed it to her aunt. When she was finished with her part in this, she would be free to move on, and that day couldn't come too soon.

CHAPTER 13

The sun's rays met the dawning of a new day as the first slivers of light peaked from behind the mountain range in the distance. Little by little, the valley filled with light as the crisp morning air melted away with the increasing warmth of the sun. It was Lena's favorite time of the day, before the world awakened as most were still in bed sleeping or just beginning to rise from their slumber. This was the time she spent interceding and drawing close to the Ancient of Days. She had learned long ago that if she waited until a later time in the day for her ritual of prayer, she would almost always be disrupted by the tyranny of the urgency that life often brought. The Intercessor held this time as sacred, and after all the years of her life, she cherished these minutes of her day as the most important.

Just before the sunrise she had been immersed in intercession, and at the fringe of her own awareness, she sensed a presence hovering at the edge of her sacred space. Lena was unaware of how long it had been watching and listening to her. The dark ones would often come to listen to her prayers, but they did not intimidate her. In fact, she had come to expect it.

Sometimes they came to collect information from the content of her prayers, but most of the time it was to draw her away from this vile activity that repulsed them to the core. It was an assignment the dark ones loathed because it required them to be in the presence of an Intercessor and her prayers. This of all things was a form of torture that was almost beyond their ability to withstand, but it was a necessary strategy of their dark warfare. To distract an Intercessor away from their prayers with anxious thoughts or other meaningless concerns was considered a supreme level of victory for the dark ones. It was a strategy as ancient as faith itself, implemented for generations to hold back the violence inflicted against the dark kingdom by the powerful impact of intercession.

For years the distractions sent by the dark messengers had worked on Lena. She would grow anxious and allow herself to be drawn away from her post. Things were undone that needed her attention. The anxiety would build inside until she would conclude; I don't have time for this. Then she would leave her post and go about tending to the undone things, thinking she could somehow complete them all. Then one day through the loss of a dear friend, she came to the painful realization that all her efforts to help her friend still ended in her death. After her friend died, it occurred to her early one morning, when she was battling to stay focused in her intercession, that she had not prayed once for her sick friend during her illness. She had done everything else she could think of to help her, except pray for her, and now she was gone.

Lena had begun to weep as the reality of her choices came crashing down upon her. The dark voices shot barbs of shame and condemnation, taunting her with messages of doom and self-doubt. She would never forget the dark thought that almost ended her destiny to follow the call of the Intercessor. It rose up from a dark corner of her soul calling out to her aching spirit to follow another path.

If you were a true Intercessor, you would have prayed. How can you live with yourself?

Lena thought, It's true. I have failed. How can I live with myself?

Shame flooded her mind almost drowning out any ability to hear the other voice seeking to break through the lies that threatened to wrest her from the path before her. The shame of her failure had almost convinced her to walk away from her destiny that day, but something happened next that saved her. She stumbled into her room and saw her grandson Cyle lying in bed asleep. He was only one year old at the time. For a brief moment she felt a penetrating peace come over her that began to push back the menacing lies of shame. The despair suddenly subsided, making room for another simple thought that came to her like a messenger of hope bringing good news from a faraway place.

Next time you will pray.

She began to weep as she uttered the words, "Thank you. Thank you."

The shameful thought returned. It's too late for you. You are unworthy.

I will never be worthy, thought Lena. But I have been called by the one who is.

"Go away," commanded Lena out loud. "You and your kind are not welcome here."

Then there was a shattering of the darkness. The shame left and was replaced by the understanding that she had been chosen and appointed to this path. She had not been elected because she was worthy of the office. On the contrary, she had been chosen because it had been predetermined by the Ancient of Days before she had a chance to prove she was worthy. Knowing this had changed the course of Lena's life. She was finally able to accept her own destiny regardless of her own flaws. She had almost walked away from this path because of her own belief that her calling somehow was connected to her worthiness. And that belief had almost blinded her from seeing the truth.

Lena could still remember what Graybeard had said to her after she had overcome the shame. "Shame is the enemy that keeps many from embracing the path they are called to walk, and that path is never gained without a fierce battle to defeat shame's deception, which is as ancient as time itself. Many live and end life walking next to the path, but not on it, because they continue to believe that they must gain worthiness through effort of their own before they can travel the path. Fear becomes their master and lost destiny their regret."

Lena pressed on in her prayers and after several minutes a familiar form of darkness began to enclose about her. She had experienced this many times before during intercession where the darkness appeared to overcome the light. But she was wiser now and she he had come to learn that the appearance of things could sometimes be deceiving if one saw through eyes of fear. In time she understood that light always drove away the darkness, but that did not mean that the darkness was easily dispelled. The smallest amount of light would break through and provide a way, but the light may have still been enshrouded by the dark. Her prayers generated light, and that meant that there was darkness to be overcome which at times could be most vile.

Lena's breathing shortened when she felt the presence of evil encroaching. Defiance drove her as she began to sing the spirit song of adoration with words unknown to her that flowed from her trembling lips. Even though she did not comprehend the meaning of her song, she knew that it would be embraced by the beings of the light and hated by the creatures of the dark.

Shafts of light streamed into the gloom surrounding Lena. Sparkling prisms danced in every direction until they softened and gave way to an image. The void appeared torn open by a massive breach in the barrier between the world of spirit and flesh, where shadow wraiths traveled freely back and forth, unencumbered by any resistance. Inside the void, a battle raged with a handful of Gap Warriors surrounded and greatly outnumbered by their foes, at least six to one. Those attacking the Gap Warriors were clothed in the flesh of men, armed with weapons of metal yet driven by an invisible force that gave power to them in battle.

"What manner of evil is this?" cried Lena.

There was only silence in response to her question, so she pressed forward in intercession with deep moaning that turned into wailing. Tears flowing from her eyes, her stomach twisted into a knot as she hunched over and began renouncing the invading darkness.

"There needs to be more of us," she pleaded. "This battle cannot be won with the few that we are." She hunched forward groaning in pain. "Send us more Intercessors," she wailed. "Send us more, or we will perish."

She realized someone was next to her; glancing to her left,

she saw Jef. He was kneeling nearby, interceding with her. He looked up to return her gaze.

"We are not enough, Jef," said Lena through trembling words as the vision faded before her eyes. "I have never beheld a darkness such as this where evil resides in flesh, and the dark ones breach the void at will." Lena shook her head and slowly wiped the tears from her eyes. "What manner of evil is this, Jef?"

Jef had no response to the questions. He just stared at her.

Lena assured, "It's okay, my friend. We may not see the way, and we may not know the outcome of what is before us, but we do not put our trust in what we can see. We put our trust in the one we cannot see. His ways are sure, and I choose to trust Him even though I know my heart will be challenged."

CHAPTER 14

"I am not going to eat that," whispered Choppa to Cyle who was sitting next to him. "I can barely stand the smell of it."

Before the two of them rested a huge bowl on the ground filled with twigs and what looked like dirt mixed with fruit, vegetables and half cooked meats. Eight tribal elders sat quietly encircling the bowl, waiting with stern stares for Cyle or Choppa to take the first bite while Drew stood behind them looking on.

"I thought you said you were hungry?" said Cyle.

"Not that hungry."

"Before they will speak to you about the medicine you seek, you must eat with the elders," said Nolan who was standing next to Drew. "Trust cannot be made with outsiders until a meal is shared."

Choppa smiled nervously as he looked around the circle of wrinkled faces. They did not return the smile. Beyond the circle, young warriors watched from a distance, holding their weapons in hand, and Choppa was sure they found some sick kind of pleasure in his predicament.

"It's okay," said Drew from behind them. "It's not as bad as it looks. I have sat where you sit, and I survived to tell of it."

Cyle reached into the bowl and drew forth a small fistfull of the mush and held it to his nose to test it. The scent was pungent and earthy, mostly unfamiliar to him. He studied the leathery faces staring back at him and smiled slightly, then put the stuff in his mouth. Small grains of sand crunched between his teeth as he bit down on it. He did his best to present a pleasant look on his face and smiled, nodding his head in approval. It was not as bad as he had imagined, but it required effort to take a second bite.

The Elders smiled through toothless grins. One of them sitting next to Choppa slipped his hand into his loin cloth to scratch his crotch, and then he put the same hand into the bowl and withdrew a fistful of the mush. Smiling at Choppa, he grabbed his arm and placed it in his palm, motioning to him to eat it.

"It's your turn," said Cyle, repressing a grin.

Choppa stared at the glob of food in his hand and tried hard to disguise his repulsion behind a frail smile. His stomach churned until it crunched into a queasy knot, and he had to fight back the urge to gag. Suddenly, the full impact of the smell could be ignored no longer he jumped up and ran from the circle and disappeared behind the nearest tree. The elders peered at one another, toothless smiles formed on some of their faces, and after a brief silence they erupted in laughter.

Those remaining at the circle continued their feast until they had finished their meal. Nolan led Cyle, Drew and Choppa from the circle after the elders had decided to grant them the medicine they needed. It would take time to gather the herbs and prepare them, so the young Buntoc warrior took them to a large tent made of animal hides where he waved them inside. Hanging on the wooden posts inside were several weapons, mostly spears and bows and some knives. The floor was covered with animal hides and woven baskets of all sizes. Nolan unlatched one of the bows along with a quiver of arrows from one of the posts in the center of the tent. He held it with both palms extended and slowly handed it to Drew. Drew accepted the weapon in much the same manner it was presented. He held it gently in his hands admiring its design. He let his fingers run along the familiar markings of the Buntoc that decorated the weapon. A single feather was attached to the bow at one end and from tip to tip it stood almost as tall as Drew. It was the finest bow he had ever held in his hands. The grip was sure and the flex tight to the test, and the weight was perfect.

"If you are offering this to me, I cannot accept it." said Drew softly and tried to hand it back to Nolan. "It is Buntoc and should only be carried by a Buntoc."

"You have lost much my friend, your family and your village, but you have not lost all. This is my gift to you. As long as you carry it, you will be a part of us. You will be Buntoc."

Tears layered Drew's eyelids as he stared at the magnificent weapon. He thought of all the times he and Nolan had hunted together and of the many days he had spent among the Buntoc people while he was away from the village on hunting expeditions.

"This is a great honor," said Drew softly, gripping the bow tightly with both hands. "I am honored to be counted among your people and I will carry this with pride."

"The Emperor takes what he pleases from the people of these lands without thought of his actions," said Nolan through a steely gaze. "We are no longer able to live in the land of our heritage, but we will remain free. Better to dwell alive in unknown regions than live without freedom. They drove most of us from our homes, and many were sentenced to fight in the arena. Those who were left living in the Misty Realms now work as slaves in the mines where they mine the silver for the very weapons they use to oppress us."

"How is it your people were able to escape the clutches of slavery?" asked Cyle, feeling a sudden surge of anger rise up within him.

"We were able to flee after a great battle and loss of many lives. We are a strong people, and we will not have our freedom taken from us by a tyrant." Nolan's voice intensified. "We are Buntoc, once proud dwellers of the Misty Realms. We still dream of a day when we will return there to hunt and fish and raise our young without fear. Until then, we keep moving in order to remain free."

"How many are you?" asked Cyle.

"There are many other Buntoc settlements scattered in small groups throughout this mountainous region. At last count, we totaled eight hundred. Three hundred of us are warriors and the rest are women, children and elders. The high places are rugged and provide refuge and enough game to feed our families."

"I understand the love of homeland," responded Cyle. "I have not been back home in two years and I often dream of the friends and family I left behind. Your people have suffered as many others in this kingdom have suffered. It is beyond what any people should have to bear." Cyle looked at Drew. "Should you ever have need of it, I offer you refuge and a home on behalf of my people. The people and land of Talinor would welcome you and give you land you could call your own."

Nolan was speechless as he searched to find the words to respond. "What kind of kingdom would offer part of its own land freely to a stranger?"

"The kind of kingdom that has been threatened more than once by the same kind of tyranny you have faced. We have fought and spilled blood for our own freedom, but most of all, we are a kingdom that seeks to honor the faith of our founders."

"Again you speak of this faith. Does it see men and women as free instead of slaves?" asked Nolan.

"The One Faith sees all men and women as free."

"But there are many faiths as you call them," countered

Nolan.

"Yes there are my friend, but there is only one that offers freedom from the oppression of the dark magic."

"I know well the power of Terashom," said Nolan with anger rising. "My people have lost much to it, and I have seen what the Ravens can do in battle. Their weapons seem to come to life with the power of Terashom. It takes many of ours to defeat one of theirs."

"There were so many of them," interrupted Drew suddenly. "They overwhelmed us like a pack of wolves attacking a rabbit."

"Do not let the weight of shame overtake you my friend," said Nolan putting a hand on his friend's shoulder. "Even the mighty Buntoc could not prevail against such a force, so how could a humble fishing village stand against them?"

"We are a doomed people," said Drew somberly. "What hope is there for us?"

"I once heard an old prophet remark that sometimes hope is as the dawn's light," offered Cyle. "Its beauty is captivating but ever brief. It reminds us that life is not yet over, and that we must live the day that is before us because soon it will be gone. If that is all we have, then so be it."

"You speak of a prophet," said Nolan. "My people tell a story of long ago before I was born. When they still lived in the Misty Realms, a young seer visited them. He traveled in the company of an older man who was in possession of a sword of great power. One of our tribesmen stole the sword, and in his haste to get away with it, he cut himself, causing a small flesh wound to his hand. He instantly fell to the ground, screaming as if demons were attacking him, then died. After that, no one went near the sword."

Chills washed over Cyle, he thought he felt the staff vibrate under his palm.

"Stories are still told of their visit around the elder fires. They say the prophet foretold of a time of great sadness and darkness that would overcome our people. I believe that time has come to pass. Sometimes I wish he had never come to us, for seers only seem to bring bad news."

"You have left part of his message untold," said Cyle. "Surely there was more."

"What you say is true. There was more. How did you know this?"

"If the message of the seer is one of gloom only, then I question the message and the one who delivers it. When a prophecy is absent of hope, I believe it to come from the darkness."

"There was more," said Nolan, a distant look crossed his face, "but I am unable to recall it now. The stories fade in my memories and have been consumed with all that we have suffered. I stopped attending the elder fires long ago."

"Then maybe you should return brother," a deep voice boomed, revealing a tall muscular man silhouetted at the tent entrance.

Nolan rolled his eyes. "And now my big brother will tell you what it is like."

Bayson, Nolan's older brother, filled the entrance to the tent with his powerful frame. "You are correct, eagle man. There is more to the message of the seer, and my little brother would have knowledge of it if he would bother to visit the elder fires."

Nolan pursed his lips and stared at the ground.

"The seer spoke of a deliverer who would come from a distant land bearing a weapon of deliverance and offering freedom to those who would follow him."

"Such are the useless tales of seers," said Nolan through gritted teeth. "Whomever this deliverer is, he is too late. Besides, we would not put our trust in an outsider."

"Please excuse my little brother," remarked Bayson sternly. "The darkness of the times and the loss of our freedom has clouded his hope, as it has for many of us."

"What did this seer call himself?" asked Cyle.

"Tekera Toc," answered Nolan.

"Ah, so you do remember, little brother," said Bayson

105

smiling.

"Tekera Toc. What is the meaning of the name?" Asked Cyle.

Bayson answered. "In your tongue, it means bearded one."

"Graybeard." Cyle felt a new wave of shivers across his neck. "I may know the seer of whom you speak. He resides in my homeland of Talinor. He is old and gray now and has lived over a hundred years. He is the prophet we call Graybeard."

Cyle rubbed the back of his neck and furrowed his brow, trying to remember something his Grandmother told him long ago. Now he wished he had paid better attention when she told him stories as she tucked him into bed at night. He had always struggled with listening if she went on for very long.

"I faintly remember something from our histories about Talinor's first king, his name was Kem Felnar." Cyle paused again, straining to recover the memories. "I believe when he first came to Talinor, he arrived in the company of the prophet, Graybeard. That part is unclear to me, but I do know of a magic sword that belonged to Kem Felnar though I have never seen it. When he died, the sword was laid to rest with him in the tomb of kings. There is more to the story, but I do not remember it now."

Cyle paused and stared at the ceiling briefly before he returned his gaze to Bayson. "I wonder if the man with Graybeard was Kem Felnar?"

"I cannot help you there, eagle warrior. Our stories do not give him a name."

"I have waited long enough for the arrival of this deliverer that the prophet predicted," said Nolan. "I grew weary long ago of waiting for his arrival. Tomorrow I will hunt for food, and today I will fight to protect my tribe. That is all I know."

"We are not all as skeptical as my brother," countered Bayson as he moved farther into the tent. "Some of the stories of the past fade over time from our tribal fires, but this one somehow has held the hearts of many of our elders. Unfortunately, many of the younger Buntoc, like my brother, have lost interest in the histories. I, for one, still choose to believe in the coming of a deliverer."

The flap to the tent brushed open, and Choppa entered with a pale look on his face. Cyle smiled, remembering what had just happened at the Elder's circle.

"Do you have any real food around here," said Choppa, holding his stomach. "I'm starving."

"Your friend does not look like he has gone without too many meals," said Nolan, glancing in Choppa's direction. "We will feed you, my friend."

"What? What will you feed me?" said Choppa, backing away.

"Do not be afraid. We have dried fruits and some meats that we can give you."

"As long as it…"

Cyle motioned with his hand to cut Choppa short.

"It's okay," assured Nolan. "We do not take our traditions as seriously as we once did. Life has become more about survival than traditions. Let's find you all some food, then we can see if the medicines are ready."

CHAPTER 15

Vanus was beginning to resent the pressure his father was putting on him to find the assassin who had made the attempt on his life. The Emperor had been in a foul mood lately due to the lack of good news coming from the Boogaran campaign. He had made the decision to send most of Abbodar's troops to the faraway land of Boogara in the hopes of securing a hasty victory, but they had proven to be a worthy adversary. As a result, things were moving slower than he had planned.

Vanus was growing increasingly impatient as he paced

back and forth outside Drok Relnik's worship chamber, waiting for the warlock to finish the sacrifice ceremony. Relnik had told the king that he would make a sacrifice to the Terashom gods on behalf of his troops, but his true intentions were for his own purposes.

Drok Relnik did not particularly enjoy the company of demons, but he relished the power they could give him. Today he would make an attempt to summon Gizshra, one of their leaders. The shadow wraith had been an ally in the past, and Relnik was feeling uneasy knowing that the Intercessor, Lena, had entered the realm. The Ravens he had dispatched to find her had not yet succeeded in locating her, and he was losing his patience. He knew that wherever she would be found, it was likely that Gap Warriors would be somewhere nearby. That was more than enough to cause him concern.

The warlock stared at the lifeless body upon the sacrifice altar, a young lad barely twelve years old. They had taken him from the home of one of the Dissenters. The mother had pleaded with the Ravens when they burst into her front door, but her cries fell on deaf ears. The father attempted to stop them, but he was no match for the warrior priests. His life was spared, at least for now, but he was sentenced to the arena where he would surely die.

Blood dripped into the golden bowl that Drok Relnik held in his trembling hands. When he lifted it above his head, a rush of intoxicating magic washed over him, and he began chanting in his warlock tongue, "Desh mell brah dook." A mist filled the room, rising from the ground up. Flickers of candlelight danced off of the walls casting ever-shifting shadows across all surfaces. The warlock ceased his chanting when he sensed a new presence in the room. He slowly turned around to see a translucent figure shrouded in black, and he watched quietly as the mist in the room gathered and swirled about him.

"Lord Gizshra, thank you for honoring my summons." Said Drok Relnik as he placed the bowl of blood on the altar.

"I am not Gizshra. He has sent me in his stead," vibrated

the voice from beneath the cowl.

"I was hoping to speak with Gizshra. Does he not have time for his faithful servant?"

"Gizshra is busy with other matters and will arrive when it suits him. Speak your mind. I have other business to attend to myself."

"Of course. As you wish." Relnik folded his hands in a priestly manner, then continued, "We have a threat that has risen against us that I am sure you will want brought to your attention. The Intercessor, Lena, has entered our lands."

"I am aware of this," hissed the shadow wraith. "What are you doing about it?"

"We are looking for her, but we have had no success so far. Can you help us with her whereabouts?"

"I cannot tell you her exact location, but the Intercessor is traveling inland from the port of Velarim. Her exact destination is unknown."

"Do you know her purpose?" asked the warlock.

"You mean you do not know?" the demon's voice intensified.

"I have not been able to divine an answer to her purpose." For the first time, the warlock sounded nervous.

"She carries a talisman with her. I do not know what it is, but we are repulsed by its power. The prophet Graybeard is in her company. He is old and is nearing death. He has gone to the trouble of traveling far from home, and that can mean only one thing—he seeks to pass on his prophetic mantle to the next generation."

"A potential prophet here in Abbodar, how can this be?" Relnik nervously rubbed the medallion connected to a silver chain that hung from his neck. The demon did not answer, so he continued, "And what is this Talisman you speak of? What power are we facing?"

"I do not yet know all the answers you seek. It is difficult to get close enough to determine its power. The Intercessor traveling with them repels us with her petitions, and we have been unable to get close enough," hissed the wraith, seething in anger.

"I will get a message to my men to have them check the trail between here and Velarim. What else would you suggest?"

"Somewhere there is a prophet waiting to be anointed. You must do all you can to prevent it. Look to the Dissenters for answers. As for the talisman, my kind cannot touch it. So you must find it and bring it under your control."

"The Dissenters have scattered into the mountains while others have chosen to remain in the city. Tell me where I can find the ones who have fled the city," said Vanus, trying not to sound desperate, "and I will compel the king's son to seek them out and bring them to the arena for sacrifice. If a prophet is among them, we will condemn him to the arena."

"I am forbidden to give you the exact location of the Dissenters," responded the wraith, "but I can tell you that many of them are still leaving the city to join those who have sought refuge elsewhere. Follow them and you will find the Dissenters."

The mist and the wraith dissolved as quickly as he had appeared. Relnik turned to exit the door into the antechamber where servants were busy about their chores, lighting candles and filling the large pots with fresh water. Guards stood statue-like at both of the tall mahogany doors. The warlock almost collided with Vanus upon entrance to the room. Vanus had been pacing impatiently to speak with the warlock.

The king's son pressed his concerns upon the warlock before he had a chance to speak. "My father will not let me rest until this assassin is found." Vanus began pacing again. "Is there any way we can locate him with the use of magic? My trackers have had little to no success so far."

"I have reason to believe that the Dissenters were behind the attempt on your father's life," Relnik lied. "As bold as it may seem for such a meek people, I believe it to be true."

"How can this be? I find it difficult to imagine such a thing."

"I, as well. However, they have lost much in recent years under the reign of your father and sometimes bitterness finds a way of seeking revenge. I believe they hired someone to carry out the task. If what I suspect is true, then we must erase their presence from this land." The warlock moved closer to face Vanus. "You cannot risk letting this go without a response."

"Now would be perfect timing to seek out the ones in hiding and those who remain here in the city," continued the warlock, sensing that he had Vanus's attention. "With the approach of the Spring Festival of Terashom, Abbodar will be hungering for the arena sacrifices. While most of the Dissenters are not warriors and provide little in the way of competitive battle, the crowd will enjoy the spilling of their blood for sacrifice."

"I don't know," countered Vanus. "It seems a waste of time and manpower to gather them on the hunch that they may have had something to do with the assassination attempt. Besides, I believe my father to be overly paranoid in his old age. He does not think as clearly as he used to."

"There is something I have just learned that may change your lack of concern on this issue. A prophet of the One Faith may soon rise among them."

"A prophet," mused Vanus. "That would be a problem. Prophets have a way of stirring things up. The last thing we need is a revival among them."

"Now is the time to take action," pressed Relnik. "There is an old prophet named Graybeard who has entered our lands and carries with him a talisman of great power. I am convinced that it is somehow connected with the Dissenters. I have decided to send four more Ravens to join the hunt for the prophet and the Intercessor who travels with him."

"What do you know of this talisman that you speak of?" asked Vanus, showing more interest. His addiction to magic would not let the comment pass unquestioned.

"I have spies in the kingdom of Talinor, which is where the talisman comes from. They tell me that it is a sword that contains a great magic."

"Then we must have it, and the prophet you speak of, Graybeard. I have heard of him. He came to Abbodar many years ago before I was born. If my memory does not fail me, I recall that he was tortured and imprisoned in our dungeons. Eventually, he was sentenced to die at the stake in the arena, but a powerful warrior stood in as his champion." Vanus paused trying to remember the histories he learned in school as a boy. "The warrior had a name. I think it was Felnar."

"His name was Kem Felnar," said the warlock. "He was the first king of Talinor."

"Graybeard the prophet has returned, and he is near death. I have no doubt that he seeks a successor to pass his prophetic mantle to," said Relnik.

"Then he is in violation of his exile, and I agree. You have done well to send the Ravens to find him. The last thing we need is an uprising of Dissenters."

Drok Relnik knew it was the sword that interested Vanus more than the prophet, but it would still serve his purpose just the same.

CHAPTER 16

It had been three days since they had left Karn, and during that time the travelers had passed through several smaller villages. Bryann's mood had grown darker with each passing day. In one of the villages, she had almost attacked a merchant that she believed was cheating her when she tried to buy a knife from him. Gerrid believed that if he had not been there to intervene, she would have killed him with his own knife. His attempt to stop her gave her yet one more reason to resent the quest and Gerrid.

The former Tal commander increased in strength with each passing day. He felt the muscle tone returning to his arms and legs, but most of all, he noticed that his stamina was improving. He had Packer to thank for that. The collector kept them well fed with the bartering he did in the village markets. Somehow he always had something to barter with and, to Gerrid's amazement, he seemed to have an uncanny way of always trading up.

On one occasion, Packer was bartering with a shopkeeper for some bread. When he produced some colored beads for payment the baker appeared disinterested in the beads until Packer told him that they had once belonged to a great warrior chief from the Buntoc tribe. The merchant shifted to show a sudden increase of interest in his offering. Once Packer sensed the advantage he was gaining with the man, he feigned a lack of interest in the bread and turned his back on the man to walk away. Gerrid saw the smile on Packer's face as the merchant chased after him. By the time they were done bartering with each other, Packer had obtained bread, cheese and a small bag of meat to show for his trade.

Gerrid was amused by the transaction and asked Packer about the beads. The young street hound told him he had traded for the beads a few days earlier and was told by the seller that they contained magic. Packer laughed and said, "They were magic. Look what we traded them for." He smiled and handed Gerrid a piece of cheese.

The small company of four had been walking since sunrise without stopping to rest, so they could cover a lot of ground. After hiking through the arid valley filled with patches of scrub oak and thorn weeds, the terrain began to change. They had passed several wind shelters, and to their luck, did not have to use them. The hills that rose in front of them were a welcome sight. A little higher, and they would be above the reach of the howls. In the distance, jagged peaks pierced a shroud of clouds and mist. Gerrid felt an unexpected excitement as they drew nearer to their destination, and he began to wonder what he would find upon his arrival in Hebron Forest—what old friends would be there to greet him and which ones would not. Hopefully, Dallien would be among them.

Gerrid could not stop thinking about the conversation he had with Pamela before he left her home back in Abbodar. She had pressed him to make this journey, and she was convinced that he was somehow destined to do so. Destiny, he thought to himself. Was it his destiny to spend two years in prison and suffer torture at the hands of his enemies? He was unable to resolve that question, and it seemed to haunt him daily and in his dreams. If Pamela had not brought destiny into the conversation, he would have probably moved on by now and left prison behind him.

Suddenly a deep sadness threatened to overwhelm him as he paused to look back over the valley below toward the city. He once carried an unspeakable burden for these people. The golden rays of the fading sun brought their final farewell to the land, and for some strange reason, it felt like he was saying goodbye to a dear friend for the last time. He was free now, but the same loneliness he had felt when he was in prison continued to envelope his thoughts and emotions. He couldn't shake the feeling like he was leaving something undone.

The shadow fairies appeared once again at the corners of his mind, whispering to him. You were left alone and unprotected by the god you put your trust in. Where was he when you needed him most?

I was left alone and unprotected by the god I put my trust and hope in, he thought. Gerrid would not abandon his faith in that God, but he also knew that he would not so easily trust him as he once had. The price he had paid for trusting him had cost him too much, and he doubted he would ever completely recover. His body may be growing stronger, but his spirit remained weak and vulnerable. He ached to go back home to Talinor where he belonged. Fond memories of home deepened his yearning to return there. He pictured the palace of the king with its tall round columns lining the courtyard and the countryside with its giant oak trees and rolling hills littered with streams and lakes filled with an abundance of fish. He smiled as he recalled catching his first fish with his grandfather. He thought it was huge, but he knew now it was barely a fingerling. His grandfather had praised him for such an amazing catch.

I will complete the journey to Hebron Forest, thought Gerrid. I will say goodbye to my friends one last time and then return home.

He slowly pulled himself away from looking at the city and turned to catch up with the others, but he had to come to a sudden stop when he noticed Sera standing in the path staring up at him. Her sad eyes pierced his heart.

"Why do you listen to them?" she asked in a bewildered tone as her head slightly twisted, straining to grasp the answer before it was offered.

His brow wrinkled at the question. "Sera you are a strange one," said Gerrid as he walked past her, ignoring the question. "Come, we need to catch up with the others."

Sera followed in behind him as her mood suddenly shifted, and she began to skip along as if dancing to a tune in her head. Humming at first, then she began to sing.

> "Beware of the shadow fairies
> who come and go.
> At early light and end of day
> come the thoughts they sow.
> Gentle and soothing,
> when they appear.
> Enchanting voices disguising fear.
> Hush, shadow fairies, and go away
> Never to return another day."

Sera continued to skip and sing the song over and over again until they caught up with Packer and Bryann.

"Are you singing again?" Said Packer, squinting as if in pain.

Sera smiled at the street hound. "Thank you," she said as she bowed to her audience and again, she repeated, "Thank you."

"You aren't going to keep doing that are you?" asked Packer through strained words.

Sera smiled, and in a short sweet voice replied, "I'm done."

"It's been a long day," said Gerrid, taking a deep breath and slowly exhaling. "I say we set up camp for the night." He looked at Bryann to check her response. She registered a blank stare at the ground as if unconcerned.

After Packer prepared a fire, he cooked a stew made of vegetables and venison, and the four of them ate in silence except for Sera who was humming tunes no one recognized. Darkness settled with the last light of dusk, giving way to a canopy of glittering stars that lit up the sky. A chorus of crickets and frogs began their nightly serenade as if in competition with Sera's humming.

After they finished their meal, Packer and Sera went to gather more wood for the fire. Bryann had wandered off. After sitting and staring at the fire for a while, Gerrid went looking for Bryann and found her perched quietly on a rock, looking out at the star filled sky.

Quietly moving next to the rock, he joined her and sat silently before speaking, hoping she would say something. She acted as if she was unaware of his presence.

"Even in this land of suffering and darkness, there is still beauty to be found," said Gerrid softly.

Silence. She kept her gaze fixed on the twinkling lights.

"What are they telling you?"

Silence again. Bryann stiffened and looked down. The moon shed enough light to reflect gently on her face and the hair that fell past her shoulders to her hips.

"I can hear them," whispered Gerrid, observing that beneath all her anger and hard demeanor, she was strikingly beautiful.

"You can hear the stars?" A subtle irritation shaded her tone.

In the background, they could hear the muffled sounds of

Sera singing at the campfire and Packer begging her to stop.

Gerrid smiled and said, "Yes, the stars always have something to say. Can't you hear them?"

"I only hear the tears of suffering and sadness everywhere I go in this wretched land."

Then something happened to Gerrid that was unfamiliar to him. A picture suddenly filled his mind, he saw a little girl sitting by a small stream bathed in sunlight. Tears streamed from her eyes. She was holding a crumpled daisy in her trembling hands. He could feel the full impact of the grief that overwhelmed her, and he fought to hold back the tears.

Bryann looked at Gerrid, noticing the distant look on his face and the sadness in his gaze. Somehow she could feel the grief he was feeling, and it frightened her. Those kinds of feelings were not welcome in her life. He turned to look at her, and their eyes met for one unsettling moment before they both shifted their gaze away from each other. In that second, there was a small connection between them. She felt strangely safe with that connection, yet threatened by it at the same time.

Bryann broke the uncomfortable silence. "What is it?" she asked before realizing she wished she hadn't said anything.

The picture faded from his mind. Somehow he thought that he had seen a vision of Bryann as a child, but he was unsure and did not know how to respond to her question. The thought came to his mind, softly at first, and then more clearly as if sent from the vision he had just seen.

Gerrid stuttered, at first doubting that he should reveal any of the mysterious image, then a sense of urgency came to him. Before he realized what he was doing, he was speaking, "A torn and tattered daisy will drop its seeds to the ground, but the tears that water them will bring new life."

Where did that come from? thought Gerrid.

Bryann shuddered inside, clearly shaken by the comment. "I will never cry again," she said fighting to hold back the tears she had just vowed to forsake. "Who are you? How did you know?"

She stood up from the rock and was standing now in a defensive posture.

"I—I don't know what just happened," mumbled Gerrid.

"Stay your distance. I don't know who you are—a priest, a holy man, a warrior? Whatever you are, stay back."

Bryann turned quickly and walked away into the dark night. Confused by what had just happened, several thoughts filled her restless mind. How could he know? How could he know my heart this way? She had spent a lifetime building walls to keep others away, especially men, and now he had found a way in. She wanted to keep walking and never turn back.

The next morning, when Sera, Packer, and Gerrid woke up, Bryann was gone. Concerned at first, Gerrid began to scout out the immediate area to see if he could find her. In the distance beyond the clearing of their campsite, he could see her sitting alone on the same rock where they had talked to one another last night. Gerrid had slept restlessly after the strange vision and conversation with Bryann. He was just as confused as she was, only for different reasons. The vision seemed so real and yet he did not understand its meaning. Clearly it meant something to Bryann, and he wondered what painful secrets she held in her heart.

"We need supplies," said Packer as he and Sera approached. "There is a small village beyond the next rise. Sera and I will be safe this far out. We'll go buy what we need and be back before midday."

Gerrid paused for a moment to consider the idea, unsure of their safety. "You go ahead, but we will be right behind you and meet you when we get there."

Packer nodded.

"Packer, beware of military patrols," warned Gerrid. "I know we haven't seen one for days, but you can't be too careful."

He knew Packer could take care of himself, but he was concerned for Sera after almost losing her in Karn.

Packer produced a cloth hat from his pack and handed it to Sera. "You may want to put this on to cover those ears," he said as Sera smiled, placing it on her head. It fell down just enough to cover her pointed ears. "You can come with me. Just promise me, no singing."

"No promises," smiled Sera as she skipped away in the direction of the village.

Packer grimaced and turned to head over the rise to follow her. Sera had pestered him all morning to let her go with him when she found out he may be going to the village for supplies. He had conceded reluctantly, still holding some concern for her safety. The bounty on Elves was tempting for most, but the villagers in these outlying areas were simple people, and most wanted to avoid such things.

CHAPTER 17

Lena could see that the journey was taking a toll on Graybeard who grew weaker with each passing day. If not for the horses, he wouldn't be able to make the journey. It was especially difficult through the mountains where the trails sometimes wound along the side of steep cliffs. Their mounts proved stable under the mountainous conditions, and for that, they were thankful. It had been several days since leaving Fairwinds, and they had managed to avoid passing through the towns and villages along their journey. Several small caravans of traders had passed them on their way to the seaports, but none of them were willing to sell them food. Seeking to restock their supplies, they found a quiet hamlet where they could buy fruits and vegetables and all the meat they needed for the next leg of their journey. Lena, along with Jef and two other Tal warriors, Rafe and Lebo, entered the village marketplace. The streets were beginning to get busy with the early morning bargain hunters.

"We must find the baker, Jef," said Lena as she caught the scent of fresh bread in the air.

"You'll have no argument from me, Lena. My only regret is that it will pale in comparison to your own bread."

"I fear you are right, my friend. I find that one of my greatest pleasures is in the baking and sharing of bread."

"And one of my greatest pleasures is in the eating of your bread," said Jef with a sigh.

"I miss my grandson, Jef," said Lena, suddenly changing the subject. "I have not seen him in two years, and I have no idea where he is or if he is okay."

"I pray for him often," said Jef thoughtfully.

"As do I, and at times I sense he is in great danger, like when we were on the ship just before we landed in Fairwinds. I travailed during intercession, and I knew in my spirit I was praying for him. I hope he is alright."

"He has you praying for him, Lena. How can he not be?"

"I wish it was that simple, but I know the life of a Gap Warrior because I lived it for so many years. I carry this staff as a reminder. It also serves as a good walking stick."

"Cyle is a strong one," said Jef, attempting to comfort her. "He proved his mettle at the battle two years ago in Talinor."

"He was just a boy."

"And by now, a young man."

"He could be stubborn at times," said Lena with furrowed brow. "He was always dreaming and hoping for something different—a new adventure, a different kind of life. I guess he found what he was looking for."

"The young are restless for adventure. That is for sure," mused Jef.

"I just pray he is over it and keeps his focus. Battling the dark spirits requires more than skill with a weapon. It demands a clear heart and a strong bond with the Ancient of Days. The dark ones do not always attack us head on with weapons drawn. Pride or confusion can leave us vulnerable to attack. It is easy to forget that it is the heart that must be protected. We can become too busy defending others and forget that we too need protection."

"I wish I had known the truth of what you speak many years ago. Maybe I would not have wandered from the One Faith as I did," Jef sighed. "So much time wasted. I was young and thought I knew it all. I knew so very little, and what little I did know was incomplete."

"It is difficult to see the big picture when we are young, and yet the greatest deception is that we think we do," offered Lena as she shifted her gaze away from Jef. "Even now in my old age, I have come to understand that I see so little."

"So true," Jef agreed.

They followed the smell of baking bread until they arrived at its source. Rafe and Lebo consumed more than seemed possible, and Jef did the same. After purchasing enough to fill their bags with hot bread, they finished gathering all the supplies they needed, remounted their horses, and headed back to their camp.

The trail back to camp took them clear of the trees into an area of giant granite boulders that stood at the edge of massive cliffs which rose into the heavens. Their horses nervously came to a sudden halt with Rafe's mount rearing on its back legs, staggering backward. A rumbling sound vibrated softly in the ground beneath them, softly at first. Before they could make any sense of it, there was a thundering crash as rocks showered outward from the base of the granite cliffs. Three giant boulders bounced onto the path in front of them. Jef grabbed the reigns on Lena's mount and backed their horses to a safer distance.

The four travelers were calming their startled mounts, pulling on their reigns and attempting to settle them, unaware of what was unfolding before them. The three massive boulders began to shift and change shape. Rafe saw it first, and his eyes grew to saucers, and all he could do was point. The others stared speechless as the boulders formed into giant rock-shaped men with stony flesh.

"Pull back," cautioned Jef as he tugged on the reigns of his horse.

The three giant rocks had morphed into full size, standing at least twelve feet high, towering over them. A dirty green moss-like covering hung about their waists with bits of mud and twigs holding it together and the hair on their heads looked like the same material. The shapes of their bodies were like that of any man, except bulky and wide, like crudely chiseled sculptures.

They all grunted and looked about them as if searching for something. One of the rock giants spoke in a deep, gravely growl, ignoring the audience that had gathered. "Come out and stop running like a coward."

Another form emerged from a cave similar to the other three only much smaller.

"Outcast," rumbled the one who appeared to be the leader of the three bigger giants. "You are no longer a part of us."

The smaller giant, who was at least eight feet tall, had a look of fear in his eyes and was breathing heavily as if he had been running. Two of the rock men rushed the one they had called outcast and crashed in upon him as the third joined in behind them. The four of them rolled in a thunderous ball, crashing into the side of a granite wall. Rocks burst out in every direction. The mountain shook as more rocks tumbled down from the cliffs above. The smaller giant kicked one of the bigger ones in the chest and sent him reeling into another rock outcropping. The other two were on him instantly, pinning him. He struggled unsuccessfully to free himself from their grasp.

"What are they?" yelled Lebo. "I have never seen such creatures that appear as stone and yet speak as men."

"Rock trolls," came an answer from an unfamiliar voice, "or stone giants, whatever you prefer."

The voice came from a young man with bushy brown hair standing alone with a pack on his back. He had approached from behind them without notice.

"No," pleaded the smaller giant who was still being held down by two of his attackers while the third giant approached with a metal rod in the palm of his hand.

"You shall be branded as an outcast," threatened the giant with the rod in his hand as he moved toward the other cautiously.

A look of terror filled the smaller giant's eyes as he struggled helplessly to get free from his captors who had him firmly pinned to the cliff wall.

The rod seemed to glow with heat when he moved it closer to the chest of the smaller one who was still fighting to get free. Then a second person moved into the clearing from behind one of the fallen rocks. A small girl wearing a cloth hat walked toward the giants. She was tiny in comparison to the rock men but showed little concern for the potential danger of her actions. Without saying a word, she kept walking until she filled the space between the brand wielder and the captive outcast.

The giant holding the iron rod grunted in confusion and shuffled slightly backward.

"Sera," cried Packer. "Are you crazy? Run away now."

Sera acted as if she hadn't heard her friend's frantic warning. Instead she held her ground between the rock troll with the iron brand and the smaller giant. The one with the brand glared down at the tiny spec of a person before him. "Move aside, little bug, before I crush you." His voice rumbled like grinding stones.

"My, aren't you a scary one," squeaked Sera through a timid smile.

"You are in the way, bug. Move or I will step on you."

"Run, Sera," Packer whispered.

Sera ignored her friend and paused briefly seemingly unmoved by the giant's threats. She was in awe of the giant's size and the stone-like texture of his skin.

"Don't you ever get tired of being rude?" asked Sera.

The giant growled under his breath, shifting nervously

123

before speaking again in his best menacing voice. "I am Stone Hammer, son of Stone Crusher. You must step aside or I will have to swat you like a gnat."

"I wouldn't think a little bug would be much of a bother to a rude pile of rocks like you."

The giant's stony brow furled in confusion at the little one's defiance. Packer tried again to call his friend over to him, but she continued to ignore him. Lena smiled as the others watched the whole thing, mystified by what was happening.

"What does a rock giant eat anyway?"

"Stop talking to me. My brand is fading. Now move, pest, before I brand you."

"What has he done that he deserves branding?"

"He has done nothing," grumbled the giant as he stooped down to the level of the defiant little girl and looked her straight in the eyes in an attempt to intimidate her. "He is Mingi, and he must be cast out from the Stone Clan. It is our way. Now stop asking so many questions, for I am running out of patience."

"Mingi. What is Mingi?" asked Sera ignoring the giant's request.

"Mingi is cursed."

"Cursed. Why is he cursed?" Sera pressed with a look of determination on her furrowed brow.

"He has not grown to an acceptable size. He is Mingi, and he must be branded and exiled from the clan. He no longer has a home with us. Now step aside."

"Stop," cried Sera, holding up her hand. She could hear Packer calling to her in the back of her mind to come away. "Is there no other way to avoid the branding?" Anger filled her voice, and it did not escape the giant's attention.

"He has no clan and no one will accept him with the Mingi curse, so he must be branded."

"My clan will take him," said Sera, putting her hands on her small hips as she twisted to look back at the captured giant behind her.

"And who are you that you can make such an invitation?"

"I am Sera, the daughter of Galandell, High Prince of the Elves of the Crystal Mountains."

"Ha, ha, ha! You are an Elf. I doubt it is so. I have never seen one, but I have heard they are fierce warriors of great power and you are but a little bug. Where are your pointed—"

Sera tore off her hat exposing her ears.

"Oh no, here we go again," groaned Packer.

The giant jerked backward, and for the first time he was without a response.

Lena walked toward them until she was standing next to Sera. The giant looked at her, registering confusion in his eyes.

"Hello, my lady," Sera dipped in respect to Lena as she greeted the Intercessor.

"Greetings daughter of Galandell. You are far from home," said Lena, and then she turned to fix her gaze on the giant. "She speaks the truth, and as a daughter of royalty, she has the authority to adopt anyone she pleases to join her clan, even one who is cursed. What is your response to this royal request?"

Stone Hammer stood back up to his full height and glared at the smaller giant still subdued by his restrainers. "I, too, am of royalty, and I am bound to accept such an offer, even if it is for this one who is Mingi. Release him to her." Stone Hammer's voice shifted from one of anger to relief as he dropped the firebrand to the ground. "May you live in peace brother," said the giant with a look of sadness filling his eyes, and then he turned to walk away. The other two giants released the smaller giant, turned and followed their leader into the rocky canyon.

Sera and Lena turned to face the one who had been left behind. He looked as big as the others now that they were gone, but in reality he was at least two to three feet shorter than them.

"And what do they call you, mister giant?" asked the elf girl kindly.

He looked at Sera as if he did not understand her words at first. She was not sure what the look on his face meant because she was unaccustomed to the facial expressions of a stone giant. "I am called Stone Hutch."

"What does your name mean?" asked Sera.

"It means strong shelter," Mumbled the giant timidly while looking at the ground.

"But I am cursed." The giant's voice grew deeper and sounded angry. "At the fifth year of my life, I was taken to the center rock at the heart of our homeland. I had not grown taller than the rock so I was cursed and banished from the tribe. It is the way of my people. Why would you choose to take me with you?"

Sera reached out with both of her tiny hands grabbing one of Hutch's fingers, barely able to hold on. "Come, Strong Shelter. Curses are not unbreakable, stone man. Today you will join our tribe and help us with our quest, and we will find a way to break this curse."

"Your father is a High Prince," squealed Packer in disbelief, breaking into the conversation. "Why have you never spoken of this to me?"

"I didn't think of it," answered Sera dismissively.

"My dear Sera," said Lena, "you are a long way from home."

"Yes, my lady."

"Sera, please, call me Lena."

"Yes, my lady."

Lena smiled knowing she would not convince her. "So how is it you are in this place?"

Sera recalled a story of how she had traveled to this region with a group of diplomats and healers at the request of Elias, the elf king of Krellander. A great sickness had infected the elves of the Crystal Mountains, causing many of them to perish. Their mission was to seek out a people known as the Buntoc, a tribe that inhabited a region called the Misty Realms not far from Abbodar. The Buntoc were known to have powerful medicines for healing, but when her company of elves arrived in Abbodar they discovered that most of the Buntoc had been taken captive to

SWORD OF DELIVERANCE

work as slaves in the mines. The ones who escaped that fate were now in hiding somewhere in the high forest regions surrounding Abbodar.

Once in Abbodar the elves discovered what a dark place it was, and so they decided to leave immediately, but most of them were captured and sacrificed at the altars of Terashom. Sera was fortunate enough to escape into the streets of Abbodar where she met Packer, who befriended her and brought her in among the street hounds. She was later abducted by a rival gang of street hounds and sold to a wizard named Drok Relnik who planned to sacrifice her to Terashom. That's when her friend Packer rescued her and they fled from the city.

"Drok Relnik." Lena stumbled over the words. "What evil is he up to?" Her spirit quaked at the news. "Please, Sera. Continue."

"There is one more thing you should know, my lady. I travel with a man from Talinor, a former commander of the Tal Army who led them in the last battle for freedom against the Boogaran horde."

"Is this one of whom you speak named Gerrid?"

"Yes, my lady," responded Sera with surprise and delight.

"I remember Gerrid. He left us in Talinor over two years ago full of vision with the message of the One Faith burning in his heart." As the Intercessor spoke Gerrid's name, something stirred within her spirit. "We prayed for him when he left, and I have continued to intercede for him since that day. I had no idea he had come to this place as I have not heard from him since he left."

"He spent almost two years in prison and was recently released, but before his imprisonment, he was able to build a modest following."

"I wish to see him, Sera."

"That will be easy, our camp is not far from here."

127

CHAPTER 18

Drew moved through the forest quickly, running and jumping over rocks and logs as he led Cyle and Choppa back toward the small ship where the others anxiously awaited their return. Cyle reflected on his time with the Buntoc. For some reason, he had felt connected to the tribe in the short time he was there, especially Nolan. His story of how his people had fled from their home in the Misty Realms to escape being enslaved had grieved the young Gap Warrior. He had grown up free his whole life, but he had almost lost his freedom at the battle against the Boogarans. It dawned on him that he could have lost his own freedom just as the Buntoc had.

How could a nation be so cruel as to enslave a people against their will, he wondered? He knew slavery happened in the world, but he had never met someone who had lost so much because of it. Before he left the Buntoc camp, Nolan's brother, Bayson, had said to him, "Maybe you are the one, eagle man."

The comment confused Cyle at first until Bayson made clear what he meant. "Maybe you are the one whom the Graybeard spoke of. Maybe you are the warrior sent to deliver us." Cyle couldn't shake those words from his mind. Surely he was not the one, he argued with himself. Could his mission have something to do with Graybeard's prophesy of a deliverer who would come to set the Buntoc free of their oppressors?

When Cyle and the others arrived back at the boat, they could hear voices yelling. As the boat came into view, they saw a door on board crash open, and Gafney staggered out onto the deck and grabbed the railing to steady himself. Ginzer and Bernard rushed through the door right behind him. Gafney kept yelling something about being fine and wanting some fresh air.

It had been difficult keeping the big man in bed. Only Addie had succeeded in calming him down and keeping him still. She had gone ashore to collect herbs and left Gafney in the care of

Ginzer and Bernard, sternly warning them before she left to keep him in bed and calm. Gafney kept trying to get outside, insisting he was fine and that he wanted to do some hunting and fishing. His fever had spiked several times. Once late at night, Bernard had found him wandering the deck staring at the moonbeams reflecting on the water.

Within half a day, Gafney's fever had broken, and the stitching on his wounds had improved markedly But there was still a great deal of soreness and need for further rest.

Once they had returned with the medicine, the Sea Horse pulled anchor and headed upstream under full sails. Ginzer and Bernard had pledged themselves to the two Gap Warriors on their quest.

"Our ship is at your service." Bernard had made it clear. "It would be unacceptable for us to abandon our friends from Talinor. Besides, I think we are about due for an adventure."

Drew and Addie would stay on as well, knowing that they could not return home. By now, the surviving villagers would have scattered into the forests in the wake of complete destruction of their homes.

When darkness fell that night, a full moon lit the sky overhead as Ginzer anchored the boat far enough from shore to provide safe harbor. For most of the evening meals, both Ginzer and Bernard would cook. They usually prepared game from the shore or fish caught from the river. The two dwarves had their ritual argument over how the meal should be prepared. Bernard's voice could be heard above deck rebuking his cousin Ginzer for using too much salt or for cooking the meat on one side for too long. Somehow through the angry clanging of pots and pans, the meals got cooked, and everyone's bellies got their fill.

After their meal Cyle settled down on the deck and looked up at the stars. He found it hard to sleep as his mind was unable to let go of the words Bayson had spoken to him about possibly being the deliverer sent to free them from their oppression. He resisted the idea. He had come to embrace his call as a Gap

Warrior and did not like the idea of things changing. He struggled at times with the uncertainty that comes with not knowing where his assignments would take him. Sometimes it was hard to accept the idea that he had to wait and trust until the details were revealed. Even now, he felt uneasy not knowing why he and Gafney were led to this place, and he always found it difficult to sleep at night with that kind of uncertainty. He recalled how his friend Bixby, the first Gap Warrior he had ever met, seemed unconcerned with the lack of details, and how he would patiently wait until they were revealed to him. He wished he could have Bixby's kind of faith, and yet every mission Cyle had been sent on since becoming a Gap Warrior left him wanting to know more. He hated not knowing the bigger picture. Gafney was similar to Bixby, only he was a more restless spirit. Cyle wished Bixby was here to bring balance to Gafney.

Mellidar, his Guardian and trainer, had repeatedly told him that things were revealed according to each battle as it unfolded over time. The Guardian challenged him that knowing too much in advance could play upon a person's doubts and fears, and besides, things changed constantly in matters of warfare. Cyle still preferred knowing as much as possible in advance, and on many occasions would pressure Mellidar to tell him more. But the Guardian would often say that he himself did not know any more than he was revealing.

Cyle shifted restlessly, seeking a more comfortable position on the wooden deck. When he sensed a presence, he knew instantly who it was. Jumping to his feet, he peered toward the shore and saw Mellidar standing ghost-like in the shadows by the water's edge. Motionless, he waited for Cyle to come to him. The young Gap Warrior drew in a deep breath and tried to exhale the irritation he was feeling at the inconvenience of the moment. He found the small boat near the front of the ship, dropped it into the water and paddled quietly to shore. Exhaustion weighed heavily on him. It had been a long day of hiking into the woods, and now he would have to delay his much-needed sleep.

Once he reached the shore, the Guardian led him to a moonlit clearing where he stopped and turned to face the young Gap Warrior. Dressed in woodsman garb with staff in hand, he turned to face his disciple and spoke in his familiar deep voice. "Ready yourself for battle." Mellidar shifted his position and went to the ready combat position.

Cyle hesitated and sighed deeply once again, wishing he could be back at the boat sleeping. Mellidar recognized the look of annoyance all too well, but he chose to withhold comment and waited patiently for Cyle to assume the battle ready position. He moved slowly in response to the command of his Guardian. Mellidar attacked before Cyle was able to ready himself. In startled defense, he lifted his staff just in time to block the Guardian's blow, but not fast enough to prevent it from deflecting against his shoulder. Pain lanced down his arm, and anger erupted within Cyle. He reacted with three counter strikes that were easily blocked by the Guardian.

"You must choose the time to let your anger drive your weapon," warned Mellidar. "Otherwise it will control you, and you must always control your own anger if it is to benefit you in battle."

Cyle seethed and said nothing as he attempted to step backward, hoping to delay the lesson, but Mellidar came at him again with an even fiercer assault. This time the Guardian's staff flashed out toward his disciple from every conceivable angle, and each strike was answered with a counter block. Now Cyle was awake and at the ready. Mellidar began his third offensive move, and once again he increased the intensity, surprising his student. He launched a flurry of straight jabs with his staff combined with combinations of vertical and horizontal swipes. All of them were narrowly blocked by Cyle until Mellidar stuck his pole into the ground and vaulted into the air. The Guardians boots slammed into the Gap Warrior's chest and sent him to the ground, knocking the air from his lungs with a grunt. It was the first time Mellidar had assaulted him using a body part as a weapon. It took Cyle completely off-guard, and somewhere in the back of his mind, he felt as if he had been cheated.

Rolling back to his feet, Cyle was preparing to spring into a counter charge when Mellidar commanded, "Hold your ground."

It took every ounce of restraint to hold back, but he froze and held his position while he stood breathing raggedly with a confused look on his face.

"You must learn to counter-strike before the flurry of blows against you has ended. Not every opponent will wait for you to gather yourself and give you time to go into offensive mode," cautioned Mellidar sternly. "Now, try again."

The Guardian pressed in again with another series of strikes that seemed faster than the last ones, and once again Cyle went on the defensive, blocking and shifting positions and looking for an opening. He was unable to find one, and for a second time he ended up in the dirt after receiving an elbow jab to the side of his head. The ground was spinning beneath him as frustration set in.

Cyle could have asked for help, but his pride got the better of him, and after several more attempts to find the opening on his own, Mellidar finally spoke into his silent frustration. "Is there something you want to ask me?" questioned the Guardian in a cold, distant voice.

"I'll figure it out," Cyle shot back.

"Are you sure you have the energy for such a task?"

Cyle was spent, and he knew he could not keep the pace up much longer. "If you have something to say, then say it," countered Cyle. It pained him deeply to make the request.

"Is it still so hard for you to ask for help after all these trainings?"

Silence.

"There is an important truth that drives the battle strategy I am trying to teach you tonight. If you embrace it, then it will serve you well in your warfare." Mellidar leaned on his staff waited silently for a response, but there was none given, so he continued.

"When battling the dark ones, your ability to overcome them is limited if you remain on the defensive. While your defensive skills are necessary, they are not enough to bring victory at the higher levels of battle. You must understand the importance of building a defiant offense, especially against the ones that inhabit this realm."

"And how do I do that?"

Finally, thought Mellidar, he questions. "Before you can fully grasp what I have to say, there is another question that must be answered."

"What question is that?" asked Cyle, huffing with impatience.

"What do you think the question is?"

"Please, I am too tired to solve riddles at this late hour."

"Steel yourself then and fight against it. Calm yourself and focus. Close your eyes and picture in your mind a path that comes to a fork and splits in two directions. One on the right and the other on the left" instructed Mellidar.

Cyle stared at him blankly.

"Do it," demanded the Guardian forcefully. "Your life may depend on it."

Cyle closed his eyes, and Mellidar continued, "Sometimes the answers we seek are found through knowing what questions to ask. Now picture in your mind the fork in the path, and be still in that place and look to the path on the right and wait for the question to come to you." Mellidar paused to give his disciple time to gather the image to his mind before he continued his instructions. "Now wait and see if a question comes to mind."

"What is the key?" guessed Cyle.

"No," interrupted Mellidar. "That is your mind running down the left path seeking old knowledge to try to find the question you should ask. You cannot find what you seek through old knowledge. It will not give you what you need in this situation. Look at the path on the right and say, what is the question I need to ask? The Spirit Wind will bring you the answer from that path.

Do it now, and then wait for it to come to you."

Cyle felt frustrated and a little confused. He could see the image in his mind, but his brain wanted desperately to seek the question from the path on the left. Impatience threatened to tempt him down the left path of reason in his mind, but he resisted and turned to his right, forcing himself to look down the right path. There is nothing there, he thought. This is a waste of time. Cyle shifted restlessly with the stillness of waiting, and again he wanted desperately to go back to the path on the left where he believed he could find the answer to solving the problem.

"If you only use the path of reason, then you will be limited by your own intelligence," said Mellidar as if he was reading Cyle's mind. "At times your own reasoning may serve you well, but when you are battling the dark ones, you need more than human reasoning. You need the wisdom of the Ancient of Days brought to you upon the Spirit Wind. Your battle is not with flesh and blood; therefore, you need guidance that is born of the light, not merely of your own flesh."

Something in the Guardian's words triggered a deeper hunger in the young Gap Warrior, driving him to want to understand more. Cyle knew Mellidar was speaking wisdom, and he felt his spirit reaching out to take hold of it. He had been called to fight the dark spirits of the void, and he knew that they could not be defeated by the weapons or wisdom forged by man. He felt shame for allowing his pride to blind him from a truth that should have been obvious to him by now.

The young Gap warrior shifted to the right and looked down the empty path that was imaged in his mind. He could see nothing before him as he calmed himself and waited. Still nothing happened. He pressed in and remained resolute to wait longer. Then the questioned formed in his mind. What is the nature and power of those I am to battle against in this realm? Cyle knew instantly it was the right question, and he understood the value of the question, for how could he defeat his enemies without knowing the answer?

"I have it," He said victoriously. "I have the question."

"And now that you have the question you need the answer to the question," instructed Mellidar.

"And where will I find the answer?" asked Cyle.

"You will find the answer from the same place you found the question."

At first Mellidar's statement sounded like another riddle but the meaning of it somehow made sense to him, so Cyle closed his eyes once again and imaged the two paths in his mind as the question burned in his thoughts and would not let go. He knew what to do this time. He looked down the path in his mind to the right and prayed the question out loud to the Ancient of Days while holding the image in his mind of the path on the right.

"What is the nature and power of those I am to battle in this realm?" The Gap Warrior stilled his mind, and after several moments of silence, an image on the path began to materialize before him. It was a woman dressed in glowing battle garments of blue metal and crystal chain mail. She was carrying a scepter in her right hand. Her presence both excited him and gave him a sense of comfort.

"Do you know who I am?" asked the woman.

Cyle recognized the voice immediately and the word Shariana formed in his mind. Then he spoke her name out loud.

"I am glad you recognize me in this form, young warrior."

"How could I forget you, my lady?" Cyle felt a tear form in the corner of his eye. "You showed me the path of my destiny, and I will be forever grateful to you for that."

Images flowed through Cyle's mind as he recalled the first time he had met the Guardian Queen over two years ago. Shariana had led him into the Caverns of Lorus where he discovered for the first time what his life would be like if he accepted the call of destiny that was placed before him. He would never forget the two images he saw there in the waters of the lake. In the first one, he saw how pitiful the lives of those would turn out if they refused their own calling. In the other image, the one where he saw a picture of himself if he chose to follow his destiny, he beheld a vision of himself as a powerful and noble warrior. It was that moment that he answered his call. That seemed like a lifetime ago.

"And now for the answer to the question you seek," Shariana interrupted his thoughts. "Some of the dark spirits you will battle in this realm will be unfamiliar to you." The glow of her armor began to increase in brilliance as she drew closer to him. "The barrier that stands between the void and the world of flesh grows weaker each day. The priests of this land have been sacrificing the followers of the One Faith, and more recently, the emperor has chosen to allow them to sacrifice elves. Now that the blood of elves stains the altars of Terashom, a breach has opened in the void like none this world has ever known."

"The elves," whispered Cyle. Sorrow threatened to overcome him. A memory of his friend Tryska, the elf girl, flashed in his mind. His body beginning to shake, he remembered the Gap Warrior and wondered if she was okay.

"Such things are an abomination before the Ancient of Days who weeps for his followers, and his tears have drenched the corridors of his kingdom," declared Shariana with her voice, rising in defiance against the detestable practices. "These despicable sacrifices have provided a point of access for the dark spirits of the void to take up residence in the bodies and minds of those who have welcomed them to infest their bodies."

Cyle could feel the hair rising on the back of his neck. He could sense the darkness in this land from the moment he first stepped foot on its shores, but he had no idea what had caused it.

"This is why you have been summoned here. You will battle shadow wraiths that have infested the flesh of men, infusing them with their own powers and personalities." Shariana paused as the scepter in her right hand flickered brighter. "You must stand strong in the faith you have been given, Gap Warrior. Listen well to Mellidar, he will teach you how to battle the infested ones. Greater courage and new skills will be needed if you are to defeat them. My Guardians and I will be battling on your behalf. You will not be alone." Shariana's voice trailed off, then she smiled and the image faded from Cyle's mind.

"Wait. How will I recognize them when I find them?"

"That, too, is a good question," Mellidar's voice broke in. "They are called the Ravens, and you will recognize them when you meet one of them. Your staff will reveal to you their presence just as it does anytime you battle the dark ones."

"The lady told me that I need to learn how to fight these infested ones."

Mellidar walked to the middle of the clearing where the moon shone down upon his face, creating a ghost-like appearance. "Remember that when you battle the Ravens you are not just fighting flesh and blood. You are fighting spirit that has infused flesh, giving it supernatural strength. So in reality, you must be prepared to battle the intelligence and strengths of both worlds. The Ravens are skilled in warfare to the greatest level this world can train a warrior. They began their battle training as children, so they will have that advantage."

Cyle reflected back on his training growing up as a cup bearer to the king. Little good that would do him now.

Mellidar continued, "The Ravens are stronger than any mere man because of the dark spirits that inhabit their bodies. Their strength comes from the dark magic that flows from the inhabiting demons through the host bodies and into their weapons."

Cyle felt fear stirring inside of him. "I have only been training and battling for two years." The young Gap Warrior paused as he twisted the staff in his palms. "Most of my battles have been with the dark spirits or the melded creatures, like the scavengers, that lack any significant intelligence."

"What you say is true," said Mellidar flatly, offering little comfort to his fears. "The Ravens are experts in the art of combat against flesh. Your training has been focused on battling against the rulers and powers of the void. The advantage you have is that the Ravens believe that they control the dark spirits that they have allowed to infest them, but in truth, it is the spirits that hold the balance of control. It is the folly of men to believe that they can control anything, let alone the shadow spirits of the void."

Cyle stared at the ground silently. He softly pounded the staff in his hands into the dirt at his feet. He could feel the muscles in his arms tensing in unison with the knots forming in his stomach. "What now?" he whispered.

"Your training must now focus on the combat strategies of flesh and blood combined with the tactics of the dark magic."

"How much time will I have to prepare?" asked Cyle, sensing he would not like the answer to his question the moment he asked it.

"That I do not know," said Mellidar without emotion, "but what I do know is that we are in the heart of darkness as we speak, and we must make every effort to prepare you for when the time of battle comes."

A flood of thoughts rushed over Cyle, bringing a fresh wave of doubt and confusion. He first thought of Gafney and his skill with the axe. Cyle had watched with admiration as the powerful Gap Warrior had battled in the last moments of the conflict at the walls of Talinor. Warriors came at him from every direction and yet he had prevailed against those of the flesh. Gafney had fought with a mysterious combination of reckless abandonment and years of honed battle skills. Then Cyle remembered Bixby, the other Gap Warrior who had taught him so much about battling demons. His style was so different from Gafney. Bixby was fluid, quick and smooth in his motions. He seemed to sense what was going to happen before it happened. All these thoughts overwhelmed him, because Cyle knew these men had taken years to attain their battle instincts. The idea that he had only days, if that, to prepare for what he would have to face worried him.

"I can see that you are thinking again," interrupted Mellidar. "Fear would have you spend all your time trying to figure it all out. You have always had good instincts and you are a fast learner when you put your mind to it. I am not here to teach you how to figure things out with your head. I am training the instincts given to you by the Ancient of Days. All the unanswered questions will have to wait. It is the way of faith. You will know what you need to know when you need to know it."

Cyle ruffled against Mellidar's comment. He didn't like the waiting part. "I have one more question before we continue," said Cyle solemnly.

"Speak your mind if it will help you to move on."

Cyle looked at Mellidar through intense eyes. "Why the elves? Why do they seek to sacrifice them?"

"The elves are the elected ones. Blessed of the Ancient of Days to carry his unfailing favor." Mellidar paused as if looking to find some elusive thought before continuing. "The warlock Drok Relnik has convinced the priests of this land that great power can be gained by eliminating the bright ones."

"You mean the elves."

"Yes. The elves carry a light greater than any other race. They are a great threat to the dark kingdom."

Mellidar's answer only brought more unrest to his already troubled spirit.

"There is one more thing you must know." Mellidar paused before continuing. "There are two kinds of Ravens, red and black."

"Red and black?" repeated Cyle. "What is the difference?"

"All you need to know is that the red ones are supreme in power compared to the black ones. Do not attempt to fight the red ones on your own. If you do, you will be defeated. You have not had sufficient training yet to overcome their level of skill. Even now, your skill against the black ones is questionable."

"Then why am I here if I am not capable of victory?"

"Without the power and wisdom of the Ancient of Days, none of us are capable. That is what you must learn. We are rarely summoned to achieve the possible. Alone and apart from faith, all is impossible. But you are not alone. Others are with you, and others will join you in this campaign." Mellidar paused and reached out to put his hand gently on Cyle's shoulder. "I know you struggle with fear in times like these. Don't let your fear dictate to you the choices you make. Let it drive you to your faith, not away from it. That part is up to you."

Cyle nodded silently and offered no other response.
"The dawn will soon break, and my flesh form is weakening, so I must leave this world now," said the Guardian as he looked to the horizon. "Go now and sleep. We will continue your training soon."

CHAPTER 19

Gerrid was surprised to hear that Lena was nearby. What would bring an Intercessor to a place like this, so dark and so far from home? The question burned inside, stirring both excitement and fear. Gerrid tried to understand what he was feeling about the news but found a growing uneasiness settling within. He pushed back his fears and chose to embrace the excitement he felt at the thought of Lena's presence here in these Shadowed Realms. Bryann, on the other hand, resisted any delay for any reason. Sera pressed her to join them until she agreed. They were less than two days away from the Hebron Forest, and Sera assured Bryann that they would keep the visit brief.

When they entered Lena's camp, the Intercessor reached out and took both of his hands and greeted Gerrid warmly. "How have you been, my friend? It is good to see that you are well."

Rafe, Lebo and Jef approached. Gerrid recognized Jef and knew immediately that the other two were Tal warriors. Jef offered Gerrid the customary greeting of a Tal warrior to his commander, but Gerrid respectfully turned it away.

"I no longer command warriors of any realm," he said. "Please. a simple greeting will do."

Rafe and Lebo offered their greetings, marveling at the opportunity to meet the former Tal Commander whom they had admired for the legacy he had left behind him in Talinor. The two had joined the military after Gerrid had resigned his position and had grown up hearing stories of his exploits.

"It is a great honor to meet you, sir," said Lebo. "Your service to the military was legendary."

Bryann scowled and backed away to distance herself from the conversation.

"Legends are mostly exaggerated to entice the young to join the battle," said Gerrid. "I am glad those days are behind me."

Gerrid turned his attention back to the Intercessor. "What brings you to this land, Lena? Surely, they must be weighty matters to bring you so far from your beloved homeland."

Sera started humming a tune softly, but Packer shot her a glance to cut her off. He was more interested in the lady's answer than listening to his friend sing another one of her songs.

Lena looked at the elf girl and smiled before responding to Gerrid's question. "I have traveled here at the request of the prophet Graybeard, who is growing weak and will not be in this world much longer. I resisted leaving home, but the old prophet can be very convincing when he puts his mind to it, and I have never been very good at resisting his directives." Lena smiled and glanced back at the prophet's tent. "He seeks to pass on his mantle of prophecy to the one who will carry the Sword of Deliverance, the legendary sword brought to Talinor by our first king, Kem Felnar."

Sera began humming softly once more. Packer grabbed Sera's arm and scowled her to silence once again. She only smiled and lifted her brows.

"I know of the sword, but have never laid eyes on it. We were all taught of its history as part of our military training." Gerrid paused, furrowed his brow and then continued. "And the old prophet believes he will find one worthy of such a calling here in a place like this?" Doubt registered in his tone. "Are you sure he has not lost his senses in his old age? I fear you have traveled all this way in vain."

"Sometimes the brightest lights can be found in the darkest of places," offered Lena with a smile. "Is it not in the dark places where the light is most needed?"

"This place devours the light," responded Gerrid with disdain. "I, for one, am done with it, and I believe that it is done with me."

"Does that mean you are leaving Abbodar?" asked Lena.

"I hope to leave soon and return to Talinor, but first I will journey to the Hebron Forest to seek out friends who find shelter there. There is one among them that I believe will want to leave with me as I return home."

Lena felt a familiar stirring as she listened to Gerrid tell of his plans to re-connect with the believers in the forest. She also felt a deep inexplicable grief at the thought of Gerrid departing from this place. Since she had stepped foot on its shores, she discerned that it was a place desperately in need of the light, and with that discernment came a heavy burden.

"I don't want to sound disrespectful, my lady, but I do not believe that you will find anyone in this land who is worthy of the mantle and the sword unless the one you seek lives among the Remnant that resides in the Hebron Forest." Gerrid paused to ponder who that might be. "Are you sure that the old prophet still has all of his senses?"

"And how many senses does it take to recognize the voice of the Ancient of Days?" said a familiar voice. They all turned to see Graybeard standing near his tent. Gerrid blushed. Rafe and Lebo moved quickly to assist the old prophet to walk toward them. He shuffled slowly, and through labored effort, he covered the ground between them.

When the old prophet reached the group, he stopped briefly to catch his breath. At first he said nothing as he slowly looked around the circle, meeting each of their gazes with his own piercing blue eyes. When he came to Bryann, she shuddered and quickly looked away.

The old prophet's snow-white hair glistened under the rays of the afternoon sun. As if waiting for the perfect moment, the wind stirred to life, blowing through his thin wisps of shoulder length hair. Packer shuffled backward to try to conceal himself. This was his first time meeting a prophet, and he secretly hoped it was his last.

Graybeard shifted his gaze to Gerrid. When their eyes met, a subtle trembling vibrated at his core. Gerrid felt an unsettling urge to cry. He tried to speak but words escaped him.

Time seemed to come to a standstill. Everything faded away except for this moment and the space surrounding him and the prophet.

He heard Graybeard's voice. His statement came through clear and precise. "You are the one."

It was as if his words had crossed the ancient corridors of time to find their resting place, penetrating Gerrid's soul like rain falling on dry ground. Even though a small part of him hungered for what he was hearing, the biggest part of him felt overwhelming fear and wanted to push against it with all his strength.

Unaware of what he was doing, Gerrid began stepping backward in retreat, stumbling and almost falling to the ground. He tried to put into words what he was feeling. Any words will do, he told himself. Then he stammered, "I, I, what?"

"Bring me the sword," demanded Graybeard, holding out his trembling hand as if something would suddenly materialize in his palm.

Lebo ran to the tent and brought back the sheathed blade to place it in the prophet's outstretched hand. Gerrid watched what was happening, and it seemed as if he was observing the whole thing from the outside looking in. Sera began singing in an unfamiliar tongue and she lifted both her tiny arms toward the sky. Bryann looked on from a distance, completely confused by the whole thing, and even Packer was uncharacteristically silent.

"You are the one to inherit my prophetic mantle and the

sword of deliverance once carried by Kem Felnar. You are the one. You are the reason we are here." Graybeard's voice resonated along with the air about him. He began to take off the faded blue cape strapped to his shoulders.

"You must be mistaken, prophet." Gerrid finally found his voice, trying hard to sound respectful, but anger seeped through his words. "If you knew the condition of my heart, you would not speak of such things. My faith hangs by a thread, and my vision of any personal mission was lost long ago in the dungeons of Abbodar. It is hard for me to admit it, but it is true."

Gerrid thought back to the beginning almost three years ago when he first came to Abbodar. He believed his faith was invincible and that nothing could ever shake it. Even when he first went to prison, he was convinced that he would persevere and grow stronger through it all, but somewhere close to the end his faith began to falter. Through all the torture and endless lonely nights, his faith faded and he felt that he lost his heart. Now he just wanted to go home. He longed for the freedom of Talinor and the beauty of his homeland. His heart ached to reunite with his family and friends. He believed that going home would heal him. What troubled him most was that he could not fathom how the God he had sacrificed so much for could have abandoned him and left him to suffer at the hands of a sadistic torturer for almost two years.

Graybeard held the sword loosely in his trembling, gnarled hands, gripping the sheath that encased the blade. A subtle look of deep sadness filled the prophet's eyes as he looked past the former Tal commander, as if gazing into some invisible realm that only he could see. Then his eyes shifted, and he appeared to refocus back on Gerrid before speaking in a commanding tone. "The thread that holds you to your faith is stronger than the suffering that seeks to destroy it."

"I am not worthy for such a calling," countered Gerrid before he knew what he was saying. He noticed the carved eagle perched on the hilt of the sword in Graybeard's hand. A wave of shame came crashing in on him. He hated that he had for the most part given up, that he had not been stronger through his imprisonment. The shame was almost unbearable. He said it again in a soft whisper, "I am not worthy."

"You speak truth," said Graybeard softly as a subtle smile appeared. "You are not worthy. And no matter how hard you try, you cannot make it so. These matters are not decided by the successes or failures of men. They were decided long before time began in the heart of a ruler much wiser than any of us. It is the way of the summoning of destiny. The Ancient of Days has chosen you to carry the mantle and the sword. It is what He desires. Now you must choose whether or not you will bend your will to follow His."

It was impossible at the moment to fully grasp the meaning of it all. To be chosen by the Ancient of Days to follow the prophetic path. The former Tal commander truly had done nothing to deserve such an honor, but he understood what Graybeard had meant when he said there was nothing he could have done. Something in the prophet's words had broken through. His own reasoning would want him to believe that such honorable callings only go to those who achieve them, those who deserve them. But this was about being chosen, not based on his own merit. Instead, it was based on a decision to choose him that he might never fully understand.

Something noble buried deep in Gerrid's spirit longed to embrace the prophet's words, but that spirit carried a weak voice within him. It would mean completely changing the direction he had decided to take. His resolve to go home was as strong as ever, and the emotions that pulled him in that direction were weighted with desperate longings that words could not describe.

The bewildered would-be prophet turned away from Graybeard, muttering under his breath, "I am not ready for this." Shuffling backwards a few steps, and then completely turning, he walked away, beyond the edge of the camp. The others looked on in silence. Even Sera had stopped singing as great sorrow filled her heart, and a tear began to form at the corner of her eye.

"Hand me the sword, old friend," said Lena, extending her hand toward Graybeard. "Keep the Cloak for now. It is yours and yours alone to give."

The prophet seemed to hesitate at first, and then with trembling hands, he placed the magnificent weapon into her palms. She turned toward Gerrid and said to Sera without looking her way, "Don't stop singing." Then she glanced at Jef and said to him, "And you, my friend, don't stop interceding." Jef smiled back at the Intercessor as she turned away with a look of resolve in her eyes.

Lena knew that this was a critical moment for the former Tal commander. She understood the way of the Call of Destiny and the resistance that Gerrid was feeling. She also knew that the next few moments were critical. Left to his own musings, he may give into the fear and miss the path before him. Matters of destiny were never settled without a fierce battle over the heart. As she approached Gerrid, she heard Sera singing. The elf girl had climbed upon a large granite rock and perched herself on its edge with her legs dangling, and she started to sing in a tongue they couldn't understand at first. Then the words changed, and they were able to recognize their meaning. Lena stopped before speaking and allowed the message of the song to float unhindered to the confused young man before her.

> "From a distant land he comes, carried on eagle's wings,
> A warrior who lost the song his heart no longer sings.
> Day will turn to night, and night will turn to day.
> The truth will call him home, and he will find his way.
> A weapon forged within the fires of a time from long ago,
> And when he holds it in his hands, he will surely know.
> Freedom reigns within the light. There is no other way.
> Freedom reigns within the light where he will lead the way."

"Listen," commanded Lena firmly. "Those words are for you. There will never be another moment like this one."

Gerrid looked at the Intercessor. He said nothing.

"This is a land of great dread and ruin cloaked in an overwhelming darkness, and there is no doubt that darkness has left you stumbling for hope." Lena's words softened, but the intensity remained. "Don't be confused about your own confusion. It is the fruit of evil. If you give into its beguiling lure, you will lose what little of the light remains in you." The Intercessor paused to let the words sink in, then she continued. "If I am not mistaken, you took the path of fear once before and walked away from the One Faith. Do you really want to go back there a second time?"

Lena's words pierced Gerrid deeply, but a swirl of dark thoughts swept in to rob him of their clarity. From the rock upon which Sera sat, she could see the shadow fairies swirling about his head, whispering into his mind the lies of the darkness. She wanted to scream at them, but instead she began to sing again.

> "Beware of the shadow fairies
> who come and go.
> At early light and end of day
> come the thoughts they sow.
> Gentle and soothing
> when they appear,
> Enchanting voices disguising fear.
> Hush shadow fairies and go away.
> Don't come back another day."

Lena could not see the shadow fairies, but she knew the meaning of Sera's song. "You must learn to discern the difference between your own thoughts and the thoughts sent to you from the dark magic," Lena cautioned. "If you assume every thought is your own, you will fall swiftly to the dark lies of the shadow fairies."

Sera's song made no sense to Gerrid, and neither did Lena's warning.

"What do you mean?" he asked.

"Listen to your thoughts. Some tell you to embrace the call before you, while some seek to convince you to turn away from it."

Gerrid thought about Lena's words. Some of the voices in his head telling him to walk away may not be his own. He was beginning to separate them out in his mind. Some pulled him toward the light, while others pulled him toward the darkness.

"You are a proven warrior, Gerrid," said Lena. "Your training has prepared you for this time, and I believe that if you give it time, your faith will carry you through to the end."

"But why prison? What possible purpose could it have served?" asked Gerrid painfully.

"That is not for me to answer, but this one thing I do know—you have survived captivity, but now you must overcome it. Then you will know the answer to the questions your heart seeks."

He knew she was right, and even though the voices of the shadow fairies were now screaming at him and taunting him with messages of fear, he reached out his hand, taking hold of the sheath that housed the sword. He gripped it tightly and gazed upon it, taking note of the carved eagle perched upon its pommel. Slowly he moved his right hand to pull it from its resting place. Hesitating briefly he thought, this is going to change everything. When his fingers embraced the hilt to slide it free of the sheath, a wave of nausea swept through him and he almost fell to the ground, but he caught himself and landed on one knee. He felt a strange sensation pressing down upon his shoulders. The nausea left his stomach, and a surge of power coursed through him and over his body. With the blade halfway unsheathed, now sparkling in the sunlight, he could feel its excellent grip and perfectly balanced weight. Gerrid had held many swords in his lifetime, but none as fine as this one. A ringing sound vibrated into the surrounding air as he freed the blade completely from its casing.

SWORD OF DELIVERANCE

A rush of wind blew through the camp, stirring the dust on the ground and wresting leaves from the trees. Gerrid hunched over as tears filled his eyes, and his body began to shake uncontrollably. Suddenly, he remembered his first torture session with the atrolis back in prison and the shame he felt as his own depravity was revealed to him. That moment almost destroyed him. He stood slowly and looked about, and to his surprise, it appeared as if he was back in that place where the demons of the void had attacked him with taunts of shame and condemnation. His defenders stood once again with their backs to him, ready to protect him from the demons that had returned to assault him once more.

How could this be? thought Gerrid. The sword has brought me to the same dark place as the atrolis. Wind swirled around him, and he could see beyond the shadowed backs of his defenders to a wall of demons waiting to attack. Slowly, the defenders departed one at a time until only one of them was left between him and the wall of demons. The lone defender turned to look at him. Gerrid thought he recognized his face but struggled to recall from where. Then it came to him, a burst of memory from the past. It was Bixby, the Gap Warrior from the battle of Talinor.

Bixby smiled at him and said, "We have been here protecting you and watching over you since the day you went to prison. The dark ones can smell destiny all over you, and their lust to destroy you increases with each passing day. They seek to thwart you from fulfilling the path that has been set before you."

Gerrid could see them huddled in shadows, and he could hear their raspy cries through the swirling mist of the void, snarling and whispering to one another their deathly schemes to undo him. *He is ours now, alone and unprotected. We will have him.*

Bixby only smiled as if he knew something that Gerrid and the demons did not know, and then he said, "Use the gift you have been given to make this stand." The Gap Warrior smiled as he turned and walked into the mist, disappearing in a flash of light leaving no one to stand between Gerrid and a wall of demons.

Panic threatened to consume him. The demons could smell the fear in him and slithered cautiously forward from every direction. Shadow fairies buzzed around his head, crying out their hissing taunts, "You are not ready, and you are not worthy. Walk away before it's too late. Protect yourself. It's time to go home where it's safe." Their glowing forms darted about him like bees buzzing a hive.

Then he heard it—Sera's singing.

> "A weapon forged within the fires of
> faith from long ago.
> And when he holds it in his hands
> he will surely know.
> Freedom reigns within the light,
> there is no other way.
> Freedom reigns within the light,
> where he will lead the way."

Gerrid looked down at the legendary Sword of Deliverance forged in the elfin fires of the Crystal Mountains and once wielded by Talinor's founder, Kem Felnar. The former Tal commander raised the sword aloft, and the demons halted their advance. Painful screeches rose from the darkened horde as whimpers of pain swept through their ranks.

Then the words of Bixby the Gap Warrior flashed through his thoughts once again. Use the gift you have been given to make this stand.

Gerrid held the sword in place above his head, and he cried out in defiance the words that came to him from someplace deep within his spirit. "By the power of the One Faith and the Ancient of Days, I renounce the darkness in the name of the light."

The blade began to glow, first near the hilt and then upward toward the tip until it exploded into a burst of brilliant light washing over the dark ones that encircled him. It appeared as though their leathery hides began to sizzle and spark in the wake of its penetrating glow. Then Gerrid could hear their agonizing howls as they turned and fled in all directions.

Silence.

The light slowly dissipated, and Gerrid heard a voice that sounded like that of a woman. "Now you know that the darkness cannot withstand the light."

Gerrid looked in the direction of the voice, and in the faltering mist about him, he thought he saw the faint image of a woman dressed in regal clothing that shimmered at the edges. She was holding a flaming scepter in her right hand, but her form quickly faded before he could take it all in.

Then came one final flash of light that was so bright he had to close his eyes. When he opened them, he was back in the camp.

"It is time," said the old prophet as he shuffled toward Gerrid with the aid of Lebo and Rafe. The rest of the company gathered around except for Bryann who was nowhere to be seen. Sera was smiling and humming quietly as she pulled the giant, Hutch, by one finger to join with them, for she knew what was to happen next.

CHAPTER 20

Overwhelmed by the day's events, Gerrid tried desperately to take it all in. Graybeard stood before him as the others in their company looked on. With trembling hands, the old prophet removed the faded blue cloak that had draped his shoulders for so many years. Gently, he laid it upon the shoulders of his chosen successor. As soon as the old prophet's mantle touched Gerrid, intense warmth washed over his whole body. Gerrid knew so little about prophecy and nothing at all about being a prophet. Accepting the sword was difficult enough, but receiving the prophetic mantle from Graybeard was far beyond the scope of his own understanding.

As if Graybeard was reading his thoughts, he began to speak into Gerrid's confusion. "In time, there will be more answers to the questions you seek. Understanding will come to you when you need it. For now, all you need to know is that you have been chosen to bear both the mantle and the sword. No one has been called to such a path since Kem Felnar reigned as king of Talinor."

Gerrid knew most of the histories of his people, and certainly he could recall those of Kem Felnar, but he was struggling to bring them to mind after what he had just gone through. His thoughts were jumbled together, and he was struggling to separate them from one another. Looking into the eyes of the old prophet, he suddenly found himself drawn into his piercing gaze. He felt as though he was looking at the ancient wisdom and endless pain of the ages. For that moment, time stood still. He knew that he could not look away, for he thought that if he did, he might melt into the ground.

Graybeard removed a small crystal vial filled with oil from his robes. Lena and Jef stood behind Gerrid, placing their hands on his shoulders as the old prophet held the container of oil over the former Tal commander's head. The old prophet paused and looked up at the sky overhead, then he spoke the words that all prophets had spoken for countless years when it was their time to pass on their prophetic mantle to the one who would carry it on to the next generation. "As the Spirit Wind comes through the sound of a whisper and the rolling of thunder, heed carefully the messages that it brings, and speak them just as you have heard them. No more. No less." Graybeard paused to look down at Gerrid, then he continued. "Until that time when you shall pass this prophetic mantle on to the next generation, I pass it on to

SWORD OF DELIVERANCE

you from prophet to prophet, from faith to faith," said Graybeard. Then he poured out the oil from the vial upon his successor's head. As it flowed down his face and onto the cloak that rested upon his shoulders, a vision formed in Gerrid's mind. He saw a brightly lit meadow of tall green grass where the wind blew gently through the surrounding trees. A lone lamb walked from the tree line into the center of the meadow. Soon, others followed until the area was filled with sheep feeding contently upon the green grasses. Suddenly, the skies shifted and churned with the darkness of fluttering wings. Black birds descended in a raging frenzy, blocking out most of the light from above. They attacked the sheep, pecking and clawing at them with their talons until blood appeared on their white, wool coats. The terror stricken herd ran toward the edge of a nearby cliff.

Gerrid watched as the scene unfolded before his mind's eye. Panic threatened to overwhelm him. His breathing grew difficult, and he felt the urge to gasp for air. Most of the sheep were gravely wounded and bleeding by now, and the dark winged creatures kept clawing and tearing at their wool. The picture faded from his sight, but he could still hear the cries of pain coming from the sheep. That finally passed, leaving only deathly silence.

The young prophet became aware of his vice-like grip on the sword. He began to slowly release his grip, feeling the painful strain it left in his fingers. He inhaled deeply and exhaled slowly, as if he could blow away the burden that came with the vision he had just witnessed. He couldn't explain it, but somehow he knew what it meant. The herd of sheep was the Remnant of believers hiding in the Hebron Forest, and he was supposed to deliver them from this place of death and bring them back to Talinor.

It cannot be done, whispered the shadow fairies. No sword has the power to accomplish such a task.

"Have you no ale on this tub?" wailed Gafney, pounding the table and knocking some of the playing chips to the floor. Ginzer and Drew laughed at his losing tirade.

"Ale won't improve your chances any in this wager, my friend." Ginzer laugh again and pounded the table. "You will have little luck finding it on this vessel anyway. Bernard forbids any strong drink on board."

"Don't give him any ale," came Cyle's voice through the window from the deck outside as he walked past.

"You've a run of luck, old man, but I'll have you know that I play this game better with a little ale in me," complained Gafney once more.

The Sea Horse had been sailing upriver a total of five days, and though the going was slow, favorable winds and strong sails held them to a steady course against the opposing current. Gafney's wounds were healing well, and his fever had left him three days ago. Two days earlier, without telling anyone, he had removed the stitches from his own shoulder and thigh. That earned him an earful of stern scolding from Addie.

She had told him, "You are as stubborn as a caged wild boar."

Gafney smiled and said, "Have you ever been wild boar hunting? I'll take you tomorrow. They're most likely rutting this time of year, so it should make for an easy hunt."

Addie laughed. "Maybe in a week or two you can take me."

Choppa found Cyle near the bow looking out over the moonlit waters. With his mouth full of food, Choppa offered his friend a small wafer.

"Do you ever stop eating?"

"You have to try this. It's sweet cake. Bernard made it after dinner, and it's still hot."

Cyle had smelled the aroma of the bread seeping out of the galley windows for the past hour, but he had been too busy thinking about his last conversation with Mellidar to concern himself with food. He declined on Choppa's offer and asked, "Do you ever miss being back home in Talinor?"

"Sometimes I do," said Choppa before he took another big bite out of the sweet cake. Cyle watched as pieces of it crumbled out of his mouth and onto his tunic. "I miss my friends and the festivals, and… well, I guess I just miss home. It would be nice to wake up in the same bed every day."

"I miss all those things, but I really miss my grandmother and my cousin, Micah. I haven't seen my grandmother for over two years, but it feels like forever." Cyle sighed. "I wonder how she is, and if she is being taken care of."

"She makes the best bread," said Choppa. He took another bite out of the sweet cake. "Don't tell Bernard I said that. He's touchy about his cooking." Choppa looked back at the galley to make sure the dwarf didn't hear his comment. "Maybe we can go home after this is over. If we finish here soon enough, we can make it to the Fall Festival."

Cyle smiled at his friend's enthusiasm. "And get some of Grandmother's home baked bread."

"Oh, the kind with the walnuts and raisins and slathered in honey butter." Choppa paused looking back at the Galley. "I wonder if Bernard has any honey butter."

"Thanks, friend," said Cyle, changing the subject.

"For what?" asked Choppa, sensing the change in his friend's mood.

"For coming with me. You didn't have to do that."

"Oh, well, I…" Cyle's friend struggled to respond.

"Who's going to keep an eye on you? That's all." Choppa grinned. Then his mood changed, sensing it should be more serious.

"Well, you're welcome," continued Choppa awkwardly, "but it's been a great two years. Besides, in all this traveling, I have had adventures and seen things that I would never have seen back in Talinor."

"We have seen a lot, haven't we?" agreed Cyle.

"Do you know what we are here for?" asked Choppa, changing the subject.

"Not really. All I know is that Mellidar is training me to fight warriors that are infested with the power of the dark beings."

Choppa's eyes widened, and he felt a shiver shoot up his

spine. "Infested? How does such a thing like that happen?"

"I don't really know, but I'm sure we will be finding out soon enough. I don't mind saying it's got me on edge. I'm just glad Gafney's here for this one, and I'm praying others are on the way," said Cyle, looking around as if they would show up at any moment.

They could hear the sound of Gafney and the two dwarves laughing from down below. The sound of their voices brought both of them a feeling of comfort, reminding them that they would be a part of this journey. Cyle had been on several missions in the last two years, and it was always at this point that he became anxious, the time when the details of the mission were still unclear to the moment when everything started making sense. He called it the middle time, the time that tested his nerves and rattled his sense of peace. Cyle knew he would never get used to it, and found that in his restlessness, it was almost impossible to sit still for any amount of time except at early evening just after sunset. The world seemed to slow down just long enough to enjoy the calm. It was during this time late in the day that Cyle felt the most at peace.

Gafney appeared from the cabin below deck to join Cyle and Choppa near the bow. The limp from his wound was barely perceptible, but it was obvious he was making an effort to conceal it. Cyle recalled his time with the powerful Gap Warrior from two years ago during the battle at Talinor. Gafney had always minimized his wounds and seemed almost reckless with his own safety. Even though he demanded a lot from others in battle, Cyle knew from experience that Gafney was always watching out for him. While the two had never acknowledged it, Cyle carried a deep sense of gratitude for his loyalty.

The three of them shared about their adventures of the past two years. Though they had not seen one another once during that time, there was a common thread that ran through the stories of the two Gap Warriors. Both Gafney and Cyle had battled dark spirits, and in every encounter, they were fighting to hold off a breach in the void and prevent the dark ones from gaining a foothold somewhere in the world. Some of those battles involved protecting individuals, while others involved cities and sometimes kingdoms.

During the conversation Gafney stated several times, "Things are changing in the world." Finally, he said, "I hate to admit it, but it seems to me that the world is becoming a darker place. It's as if the dark magic is getting stronger while the One Faith grows weaker. In my travels I have met so few who are willing to stand against the darkness."

"Sometimes it does seem as though we are the only ones who care about the battle between the light and the dark," said Cyle thoughtfully.

Gafney leaned forward on his muscular arms and began to stroke his black beard. Cyle noticed it was beginning to show flecks of gray. "Alone or not, I for one am going to fight the dark ones," Gafney responded.

"Are you happy?" asked Choppa awkwardly.

"Happiness? I don't think about it much, but I know one thing. I left the battle once, and I was almost destroyed by my own bitterness because life didn't happen the way I thought it should. I couldn't get past the pain. It still haunts me at times." Gafney looked up at the star littered sky as if he would find the answer somewhere up there. "I think I rediscovered something better than happiness when I came back to the One Faith. I found a reason to live—a purpose, if you will. As crazy as it sounds, I feel the most alive when I'm killing demons. I guess I had to kill my own demons first before I could truly grasp that."

"Your words remind me of the loneliness we must endure to do what we do," said Cyle, "away from friends and family."

"Not all friends," added Choppa.

"Yes, my friend. I don't know that I could do this without you at my side."

Choppa smiled contently and took a last bite of sweet cake.

"It is always a joy when the path brings us together with old friends we have battled with in the past," said Gafney with a smile.

"And battling with friends always brings an advantage, does it not?" asked Choppa.

"It does," said Gafney. "We will need all the advantage we can muster. This place carries a power like none I have ever known. I bear the scars to prove it."

"The scavs in the village," said Cyle.

"Exactly," said Gafney, rubbing his wounded shoulder. "They were stronger, quicker, if you know what I mean. The first beast I fought was unknown to me, though it seemed to be a meld of different creatures I have seen before, mostly gargenmall. What concerns me is that it was able to wield a weapon, although crudely. It clearly was a creation of the dark magic. I felt its power in my blade."

Cyle stood up and gripped his staff, twisting it nervously in his hands as he often did when he was feeling anxious. "I felt it, too, when I fought the scavs," mused Cyle, recalling the speed and power of the creatures he fought had at Pallarim.

"There's always something, isn't there?" added Gafney.

Cyle nodded and then asked, "Where will we find Intercessors in such a land as this? Drew tells me that the only Intercessors he knows of are the Maggrid Priests who worship at the temple daily. They sacrifice to the dark magic and use it to create the kind of monsters we battled back in Pallarim."

"You worry too much, lad. It will work out. It always does," assured Gafney, "I know the importance of Intercessors in defending the breach, but sometimes we have no choice but to fight without their covering." Gafney paused to glance over at Choppa. "Besides, we have Choppa to watch out for us."

Cyle laughed and noticed that his halfling friend was staring toward the shore. "What is it?" whispered Cyle.

"Something moves at the shoreline," said Choppa, squinting his eyes in that direction.

Cyle's heart jumped as he turned to survey the bushes and

trees that covered the riverbank. "I don't see anything. Are you sure?" He felt a fresh wave of energy surging through him.

"Choppa's right," said Gafney calmly. "Something's been out there watching us since I came up on deck."

"Why didn't you say something?" asked Choppa nervously.

"I wanted to make sure before I mentioned it. You two are already on edge as it is, and I didn't want to stir you up if it wasn't necessary. Get some rest. I'll take first watch. Tomorrow we take to land and head toward Aboddar."

Abbodar. Why Abbodar?" asked Cyle and Choppa in unison.

Gafney smiled and leaned back against the railing of the Sea Horse. "That's where the darkness is the greatest."

CHAPTER 21

Graybeard had requested that he be buried at the foot of a majestic oak, and that was where they laid him to rest. They stood on the crest of a hill beneath a starlit sky. A gentle breeze caressed the leaves of the ancient tree, and with tears in her eyes, Lena spoke of the old prophet's service to the Ancient of Days. She told stories of his life and the legacy he would leave. Sera sang a song, and the others stood by in silence. Though he barely knew the prophet, Gerrid felt an inexplicable depth of grief and loss. He didn't think it possible, but he felt even more alone than before with the prophet's passing, and he wondered who would teach him.

The night before he died, the prophet summoned Lena to his side. Through his faltering voice, he exhorted the Intercessor regarding Gerrid and the mission before them. "He still walks with a deeply burdened spirit that is weighted with doubt and confusion. As a warrior in Talinor, he was confident in his identity, and he longs to go back home because he thinks he can recapture his identity from his former glory. What he does not understand is that the path of destiny will never lead us back to the past. It is ever moving forward to a greater glory. It is there that he will find what he seeks."

"He knows of battle and commanding warriors, but he has much to learn about the prophetic, and you will teach him. Now you must rest, old friend," urged Lena gently. "There will be time tomorrow after a good night's sleep to finish our talk."

"I will not be here tomorrow," said the prophet as a subtle smile lifted his countenance. "A new era begins," he said, coughing. "And you, Lena, must help to usher it in. He will need your counsel and your prayers."

Lena felt an ache in her heart. She took the prophet's hand in hers while fighting back the tears. She remembered the many arguments they had shared over the years. Especially when he had told her that her grandson, Cyle, was a Gap Warrior. She had always held deep respect for him, but that had never prevented her from sharing her opinions. Now she only felt the emptiness he would leave behind as he left this world. "And he shall have it," Lena had said softly, assuring Graybeard of her support for Gerrid. She could feel the warmth of his palm against her own two hands as she bowed her head to pray. "Welcome this Warrior home," whispered the Intercessor. "He has fought the good fight of faith, and he has stayed the course to finish strong. May he stand proudly with the ancient prophets that await his arrival at the gates of Logloria."

The warmth of his palms faded as Graybeard breathed his last breath for this world. Tears flowed as Lena kissed his forehead. She pondered the words the prophet had spoken to her. "With the passing of one era, there begins a new one," he had said. Even though she did not completely understand what was coming in the new era, she knew it was beginning.

That was over a day ago, and since then, the band of eleven had traveled throughout the day only stopping at night to sleep.

Sera had spent most of that time sitting upon the shoulders of the stone giant where she serenaded the group with numerous songs. Many of them spoke of the histories of the elves and their heroes, and others were songs that exalted the Ancient of Days. Some of the songs, to Gerrid's surprise, recounted the story of the last battle of Talinor and how the Gap Warriors had defeated the shadow wraiths.

Gerrid grew increasingly anxious as Hebron Forest drew nearer. With less than a day's journey before them, he found his own thoughts gathering a mounting resistance against the mission he had been given by Graybeard. Would they listen to him after being gone all this time? He tried to play over in his mind the words he would say to the remaining Remnant of believers when it was time to tell them that he had come to take them to Talinor. Nothing seemed to fit right in his imaginings no matter how many ways he pictured it. Convincing them was not the only challenge. How would he take some two hundred people—maybe more, he wasn't sure—on a journey that required crossing the Sea of Baddaris? He had no means of transportation to accomplish such a feat. Besides that, he knew there would be attempts to stop him by the ruling powers of this world and the void.

Bryann had kept her distance from Gerrid since Graybeard's death. He had tried to talk to her, but she seemed sullen and distant. Something in him still wanted to crack that hard shell that she hid behind, but so far he had not been successful. Most of their conversations ended in arguments that confused Gerrid because to him, they were seemingly insignificant. He often watched her from a distance, admiring her natural beauty. Every small movement she made held a kind of grace that he rarely saw in a woman. Her eyes drew him in and reminded him of a fawn, and on those rare occasions when she smiled, he caught himself smiling with her. It wasn't until earlier today on the trail that he caught himself imagining what it would be like to hold her in his arms. Gerrid felt a stirring of passion as the picture of such an embrace paused before his mind. He wanted to comfort her and chase away the demons that haunted her.

"Everything happens for a reason." Gerrid started at the sudden comment by Bryann. She was walking next to him, and he was so deep in thought that her presence had gone unnoticed until now. "Is it not true?" she asked, looking up at him with those doe-shaped eyes.

Gerrid hesitated, momentarily lost in her gaze, then breath filled his lungs and words found their shape. "I, I guess so. I mean, that's what some have said." And that was all he could think to say.

Bryann was smiling now, and it only confused the young prophet, for he never quite knew what to expect from her. He felt a confusing urge to pull back, but her warmth drew him to her.

"You are a hard one to read, but then I think that's how you like it," said Gerrid awkwardly.

Bryann smiled, "Thank you."

"For what?"

"For saving me back there. I didn't want you to think I was ungrateful."

"You are welcome." Gerrid stumbled over a rock in the trail, but Bryann caught him by the arm before he fell. She giggled under her breath, and he thought she might be toying with him.

"There, now you owe me."

"I owe you for what?" asked Gerrid.

"You saved me once, and I saved you twice. Just now from falling and from the street hounds back in Abbodar."

"Thank you so much for putting yourself out there on my behalf," said Gerrid. "It's good to know you are watching out for me."

"Well, don't get too excited. I'm really not that good at taking care of others. As you can tell by what happened back in Karn, I'm not very good at letting others take care of me."

"And why is that so hard for you?"

"I don't like owing anyone. It's just simpler that way," said

SWORD OF DELIVERANCE

Bryann softly.

"And when did caring for someone become about owing and paying a debt?"

Bryann pursed her lips and appeared to measure her words before responding, "It is all I have known of life, and…" She started to say "love" and then changed the word to "friendship."

"And what have you known?" asked Gerrid hesitantly.

"It is a dark subject, and I don't know that I want to cloud this moment with dark tales of my life."

"Once again you back away when the topic turns to you or your life."

"I just wanted to thank you for risking your life for me," Bryann changed the subject again. "I know you were weak from prison, and it was a risk to take on those men."

Gerrid stopped in midstride and turned to face her. "You are absolutely right. I saved you at great risk to myself, and why do you think I did that?" Gerrid's voice hinted at anger.

"I, I don't, I…"

"Well I can assure you it wasn't so you would have to owe me. The thought never crossed my mind."

"Then why? Why would you risk your life for a stranger you barely knew?"

"I'm a Warrior. I have risked my life for countless people that I will never know. And I have done it so many times, I have lost track of it."

"No Warrior I have ever known fights for the people," countered Bryann sternly. "They fight for money, land and the thrill of shedding blood."

"Then you have never known a true Warrior. You have only known killers and murderers," said the young prophet passionately.

"Well I don't believe it," countered Bryann, matching his intensity. "I don't believe such men or women exist."

"Then I am a liar, and all I have said is a lie. I pity you that you have never known the kind of men and women that I speak

163

of, but I can assure you they do exist."

For the first time Bryann was speechless as the two of them stared intently at one another. Then Gerrid broke the silence. "So tell me then, why did you rescue me, a complete stranger, if you owed me nothing?"

Liquid pools formed in her eyes as she struggled to find an answer to his question. A look of fear covered her face. Gerrid wanted to withdraw the question because he felt that somehow he was hurting her, and he did not want to do that. But he resisted backing off and held his ground waiting for her to respond.

"I don't know why." Bryann looked down at the ground, shaking her head. "It was the first time I had ever done anything like that."

"Well I'm glad you did. If you hadn't, I would not have met you," said Gerrid as he reached out to take her arm to comfort her.

Bryann pulled back abruptly at his touch, yelling, "You see what I mean? Now you expect something from me."

Gerrid withdrew his hand. "I merely meant to comfort. Nothing more."

"I do not seek your comfort, and I don't want your pity."

"Is comfort so unfamiliar to you that you would reject it even when it comes from a sincere heart?"

"And how would I know that it was sincere?"

"I saved your life," answered Gerrid intensely. "Does it count for nothing?" He turned and started to walk away, then he stopped suddenly and looked back at her. "Our destination is upon us, and you will have fulfilled your debt to your aunt. After that, I'm sure you will be on your way, and then you will no longer have to struggle with the unfamiliar feelings that come with genuine caring any longer."

Bryann's heart sank into her stomach as Gerrid turned away. Filled with confusion, she fought to hold back the tears. What was happening to her? The shell she had worked so hard to build around her heart was being taken apart piece by piece by this man. He was right. Once they arrived at Hebron, she would be on her way. No longer would she have to deal with these confusing feelings. She tried to comfort herself with the thought. Somehow it did not feel like comfort.

The surrounding trees vaulted skyward, forming a canopy of green that filtered the light into beams that sprayed all about them to the forest floor. Lena and her company of travelers moved slowly as they worked to negotiate the rocks and fallen trees on the forest floor.

Somewhere within this place of grandeur and matchless beauty, the Remnant had made their home. Finding them could prove difficult. On the other hand, they could be just around the next bend. The smell of Redwood filled their senses. Squirrels flitted about the branches, looking for food to bring back to their nests. There was no trail to follow and no trail markers to lead them, but somehow Lena felt at peace and sensed that they were headed in the right direction.

At times the undergrowth grew so thick that they could not pass. If it had not been for the powerful stone giant's ability to smash through the gnarled branches that blocked the way, their progress would have been much slower. He cleared openings wide enough for the horses to pass through, but the cart that used to carry Graybeard had to be abandoned.

Packer heard it first. The singing was very soft in the beginning. Then the sound of voices grew louder until they filled the air around them. The small band of travelers stood mesmerized in the middle of the forest surrounded by giant Redwoods. They heard singing from every direction as a chorus of voices encircled them, lifting their spirits. Lena raised her hands to the sky and began to pray softly. The singing continued to grow louder, surrounding them in a chorus of perfect harmony.

They closed their eyes as their spirits were carried away to a place where only hearts can soar. Bryann fell to the ground curled up in a fetal position where she began to weep.

The words to the enchanting song were indiscernible

in the beginning. But soon they gathered form, so that all who heard them could comprehend their meaning.

> From the dawn of time the world has known,
> Birth to life and life to death.
> Creation sings its song,
> And out of darkness, into light.

Lena and Sera joined in with the singing, caught up in the moment and unaware of the passing of time until it gently faded back into the forest, replaced by the chirping of birds and the chatter of squirrels. A soft breeze washed over their faces as they opened their eyes.

Gerrid returned to his senses, and when he opened his eyes, he noticed Sera pointing from her perch atop of the stone giant's massive shoulders, her tiny finger outstretched in the direction of two enormous Redwoods split by a small path between them.

"There—It comes from there," whispered Sera.

Lena and Gerrid helped Bryann to her feet, and without speaking, they all walked toward the edge of the glade until they reached the path that led between the two trees. After passing between them, the forest opened wide into a meadow. It was late afternoon, and the golden rays of the sun sprayed across the tall grass, sending shimmering light over a sea of green. On the far end of the meadow, a fire flickered beyond the tree line. Four figures with weapons walked into the meadow in their direction. Jef and the four Tal warriors pulled their swords.

As the strangers approached, they showed no obvious signs of aggression, but Jef cautioned Lena, "Stand behind me." Then he stepped in front of her with his sword in his hand.

Three men and one woman who were dressed in dark green clothing that blended perfectly with the surrounding forest approached. They came to a complete halt about twenty feet away. Both parties studied one another silently in the afternoon light. The one with shoulder-length, bushy red hair stepped forward with sword in hand and said, "What brings you to these woods?"

It was Gerrid who replied first. "We seek the people known as the Dissenters, also called followers of the One Faith."

"For what purpose do you seek them?" asked the red headed man.

Gerrid moved closer to the man who was speaking to get a better look, but the man pulled slightly back into a defensive stance with his sword held before him.

"Would you attack a man who holds no weapon at the ready?" pressed Gerrid, using a soft tone.

"Perhaps your weapons are of the dark kind," said the leader of the four.

"If that were true," countered Gerrid, "then your sword would be powerless against such magic."

The red-headed man lowered his sword slowly to his side. His countenance shifted, and he suddenly realized to whom he was speaking and said in a whisper, "Gerrid, is that you, or has your ghost come back to haunt me?"

"Dallien," said Gerrid affectionately as he moved to embrace his friend. The two men patted each other's backs and laughed aloud as they pulled apart to study one another. "It is good to see you well after all this time, my friend."

"You are free," exclaimed Dallien. "Thank God. He has brought you back to us. I never thought I would live to see the day. How is it you walk among the living?"

"They needed room for more prisoners, so I, along with many others, was released."

In the dim light, Gerrid saw movement behind his friend, as shapes materialized from the tree line. Quietly they formed a semicircle behind Dallien.

"Behold," said Dallien so that all could hear his words, "our leader has come home."

CHAPTER 22

Almost two days had passed since Cyle and the others had left the Sea Horse. They left it anchored on the shore near the mouth of the river where it ran into Lake Terran. Ginzer and Bernard both insisted on going with the two Gap Warriors in spite of Gafney's attempt to discourage the two dwarves from joining their quest.

Ginzer had argued, "Who will stand with you to fight the steel that you are bound to battle?"

Bernard had insisted that they would need someone to cook for them as well. "Gafney's cooking will kill you both before you reach Abbodar," he laughed.

Drew and Addie would not separate after all they had been through, and it was clear that the hunter's knowledge of these lands was an asset to their quest.

Choppa was delighted that he would not have to eat any of Cyle or Gafney's cooking. He had grown fond of Bernard's cooking as well as the stories the two old dwarves told of past glories from their long-lived lives. So, under Drew's guidance, the small fellowship of seven set out toward the city of Abbodar. Upon their arrival in Abbodar, Drew and Addie would part ways with their new friends and return to the mountains to make their home with the Buntoc.

There were many small villages scattered throughout the region, and by midmorning on the second day since they had left the boat, they entered one of them to restock their supplies. Bernard wasted no time and headed for the farmer's market to sample the fresh produce. There was a tavern at the center of town that Gafney intended to visit. Cyle tried to dissuade him from following that course. They needed to keep their visit as short as possible, and he knew that might be difficult for his friend once he sat down at the bar. Ginzer promised Cyle he would keep an eye on him, assuring him that their visit to the bar would be brief.

The market was filled with travelers passing through who had stopped to buy and trade supplies for their journey to the festival in the city. The streets buzzed with the sounds of vendors and buyers haggling for their best price. Some yelled to intimidate while others spoke with kindness, hoping to win the sale.

Business was good this time of year for the smaller villages. There was money to be made as travelers went to the games and when they returned. Some would go to watch. Others went to sell their wares in the streets where the population of Abbodar would swell to almost twice it's size for the month-long celebration. Still others went there to fight, hoping to find fame and fortune or simply to win enough coins to feed their families for a year. Many challengers had trained their whole life preparing to battle in the games, and yet the odds were heavily against them. It was rare that outlanders had lasted long enough in the competitions to win a prize, and no outsiders had ever defeated a Red Raven in the arena.

Bernard, Choppa and Addie had gone to the market to buy food supplies while Ginzer and Gafney headed to the Tavern to wet their tongues and eat a hot meal. Cyle and Drew watched from the shade of an oak tree as a group gathered to watch two men practice sword skills.

"They are fools," said Drew. "They will all die at the end of their journey."

"Like these men, I once believed there was glory in battle until I saw the pain and destruction that it brought to innocent lives very much like what you saw in your own village," said Cyle ruefully. "Only I have seen it on a greater scale. I fear I will see it again."

"I will never forget that day." Drew sounded angry. "I don't know what to do about it. I feel as though I should do something to make it right."

"Live well then," said Cyle softly. "Love your girl and seek peace whenever you can. A wise man once told me, when you must fight, fight well. It is rare that a man can pass through this life and escape the need to fight for something."

"And why do you fight?" asked Drew.

"The world needs those who will stand against the evil that threatens to overcome it. I almost turned away from it all once. I could not live with myself running away from the battle, so now I run to it. To do anything less would be to deny my faith and what it calls me to be."

"Again, you speak of your faith. How can you trust in anything that would allow a world like this to exist? So much suffering and so much injustice."

"I don't have all the answers, but what I do know is that there is evil in the world, and that evil seeks to undo all that is good. The One Faith stands against all that is evil, and if that faith was to die, then the world we know would have no one to dispel the darkness that the evil brings."

"I don't know that I understand," said Drew.

"Think of what happened at your home village. Most died, some may have survived like you. Nonetheless, evil tried to destroy the good in that place. If we had not been there to battle against that evil, none would have survived. Darkness would have had a complete victory. Goodwill and good intentions cannot overcome that kind of evil. Defiance in the name of the Ancient of Days and standing strong against all that would destroy the light is what saved you in Pallarim. Never forget that. You are alive today because the light stood up against the darkness on your behalf. Would that more had been spared. Thankfully some were. That is better than none."

Drew carefully considered the words of his new friend. He had never looked at it from that perspective before. "I can never thank you enough for what you did for Addie and me. You risked your lives for us. I don't mean to sound ungrateful," said Drew.

"You are welcome, but if you want to thank someone, thank the one who sent me."

"And who is that?"

"He is known by many names. We, the people of the One

Faith, call him the Ancient of Days."

"I will consider your words carefully. I owe you that much," said Drew.

"I could ask for no more. Now, let us go to the tavern. I fear Gafney may have been there for a time beyond his own good, and I'm not sure Ginzer will succeed in pulling him away."

When Cyle and Drew entered the tavern, they found Gafney and Ginzer standing in the middle of the room facing three men, ready to exchange blows. The tavern patrons surrounded them, yelling for them to fight.

Cyle sighed deeply and mumbled under his breath, "Here we go again." Stepping toward the men, he shouted above their raised voices, "Gentlemen, please consider what is about to happen."

The men facing Gafney and Ginzer looked in Cyle's direction. The tall one with the hawk face and jet black hair hanging to his shoulders spoke first. "And who are you?"

"I am here to warn you of the calamity you are about to suffer," said the young Gap Warrior with a hint of sarcasm touching the edge of his voice. It was clear his friend had already had too much to drink.

"Calamity, you say," said the man defiantly. "I believe your friend is the one who is about to suffer calamity." Just then, at least four more men stood up behind the other three men, and others in the back of the tavern began to move forward. Cyle groaned under his breath. This could prove to be more difficult than I imagined, thought Cyle.

"Please, gentlemen," said Gafney, holding his hand above his head. "Let's not bring undo destruction to this fine establishment. Come, let's step outside where the air is fresh and tables and chairs will have a better chance of surviving."

"Not good," said Cyle under his breath. "At least in here, others in the streets cannot run to fight against us."

Drew glanced nervously about as he and Cyle were pushed out of the tavern along with the other patrons of the bar.

They poured out into the street where a crowd of spectators was already forming. Among them were Bernard, Choppa and Addie.

"What should we do?" asked Drew as he watched Ginzer and Gafney prepare to fistfight the seven men standing ready to face them.

"Watch."

"Watch?" asked Drew, confused by Cyle's response.

"They'll either work something out or take a beating. Either way, they're going to need someone to carry them out of here."

The hawk-faced man lunged at Gafney, punching him hard in the jaw while Ginzer steadied himself ready for the others to advance. Gafney shook his head from side to side and spit a wad of blood on the ground. Then he looked up at Hawk Face who delivered the punch, smiled and said, "Are you sure you don't want to reconsider calling this whole thing off? I'll let you and your men walk away and no one will get hurt."

The man looked around at his men and snickered under his breath before saying, "I'm afraid it's too late for that. The only one here who's going to get hurt is you and your friends." Then he swung again towards Gafney's gut, but this time the Gap Warrior caught the striking fist in the palm of his hand and held it firmly as the man struggled to pull free from the vice-like grip. The attacker jerked backwards twice but was unable to free his fist. A panicked look crossed his face. He attempted to summon his friends to his aid, waving them forward with his free hand. They did not move. Something had caught their attention at the edge of the crowd where the onlookers had begun moving backwards.

Three riders on horseback could be seen at the far end of the street.

"Ravens," whispered one mother as she gathered up her kids and headed in the opposite direction.

Shrager, the Raven who led the other two, wrestled against the voice inside his head that seemed to have turned against him in the past few days.

You fool! Can you not do this one simple thing? The voice taunted from the dark edges of his mind. *Find the woman and kill her before it's too late.*

The Raven looked back at the grim faces of the other two that followed closely on horseback. They, too, were Ravens, and they were depending on him to lead them to the Intercessor, but Shrager was struggling with his gift. He was a tracker and one of the best, but something was blocking his abilities. The voice within was not happy with the lack progress.

Again, the voice taunted. *You are pathetic. Can you do nothing right?*

He wanted to defend against the spirit's accusations, but he knew it would do no good. There was no escaping the presence inside that harassed him almost daily. The irony of it all was that the very voice that shamed him was the same voice that gave him his tracking gift and other powers to help him in battle. He had invited the presence into his soul to be a part of him. At the time, the spirit seemed so kind and inviting, but now that it had control over him, it never seemed to be pleased with his efforts.

The Ravens had hunted for several days tying to find the old woman. Several times Shrager had found the trail, or at least he thought he had. His senses had told him he was on the right track, but then, without explanation, the trail was gone. Then he would go numb and fly into a rage. Two days earlier he had lost control of his rage and had slain three innocent villagers during questioning just to appease the dark presence inside of him. The villagers knew nothing, but that didn't matter to him. He killed them because the spirit dwelling within him found great delight in the killing of innocents.

Something stirred intensely within Shrager's spirit earlier this day that led him to take the course he now followed. He prayed to the gods of Terashom that this leading would not fail him. Ahead he saw a small village, and instantly he pictured in his mind torturing another victim to death, but he knew he would not do that this time. The Raven was confident. Something was here because he could sense a foreign power emanating from that direction. His abilities were working again, and the lust to kill was rising in him, crying out to be unleashed. He could feel it growing in the two Ravens that rode with him. Even the taunting voice inside his head had grown quiet as if it knew what was to happen next.

As their horses approached the edge of the village, he could see that a crowd had gathered in front of the local tavern. The Ravens were quickly noticed, and the crowd thinned as their horses came closer while those remaining tried to shuffle to the back of the crowd. Shrager relished the fear he saw in the eyes of these commoners when they entered their towns. Their power was known and feared by all, and since they were rarely seen in these parts of the realm, they had an even greater mystique to the people in these outlying areas. Stories were told at night around the hearth of the dreaded Ravens and how they could steal the spirit from a person with one glance. Lately, stories had been swirling among the villages that the Ravens were on the move, and those tales had left many a child lying awake at night, terrified with the thought that one might come to their village and steal their spirit away to the void.

The crowd parted, and Shrager could see a group of men standing at the center. One had a powerful build with an axe strapped to his back, probably one of many traveling to the city to compete in the arena games.

At the approach of the three Black Ravens, Cyle could feel a wave of fear sweep through those gathered, and he saw the hawk-faced man step backwards, trying to blend into the surrounding crowd.

The three dark riders sat silently high atop their mounts, staring out over the villagers. They were clothed in the traditional black leather of the Black Raven warriors with bucklers at the shoulders and a thick breastplate engraved with the image of a silver raven. Each of them had red stars tattooed near their left temple, but the one in the lead had more than the others—seven stars.

Gafney turned to walk away from the three riders and stopped midstride when Shrager called out to him, "You are the one."

Gafney turned to face them and answered, making his best effort to sound respectful. "No, I am not the one. I am merely one of many."

The voice in the Raven's head was screaming. Kill him! He is a threat. He cannot be allowed to live.

Shrager said, "You are the one who killed the beast and some of the emperor's soldiers."

"I only did what the law allows, and as the captain requested," said Gafney in an even tone.

Cyle's heart pounded inside his chest. He held out his hand for Drew to stay back. Addie and Choppa had already joined him. Cyle felt the staff in his hands vibrating in unison with the fearful pounding of his heart as he stepped out from the crowd to stand next to his friend.

"I thought we were going to avoid this kind of attention," hissed Cyle.

"I would apologize, kid, but I think it's a little late for that now," said Gafney, looking straight ahead. "Remember, these ones are infested, so be careful."

"Careful? What does that mean?"

"Don't get killed. I'm going to need you later."

"I'll keep an eye on him," said the one-eyed dwarf.

"So will I," added Gafney.

Bernard nudged his way to the edge of the gathering, and when he saw what was happening, he dropped the two sacks of fruits and vegetables and moved to join his comrades with axes in hand.

"I see you have friends," said the Raven calmly.

"It is good for a man to have friends, especially in perilous times such as these," said Gafney.

"They carry the power of Terashom," cautioned Drew

from where he stood.

"Stay back," warned Gafney, "and you two as well." He nodded toward Ginzer and Bernard.

Bernard pushed back, "We are not in the habit of backing down from a fight, my friend. We are here to fight against the steel."

"There is more than metal at play here, my friend. Now step back and protect the others if need be. Let us handle this."

"As you wish, Gap Warrior, but we will not stand idle if your life is threatened."

"Fair enough," agreed Gafney.

Bernard and Ginzer slowly moved backward into the crowd.

The sweat gathered beneath Cyle's palms. He unconsciously wiped them on his leggings. As soon as the three men rode into the circle of onlookers, his staff began vibrating. These were the ones Mellidar had been training him to face, warriors infested with the power of demons. Fear vibrated through his chest as he gazed down at his arms. He felt small in comparison to these muscular warriors dressed in black sitting atop their mounts.

"We're just going to leave now," said Gafney as he slowly turned, motioning Cyle to do the same. Behind him he could hear the three riders dismounting as their boots hit the ground. "Or not," he whispered under his breath. Before he turned around to face them, Gafney reached back to pull Demon Slayer from its holder on his back. The axe sparked to life at his touch.

Shrager felt the presence of an alien spirit the moment he caught sight of the light dancing beneath the axe man's grip. An unusual wave of fear coursed through Shrager.

The voice in his head started screaming. Now! Kill him now, you fool. Shrager obeyed the voice and attacked, sending his sword sweeping forth in a violent arc. Gafney swayed backward to avoid its deadly edge. The striking blade flashed past his face in a blur, coming close enough for the Gap Warrior to feel the heat carried within it.

Shrager advanced with three more rapid thrusts aimed at Gafney's head, but the Gap Warrior blocked each one with the edge of Demon Slayer. Sparks sprayed outward. The other two Ravens advanced quickly. Cyle responded to their offensive with a maneuver of his own by twirling his staff above his head, then he shifted and blocked a strike meant for his friend. The power of the Raven's strike almost jolted the young Gap Warrior from his feet, but he held his footing, stunned by the power within the blade of his attacker.

Gafney dipped backward to avoid Shrager's second deadly cut. Then he shifted direction and lunged forward at the first opening, driving the end of his axe toward Shrager's head. The Black Raven faded, and the blow lightly grazed his brow. Shrager smiled and countered with a jab to the big Gap Warrior's jaw with the hilt of his own sword. Gafney staggered backwards, slightly dazed. The demon inside Shrager screamed with glee. Cyle sensed that his friend was in trouble. Something alerted him in his spirit. He knew it was the urging of the Spirit Wind. He pulled away from his own attacker long enough to swipe his staff at the back of Shrager's calf, sending him stumbling to the ground. By then the third Raven was upon Gafney, swinging his blade at his midsection, but Gafney stepped to the left and spun in a complete circle to where he could slash with his axe into the back of his attacker. Sparks erupted upon impact, and the Raven screamed as he buckled to his knees. Gafney dislodged Demon Slayer from the man's back, kicked him and watched him topple to the ground.

Shrager had recovered quickly and attacked Gafney a second time. Cyle struggled with the other Raven who deflected most of the blows he sent his way, and the ones that were connecting seemed to lack the force needed to bring the Raven down. Where Cyle lacked in power he made up for in speed and quickness. He hoped that he could eventually wear him down by sending enough strikes. He was stunned at the jolting power delivered with each hit of the Raven's blade as it made contact with his staff.

Suddenly things shifted, and his attacker found an opening, slamming Cyle with a thundering kick to his midsection that sent him backward in a cloud of dust. Nausea threatened him, and he gulped to bring the air back to his lungs. Seizing his moment, the Raven was upon him, his sword ready to bring the greeting of death. Cyle's eyes widened. To his left Gafney was battling and unaware of his plight. Then suddenly the wind swirled, and two arrows parted the air, finding their mark in the warrior's chest plate. The first one rang out as it hit steel, and the second did the same. Cyle recognized the bolts. The shorter one came from Choppa's crossbow and the longer one from Drew's bow. The faltering warrior winced and staggered backward. Then he regained his footing, reached up and cut the arrows from his chest plate with his sword. It was enough to give Cyle a chance to recover. *I can't win.* The reality came crashing in on him. *But I won't run.* He steadied himself as he set his footing to face the Raven once again, but before he could respond, Gafney flew airborne into the side of the dark warrior, kicking him in the ribs. In one jolting motion, he drove Demon Slayer into the big man's chest, sending another spray of sparks into the air as the dark warrior toppled to the ground, lifeless.

All three of the Black Ravens lay dead on the ground. Cheers erupted from the onlookers. The hawk-faced man who had threatened Gafney earlier stepped forward and extended his hand to the Gap Warrior. "Forgive me. I misjudged you."

"I doubt it, but I accept your sentiments anyway," countered Gafney, laboring to regain his breath and suddenly realizing that he had lost some strength due to his injuries.

"No one fights the Ravens and lives," said Hawk Face. "You not only survived, you conquered them. The magic you use is powerful and unfamiliar to me. Did you know that magic, unless sanctioned by the emperor, is forbidden?"

"It is not magic. It is a force born of faith, and there is a difference."

"Beware, nonetheless. It will be frowned upon in this realm, especially since it can overcome the emperor's Ravens."

"Thank you for the warning. We will keep it in mind," said Gafney.

"And where would your travels be taking you?" asked Hawk Face.

"It is better that you do not know for your own safety, and I would also suggest that you get rid of these bodies. If others follow, there will be questions."

Hawk Face motioned to the men who had been with him. They responded by dragging the bodies of the Ravens off of the street.

"We should be leaving," said Bernard. "There are bound to be others close behind."

"Aye, our time here is spent," agreed Ginzer.

The sun was nearing the horizon by the time the travelers entered the woods at the edge of town. Fear nagged in the pit of Cyle's stomach. He had struggled fighting the Raven, and the force of his blows against his staff still vibrated in his arms. He would not have defeated him without Gafney's help and that troubled him deeply. He knew his friend could not keep watch over him in the heat of battle. What Mellidar had told him was true; there was supernatural power in the Raven's strikes, and it had surpassed a normal man's strength. The dark one's ability to withstand the strikes Cyle threw at him worried the Gap Warrior. He felt the Raven had showed patience in his maneuvers that reflected his skill and training as an elite member of the warrior class.

You cannot defeat the Ravens. They are too strong, whispered the shadow fairies in unison as they fluttered about Cyle's head, leaving trails of blue mist in their wake.

Cyle fought back against the invading thoughts. *I will learn to defeat them it will just take more time.*

You won't have time. They will come for you and you will not be ready, countered the Fairies.

What if they come for me before I have time to prepare?

They will be too strong for me, thought Cyle. For the first time in a long time the young Gap Warrior questioned his own abilities and, with those questions, fear gained a foothold in his heart.

It had been half a day since they left the village when a sound like howling wolves thundered from a distance, softly at first, then growing louder. The band of seven came to a halt in the middle of the trail, silently staring off in the distance at the howling.

Drew yelled a warning cry. "It's the howls! Run. Quickly. Follow me to the rocks!"

Drew bolted, and the others followed in close pursuit. Swirling gusts of wind whipped their clothing and sprayed dust in their eyes. A tree cracked and fell to their left, sending vibrations through the ground beneath their feet.

Drew grabbed Addie's hand and yelled again above the roaring of the howls. "Hold onto each other until we gain cover. The rocks will protect us."

The wind exploded against Cyle's frame, pelting him with small rocks and sand, knocking him from his feet. He dug his staff into the ground to find purchase, but it was no use. He continued to slide away from the others who were moving farther away from him. Something grabbed him from behind, jolting him forward. Gafney and Bernard pulled him into a crevice among the huge boulders. The howling outside raged louder until they were all covering their ears.

"It will pass," yelled Drew, his voice barely discernible. "Until then, we wait."

CHAPTER 23

When the news reached Drok Relnik of the defeat of the three Black Ravens by an axe-wielding warrior, he knew from the description it had to be Gafney. He hated the feeling growing inside the pit of his stomach even more than he hated the Gap Warrior that caused it. He wasted no time convincing Vanus to send out a contingent of twenty soldiers to track down the Gap Warrior. He would have sent more Ravens, but they were busy with their search for Lena and the Dissenters, and he felt the need to keep the other Ravens in the city close to him for protection.

The presence of Gafney could only mean that there would be other Gap Warriors nearby, and that meant resistance to his plans. He cursed under his breath at the thought of Gap Warrior and Intercessor joining forces again. He shuddered at the thought of all the trouble their combined efforts had brought him during the battle of Talinor.

While Vanus kept busy torturing a new influx of war prisoners from Boogara, the city prepared itself for the upcoming festival and the arena games. The Abbodar army was winning the battle against Boogara, and troops were leaving the city daily for the battlefront. Abbodar seemed to have an endless supply of soldiers, and while most of them had gone to battle, some of the finest warriors among them were left in the city to compete in the arena games and protect the city. While the bulk of the military was fighting in the campaign against Boogara, the city was still packed with other warriors from other lands clamoring to compete in the arena games. Preliminary competition had already begun. Blood had already been spilled as weaker competitors were being cut down. Opening day to the main festival would begin in nine days.

Once the arena games officially got underway, the stadium would fill to capacity. There would be sacrifices of human life each day to appease the Terashom gods. Not all the fighting would be to the death, but the crowds had little interest in those matches. One warrior would stand victorious at the end, and his prize would be land and wealth beyond imagination. Until the gates of the arena parted on opening day, the city would continue to swell with foreigners and locals seeking to revel in the festival celebrations. Street performers and food vendors were on every corner, looking to make their greatest financial gain of the year.

Close to five hundred worshipers of all ages gathered in the early morning dawn to greet the light of a new day. Songs of the One Faith filled the forest about them, lifting to the sky as a new day's sunlight streamed through the towering pines that surrounded them. Just two weeks ago, they only numbered a little over two hundred, but several more of them had come seeking to escape the possibility of being sacrificed in the arena.

The night before, just after Gerrid had arrived, the Remnant leader, Kevis, had met with him to hear his intentions. Kevis was cold and distant. He wore his dark hair cropped short, his never-changing face remained stern, and he stood about six inches taller than Gerrid.

Gerrid did not know Kevis well, and he regretted that there was no time to build trust with the leader of the Remnant before he told him what he had come there to do. The time had passed for building an alliance with him, and he knew he had no other choice but to get straight to the point.

Gerrid reported the events that led up to his encounter with Graybeard and how he received the prophet's cloak and the sword of Kem Felnar. He also told him of the vision of the sheep, and finally, he told him that he had returned to the Remnant to lead them out of Abbodar to Talinor.

Gerrid addressed the gathering. "Thank you. It is good to be home with friends," Gerrid smiled nervously and paused to fill his lungs with a breath of courage. "I have returned here to bring you a message given to me by the Ancient of Days."

Whispers floated through the crowd, rising in volume and

then subsided like a wave going out to sea.

"You have done well to come to this place to find safety, but it is a refuge that will not last." Gerrid looked about the clearing, then continued. "This is a harsh land, and it cannot stomach creatures of the light. Even now, as many of you know, the emperor is wresting our people from their homes, taking them to the arena for sacrifice at the festival of Terashom. I believe it is only a matter of time before they come for all of you."

The crowd bubbled with a mix of whispers and gasps. One man said, "Then we will move like we always have and seek a new place of refuge."

"You may do that if you please," responded Gerrid, "but it is no way to live and you have no guarantee you will survive."

"But it is living," said the man, and others nodded in agreement.

"You are correct to say that it is living, but it is not living free. Even as we speak, I fear that they will come for you."

"What kind of message is it that you bring us from the Ancient of Days?" said a young woman standing near Gerrid. "We already know the dangers you speak of. We live in fear everyday."

Many nodded in agreement.

"To live in fear is not the same as living free," said the prophet, "and if you live that way long enough, you risk the ability to know the difference between the two."

"If you are a deliverer of the word, then tell us the news you bring us from the Ancient of Days," demanded one of the crowd members.

"There is a place far from here where others like you follow the One Faith. I spoke of it to you often before I went to prison. It is called Talinor, the place of my birth."

"What has this to do with us?" put in an old man near the back of the crowd.

"I was sent here to take you to Talinor. You will not have to continue living in fear wondering each day if it will be your last day of freedom. In Talinor your faith will be honored and respected. You will be free to worship God openly instead of hiding in the shadows."

Kevis finally spoke. "How do we know you have not been turned against us and are leading them to us?"

Whispers in the assembly revealed the influence their current leader had over them.

"You have no grounds for such talk," charged Dallien. The anger in his voice was evident. "He is one of us and we should hear him out."

"I assure you I am no spy, and yet you make my point for me." Gerrid noted the fear in Kevis' eyes. "Your fear has crippled you even to the point that you would doubt one of your own. Is freedom so alien to you that the chance to take hold of it brings no hope to your hearts? I was in a rotting cell for two years. I lost almost everything that was dear to me except one thing. I held on to the One Faith." Gerrid's own intensity rising within surprised him. "As difficult as that was, it was my faith that sustained me. You can live in fear for so long that it becomes your identity. Once that happens, it becomes almost impossible to hear the voice of freedom. I know of what I speak because I once lost my vision of who I was meant to be."

Gerrid felt the Spirit Wind rising up inside of him. It had been a long time since he felt a stirring like this. An invisible presence fell over him, and he began to tremble. He felt a strong urge to reach for his sword, but for some reason he hesitated and drew back. He could see Lena and Sera in the distance beneath a towering Redwood where the stone giant stood behind them. Lena was smiling, and Sera with her. They watched as if they knew something.

"We are not a people called to fear," Gerrid's words intensified, and the strength in his voice surprised him. It seemed as if his words split the air as they echoed off the surrounding trees. "We are a noble people, and to believe anything less is to believe a deception that is as old as time. You and I were not created to live as cowering slaves to fear, desperately clinging to the hope of surviving another day. The fear in your hearts has bewitched you. You question me as if I cannot be trusted." Gerrid glanced at Kevis as he spoke, then he turned back to the Remnant. "I say to you that your own hearts cannot be trusted because you are ruled by fear. If it is fear that you choose as your master, then you will not hear my words today. My words are born of faith in the one who sent me, and that faith cries out to those who have the courage to believe in it."

Gerrid paused to take a breath and survey the crowd. He could see that every eye was upon him now, and nothing but the wind rustling in the trees could be heard through the sheltering forest. With his heart still pounding, he continued by saying, "The time is close when you must make a decision to follow me or to stay. If this place is to be your destiny, then know this, fear will continue to be your master, but where I lead you requires both courage and faith. I offer no guarantees, for faith is a risky business, but then again, so is fear. You must choose which one will rule over you today. Think and pray hard on your decision and let me know by the end of the day what you will do." The young prophet felt the power of the Spirit Wind in his words, and suddenly he noticed the steel grip of his hand wrapped tightly upon the sword at his side. He thought of Graybeard and smiled. He knew the words he had spoken were not his own. Now they would have to decide.

Gerrid saw her standing at the back of the crowd near the edge of the meadow. He could see her expression clearly, but it was difficult to interpret the look on her face. Bryann appeared to be captivated and frightened all by once at his words. He wondered what she was thinking and realized it was important to him. She suddenly turned and disappeared into the wooded area behind her.

When Gerrid found her, she was sitting by a small stream, watching the water dance in sparkling swirls across the rocks beneath the surface. He sat down beside her, and without speaking a word, he joined her in the silence of her gazing ritual.

Several moments passed before she spoke. "I heard you today," she said softly, keeping her eyes on the water before her.

Gerrid said nothing in response. Somehow he knew he did not need to speak.

"I mean," she hesitated, "my heart heard you." Again her words were followed by silence as tears threatened to fill her eyes.

The young prophet said nothing and continued to stare intently upon the liquid pools swirling at his feet. He could feel her presence and the emotions she bore melting into him, drawing him to her. She leaned into him, letting her head lay gently upon his shoulder. Gerrid responded by slowly and tenderly leaning his own head against hers. The two sat speechless, drinking in the moment as if time had stopped just for the two of them. Gerrid delighted in the scent of her hair and the touch of her head next to his. He would never forget this moment for as long as he lived.

By midday, a light breeze floated through the camp, lifting the smell of freshly baked bread. Most had formed a line near the cooking cave, hoping to get a piece. When Packer and Sera entered the cave opening, they spotted Lena setting several large loaves of bread out on a wooden table. They were surprised to see the stone giant busy at work leaning over another table, kneading bread with his massive rock-like hands.

Jef entered the cave behind them and inhaled the aroma he had grown fond of over the years. Lena nodded at him, and then she tore off a corner of one of the golden brown loaves, summoning him to try it. Much to Packer and Sera's pleasure, she included them in the gesture.

The three felt little guilt as they tested the bread while the others outside the cave looked on with envy. Jef swallowed his first bite, and then he offered, "I have never seen loaves of bread as big as these."

"You have never eaten bread prepared by a giant before

either, and after this he will begin preparation on the evening meal," said Lena, smiling. "Apparently stone giants are excellent cooks."

Hutch heard Lena's comment, and a subtle grin formed on his lips that Jef had not seen before now. It dramatically changed the look of his facial features. The rough edges around his mouth and eyes softened with gentleness. Sera smiled back and giggled under her breath.

The giant spoke in his deep voice that resonated off the walls of the cave. "We will need more meat if we are to feed them all."

"Then we will gather you some game," said Gerrid as he, along with Bryann and his friend Dallien, entered the kitchen. "I saw plenty of game trails on the way in, we should be able to bring back boar or elk soon enough to throw on the spit if the fire is ready when we get back."

"And we will join you," squeaked Sera with delight, grabbing Packer's hand and pulling him in Gerrid's direction. Packer rolled his eyes as if resisting the idea.

"We will be back by midafternoon," said Gerrid as he tore off a chunk of bread and turned, motioning Bryann and Dallien to head toward the woods with Sera and Packer following close behind.

Within minutes, Dallien had led the five of them toward a stand of pines at the base of a range of granite spires that could be seen jutting above the treeline in front of them. Between the hunters and the pines was a large, open meadow, and through the middle of the meadow was a game trail beckoning them to follow it.

It was not the best time of day to hunt, but Dallien assured them that there would be plenty of game to track in the area, and his assurance had proven true. It wasn't long before they had taken down a buck and two boars. After cleaning them and lashing them to poles, they began their trek home.

On the way back to the camp, Dallien had shared his

concerns with Gerrid. He believed that Kevis would undermine their attempt to bring the Remnant back to Talinor. The prophet seemed unconcerned with the resistance in Kevis, but Dallien was not easily dissuaded from his fears.

"Kevis is a strong leader and is probably talking to them even now," warned Dallien. "He will turn them against you, my friend."

"It is not me they must reject," countered Gerrid. "It is the word of the Ancient of Days. They will either have the faith to believe it, or they will reject it. I am only the messenger."

Dallien smiled as he recalled how his friend used to deal with things before he went to prison. He always seemed to take matters calmly even when conflict was in the air.

"Do not underestimate the importance you play, my friend. I think the messenger must be trusted in most cases before the message is received."

"Do you think they will remember me and what I was to them?" asked Gerrid.

"It is hard to say. The last two years have seemed like an eternity, and their ears and hearts have grown accustomed to the voice of another leader. As for me, you know I've never been much of a follower."

Gerrid smiled. "Kevis is not a bad man. He leads as his heart guides him," offered Gerrid.

"Kevis is afraid," countered Dallien. They are all afraid. It is just as you said. Fear rules them."

"Give courage a chance, my skeptical friend. I believe in what I spoke, and my words were not born of flesh. We shall see if they have ears to hear what the Spirit Wind is speaking to their hearts. They are a noble people, and we must give them a chance to let the message of freedom draw out the courage that is within them."

Dallien smiled at his friend, "You have not changed since I saw you last. I believe we have all changed, but you are still the man I once knew. I am with you, whatever they decide."

"If you are the only one to return with me, then so be it.

I'm confident that you will find Talinor to your liking."

Children ran to greet the hunters when they appeared at the edge of the trees. Little feet raced to see whose hands would be the first to touch the animal carcasses. It had been a long time since Gerrid had seen children laughing and playing. Their antics lifted his heart, and even Bryann giggled and teased them as they raced passed.

The stone giant had three pits dug with the cooking fires burning and ready to roast the meat. Next to the fires was a large vat of meat-basting sauces cooking over its own fire, sending a savory smell of herbs and berries throughout the camp. Once the spits were hung with the game, Hutch dipped a large stick with a cloth tied to the end into the basting sauce and began to spread the contents over the meat.

"A cooking giant," said Packer curiously.

"Giants have to eat, too, you know," offered Sera with a tone of sarcasm, then she ran over to the fire pits where Hutch was cooking.

CHAPTER 24

The Remnant camp had finished filling their bellies on spit-roasted pig, venison, a variety of roasted vegetables and Lena's fresh baked bread. Children giggled as they scurried to climb up on Hutch's back. The gentle Giant crawled through the grass on his hands and knees, swaying in a gentle motion. The children fought to gain a position atop Hutch's back while the unlucky ones would topple to the ground, screeching. The stone giant growled like a bear, and the children screamed and ran away in every direction. This was repeated several times.

The Remnant gathered for the evening meeting to offer their final decision to Gerrid's offer. The elders had been discussing the prophet's proposal to return with him to Talinor throughout the day. Several times their conversations had erupted into heated debates, and always, Kevis was in the middle, pressing his views.

Lena told Gerrid about the tension in the camp and that she and Jef had spent most of the day interceding for the elders. "The fear you spoke of earlier has increased, and the darkness is threatening to overtake their hearts," cautioned Lena. "They are like scared little children."

"There is one more thing," she had told the prophet. "It is paramount that they choose to follow you. The Remnant needs Talinor, and Talinor needs them. I am not sure why, but I know that it is so. Somehow Talinor needs these people. I do not know why, but I do know in my spirit that it is a strong and desperate need."

As Lena spoke, her words settled heavily into Gerrid's cluttered thoughts. How could it be that Talinor needed this small Remnant of fear-filled believers? It seemed to him that they were the ones who needed Talinor. They were the ones who had been rejected from their own homeland by Terashom, and they were in every sense orphans needing a home. His own thoughts gave rise to anger because he cared deeply about the Remnant, for it was he who had brought them to the One Faith in the beginning. Still, he wondered, what could this band of timid believers possibly have to offer a nation like Talinor?

Kevis appeared before the crowd, flanked by four armed men. "It is time," announced the Remnant leader, and as the crowd quieted, Gerrid moved to stand next to him.

The prophet could tell before a word was spoken that they had decided against the exodus. Something about their faces and the mood of the crowd left him doubting their choice to follow him to Talinor. One of the Remnant elders, a tall man with long white hair, stepped forward to speak on their behalf. Gerrid recognized him from his time before he went into prison. He and Santor had been friends once, but it seemed a lifetime ago.

"We have made our decision. We will stay here and take

our chances," announced Santor with a hint of remorse in his voice. The elder averted his eyes from Gerrid's gaze. "We have managed to survive up until now. We will continue to do so with God's help."

Gerrid scanned the Remnant crowd and found that many of them were staring at the ground and unwilling to look him in the eyes. An overwhelming sadness threatened to consume him.

"The decision is made then," said Kevis confidently as he looked at Gerrid. "You have made your case, and we have discussed it. Now it is time for you to leave."

Dallien stepped forward, ready to release the rage that was flowing through him, but Gerrid placed his hand on his friend's shoulder bringing him to calm. "They have decided, my friend. At least, they still have the freedom to make this choice."

"I see no freedom in this choice," whispered Dallien.

As the prophet turned to walk away, a deafening silence fell over the camp. Not even the wind could be heard in the surrounding trees.

Then the singing began.

> From a distant land he comes,
> carried on eagle's wings,
> A warrior who lost the song
> his heart no longer sings.

Before Sera started the next line the Remnant joined in to sing with her.

> Day will turn to night,
> and night will turn to day.
> The truth will call him home,
> and he will find his way.
> Freedom reigns within the light.
> There is no other way.
> Freedom reigns within the light where
> he will lead the way.

Then Sera, along with the Remnant, began to sing a new verse that Gerrid had never heard before.

> He'll take them from a darkened land
> to a place where children freely play.
> His weapon forged from long ago in
> the fires of the Misty Realms.
> And when he holds it in his hands, they
> will surely know.

The song ended, and silence fell. Kevis shifted restlessly and crossed his arms over his chest.

Something stirred deep within the prophet that sent a wave of vibrations through his whole body followed by a wave of emotions that threatened to overtake him. He fought to hold back tears and the tightness in his chest as he fought to gather his thoughts. He turned and stepped forward to face the crowd. Unconsciously, he reached down and grabbed the sword sheathed at his waist. The sound of ringing steel penetrated the air as he impulsively freed it from its holding place. Energy pulsated from the shaft through the handle, and into his hand as he thrust the weapon skyward. He watched as sunlight danced up and down the glittering blade. Gerrid had fought back a strong urge to fall to his knees and worship the Ancient of Days, but he held his ground and looked up at the sword in his hand. He could hear the gasps of those who stood before him, and he thought he heard some of them crying.

"It is he," cried someone from the front of the gathered Remnant.

Santor the elder stepped forward and held forth his hand to bring silence. Then he turned to Gerrid and said, "So you are the one our father's sang about and their father's before them. You are the Deliverer. The one sent to lead us to freedom." Santor paused to gather his breath, then he continued, "I thought the song had been lost to the ages, but now it returns to us, and so its message is fulfilled this day."

Gerrid lowered the sword to his side and searched the gathering to find Sera. He spotted her near the front of the crowd dancing with a smile on her face. He could not help but smile back at her. Then he sensed the presence of Kevis who suddenly appeared next to him. "This proves nothing," he addressed his warning to the Remnant leader. "How do we know this was not all contrived?" Kevis calmed the rage in his voice as he continued. "Would you be so easily misled by a stranger?"

"He is no stranger," interrupted Dallien. "You may not know him, Kevis, but to many of us, he is our friend. We do not easily forsake those we call friend."

Kevis ignored Dallien. "You are fools if you choose to follow this man. How do you know he was not sent here by the enemy?"

"I have followed you, Kevis, and I have given you my allegiance as our leader," said Dallien, "but you no longer speak words that my heart can trust. It is time to put aside your fears and see the truth that clearly is before you."

Santor stepped between Kevis and Dallien in an attempt to bring calm. "We have listened to your concerns all day, Kevis, and though we had agreed on a course of action, we must now reconsider our prior decision."

Before Santor had finished speaking, the other elders had gathered to his side to confer with him. After speaking briefly with one another, Santor reported, "We are all in agreement that this is the fulfillment of the song of prophecy and that we should follow Gerrid as the one sent to deliver us."

The Remnant erupted in cheers. Sera began spinning and leaping about in small circles around Packer. Kevis scowled and left the gathering in anger. He knew that if he resisted at this point, the elders would replace him as the Remnant leader, and he was not willing to surrender that role to Gerrid.

Santor and the other elders met again later that night and decided that it would be wise to begin preparations for the trip back to Talinor. They would travel back to Fairwinds on the coast where the Tal ship was anchored, but they would need to hire more sailing vessels to accommodate the rest of the Remnant. Fairwinds had plenty of ships for hire, and they would have no problem finding what they needed.

As first light broke the next morning, many of the Remnant families were already packing their belongings to prepare to leave the next day for their journey to the sea. Dallien had made plans for another hunting trip to gather more game for their journey. Gerrid agreed to go with his friend, Tregg, an excellent tracker, and four other bowmen. Bryann, Packer and Sera would join them as well as the stone giant who would be strong enough to carry a far greater load of game than the rest of them combined.

Tregg had lived up to his reputation as an excellent tracker, and by midmorning they had bagged four elk and two wild boars. Once the game had been cleaned and prepped, Dallien roped them together and tied them to Hutch's shoulders. The giant had no problem packing the weight. By late afternoon, after adding thirteen more turkeys and twenty wild hens to their bounty, they made plans to stop for the day and setup camp.

Packer and Sera helped the stone giant build a smoke house of stone and then began the work of preparing the meat they had harvested that day with salt and herbs for smoking through the night. Hutch attended to every detail of the preparation to smoke the game, and it was clear to the others that he enjoyed doing it.

After sharing a light evening meal together, most of the hunters retired to their beds for the night while a few remained to gather warmth from the fading campfire. Packer stirred the coals and added more wood to bring the dying embers back to life.

Gerrid looked across the firepit to where Bryann was sitting, hoping his stares would go unnoticed. She is beautiful, he thought as he watched the light dance upon her face. She glanced up suddenly and caught him looking. She smiled slightly, then turned her eyes away. Warm emotion rushed over him, and he realized that he was smiling back at her. He felt the blood rush into his face.

She was still mostly a mystery to him, and that part of it still made him uneasy. He could feel his heart being drawn to hers, and yet he knew he needed to resist those feelings. He had a difficult mission before him, and he did not want to complicate things, especially with someone as unpredictable as she was. Besides, he didn't know what she would do now that she had fulfilled her promise to her Aunt to bring them to the Remnant. There was no longer anything keeping her here, and he was surprised she hadn't left already as she promised she would.

That night as he lay awake looking up at the stars, he could hear her fighting the demons that often come during sleep. At first she moaned in fearful tones, and then he heard her whimpering like a little girl. He heard her speak a jumble of nonsensical words, and then she would restlessly toss and turn until she went silent. This went on for most of the night. Several times Gerrid felt the urge to go to her and offer comfort, but he held back. He had learned that she was uneasy receiving comfort, and it was better to let her ask for it.

It had been two days since they had left the Remnant to go hunting. They had been hunting longer than they had originally planned, but game had been plentiful, and this would allow them more time to travel with less need to have to stop and hunt along the way. Gerrid knew that once the Remnant started their trek toward the coast, there would be greater risk in getting back to Abbodar. He wanted to get back to the sea and onto ships as soon as possible, and fewer stops along the way would help them avoid unwanted encounters with the military or the Ravens. If Drok Relnik found out the Remnant was trying to leave the realm, he would not stand for it. He was sure that Relnik was unhappy with his own release from prison and would have killed him long ago if Vanus had not been so fascinated with torturing him.

With the arena games just a few days away, Drok Relnik would already be rounding up the Remnant for arena sacrifice.

It was during the time of the roundup that most of the believers would attempt to flee the city. The unlucky ones who got caught were dragged to the arena to be burned at the stake or fed to the scavs. He was beginning to feel an urgency to return and begin the journey back. It would be difficult moving close to four hundred men, women, and children through the wilderness without drawing attention to themselves. He hoped that Abbodar would be too distracted with their preparations for the festival to bother looking for the Remnant but doubted they would be so lucky.

Gerrid was fortunate he had not been summoned to the arena to fight during the time of his imprisonment. Vanus knew that the former Remnant leader had once commanded the Talinor army, a small kingdom across the sea. He was not about to put a Dissenter in the arena with proven fighting skills and risk him succeeding in battle. Dissenters were hated for rejecting the ways of Terashom, and the last thing Vanus wanted was to see one of their own become victorious in the arena.

The sun was directly overhead when the hunting party neared the Remnant camp. As they entered the meadow nearest the camp, swarms of mosquitoes buzzed about their heads. Gerrid suddenly stopped, motioning them to silence. The air was completely still and all that could be heard was the stone giant's breathing and the buzzing of hovering mosquitoes.

"Something isn't right." Dallien was the first to break the silence.

"Listen," whispered Gerrid.

"I hear nothing," said one of the men under his breath.

"That's what concerns me," replied Gerrid.

The silence became as unbearable as the heat that bore down upon them. A sick feeling rose in the prophet's gut, and without speaking another word, he and Dallien bolted forward as the others fell in behind them.

Dallien was the first to clear the stand of pines with Gerrid

SWORD OF DELIVERANCE

close on his heals. Gerrid's fears were confirmed when he saw that the Remnant camp was abandoned and most of the supplies were strewn about the camp. Dallien and the hunters scouted the area until one of the trackers reported as he knelt to touch the earth, "They've been taken. These boot marks are of the Emperor's men, and these here," the tracker paused briefly to gather his breath then he pointed at another set of footprints, "belong to Ravens."

"He's right," confirmed Dallien, bending down to touch one of the bootprints. He took notice of a small anthill within the boundaries of the indentation. "I would say they were taken right after we left." Dallien crossed the open area and knelt again before continuing. "And here, wagon tracks. They've put them in wagons to transport them."

"We've lost them to the arena," lamented Tregg. "My son is with them. He is but a boy of ten years." The bowman stared helplessly in the direction they had been taken.

"And my wife and daughter," said another. "What can we do? We are but a few against many."

"It's not over," comforted Dallien, laying his hand on his friend's shoulder, and then he looked to Gerrid for his reply.

The others looked at him waiting for him to speak, but the prophet would not answer quickly. It was not his way, and his silence made them uncomfortable. First he looked at Sera whose face was marked with fear and then to Bryann whose eyes showed no emotion.

Gerrid's thoughts raced in every direction. This changed everything. It was going to be hard enough to get the Remnant out of the country, but this made it impossible. By now they would be almost back to Abbodar, and they would never reach them before they entered the city. He had led battle campaigns in the past, and he knew that just because the tide of battle shifts against you, it didn't mean it was over. If nothing else, his last campaign in Talinor had taught him that much.

"I need to think," said the prophet before turning to walk away. The others watched him retreat to the edge of camp where he faded into the shadows of a stand of pines.

Gerrid was known as an excellent military strategist with an uncanny ability to solve the problems that wars produced: but this was no war, and he had no military to organize a counter strike. He reflected on the words of his father who had commanded campaigns before him. Gerrid was eight at the time, and Talinor had just defeated the Boogarans twenty years prior to the second battle where Gerrid had led against them as commander of the Tal Army.

Every battle is similar, and yet there are always differences. We make our plans as best we can, and then we change them, and we almost always have to change them. Gerrid smiled as he recalled his father's words. The best military strategists understood that the first plan was to build confidence among your troops, but those plans rarely held. It was the plans that had to be changed due to the nature of warfare that really counted. All of this gave the prophet little comfort because when he left Abbodar, he thought he would never return there again, and now it was calling him back. The thought sickened him, especially under these conditions.

His father had also told him that every conflict involves unseen forces that were at work, both good and bad. Man to man and metal to metal, we must battle but never forget that we also battle the powers of the unseen realm. The dark warriors of the void, as his father would often call them. Our prayers and choices here can influence what happens there.

As a child, Gerrid had heard his father tell many stories, and he had listened with a mix of fear and excitement. He felt a tinge of shame recalling how he, along with the whole nation of Talinor, had once wandered away from the One Faith that his father had sought to instill in him through the teachings of the prophets and the holy men. It seemed to him that so much of life worked against those teachings, but when the last battle came to Talinor, he returned to the faith of his childhood with a deeper passion. Once again it had been tested with prison, and now it would be tested with this seemingly impossible task set before him.

Gerrid felt insignificant as he looked up at the towering pines. High above the blue sky, billowy puffs of white clouds seemed to skip across the tips of the trees. It was a refreshing sight, and he found himself feeling angry at the latest developments that would delay his return to his homeland of Talinor. The prophet stood in the middle of the forest and waited for a sign, some kind of a message born of a vision or clarifying thought that would show him where to go from here. Isn't that how it works? He thought to himself. Nothing came, only the sounds of birds chirping and squirrels squawking. How was he to move forward without a sign or some kind of instruction?

An uneasy restlessness began to set in. "I will not move without your instruction," he prayed under his breath. "Please don't make this difficult." He could feel the tension rising in his own voice. Shadow fairies fluttered nearby, taunting with barbs of doubt.

"It is time." He recognized the voice that startled his prayerful thoughts as he jerked to look in the direction from which they came.

"Sera," acknowledged Gerrid. "Are you my sign?"

The elf girl did not return the smile. Instead she walked closer to stand next to him, and reaching out, she took his hand into her own. "There are no other signs to be seen at this time. The signs have already been given, and you already know what you are to do. That is enough for now. It is time to go."

A crimson shade crossed the prophet's face as he felt shame over his own fear. He knew that she was right, and he understood what he needed to do. The only thing that had changed, was the level of difficulty, but the mission remained the same. He surrendered to Sera's tugging at his hand and headed back toward the others who were waiting at the deserted Remnant camp. The return to Abbodar was inevitable.

CHAPTER 25

Bernard pounded his fist on the ground as Gafney and Ginzer laughed at the dwarf's frustration with another loss at the game they called Brakkos. They had been playing with the stone pieces since they had shared a meal of brush quail and potatoes earlier that evening. Drew was learning to play for the first time, and he had defeated Bernard enough times that it was beginning to irritate the old dwarf who prided himself on his knowledge and skill with the stone chips. Somehow Drew kept winning.

"I must admit I've never seen anyone take to the game faster than you, young man," mused Bernard as he lined up the wooden chips for another round of Brakkos. Drew smiled back at the old dwarf as Addie looked on from behind with a grin of delight on her shadowed face.

"Sometimes luck is kind to the inexperienced," muttered Gafney. "All that knowledge tends to puff us up, if you know what I mean."

"Either way," groaned Bernard, "I think the boy has a gift."

"The game is mostly luck, Cousin," offered Ginzer.

"Luck," cried Bernard. "Maybe a tiny bit, but there is definitely a strategy involved."

"Then explain to me how the lad has beaten you so many times," argued Ginzer as he winked at Drew.

"I don't know. Maybe he's played before, and he's just not saying it."

"No," Drew shook his head, "I've never heard of this game until now."

"The lads gifted then," said Gafney. "There's no other explanation. I've never seen anyone master Brakkos this quickly."

"I'll agree with you there," offered Addie with a smile. "He is gifted. He has a knack of figuring things out quickly. It's always been his way."

"That would explain it then," said the one-eyed dwarf,

"but it doesn't explain why Bernard hasn't figured out how to beat him, now does it, Cousin?"

"Quiet and listen," warned Cyle holding up his hand pointing toward the shadow. "I thought I saw something moving in the woods."

"I saw it, too," whispered Choppa, staring intently at the shadows among the trees. "I don't have a good feeling about this."

"If they meant us harm, they would have threatened us by now," responded Gafney in a tone that revealed his lack of concern, but his words did little to calm Choppa and Cyle.

"Could be waiting for us to separate and then attack," said Bernard. "I say we track it tomorrow and find out who or what it is."

"I'm for that," offered Drew. "I prefer being the hunter rather than the hunted."

Suddenly a wolfish howl vibrated through each of them, sending the hair up on the backs of their necks.

"Sounds like a wolf," said Ginzer as he grabbed his axe and rose quickly to his feet.

"Doesn't sound like any wolf I've ever heard," warned Bernard. "And yet, it does have that kind of…"

Again the howl rent the night air even louder this time. Everyone stood and scrambled for their weapons. Only Gafney stayed seated.

"That's got to be a wolf," whispered Drew. "What else sounds like that?"

Gafney stood up, put his hands on his hips and stared at the shadows as the rest watched him, waiting to see what he was going to do. Without his weapon, he started to walk toward the treeline in the direction of the howl.

"He's crazy," said Ginzer. "I've wondered if he was, but now I know for sure."

The rest of them slowly fell in behind the unarmed Gap Warrior with their own weapons firmly in their grasp. The light from the fire offered little help in penetrating the darkness of the woods. Scattered shafts of moonlight seeped faintly, providing glimpses of shadowed forms amid the trees and rocks.

Cyle felt his grip tighten on his staff, and a slight vibration danced beneath his fingers as if to warn him that something born of the spirit world awaited them. He wanted to question Gafney's wisdom in leaving his axe back at the fire, but they had passed the point of talking. Something moved to their left. Between the light and the shadows, a ghost-like form floated to the giant trees.

"Did you see that?" Choppa whispered softly.

Gafney grunted, then turned to move in that direction. The others huddled close behind him. Why are we following Gafney? Cyle wondered. We have the weapons. He moved closer to his friend's side, thinking he may need to protect him.

Two glowing eyes appeared out of the blackness. Gafney came to a sudden halt, as did the others.

"What now?" Drew whispered, holding tightly to his bow with an arrow ready and Addie clinging to his side.

"Hold here and lower your weapons," ordered Gafney firmly, motioning to the rest as he stepped closer toward the growling. As the Gap warrior moved forward, the snarls grew louder.

"It's a creature of spirit," warned Cyle, trying to calm the pounding in his own chest.

"Aye, but what spirit?"

The shadows shifted before the glowing eyes pounced on Gafney, slamming him to the ground. Drew pulled back his arrow and Choppa his crossbow. The others pressed in with weapons drawn, then Cyle held up his hand. "Hold fast," he commanded.

Gafney fell, spread out flat on his back, appearing as if something had thrown him to the ground.

"What matter of dark magic has taken control of him?" whispered Choppa.

Crystal waves of shimmering light washed in flowing patterns above the fallen Gafney and slowly took the form of a giant silver wolf. Cyle's pounding heart calmed as a he realized what was happening. He recognized this massive creature resting her forepaws on his friend's chest licking his bearded face.

"She appears from nothing," noted an astonished Addie. "I have never seen such magic."

Gafney sputtered through the creature's slobbering tongue, "Off, Keesha. Off, you beast."

Cyle and Choppa roared in laughter born of relief as they ran to the silver wolf to greet her. Her massive head turned to welcome them as her tongue searched for each of their faces, and it was then that Cyle caught the look in her wild eyes. A mixture of sadness and excitement gathered deeply within her giant orbs. Instantly he knew something was wrong. "Where is she, girl? Where is Tryska?"

Keesha shuffled backward, putting her weight on her hind legs, then she lifted her muzzle to the stars and howled louder than before. It was the sound of fear and mourning, the sound you heard on a cold moonlit night in the high country when a wolf had lost its mate or one of its cubs. Cyle had heard that chilling sound before only this time he knew it was for Tryska, the elfin Gap Warrior.

The two were inseparable, remembered Cyle, recalling the time when he had fought side by side with them to defend Talinor. Tryska, along with Gafney and Bixby, were the first Gap Warriors he had ever met, and before meeting them he had wondered if they were nothing more than a myth. It seemed like an eternity since the time two years ago, when the Prophet Graybeard had charged him with the task to bring the Gap Warriors back to Talinor to fight against the dark magic threatening to destroy his homeland. Soon after he found them, it was revealed to him that he, too, was a Gap Warrior, and he was being summoned to defend the weakening breach in the barrier between the worlds of spirit and flesh. He thought of the flute the elf girl carried as her weapon and how she played it when they fought in the void and on the ramparts of Talinor. To him, it had always been an unusual weapon, but when she played it, something magical would happen. The music would confuse the enemy, and it seemed to give their own weapons more power.

A longing for home surged deep within him. He desperately missed his homeland and his grandmother.

"Where is she, girl?" Cyle asked, as if she could tell him. She licked his face again and nuzzled him with her cold nose before backing away. The silver wolf's eyes furrowed, and a look of longing flooded her eyes.

"She wants to show us," whispered Addie.

"Aye, she knows," said the Axe man. "Let me fetch my weapon. Ginzer, will you stay here with Addie?"

"I'll stay, if I must, but who will look after cousin Bernard?"

"We'll keep him safe," said Gafney. "If we don't, we'll have to eat your cooking."

Keesha wagged her tail as if she knew what Gafney had said, then turned and trotted toward the trees. They followed her deep into the darkened forest where the trees grew thicker overhead, blocking most of the moonlight from above. The travel would have been almost impossible in the dark and unfamiliar terrain if not for the wolf's ability to reflect light from her silver fur. Almost an hour had passed when the wolf came to a sudden halt, then she softly whimpered and began to shuffle restlessly.

"It's okay, girl," calmed Cyle while stroking her neck.

"Wait here," cautioned Gafney to the others, then disappeared into the shadows.

Only a few moments had passed when the burly Gap Warrior returned to wave them after him. They quickly came to a rise that gave them a view that looked out across a clearing where they could see a structure in the distance that was barely discernible. Keesha shifted anxiously, emitting soft whimpering sounds mixed with guttural groans.

"It's too dark now to do anything," said Gafney. "We'll wait for first light, but until then, I want to get a closer look. Cyle, you come with me, the rest of you wait here until we get back."

Cyle and Gafney faded into the darkness with Keesha

close behind. Cyle could feel the blood pulsing through his heart, and he tried to calm himself as he remembered Mellidar's training. A calm heart was an important weapon in battle. It not only helped conserve physical energy, it made it easier to judge your opponent's moves and intentions.

Cyle could see the structure more clearly now. Beneath the moonlit sky, it appeared to be a fortress of some kind built out of roughly hewn logs. There were four guards standing on the walls keeping watch and at the center stood two wooden gates. Gafney and Cyle moved close enough to hear the guards talking.

A deep voice spoke from the top of the wall, "I'd rather be fighting at the arena games than stuck out here guarding one of Relnik's precious elves."

"The warlock is obsessed with the elves," said the other. "They will no doubt sacrifice her for the opening of the games."

"I care little for these matters, but they say the gods show great favor for the elves."

"Be patient, my friend. Tomorrow when the Ravens arrive to collect the girl, we will return to the city with them, and with some luck we will be there before the festival begins."

"Ravens," said a deep voice. "They give me the shudders. Why send them to deliver a single elf girl?"

"Have you not heard? There are rumors of alien magic in the land. The king's son is on edge."

"Just what we needed, more magic," complained a deep voice. "I have never found comfort with the mystical. May the gods forgive me. We could have brought the girl back without the help of the Ravens, magic or not."

Gafney motioned to Cyle to follow. The two of them slipped back toward their camp.

The four guards wrestled against the predawn chill and the weight of heavy eyelids that often beckoned after a long night's watch. They leaned heavily on the posts supporting the ramparts of the small fortress as if seeking to draw energy from the support they offered. The morning sun and its warmth would tarry for at least another hour and, with its arrival, they would be replaced by the day guards.

The deep voiced guard sensed something, and a surge of energy jolted his weary body awake. Before he could interpret the source of his inner stirring, a piercing howl erupted from the bushes fifty yards to his left near the big trees. The watchmen on the walls sprang to their posts with weapons in hand. They looked on, scanning the surrounding area through squinted eyes. Again they heard it, only this time the growling seemed closer and angrier than before.

One of the terrified guards jumped from the wall and ran toward the barracks while the others considered doing the same. Before another could follow, a crash shook the gates. An invisible force ripped at the timbers below, sending shards of wood spraying outward.

"What sort of magic is this?" cried the lead guard from above. Before he could say another word, an arrow pierced his shoulder, knocking him backward off the ledge.

Drew set a second shaft in place, pulled back, aimed and let it fly. The swishing sound of parting air followed, and then it hammered into the chest of another guard on the wall. The man stumbled at first, trying desperately to grab the arrow embedded in his chest. He started to sway, lost his balance and fell crashing on top of a wine barrel. There was a loud crack, and the contents burst outward and onto the ground.

Bernard and Ginzer appeared with axes in hand, running toward the gate where Keesha, still invisible, ripped viciously at the faltering timbers. The two dwarves hammered their axes at what remained of the gate.

Soldiers ran from the back of the compound toward the gate. When they arrived, it exploded inward away from the wolf and the hammering axes. Invisible jaws clamped down on the shoulder of one guard. He felt the raw power pierce him, and he screamed in terror. Before he could respond, a powerful force flung his body through the air, slamming him into another guard and sending them to the ground. By now Ginzer and Bernard were striking out fiercely with axes clashing against swords. One warrior behind Bernard lunged with a spear, Bernard would have been killed if not for the bolt from Choppa's crossbow and Drew's bow that hit the man at the same time, one in the chest and the other in the neck. Bernard heard the impact of the arrows behind him, turned and slammed the butt of his axe into the man's forehead, sending him the rest of the way to the ground.

"We're back at it again, cousin," grunted Bernard.

Ginzer grunted, "Are we not getting too old for this sort of thing?" He then hammered the blade of his axe against the helmet of one of the guards, knocking him into another attacker.

Bernard chuckled. "Nothing like a little rescue to start the day, if I say so myself."

Cyle and Gafney had scaled the back wall of the fortress, already looking for Tryska. As they ran between two buildings, a blast of air swept between them, almost knocking them to the ground. The silver wolf took form. Gafney nodded, and they turned to follow but quickly lost sight of her. Then they heard the growling as shouts echoed off of the walls ahead. When they caught up with the wolf, there was only one man left standing while two others lay dead on the ground. As soon as he saw Gafney and Cyle, he bolted from the room through the nearest door.

Gafney ran to the door where Keesha was snarling and gnawing at its frame. He hammered his axe at its center, and the blade cut into the timber. On the third strike, the door gave way and flew from the hinges. The silver wolf bounded through its opening, knocking Gafney to the side. Once inside, she found what she was looking for. Her tongue swept out, lapping several times over Tryska's crinkled face. The elf girl squealed, "You found me, my friend. I knew you would." She hugged Keesha's neck and buried her head in the wolf's fur. Then she glanced up to see Gafney and Cyle standing in the doorway. "Well girl," she said to Keesha, "I see you brought someone with you." She grabbed a handful of the wolf's mane and pulled herself onto Keesha's back. "You were the last two people I expected to see in these parts."

"We need to head back to the gate," urged Cyle. "The others may need our help out there."

"First I need to get my weapons, and I think I know where they put them."

By the time they reached the front gate to join the others, the fighting had ended. Cyle could see Drew waving from a tree where he had positioned himself on a limb to give him a direct line of fire. He looked across to an outcropping of rock on the opposite side of the meadow where Choppa stood keeping watch down the road in case the Ravens returned. He greeted Tryska with an enthusiastic wave of recognition. She smiled and waved back.

Ginzer did not look well, he was breathing heavily and sweating profusely. Bernard offered him water and his cousin poured half of it over his head and then proceeded to drink deeply of what was left. The two dwarves had held their ground, but they both felt the consequence of being out of fighting shape. Tryska recognized the two dwarves from the battle at Talinor and was surprised to see them so far from home. She greeted and thanked them for their rescue.

"We should leave this place. The Ravens are due here soon," warned Cyle as he glanced toward Choppa to see if there were any signs of them down the road.

After a hasty return to camp, they packed up and set out toward Abbodar, taking care to avoid the established routes. Gafney's plan had not changed in spite of the clear danger to Tryska and the rest of them. The axe man was determined to follow his instincts and go to the place where it was darkest. He assured them that, with the arena games and the festivals, they would be able to blend in with the masses as long as they were careful.

Tryska rode atop Keesha as she recounted the story of what

brought her to this region and how she was captured. The Lady of the Gap had appeared to her one night when she and Keesha had just finished an assignment in the Highland territories. She had planned to go home and visit family in Krellander, but Lady Shariana told her that she was needed across the sea of Baddaris in a place called Abbodar. "Travel with care," she had warned. "It is one of the last shadow kingdoms where the barrier between the void and this world is almost nonexistent. The two are linked in a fusion of wicked harmony, unlike any other kingdom." Tryska thought she had seen fear in the lady's eyes as she finished her warning. "You must take care to conceal your elfin features, for you would be considered a great offering for sacrifice to their priests."

Tryska continued to describe how she had left Keesha behind to go into a small village to gather supplies where some of the Abbodar military had stopped to do the same thing. She had pulled her hair over her ears while wearing a hood. Then one of the soldiers ran into her while chasing a young boy. When he slammed into her, the hood fell off. The stocky soldier saw one of her pointed ears, grabbed her and called for his comrades who appeared instantly. They took Tryska to the fortress, which was not far from the village. The whole way there they spoke excitedly of the rewards they would receive for capturing her.

"That was three days ago, maybe four," said Tryska. "I'm not certain. They kept me in a dark and smelly room the whole time." She paused and breathed deeply before continuing. "That's a harsh punishment for an elf. I'm glad to be out of there, and I thank you all."

"It was Keesha that found us and led us to you," said Choppa.

"Did the Lady tell you anything else?" asked Cyle.

"Yes, but it is not completely clear. You know so much is revealed in layers because the dark ones are often listening." Tryska looked about as if she might see the dark ones. Some believed she could. "The Lady said that there is a small Remnant of believers in the One Faith who are living in this kingdom and that I am to help bring them away from here to the land of Talinor."

"How do we know they will be willing to leave?" asked Cyle.

"She said that they will not survive here if they don't leave this place and that freedom has already been planted in their hearts."

Cyle had been listening silently as they walked through the giant redwoods that surrounded them. Something was unsettling to him about Tryska's story, and he didn't know why. Then Gafney asked impatiently, "Was there anything else the Lady said that could help you find these people?"

"Only that others would be sent to help me."

"And Intercessors," interjected Cyle, "would they not be summoned as well?" His stomach churned and his grip tightened around the staff in his hand. "Are you saying my grandmother is here in this land?"

"The Lady only said there would be Intercessors. She would not have told me even if it were your grandmother. They do all they can to protect their coming and going, and sometimes that means not speaking their names."

Cyle could not imagine his grandmother in a land such as this. To travel so far from home at her age, and the danger she would be facing. Surely the Ancient of Days would not call her to such an impossible quest. Anger stirred inside him and the tone of his words revealed it. "She's here. I know it."

"Easy lad," said Gafney, scratching the back of his head. "You can't know for sure. I'll not have you stirring around about it. I need you to keep your focus."

"My focus is fine, but I see no reason for it." *It makes no sense at her age. Surely the journey would be too much for her,* Cyle thought to himself. He looked to the trail ahead, struggling to shake the feeling of fear pressing in on him. He missed his grandmother and had tried to go home to see her, but this was not the way he wanted it to happen. *If she is here at least he may* be able to protect her, but that offered little consolation for his troubled heart.

CHAPTER 26

They were behind the captured Remnant by at least three days. Gerrid had hoped that if they traveled fast enough, they might be able to catch up with them. If they could catch up to them before they reached the city, they might have a chance at rescuing them before losing them to the arena. He knew they would be taken to the holding pens at the arena, and then they would be sacrificed to the Terashom gods or used as sport for the arena warriors. Once that happened, it would be next to impossible to rescue them.

After a long day of traveling, they decided to stop and rest so they could get a fresh start early the next morning.

Sera and Packer left to find water, and after being gone for what seemed a long time, Hutch began to grow restless. The giant had been gathering wood and was well into preparing a feast of venison to be cooked on a spit. Lost in the preparation of the meal, he suddenly stopped placing his massive stone like arms on his hips and looked about. "Where are those two?" He rumbled to himself. Gerrid overheard him. Hutch shifted his feet and furrowed his bushy brow. He could no longer stand still, so he lumbered in the direction they had taken when they left the camp. He stopped and stared quietly into the tangle of trees. Then he broke his silence. "They should have been back by now," said the giant. Looking over at Gerrid, he released a sigh filled with tension.

It had become obvious that the giant had become the self-appointed protector of the little elf girl although she saw it differently. She was his protector, for she had been there when they had rescued Hutch. In Sera's mind, the stone giant needed someone to care for him after losing his family and people, and she was going to be that person.

"The giant is right," Bryann rose to her feet. "Something is not right. They should have been back by now."

Gerrid agreed and motioned to Hutch and Bryann. "The three of us will go and see what they've gotten themselves into." Dallien nodded in agreement.

Shortly after leaving the camp, Bryann had no problem finding their tracks, and only a short time had passed before they met Packer and Sera heading their direction, out of breath and waving to them to draw their attention. "We have found something," screeched Sera. "Come, you must see for yourselves."

Packer nodded in agreement. "This way." He was already moving backward in the direction they had come from. Gerrid was hungry and tired. He wanted to go back to camp and eat, but he sensed it was important. She looked more nervous than he had ever seen her before, so he agreed, and the three of them fell in behind the elf and the street hound. They led them across the stream they would have drawn water from and into a thicket of branches that Hutch shoved aside as if they were kindling for fire. With the branches cleared they could see the foothills below that rest in the direction of Abbodar. To the right they could see well enough through the fading sunlight to make out rock outcroppings covered by the dense forest growth threatening to swallow it completely. It was then that Gerrid realized that they were not rocks but the walls of the ruins of some ancient fortress or temple. He couldn't be sure.

"What is this place?" asked Gerrid, "Do either of you know?"

Both Packer and Sera shook their heads. "I believe it's a place of great magic," said Packer, wide-eyed. "And possibly there is a great treasure that lies within."

Sera pursed her lips until they turned purple. "You and

your treasures. Have you no other ambitions in life?"

"Treasures are for finding, so why not by me?" said Packer, raising his hands to his side.

Sera scowled at her friend a second time, twisted away and motioned Gerrid and the others to follow in her direction. She ran toward the wall then pointed at what appeared to be a large opening covered by thick vines. Without any prompting, Hutch grabbed them easily, ripping the vines off of the rock. Rusted hinges hung loosely to the sides of the entrance, and at the base lay the shattered remains of the Gates.

"I have heard of such a place," said Bryann softly as she approached the wall to get a closer look. "I am not sure, but it could be the original temple of Terashom."

"I did not know there was any other temple," said Packer. "Why would it be deserted?"

"I remember hearing stories from my aunt when I was a small child," said Bryann. "It's a jumble now, but I recall her talking of a Temple somewhere in the mountains. There was a lot of pain in her voice. I think people died. I thought it was a Terashom temple, but I am unsure. It was a long time ago."

"I cannot imagine what power could overcome Terashom," said Packer.

"It's time to go in," said Sera, interrupting.

"What?" cried Packer. "What would be the purpose?"

"Treasure?" said Sera, smiling mischievously.

"I believe we have other more pressing matters to attend to right now," said Gerrid.

"Perhaps the history of this place will be of benefit to us," said Sera. "Maybe there's a reason we have discovered it."

Gerrid hesitated; he respected Sera's instincts. "You make a strong argument, little Sera. Perhaps it would at that."

"What good would it do to argue with her anyway?" Packer mumbled under his breath and began searching through his backpack. He quickly produced a flint and steel along with strips of cloth. He grabbed two vines and quickly fashioned two torches.

The five of them entered through the main gate into a large courtyard filled with more vines and rocks from the surrounding walls. The elf girl led them across the courtyard to another entrance into the main building that was just big enough for Hutch to fit through. Once inside, they were greeted with a dusty smell and damp air where several broken stones and pots littered the floor of a large room. At the front of the room was what appeared to be a sacrificial altar. Sera trembled at how similar it was to the one she was almost sacrificed on before Packer rescued her. She looked at him with a renewed sense of appreciation, recalling what he had done for her.

Gerrid motioned them to another opening where they walked down a hall that eventually led them into another room even bigger than the first. Once they were inside, the air grew colder. Something scurried across the floor on the other side of the room—probably a rat, but it was hard to tell in the flickering torchlight. Dilapidated benches littered the floor, and near the front of the assembly room was another altar and what appeared to be statues lying shattered on a platform. It was difficult to tell what likeness they bore, but one appeared to have the head of a bird.

Another door took them into a corridor where they walked for several steps, passing by unlit torches hanging on the walls. The hall widened, and they continued until they came to a set of stone steps that ascended before them. When they reached the top of the steps, they were surprised to see that they ended suddenly at a stone wall.

"Maybe there is a treasure to be found after all," said Packer excitedly. "Why else would they block this way off?"

"Surely not for treasure," scoffed Sera. "Why would they leave a treasure behind and not take it with them?"

"It really doesn't matter, does it?" posed Bryann. "We have no way to get past it. Whoever put it there did not want anyone to pass through this way."

Hutch shuffled his way toward the rock wall, and the others parted to let him pass. The stone giant placed his hands on the barrier and paused to gently feel the surface. Then softly, as if he was kneeding a loaf of bread, he slid his hands toward the seam at the edge. Then he did a peculiar thing. He sniffed it several times before stepping backward about ten paces and giving a warning. "Stand back." The Giant motioned them to step wide, then he ran and slammed his shoulder into the barrier with a crash, shaking free pieces of rock and dust that fell from the ceiling. Hutch backed up a second time and charged once more, hurling his powerful stone-like form into the crumbling wall. This time several huge pieces broke off, and after one more battering charge, the whole thing crashed to the ground. Sera clapped and cheered, then spun in a swirling dance, jumping up and down. Hutch grabbed several of the pieces that had fallen to the ground and shoved them aside so the explorers could pass through.

Torchlight filled the new opening. The smell of stale air assaulted their senses, forcing all of them to gasp for fresh air, all except the giant who was unfazed. The room was different than the others they had walked through. Several wooden shelves lined the walls, and others lay broken on the floor in the middle of the room.

"A library?" wondered Packer out loud.

"Possibly," offered Gerrid, "but where are the books?"

"Over there." Sera motioned to a pile of books heaped on the ground.

Packer sifted through the debris and quickly found several more books covered in dust. He brushed back the film with his sleeve and then blew the film off the cover of one of the parchments. He discovered that most of them were burnt and only partially readable. Packer looked up to see that Hutch and Sera were both staring at something on the other side of the room. It was a wall tile that stood out from the other stone tiles that surrounded it, only it was slightly raised and covered with faded markings. The others watched as the giant ran his massive fingers around the seam, scrapping the grout clear until he could firmly grab the edges. With the sound of stone grinding upon stone, he was able to loosen it enough to pull it free.

Beneath the tile was a metal lever. They stared at it in silence and then at one another before Sera whispered softly, "Pull it."

"I'm not going to pull it," Packer whispered.

Gerrid grabbed the handle with both hands and tried to wrench it downward. It wouldn't move. Nothing happened. Packer shrugged and looked at Sera.

The scraping started softly at first and grew louder until the ground rumbled beneath their feet. The main wall at the front of the room shifted and separated at the center, sending sprays of dust from its edges. Once it settled, they found themselves staring at a huge cavern three stories high. Something massive moved from deep within the shadows.

"I knew it was a bad idea from the start," whispered Packer. An armed warrior twice the size of Hutch appeared at the mouth of the cave. His gray armor blended into the walls behind him and made it hard to see him clearly. Clutched in both of his hands was a curved sword iwth a spike at the handle. "Death to all who pass this way without the carrier." The voice echoed from within the metal helmet which covered his face and head.

Gerrid had no intention of entering the cave and held no concern for the meaning of the gatekeeper's words.

"We do not know what the carrier is, and we have no desire to enter the portal," said Gerrid. "We only wish to leave here without trouble."

"Only the carrier can pass," said the sentinel a second time as if he had not heard Gerrid's words.

"We must leave now," warned Sera.

"We will not pass as you have commanded," said the prophet, motioning the others to move backward. "We only wish to leave peacefully."

The gatekeeper slowly backed away disappearing into the mist. From within the darkness of the cavern he offered a final warning. "You are forbidden to return here again, or you will be destroyed. No one passes without the carrier."

"What's he's protecting?" wondered Gerrid out loud. He looked at Sera. She only shrugged her shoulders.

As they turned to leave, Packer spotted a small opening in the wall that had been uncovered when Hutch had knocked a hole in the stone door. The street hound could not resist walking over to look inside. Sera saw what he was doing and followed behind him. He held the torch inside the opening but withdrew it quickly. Then he reached in to pull clear a leather pouch which was bound by hemp and covered in dust.

"At last," said Packer with anticipation rising in his words. "Treasure."

The street hound blew on the leather pouch, sending dust at Sera. She sneezed then waved her hands in front of her face.

"There is a seal where it is bound," noted Gerrid who was leaning in to get a closer look. The sword hilt at his waist vibrated gently, and he whispered to the blade. "What are you trying to tell me?"

Packer licked his fingers and gently rubbed the wax seal. "It looks like a bird." Packer continued to clean and smooth. "That's what it is, a bird."

Sera screeched, "That's not just any bird." The others drew closer now. "That's an eagle."

"An eagle?" questioned the prophet. "How can this be?"

"What does it mean?" asked Bryann. "What does the eagle mean?"

Sera screeched again, "The One Faith."

Bryann wrinkled her brow.

"It is the symbol of our faith," answered Sera. "We have to open it."

"Hope," said the giant softly. Sera smiled at Hutch. Packer broke the seal and peeled back the leather cover to reveal parchments with words written in a tongue unknown to him. "What does it mean?" asked the street hound.

"Its an elfin dialect," offered Sera with delight. "The words at the top I do not understand. But here at the bottom," Sera pointed her finger, "is a song, a song of worship to the Ancient of Days."

'What is a song of the One Faith doing in a Terashom temple?" asked Gerrid.

"This is not a Terashom temple." Sera paused to look down at the parchments in her hands. "I believe it was a temple of the One Faith, and this may have been their place of worship. At least I think it was."

Packer saw it first. Something moved in the shadows near a dark opening at the far corner of the room. Gerrid called out. "Who goes there? Show yourself."

Whomever it was slipped away into the shadows and was gone. Without a word, Hutch bolted toward the opening to follow it into the darkness. The others paused, shot brief glances at each other, then ran after Hutch.

The hallway was dark and dank, but there was still enough fire from the torches to light their way. Hutch was nowhere to be seen, but they could hear his footsteps pounding the ground ahead of them. They tried to speed their pace, hoping to catch up with the giant, but soon his footsteps faded. Then they heard something. Muffled voices could be heard ahead of them. Gerrid held up his hand to slow the approach.

The narrow hall opened to a larger room. Sera saw them first and ran ahead. At the center of a large cavern was a small group of stone giants surrounding Hutch. Gerrid counted six of them.

"Don't be afraid," said Hutch waving them in his direction. "These are my friends and this is their home."

The giants stared at the onlookers briefly then turned and continued greeting Hutch. The shadows shifted near the edges of the cavern, and other giants appeared and slowly came forward into the light. Now there were some fifty or more stone giants surrounding him.

Gerrid, Bryann and Packer watched from a distance as the giants spoke to one another, and after several moments had passed, Hutch turned and spoke, "They are Mingi, all of them." A look of deep sadness filled the giant's eyes. "They were cast out just like me. The Stone Clan believes they were cursed."

Sera ran to Hutch. He scooped her up into his arms and placed her on his shoulders. "She's my protector," said Hutch as a smile returned to his face. Sera giggled.

Gerrid knew what the giant would say before he spoke his next words. "I will stay here. I have found my home among the cursed."

Sera hugged the giant's neck. "I cannot bear the thought of leaving you behind."

"You won't need to," said Gerrid. "Not for now, anyway. We are still going into the city, and it's too dangerous to take you with us. We will come for you when we return."

Sera reluctantly agreed, knowing that it was the only way. Packer did not like the idea of leaving Hutch and Sera behind either, but he knew Gerrid and the others would need him once they were in Abbodar.

CHAPTER 27

Vanus leaned against the back of his Father's golden throne, staring restlessly at the inlaid jewels that lined the seat and arms—all of them taken from the different lands they had conquered. It was appointed to him as the king's son to rule in his father's absence. The campaign against the Boogarans was nearing its end. The king had left the day before, heading to the front to join his warriors. Vanus had tried to talk his aging father out of making the trek, concerned that he might encounter trouble on the journey. But the king had insisted that victory was near, and he wanted to be with his forces to celebrate when it came. Vanus pressed to send three of the Red Ravens for protection, and the king reluctantly agreed even though he was confident that his own guards could provide the protection he needed.

Vanus leaned forward, placing his arm on his knee. To his left were three Red Ravens standing silently, and on his right stood three more. They were all dressed in the customary battle garments required when standing guard in the throne room. Their red leather breastplates were lined with black metal trim, and all of the six wore a dark red matching helmet through which their eyes could not be seen. On top of the helmet was a plume of black raven feathers. Haggron, the head Raven, was the only one not wearing the helmet. He stood over six feet tall, and his broad shoulders and muscular frame had served him well in combat. The Raven leader stared straight ahead through lifeless, gray eyes. The last man to look him in those eyes had lost his life, as did all others who dared to do the same.

Drok Relnik was summoned to approach the dais by the Terashom priest who stood stoically behind Vanus. The warlock despised the pomp, but knew it was necessary.

"The Dissenters have been captured and are being held at the arena," said the warlock, "but I still have a concern."

"What is it, my friend?" asked Vanus. "You have been restless of late."

"There is a witch among them, and she must be dealt with according to our laws."

"Is this the old lady you spoke of before?" asked Vanus. "Even with her held in captivity, you are still convinced that she is a threat?"

"She practices magic that is not sanctioned by the temple;

therefore, she must be brought before the council of priests and judged."

"So be it," assured Vanus. "If she is the threat you warn against, then bring her before the council. If she is found guilty, she will be sentenced to death in the arena."

The arena holding pens were clean enough, mainly due to the fact that they had not been used for several days, but soon the blood of warriors would stain the dirt floors. It had been three days since the Remnant had arrived. Over three hundred men, women and children huddled together, awaiting their fate. Children clung to their frightened mothers while Kevis, their leader, along with the elders, did what they could to offer comfort. Their efforts had little effect.

It was Lena who managed to bring some measure of hope when she began telling stories about the legendary fighters known as the Gap Warriors. Once she started, they did not want her to stop. Her tales captivated the children and filled them with questions. Most of them had heard stories of the Gap Warriors. Before Gerrid had been taken away to prison, he had told them how the warriors had come to Talinor once, when he was a young boy, and then again twenty years later when he was the Talinor commander.

"They came to fight the dark ones," whispered Lena for effect. She did not want to use the term shadow wraith for fear she would frighten the children.

But one of them blurted out, "You mean the shadow wraiths."

Lena noticed the eyes of the younger ones growing wide as they snuggled up next to their mothers.

"Are there any girl Gap Warriors?" asked a curly-haired blond girl.

"Why, of course," assured Lena. "They are some of the bravest of all." The little girl giggled with delight. "There is an elf girl named Tryska. She rides a giant silver wolf that can turn invisible, and when she plays her flute, the demons tremble."

The little girl squeaked with delight.

"I wish the Gap Warriors were here now," said Barrand, one of the younger boys.

"I pray every day, little Barrand, that the Ancient of Days will send them to help us."

Barrand smiled. "We should all pray that they come."

"You fill these children with false hope," huffed Kevis. "There are no Gap warriors coming to Abbodar, and you know it. We must pray and hope for another way."

"You will pray as you see fit," said Lena as she rose from her seated position to face Kevis. "Barrand and I will pray for the coming of the Gap Warriors." Lena winked at Barrand who smiled and winked back.

"Do you think they will come for us?" asked Barrand hopefully.

"Yes," Lena paused and looked Kevis in the eyes, "I do."

Suddenly the doors opened to the holding pens, and two guards walked into the room. "Is the witch, Lena, here?" asked one of the guards.

Jef stood to his feet and made his way to Lena's side. "I'll not let them take you."

"What will you do, my friend? They are armed." Lena smiled at her friend and placed her hand gently on his shoulder. "I'm here." Lena waved to the guards and started toward them. Jef tried to follow, but Lena put her hand on his chest to stop him. "Pray for me." She smiled and turned to walk with the guards through the door.

When Lena entered the meeting chamber, the first thing to catch her eye was the towering statues that lined the back wall. Carved from white marble, they rose some fifty feet from floor to ceiling. Each figure had the body of a man or woman and the head of an animal. There was a goat's head on one and the head of a snake on another. The head of a raven was upon a statue of a warrior's body, clad in armor. All of the stone figures appeared to be peering down upon the throne. To the right of Vanus stood Drok Relnik whom Lena might not have recognized, but when she saw the familiar silver band that he wore upon his brow, she looked closer. Then she recognized him and wondered how it was that he had come to this faraway realm across the sea. Six warriors, three on each side, held position next to the dais, and several other priestly looking men dressed in temple robes stood cloistered at the foot of the stage where the king and the warriors stood. Two additional guards stood on each side of the Intercessor and two more behind her.

The one on the throne spoke first. "Do you know why you are here?"

"All I know is that we were taken from our camp and brought to this place against our will. Beyond this, I know of no reason for such an action, but apparently this old woman is a danger to you if it takes four guards to watch over me."

Vanus smiled slightly as he rose and stepped closer toward Lena. "You are here because you have been accused of using magic that has not been sanctioned by the temple priests." Vanus crossed his arms and smiled. "How do you respond to this charge?"

"I am no user of magic, and I have no use for it."

Drok Relnik whispered something in Vanus's ear. The king's son nodded and continued, "Did you not bring with you into this land a talisman of magic properties in the form of a sword?"

"I did no such thing." Graybeard was the one who delivered the sword here, thought Lena, but she did not want to tell them anymore than was necessary.

"I think you are lying to me."

"I have told you the truth, but I think it matters little what I say. You will do what you wish with me."

Again Drok Relnik whispered something in Vanus's ear. He paused as if to ponder, then he turned and said, "If you tell us where the sword is, we will consider a lesser punishment than death."

"Already you speak of my death before you have had time to consider your claims against mine. I do not know where the sword is, and if I did, I would not tell you."

"Then you are a fool," shouted Vanus. "Do you not realize that I have the power to give you life or death?"

"You call me a fool, but only a fool believes such power lies within his own grasp. Flesh and blood or any mere man will never determine whether I live or die. My life is in the hands of a power that is above all other forms of magic."

Drok Relnik shrieked, "You blaspheme our sacred beliefs, and your very words condemn you. This is proof enough that you are in defiance of our sacred laws. Death is the only reasonable conclusion for such a violation." The warlock relished the moment. He had long wanted to see the Intercessor's life ripped from this world. Finally, he would see his wishes realized.

Lena could feel defiance building inside her, borne of the Spirit Wind. "You call me blasphemer, and yet you fellowship with the darkness and call it light. Your deeds have brought needless death and destruction to your own people and to other kingdoms. You make yourselves judge over all, and yet you yourself follow no law unless it suits you." Lena pulled her arms free of the two guards that held her and took two steps toward the dais before speaking again. "Your blindness can only lead to your own destruction. If I am to die before that happens, then so be it, but I will die full of the One Faith. No one can take that from me—neither you nor the powers of darkness that you serve."

"Then it shall be as you say, Intercessor," declared the warlock. "You shall be burned on the pyre in the arena as a traitor to the gods of Terashom. Take her from this place and put her in a separate cell from her own people. "

The four guards escorted Lena from the room, leaving the king's chamber behind her.

"She is a feeble and harmless old woman," said Vanus to the warlock. "Now that I have met her, I believe it to be so even more."

"Even the smallest spider can carry a deadly poison. You must trust me when I say that this one is strong in the magic of her choosing. As long as she breathes life, she is a grave threat to everything we believe."

Vanus smiled then looked Lena in the eyes. He felt an intense fear rush over him. "Take her." The words barely escaped his lips before the guards pulled her from the room.

Lena was put in a cell with bars that separated her from the larger holding area where the Remnant was being held. Three others already inhabited the small space—two young men dressed in tattered rags who looked to be about thirty and twenty years of age and a woman in her mid-forties. As she entered the cell, they greeted her warmly. Shortly after that, Jef appeared from the other side of the bars. At once, the Tal warrior reached his hands through to take hers. "Are you okay?" he said softly.

"I am fine, Jef, and how are you and the others?"

"It has been quiet since you left. We have been worried about you. What did they want from you?"

"They want my life."

"Your life," whispered Jef as he grabbed the bars and squeezed them with both his hands. "Why would they want your life?"

"It is Drok Relnik, the warlock. He is behind it. It seems he has the ear of the king's son. He sees me as a threat and wishes to eliminate me."

"Relnik?" Jef pulled closer. "He spreads his darkness even to this place?"

"It seems as though he has left the faltering land of Boogara and found a way to join with Abbodar in defeating those he once stood with."

"I will not allow it," declared the once Tal warrior through clenched teeth. "I will find a way to get you out of here."

"Please Jef, you cannot put yourself in harm's way. Soon Gerrid will come for them, and he will need your help."

"They will need your help more than mine, Lena. How can I

stand by and do nothing?"

"That is exactly what you must do. I cannot bear the thought of harm coming to you on my account. I am at the end of my life. You too are an Intercessor. If it is my time to go, then you must carry on in my place."

"Lena?" a voice from behind her questioned. "Are you Lena the Intercessor?"

"I am," answered Lena with a quizzical look on her face. "And who are you?"

"I am Pamela. I can't believe I am talking to you, Intercessor. I've heard stories and a song that told of you. I've only dreamed of meeting you in person."

"Songs are always exaggerated for the purpose of holding the listener's interest," Lena laughed. "I did not know a song had been written about me."

"I heard the song from a traveling minstrel. He sang a story of Lena, the Intercessor. I was not sure if his words were true until I recently met Gerrid, the former leader of the Remnant. He confirmed your existence." Pamela paused as a look of concern crossed her face. "Do you know what has happened to him?"

"He was not with us when we were taken, but he will be here soon to free the Remnant."

"He will come before they take you to the arena. I know it," assured Pamela. "And my niece, Bryann. Have you seen her?"

"As far as I know, she is with Gerrid."

Pamela smiled hoping it was still true. "You are here, Lena. Maybe the Gap Warriors will come to join you."

"Maybe," said Lena. "But their abilities are not endless. I fear it will take more than Gap Warriors to help us now."

"Lena, will you teach me to intercede?" begged Pamela through pleading eyes.

"Of course I will," Lena smiled. "I see the fire in you, child." Pamela smiled back.

CHAPTER 28

Gafney spit on the stone and then slid it over the axe blade he called Demon Slayer. Back and forth he stroked the edge with the stone, moving it in smooth repetitive motions. Then he flipped it over in his palm and continued the process on the other side. Lost deep in thought, the Gap Warrior had said little that day.

Cyle knew him well enough to leave him alone when he was like this. Now that they had come to the edge of the great city, Gafney needed time to think it through. Cyle knew that in time, the axe man would be ready to talk, and when he did, he would present his thoughts on what to do next.

"This is a dark place," muttered Gafney after several more minutes of sharpening his axe. "Very dark. Like none I have ever known."

Cyle could feel the tension increase as it filled the air between them, and he could not push it away no matter how hard he tried. The others were playing the stone game, and he could faintly hear them laughing in the background. He heard Bernard groaning. It sounded like Drew was beating Bernard again. Addie and Choppa worked at roasting a small pig over the fire and beyond the camp he could see the lights of the city below them in the distance. And yes, he too sensed the depth of the darkness there.

"Tomorrow we go in," said Gafney staring at the blade of his axe as if it was speaking to him. Cyle did not bother to ask him why. He knew it was what they would do and that they would no doubt encounter more of the Ravens. The thought of a second encounter tore at the edges of his nerves. It seemed pointless to knowingly walk into harm's way without a clear mission before them. Beneath the doubt he was feeling, he knew that their mission was down there among the lights below. He wasn't sure how he knew. But he knew and he did not doubt it.

That night while Gafney snored nearby, Cyle slept fitfully until he awoke suddenly for no apparent reason. The stars were crystal clear overhead, and a slight breeze cooled his warm body. First he listened intently and heard nothing, then he scanned the area around the camp. At the edge of the dying firelight amid the trees he saw Mellidar staring at him. Even though the Guardian spoke not a word when he turned to walk into the darkness of the forest, the young Gap Warrior understood that he should follow his teacher.

Mellidar almost always came to him at night, either taking on the form of flesh, for limited amounts of time, or he would appear in his dreams. Tonight Cyle could not tell which it was. Was he dreaming or was he awake? So many times these meetings with Mellidar took place in his dreams and yet they were as real to him as any of the times he was awake.

Cyle's thoughts flashed back to how it all began over two years ago when he had fled Talinor to escape the threat on his life. The king's priests had accused him of trying to poison the monarch's wine, and as the king's cup bearer, he was the most likely one to blame. It was after he had fled for his life that he encountered the Guardian Mellidar. Several times his life was in danger and Mellidar had protected him from death. At first he had no idea it was the Guardian, but in time, it was revealed to Cyle that Mellidar was to be his appointed Guardian, a spirit warrior sent by Shariana, the Queen of the Guardians, to train Cyle in the ways of the Gap Warrior.

Cyle followed his mentor to a stone slab surrounded by crumbling walls that appeared to be the ruins of a large estate or a small castle. The full moon above provided adequate lighting to accomplish their training. Mellidar stood across from Cyle, dressed in his battle garments. He usually came to these meetings dressed more like a woodsman, but tonight he was fully dressed for battle, this fact did not escape Cyle's attention. The garments he wore were not unlike that of an earthly warrior. The breastplate bore the golden emblem of an eagle, and his helmet, like the rest of his armor, had a mysterious translucent quality to them.

"You look as though you are going to war," said Cyle in an attempt to converse with his Guardian.

"Ready yourself, Gap Warrior." Mellidar ignored the statement and replied in his customary deep voice, devoid of emotion. It bothered Cyle that the Guardian could be so distant and full of intensity. He had tried several times to break through the enigmatic shell that surrounded him, but the results were always the same. Tonight was no exception.

Mellidar responded in a full attack with his staff striking out at a blinding speed. Cyle's eyes widened as he reacted, instinctively blocking the strikes. As the young Gap Warrior stepped back to gather himself, the Guardian warned him sternly, "Don't pause before offering a counter attack."

Cyle remembered the Guardian's warning from their last meeting and felt shame as the blood rushed to his face. He had not been focused and had so easily forgotten the prior warning. The attack came again for a second time with the same vicious flurry as the first. This time Cyle managed to launch a counter to the attack, but even he knew it was a weak response to his opponent. Mellidar stepped back from the attack, and as he did, Cyle responded with a whirlwind of rapid strikes that put the Guardian on the defensive. Mellidar countered after several blocks and drove Cyle backward into defending again. The Gap Warrior stumbled backward several steps, and then he turned the pressure back on his trainer, delivering a straight shot to his chestplate and another to his shoulder.

Mellidar held up his hand to bring them to a halt. Cyle smiled, feeling a sense of power. A thought crossed his mind. *How much more can this man teach me? I am becoming his equal.*

"Your progress is commendable, Gap Warrior."

Cyle bristled at the statement, primarily because it felt condescending to him, and he wished that Mellidar would call him by his name. He couldn't remember a time when that had happened.

"What is happening?" asked Cyle.

"What do you mean?"

"You are dressed for battle. Surely it is not to protect yourself from me." Cyle smiled as he said it.

"The closer we move to the city, the darker the threat. This is a place of detestable and unimaginable practices. With the exception of a very few, these practices are fully embraced by the people of this realm. The festival that is about to begin is a celebration of evil, and anytime evil is celebrated with such intensity, doors will be opened that will invite the dark ones to secure strongholds in the minds of men and women." Mellidar paused and nervously flipped his staff back and forth from hand to hand. "At the same time the breach in the void is opening, which leaves you and I battling on two fronts—the demons that cross over and the ones that inhabit flesh and blood."

"What you speak of sounds impossible. Why do we even bother with such a place? Wouldn't it be better to leave them to their own destruction?"

"In some cases, yes, but not in this one. There is a Remnant of believers that have been taken captive and are being held at the arena for sacrifice to their gods. The Ancient of Days will not forget them."

"Is that why we are here," asked Cyle, "to help the Remnant of believers?"

"We are here to rescue them and bring them back to Talinor."

Finally, thought Cyle, some answers. "I have felt the piercing pressure of the darkness in this land. As we stand on the edge of entering into the city, it increases to a level like none I have ever known. Even my staff seems to know it. I feel it flaring beneath my grip as if to warn me."

"Your staff flares for a reason. I have been near you, unseen to your eyes, battling the dark ones."

Cyle was stunned by Mellidar's statement. He had not

considered that the Guardian had already been engaged in warfare, but now it made sense that he would appear in his battle armor.

"Are there Intercessors among the Remnant?"

"If there are, it has not yet been revealed."

Cyle felt the anxiety rising within him. He had learned much in the past two years regarding this type of warfare, but one thing he knew for sure was that the role of the Intercessor was essential to every battle they entered. While there were few Intercessors in number, there had been at least two present in every battle that Cyle had fought in since Talinor.

"Then how are we to prevail if there are no Intercessors in the land?"

"I did not say there were no Intercessors in the land."

Cyle's stomach twisted as he pushed back the urge to throw up. "What is happening here? What are you not telling me?"

Mellidar hesitated.

"She's here, isn't she? My grandmother is here in Abbodar."

Still Mellidar said nothing, but he didn't have to. Cyle knew that it was true. "Why have you kept this from me?" Anger flowed through gritted teeth.

"I have kept nothing from you, Gap Warrior. It was only just revealed to me. Your grandmother and one other stands with her."

"Then we must go and help her." Cyle began to pace nervously.

"That is not the chosen course for you at this time."

"I'm going to help my grandmother. There is no other choice that makes sense," countered Cyle intensely. "That is the course of my choosing."

Mellidar moved closer and gripped his staff tightly in his hand, pounding it into the ground. "You are a Gap Warrior." The Guardian's words blasted forth in a mixture of passion and anger. "Do not forget that you responded to this call. No one has ever promised that it would be a safe and predictable journey.

Certainly by now, you understand that sometimes the way is unclear, but that is the time for faith."

Cyle fired back, refusing to give up ground, "You can't expect me to ignore my grandmother's peril. It's one thing to put myself in harm's way, but I can't bear the thought of not going to her."

"Quite the opposite is true. If you go to her now, you will put her in peril. It is not time yet. You must recognize that there is a bigger plan in place. We are unable to see all that takes place behind the veil. Even I see more than you, and yet I do not see all."

"How can I trust what I cannot see?" countered Cyle.

"It is not the first time you have trusted the ways of the One Faith."

"It has never been easy for me," said the Gap Warrior.

"That, I am aware of."

Several thoughts bombarded the young Gap Warrior's mind. The image of his grandmother kept forming, and each time came overwhelming fear and trepidation. *I cannot leave her,* he thought to himself. *I cannot bear it.* And then he realized he was speaking the words out loud.

"The way of the Gap Warrior is not always an easy one," challenged Mellidar. "If you choose to trust the fear in you, then that fear will be your master. If you choose to trust the Ancient of Days, then you will be mastered by the one who rules all."

Cyle did not hear what Mellidar was saying to him. He could only hear the other voices, the voices of fear, doubt and intimidation. At the edge of the clearing, hidden in the murky edges of gloom a safe distance from Mellidar, the shadow fairies danced a dance of glee. The Guardian could hear them celebrating, but he could not send them away. Only Cyle had the power to do that.

"I have decided," pressed Cyle defiantly. "I am going to help my grandmother." Then he moved to walk past the Guardian.

Mellidar stepped into the path to block the young Gap

Warrior, and Cyle reacted without thinking, firing forth a flurry of angry blows with his staff. The Guardian blocked them without difficulty. He could see and feel the rage in his young disciple's eyes as Cyle attacked, and Mellidar knew that the pain and rage was not directed at him. Nonetheless, he had become the object of his apprentice's misplaced wrath.

Cyle pressed forward with unrelenting intensity, and with each move he could feel the panic increasing within him. An overwhelming feeling of horror had been loosed inside, and the pain was so deep and primal that it began to over take his ability to reason. The thought of not protecting his grandmother—knowing that she was in danger—was unbearable, and he had unleashed all his fear and rage on his Guardian, Mellidar.

Mellidar lashed back with an unexpected ferocity, blocking Cyle's blows and countering with strikes aimed at the Gap Warrior's head, causing him to feint back and regather for a second volley. The two warriors clashed beneath the moonlight with an intensity they had never used with one another before now. Each time their staffs connected, sparks erupted, spraying forth and lighting up the meadow, sending the shadow fairies for cover.

"Let me by," bellowed Cyle in a shriek of rage as the two warriors' staffs connected, pulling Guardian and Gap Warrior face to face.

Mellidar refused to relent, pushing back. "Whether you choose the way of faith or the way of fear, you still need a lesson today, and I am going to deliver it."

Then, with increased speed, the Guardian tore into the Gap Warrior with a series of strikes that flashed from every direction. Cyle was able to block the first few that came his way, but a straight forward thrust penetrated his defense and caught him square in the chest, sending him reeling backward. He was stunned at the impact and felt a slight dizziness threaten his balance. That slight advantage gave Mellidar the opening he needed. Sensing Cyle's demise, the Guardian seized the advantage and in a fluid motion, he sent his staff in a lateral arc, slamming it against the side of the young warrior's head. The blow sent him sprawling on the ground.

Looking toward the spinning stars that filled the sky above him, Cyle felt the darkness edging in at the corners of his vision. He smelled the pine needles on the forest floor all about him. The screech of a hoot owl in the distance filled the silent forest followed by a flutter of wings. The small distraction was not enough to rescue him from the pounding in his head. A form silhouetted by the stars and the light of the moon stepped over him. Cyle fought to clear his mind and push aside the ache in his chest and the throbbing pulse of his head. Where am I? What's happening?

Fighting to draw fresh air into his empty lungs, he looked up at the Guardian and forced out the words through ragged breathing, "I am going, and you cannot stop me."

"It was never my intention to stop you, Gap Warrior. You are the only one who can do that. I will not be going with you. But I will send you with a mark, so you will never forget the night you chose doubt and fear over faith."

Mellidar lifted his staff with both hands and sent it whistling forward, parting the air, slashing across Cyle's forehead until blood appeared on his brow. Piercing pain surged behind his eyes as he floated toward the edge of consciousness. Then came a burst of light and Mellidar was gone.

Cyle rose slowly, stumbling from the shifting ground beneath his feet. His hands trembled. Reaching for his staff to give him balance, he drew in a deep breath. For a fleeting moment he considered going to Gafney to tell him of his decision, but no, that would be met with even more resistance.

You must go now, whispered the shadow fairies. That is all that matters.

I must go now, thought Cyle. He turned and headed toward Talinor.

CHAPTER 29

Gafney stirred awake to the presence of Mellidar standing over him. Mellidar had come to Gafney moments before dawn to tell him that the young Gap Warrior had departed in the night. The staff-wielding Guardian warned Gafney sternly not to follow the boy. At first Gafney pushed back and insisted on following Cyle, but Mellidar would not back down.

Gafney asked Mellidar, "Do you plan to follow the boy?"

"He has made the choice to follow his own course. It is a simple matter of will. He has placed his own will over that of the Ancient of Days. I cannot follow that path," said Mellidar with a hint of regret in his tone. "Foolishness always has its price." Reluctantly the Gap Warrior relented, although he wanted to pursue and protect his impulsive young friend.

"You are right to go to the city, but be careful," Mellidar warned. "The dark magic is strong in this land as you have already witnessed, so move with great caution. Do not bring any more attention to the power of your weapon unless it is absolutely necessary. You have already made enemies here. The battle you fought with the Ravens has already found its way to the ruling powers, and there are already exaggerated tales of it being told in the city streets."

Mellidar told the Gap Warrior all that he could about their quest. He spoke of the Remnant and Lena being held captive at the arena. "The Remnant is to be freed and brought back to Talinor, but before you do anything else, you must find the one who is key to freeing them. There are dark spies watching us as we speak. So all I can tell you is that he travels with a small company, and you have fought for the same cause in the past. Together you must forge a plan to rescue the Remnant. Unfortunately, Cyle will not be with you. His fear for his grandmother guides him now." Mellidar shook his head and continued, "I have told you all that I can at this time. Your instincts have led you well, Gap Warrior.

Move with urgency, for time is running out. When you arrive in the heart of the city, seek out Bittles Tavern. You will find help there. Any questions?"

"Yes, one more question. Where is my Guardian, Alleneil?"

"He is near. Even as we speak, he is battling the dark ones to keep them away from our words, but I must go now. He needs my assistance. There is just one more thing." The Guardian paused, and Gafney could see his knuckles tighten around the staff he held in his hands. "The warlock, Drok Relnik, resides in the king's palace. He knows you are coming."

Gafney gritted his teeth, "I hate warlocks: this one most of all."

Choppa was gathering his things and preparing to go looking for Cyle, but Gafney stood hard against it.

"Young fool," muttered Gafney under his breath. "He's on his own now. He has made his choice, and the last thing we need is you adding to the problem. We will stay our course. And you," he had pointed at Choppa, speaking in a stern tone, "you'll not be following him. If you get the notion to do so, I will tie you up and leave you here on the trail until a scav finds you."

Choppa desperately wanted to pursue his friend, but Gafney was not to be crossed. He would agree for now, but in his mind he rehearsed what would happen if the opportunity presented itself, he would leave them to find Cyle.

In the final moments before they departed for the city, Gafney and Tryska had discussed their options and they agreed with one another that it would be safer for the elf girl and the wolf to wait at the edge of the city, until they could return. Tryska was a Gap Warrior, and she understood that her role in all of this would become clear at some point. Until then she and Keesha would wait in the hills above the city. Addie would wait with them while Drew continued on with Gafney and Choppa, along with the two dwarves, Ginzer and Bernard.

Addie had pressed to go with Drew, but he would not have it. She could not understand why he had to go with them. He had told her, "I am in this now. I do not understand it all, but I am drawn to these men and their mysterious faith. Besides, they saved my life. How can I abandon them now? They will need me to lead them through the city and back." Addie looked at the ground as he continued, "We have lived for so long in this darkness. Now that I have seen a light in these from another land, I cannot deny that it is real. I must see it through. For the first time, I have hope that life can be different and that our lives can be more than hiding from the evil that oppresses us. Everything inside of me tells me that I must stand against it."

"Wait for us with Tryska and Keesha at Fallen's Pass just below the old ruins." He gave her directions and cautioned her to travel among the trees and keep clear of the roads.

Addie could see that Drew was changing, and it frightened her. The words that he had spoken to her the day he departed filled her with confusion and fear. She found no peace in the fact that these men were following a quest that was unclear to them but was taking them into the heart of darkness.

It made the thought of being apart and of the possible danger almost unbearable. In the early morning light, he kissed her and held her close. When he turned to walk away with the others, she feared that she might not see him again. For the first time since they had met and fallen in love, she wanted to cry.

The familiar sounds of celebration that accompanied festivals echoed through the city streets. Revelers stood shoulder to shoulder and smaller crowds gathered in front of shops and down alleys to get their fortunes told, eat food, or watch one of the many forms of entertainment. There were minstrels, poets, fire jugglers and magicians along the roadways. The city guards walked the streets making their presence known, but movement was difficult as festival celebrants walked shoulder to shoulder. The bars were full, and the ale and mulled wine barrels flowed freely. The tavern owners had learned long ago to store up for the annual celebration and when to add water to their barrels to stretch their contents.

The Inns were full, so several travelers had taken to putting up tents on the streets for lodging. The street vendors stayed open through the night, and business was almost as good as it was in the daytime hours. Bittles Tavern was one of the biggest in Abbodar and easy to find. Inside was a massive hall that included three fireplaces and two long bars with several barmaids. When Gafney and his company pushed their way through the front door of Bittles Tavern in the waning hours of the evening, they were greeted with the smell of pipe smoke. Ignored by the patrons scattered around tables throughout the room, Ginzer and Bernard headed for the bar. Gafney surveyed the room carefully before joining them along with Choppa and Drew. "Is it too late to order a meal?" asked Ginzer, squinting through his good eye.

The lady behind the bar responded in friendly tone, "The cook has gone to bed, but I can see if there be anything left in the back if ye like." Her smile along with her eyes seemed to light up the moment after a long day of pushing through the crowds on the city streets. "And in the meantime, can I get ye something to drink if ye like?"

"Aye, you can bring us some ale, missy," said Bernard with a wry smile. Ginzer snickered beneath his breath, recognizing that his cousin was trying to charm the lady. "Are all the tavern maids as pretty as you are?" The lady behind the bar returned the compliment with a smile and a slight blush. "Is there any chance I can get into that kitchen of yours and make my friends a meal? We would be happy to pay for it."

Bernard observed the softness of her skin and the twinkle in her eyes. Her hair was streaked with subtle hints of gray and braided with colorful cords on one side. He guessed she was not much younger than he.

"Well I guess there would be no harm in it. Me boss has gone to bed, and besides, ye seem harmless enough," replied the lady with a wink.

"As long as you don't let him in the kitchen," muttered Ginzer softly.

The tavern maid produced several mugs and lined them up on the bar, then she began filling them with a dark colored ale from a large stone pitcher. "This will be a first for me," said the maid. "I've never seen a man in the kitchen before. Are ye sure ye can cook?"

"I wouldn't hold your breath on that one," taunted Ginzer. Then he warned, "Be careful that you don't get in his way, or he'll run you over."

Bernard ignored his cousin's taunting and smiled graciously at the lady behind the bar, then he asked, "And what is your name, lovely lady?"

"Me name is Patti, and what be yer name?"

"Bernard of the mountain dwarves at your service, my lady." He bowed to her as he said the words.

Patti smiled, appearing to enjoy the attention. "Well then, come with me." Patti motioned toward the kitchen, and Bernard shuffled around the counter to follow close behind her.

Bernard grabbed a handful of herbs sitting on the shelf, and as he buried his nose in the fragrance they offered, he said with a deep sigh, "Beautiful and perfect in every way. I've been too long on a ship, and it's been some time since I've smelled such freshness."

"So ye are a sailor, are ye?"

Bernard nodded. "A fisherman, if you please. I once commanded one of the finest battalions of dwarves that ever set foot on a battlefield, but now in my latter years, I have settled for fishing the open sea."

"We see few of your race in these parts, and even fewer fisherman come this far inland. But I must say, I have heard stories of men from the sea. I hear yer a hard lot to settle down."

"Well, well," replied Bernard as he tried to hold back a smile. "I haven't been at sea long enough to fall in love with it, but if I was to settle down somewhere, it would be for love."

Patti blushed and turned slightly away, "I thought ye wanted to cook some food for yer friends, or did ye get me back here to propose to me?"

"I wouldn't be foolish enough to propose until you had a chance to taste my cooking."

"Well then. Yer cooking must be something."

Bernard worked diligently to put together a meal of lamb, potatoes and fresh vegetables he had harvested by moonlight from the garden out back. The venture began with Patti helping him, but that was short-lived, for as most eventually came to discover, cooking with Bernard was more an exercise of survival than collaboration. Everything had to be done according to his requirements, or he was sure to be fussing like a mother hen over her chicks. Only in this case, it was the way the food was prepared. Patti made a strong attempt to appease the old dwarf, but she soon realized that it was a hopeless effort on her part. She eventually lost her patience and mumbled something about it being a waste of her time, so she headed back out to the customers in the main room.

When he had finished cooking the meal, Bernard managed to coax Patti back into the kitchen to help him serve the food.

Gafney didn't wait for an invitation. He sliced off a large piece of meat with his own knife. Ignoring the serving utensils, he used his hands to grab some vegetables and potatoes and piled them on his plate. Choppa reached in quickly for his own serving, fearing he might be left without. Once their plates were full the talking ceased, and they devoured the meal like a pack of hungry wolves.

One of the younger girls working behind the counter brought out a fresh flask of ale while Patti wiped down the counter and continued to shovel food onto their plates when there was any evidence of available space. She took notice of the leather covering the weapon strapped to Gafney's back. If it was meant to disguise the weapon, it was not working. She could tell it was an axe by the shape of it. "Tell me," asked the tavern maid, "have ye heard the stories on the street of the man who defeated the Raven?"

Gafney didn't flinch at the question, but Drew paused from his shoveling of food and glanced at the members of his party, expecting someone to offer a response. After a brief moment, he stabbed a piece of meat and stuffed it into his mouth.

"It seems the man was a foreigner, and he single-handedly defeated two of the Ravens with his axe."

"Three," Drew put in as Gafney shot him a furrowed glance. "I mean, that's what I heard."

"Yer clearly not from around here," Patti wiped the table in front of Gafney and stopped suddenly, staring straight at the Gap Warrior. "Might ye be the man who defeated the Ravens with the axe on yer back?"

"I passed several men carrying axes on my way into the city. It could have been any one of them."

"Aye, but I don't think it was." Patti's smile was barely perceivable. She wasn't going to move until she got a response.

His companions had stopped eating and starred at Gafney with their food-covered faces, waiting for his response. The burly Gap Warrior smiled and shoved a large slice of lamb into his mouth and bit down on it, causing juice to dribble down his cheek, then he began to talk through the chewing. "Well, Patti-behind-the-bar, why is it you are so curious about the business of complete strangers?"

Patti leaned closer and whispered, "Very few men have defeated the likes of the Ravens. They don't go down easily. The warrior I am speaking of took down three of them with the help of just a few men. That's something to be celebrated. Men have traveled here from far away to face the Ravens in the arena. Most of them will die, and the ones who survive are never the same. But the man we speak of, he could defeat them. He has defeated them. If I should ever meet him, I would be honored to buy him a drink."

"Well miss Patti, you may meet him someday, and if you do, please, tell him something for me. Tell him to watch his back. He would not be welcome in a place like this where these so called

241

Ravens are treated as gods."

"I understand yer concern. Believe me, I do, but not everyone in this realm favors the Ravens, especially those who have suffered loss to the edge of their blades." Patti paused to look around the room as if to see who was listening and then leaned in again. "Me own son was struck down by one of the red ones. He didn't have a chance. He was young and inexperienced, but they wanted to make an example of him. So now maybe ye understand why I might be interested."

Gafney's face softened along with his tone. "My sympathies for your loss, miss Patti. The heart never recovers from that kind of tragedy."

"Please sir, may I see the blade that defeated the raven demons?"

The Gap warrior stood up and walked toward the kitchen without speaking a word. When Patti entered the door behind him, Gafney was loosening the leather twine that held the cover over the axe. "I don't know that it will do you any good, but on behalf of your son, I cannot refuse your request."

The tavern maid stepped closer to see the blade. Tears began to roll down her cheeks, and she shuddered gently. Gafney put his powerful arms around Patti's shoulders and comforted her. "I am sorry for your loss. I hope this brings you some solace or sense of justice in some small way."

Patti laid her head into the Gap Warrior's consoling shoulder for a brief moment, and then she looked back at the blade. That's when she saw what she had missed before, the eagle that was etched into the silver near the handle. Reaching out slowly, she caressed the pattern with her fingertips. "I have seen this before, the eagle. What is its meaning?"

"It is a symbol of the One Faith," responded Gafney softly. By now the others, Drew, Choppa, Ginzer and Bernard had entered the kitchen and looked on in silence. "It is a reminder to me that the way things are in this world is not the way it is supposed to be. Mothers are not supposed to lose their sons, nor men their wives." Gafney glanced toward Drew. "Or children their parents."

"There is another who bears the same image of the eagle on the sword he carries," said Patti, still touching the etching. "He, along with a small company, arrived earlier today, they shared a meal together and rented two rooms for the night."

"Bixby. Is his name Bixby?" pressed the Gap Warrior hopefully.

Before Patti could respond, another voice came from a man standing in the shadows of the wine barrels stacked near the back entrance. "The sword she speaks of is in my care."

Gafney strained to see the one that was speaking, realizing that it was not the voice of his friend Bixby and at the same time feeling a pang of disappointment. "Come out of the shadows," commanded the Gap Warrior as he reached for his axe on the table. "Show us your face."

"You will not need that," said the man in the corner as he stepped into the light where all could see him. "I believe we are here for the same purpose."

Choppa said, "I know you, but I can't remember from where. But I know that I have met you before."

"You know me Choppa, and so do you, Gap Warrior." The man before them spoke with an air of assurance. "We fought together side by side in the Last battle of Talinor against the shadow wraiths and the horde of Boogara." The man paused to let his words sink in. "I am Gerrid, former commander of the Tal army."

CHAPTER 30

"There is no point in seeking them out when they will come to us," argued Vanus. "Tomorrow the arena games begin and our final event of the day is the burning of the witch Lena on the pyre. Surely they will come to save their precious Intercessor," Vanus smiled, "and we will be ready for them."

The warlock pushed back the rage that was rising inside of him against Vanus for insisting on letting the Gap Warriors come unheeded to Abbodar. Through gritted teeth he responded, "We know not how many there are, and you have no idea what they are capable of."

"That is correct," Vanus sat down on his father's throne, caressing the gold covered arms beneath his palms. "I do not know what they are capable of. That is exactly why I want them to come and why I want to see them fight. I want to see their magic, and what better place to see it than in the arena?"

"There are three Ravens dead at the hands of Gap Warriors," spewed Relnik. "Has that ever happened before? Of course not."

"What are you afraid of, warlock? There are only a few of them. They cannot possibly stand against the palace guard and the Red Ravens."

The warlock hesitated to say it because he knew that Vanus would not understand it. How could he? These matters were foreign to him. He only knew of the shadow magic. He knew nothing of the magic of the light. But he would try to convince him, nonetheless. "I'll tell you what I am afraid of. I am afraid of what can happen when you get Gap Warriors in the same place as Intercessors, and there are two of them in your stables, Lena and her protector, the one called Jef. It is never a good thing when there are two Intercessors together where they can come into accordance with one another."

"Are they not together now?" argued the king's son. "Where is all the magic you speak of if they are so dangerous together?"

"They are not together. I had them separated as soon as I realized they were in the same holding pen."

Vanus snickered.

"It seems to me that this is all a game to you."

"Magic is magic. It's all the same. The difference lies in who has the power. And we, my friend, have the power." Vanus smiled and held out his hands in display of all that surrounded them. "Do you deny that we have the power, warlock, or maybe your power is not as great as you have led me to believe? Is that what causes you to fear?"

The pride in Drok Relnik exploded in a torrent of anger. "Power is not the only factor in this battle. Even the most powerful can fall. Talinor was an insect compared to Boogara, and yet Talinor defeated them. There are elements at play here that cannot be ignored, and in these matters, I have a greater understanding." The warlock knew the minute the words left his mouth that he had overstepped his bounds.

Vanus rose slowly from the dais in a kingly manor. "And how many other wars have you lost my friend?"

There was an ominous silence between them until Vanus broke it. "Because I have never lost a one. So tell me, how is it that you know more in these matters than me?"

Drok Relnik knew that his next words should be measured carefully. He also knew that he was not getting through to Vanus. And besides, they were both right. Power was at play here, but so was strategy. The warlock was not about to acquiesce to the notion that the Gap Warriors and the Intercessors had the greater power. He pressed forward. "You are correct. Forgive me for my zealous outburst of ignorance. You understand power and how to wield it much better than I," Drok Relnik lied. "Might I make a suggestion that I believe would be in the best interest of the kingdom?"

"Of course. After all, it is one of your functions to give council to the king's son."

"The other Intercessor, Jef, has already requested permission to champion Lena in the area. As soon as the opening ceremonies on the morrow are complete, let him fight one of the Red Ravens. The sooner we are rid of him, the better. Then at the end of the day you can burn the lady. Have you any idea of his

"He is a warrior, but he has not battled for a long time. I believe he is no threat to any of the Ravens."

"That's unfortunate. The crowd will surely be disappointed if it ends too quickly. No matter. I will instruct the Raven that Haggron picks for this contest to toy with him a little before the kill. It will give them something to cheer about."

A dreadful cloud of loneliness covered him, weighing heavily on his heart. He tried to ignore its taunting, but he could not shake it. After walking for hours through a city that had turned out to be much bigger than Cyle could have imagined, he found himself questioning the decision he had made to leave the others. He replayed the clash with his Guardian over and over again in his mind. Each time he replayed Mellidar's scarring blow that struck him above his eye, the throbbing from the pain increased. He was alone now, and he didn't like the ache this caused inside. The irony was even if he found his grandmother, he knew that she would scold him for his defiance and disrespect toward Mellidar. That didn't matter now. What did matter was getting to the arena and finding a way to save her.

He could tell he was nearing the heart of the city when he heard the muffled sounds of people in the distance. His bones ached from the day's journey, but his walking would soon come to an end, and then he would have to come up with a plan to free his grandmother. When he impulsively ran for the city, he had not taken that into consideration. He wished Choppa were here to help him. He couldn't remember the last time he was without his friend who had proven to be so resourceful in situations like this. If Choppa were here, he would help him think of something.

The avenue he walked was silent and dark. The lamps that

lined the streets provided just enough light to help him find his way. Earlier in the day when he had stopped to get directions, he had heard stories about the killing of the Ravens by a crazed axe-wielding foreigner. He also heard rumors of a witch named Lena that had been arrested and tried for using magic. "How in the world did she end up here?" he wondered out loud.

"Who are you talking to?" The voice from the shadows startled him. Three figures stepped from the shadows.

Cyle glanced about and saw several others on all sides standing beyond the light of the street lamps. He felt his heart pounding in his chest and tried to calm it. "I want no trouble. I'm just passing through." He felt a slight quiver in his voice and hoped they hadn't noticed.

"You travel alone, do you?" said the tall one in the middle of the three. He was clearly the leader. His dirty blond hair hung shoulder length, and dangling from his right ear was a feathered earring. He was taller than Cyle but slightly thicker and probably about the same age or a little older.

Before Cyle could respond, the heavyset, boyish looking one on the left said, "You'll have to pay a toll to pass this way."

"Quiet, Langer," warned the leader with a stern glance. "He's right. You have any coins? No one passes unless they pay."

Cyle's heart had calmed, and this time the words came out smoothly. "And what if I don't have coin to pay my way?"

"Then you will have to fight me," said the leader as he placed his hands on the two crescent shaped swords strapped to his side. "That's how it works around here once the sun goes down. Street hounds rule the streets. No matter which route you choose from here, you will either have to pay or fight."

The shaggy-haired man's tone had changed from nice to tough. He had to put on a show for his street tribe to maintain his position of respect. Cyle knew how this worked. They had street gangs even in Talinor, although most of them were harmless. "What happens if I win?" asked Cyle.

"You can pass, or you get control of the street hounds you

see around you. We have laws here like everywhere else, and that's just how it is."

Cyle didn't want to fight the guy, but if it came to that, he was confident he would beat him. He had no desire to humiliate him in front of his gang. "Can I talk to you alone?" asked Cyle politely.

The leader nodded to the two standing by his side, and they backed away out of earshot. "I can see that you have the respect of your men, and that is very important for someone in your position. But are you willing to risk losing that respect over a few coins?"

"What makes you think I'm going to lose any respect here?" said the shaggy-haired man in a taunting voice. "I've fought and won this fight more times than I can remember, but I must admit I have never fought anyone with a staff." The leader smiled, pulling the two short crescent swords from the belt around his waste to hold them in the ready position. "These belonged to the last man I fought, much more impressive than a staff I must say. When I kill you, I'll not be taking your weapon with me."

Cyle stepped closer to the leader, and he lifted his swords to defend himself. Now face-to-face, the Gap Warrior spoke softly so no one else could hear him. "I did not come here to embarrass you, but that is exactly what is about to happen. If there is any way you can see around this, take it now because you are about to lose your position of power."

"You have wasted enough of my time. Step back and prepare yourself."

Cyle took three very slow steps backward. Dropped his travel pack on the ground and shook his head in regret. "Your name?"

"They call me Blades of the Northern Hounds, and you?"

"I am Cyle," pausing, he looked Blades in the eyes, "of the Gap Warriors."

Blades shuddered. He had not suspected this harmless looking boy before him to be of warrior blood.

"You can't say I didn't try to warn you, but I should have known it would come to this. You remind me too much of someone I know."

"And who might that be?"

"Me."

The leader of the street hounds charged at Cyle with his crescent swords glinting and slashing out in deathly intent, but Cyle smoothly stepped to the side, deflecting the blows. Blades lunged again at the Gap Warrior several times, and with each assault, Cyle mounted a successful defense. He was impressed with the street hound's skills, and he could see how Blades had maintained his rightful position as leader of this gang. The next strike brought a cutlass whizzing past Cyle's cheek. A hearty cheer rose from the street hounds. They were now gathered in a surrounding circle about the fight. The commotion brought lights on in the windows up and down the avenue, and the people peered out like gutter rats from their windows.

Anger was rising in Blades as he lashed another vicious assault, driving Cyle backward against a building. Until now, Cyle had not made an offensive move, and it was not a mistake. He could see that his foe was losing energy. His attacker pause briefly to catch his breath, and that's when the Gap Warrior made his move. First he lashed out in a wide arch with his staff, forcing his opponent to step back. Then he turned his back to his assailant and vaulted with his staff while running upwards on the wall behind him. With his hand at the top of the staff and his feet firmly planted on the wall, he pushed off, soared high and landed behind the street hound, still facing in the other direction. Before the hound could turn around, Cyle slammed his staff upward into his crotch. The crowd erupted in a collective groan, and the one receiving the blow echoed the same as his quivering body plopped to its knees. Cyle quickly slashed out with his staff, knocking the two swords from his hands, then jumped behind Blades and brought his staff to a strangle-hold around the leader's neck.

"It's over," warned Cyle. "No one dies today."

"What will it be then, passage or position?" Blades grunted against the pressure of the staff on his throat.

At first Cyle only wanted to pass, but now a new possibility was forming in his mind. "I'll take position." Blades groaned despondently.

Cyle heard movement all around him. He released the staff from Blade's throat and looked up to see several street hounds, male and female ranging from ten to nineteen years of age. They were holding their weapons, mostly slings, above their heads and bowing to one knee. Softly, in a whisper they began to chant in unison, "Timo, timo, timo…"

"What does it mean?" asked Cyle.

"Honor." The former leader picked up his swords, stood to his feet and held out his weapons to Cyle. "They are yours now." Blades paused, and for the first time Cyle saw humility in his eyes. "You have my timo as well."

"Keep your weapons. You're going to need them." Cyle pushed the swords back towards Blades. "You are a worthy opponent, better than I had imagined."

Cyle felt an eerie shift in the atmosphere around him, and then a subtle tingling sensation buzzed beneath his palm holding the staff. He glanced down at his weapon to see if it would tell him something. When he looked up, Blades was looking past him and backing up slowly, his eyes widening. When he turned around, he saw what it was—at least three black Ravens standing silently, almost invisible against the shadows. The street hounds had disappeared into the darkness, leaving Cyle and Blades behind. The two of them turned to retreat in the opposite direction as three more Ravens emerged on the opposite side, blocking any hope of escape.

"Looks like I won't be keeping these after all," said Blades as he laid down his swords.

Cyle held his staff steady with both of his hands and positioned his stance, preparing to strike.

"What are you doing?" warned Blades. "Look beyond."

Then the Gap Warrior saw it. Several more men were standing behind the Ravens. Cyle gritted his teeth. The rising burn of fury tried to take over, but he would not let it. He let go of his staff. It dropped to the cobbled road beneath his feet and bounced before it settled still.

"That was a wise decision," said the voice.

It sounded familiar, but Cyle couldn't quite place it.

"I've been waiting for you." The voice spoke again.

Then Cyle recognized it. "Drok Relnik." Anger washed over him.

"I have plans for you, Gap Warrior," seethed the warlock. "Bind them and take their weapons."

CHAPTER 31

"Where is the little one?" thundered Hutch as he rushed into the room, stirring a cloud of dust where the other stone giants had gathered to eat their evening meal. They frowned at Hutch and covered their meals with their rugged hands.

Boulder, the leader of the clan, responded, "We thought she was with you, Brother."

Hutch turned and ran back into the passageway he had just come through. When he reached the light outside, he quickly scanned the treeline. Nothing. The giant moved across the open ground in front of the old temple and yelled out in a booming voice, "Sera!" Then he listened, but all he could hear was the wind in the trees and the pounding of his anxious heart.

Boulder and two other stone giants emerged behind him to offer their help. Then the giant saw something move deep within the cover of the forest. A shadow passing among the trees caused Hutch to freeze. He turned to Boulder. "Get the others," he ordered, then he turned back to face the forest as Boulder disappeared into the temple ruins.

Hutch was sure he heard the sound of muffled laughter coming out of the forest. "Witches," he muttered under his breath. By now, the rest of the stone giants had emerged from the temple and stood behind Hutch, looking in the same direction.

"It does sound of witches," whispered Boulder as he and the others stepped backward slowly. Stone giants had an intense fear of any form of magic, especially witches and warlocks.

Something moved toward them from within the shadows. The bushes parted, and into the clearing a giant wolf appeared. Atop its back sat an elf girl unfamiliar to them. Walking was another girl with blond hair. Then another head popped out from behind the girl sitting on the wolf. It was Sera. Both of them slipped down to the ground, and Sera took the other elf girl's hand and skipped along by her side.

"This is my cousin," screeched Sera. "Her name is Tryska, and she's a Gap Warrior. These are her friends, Keesha," Sera pointed to the wolf, "and Addie."

Tryska bowed before the clan of refugee stone giants, and Addie waved. "I've always wanted to meet a stone giant," said Tryska through a big smile and bright eyes. "Which one of you is Hutch?"

"I am Stone Hutch," said the giant awkwardly.

Tryska unstrapped a large leather carrier from her back. Sera jumped up and down, giggling, and clapped her hands as her cousin unwrapped it. Tryska slowly pulled something large from the case. She walked over to Hutch and handed him a large cudgel almost too heavy for her to carry. The top was inlaid with dark black stone, and at the handle was an etching of an eagle in flight just above the grip. Tryska struggled to hold it out to the giant who was watching with a look of surprise on his face.

"Do you recognize this?" asked Tryska smiling.

"I do."

"I deliver it to you on behalf of the Lady Sharianna and the Guardian Atmos. You know them both." The elf girl held it forth, straining against the weight to lift it upward. Hutch grabbed the cudgel with both hands, and a spark flared beneath his palms. Then a surge of energy swept through his whole body that sent him backward to the ground. When he landed, the whole forest seemed to shake. His giant friends ran to him for fear he had died.

Hutch stirred slightly and slowly sat up.

"I probably should have warned you about the falling down part, but it wouldn't have changed anything," said Tryska, kneeling next to Hutch. "Now it is time for you to go. The others will be needing you. As for the rest of us, we need to prepare for their return." Tryska stood as Keesha walked next to her and began licking her cheek. "Yes, you too, girl."

They had talked all through the night. After several passionate outbursts, followed by disagreements, the newly formed company was still unable to come up with a plan to rescue the Remnant—at least a not plan that they could all agree on. They sat in the pub late into the early hours of the morning after the other patrons had left. Gafney was annoyed the whole time because he was concerned about Cyle and his safety.

Of all the ideas put forth, Packer's seemed to make the best sense. There were catacombs beneath the city that could provide a way of escape. Dallien was the most familiar with the passageways because, when he was younger, the Remnant would gather there for their worship meetings. There were several challenges with the plan. There was no light in the tunnels, so they would need to get torches. Also, the tunnels had been closed for years with all the exits barred or sealed with stone. However, it made the most sense, since there was an entry point that connected to the dungeons, and the dungeons were linked to the arena. Gerrid knew his way around the dungeons because they he had been his home for the last two years.

"Inside and out is our best hope," Gerrid had told them when the night was almost over. "As the afternoon of the first day draws near, our time will run short. We will have to get them out through the dungeons. They always decrease the number of guards inside during the games, so they can use them to patrol the festivities and the arena. It will give us a slight advantage."

Most of them would attend the games as spectators, but they would not be able to bring their own weapons into the arena. While Packer and Choppa explored potential routes of escape from the outside, Gafney and Gerrid would enter the tournament as warriors. This allowed them to get on the inside where the Remnant was being held. Drew was tasked to find a high point above the area in case they needed his bow. Tomorrow was the first day of the tournament games, and there would be mostly parades and celebrations for the better part of the day. Then late in the afternoon, competitions would begin immediately following Lena's sacrifice at the stake. They would need to find a way to get her and the Remnant out before they took her into the arena.

Just before dawn, Gerrid walked out near the garden at the back of the Tavern. The sun had not yet cleared the horizon, and there was still a slight chill in the fall air. The prophet pulled his thin overcoat close to him and crossed his arms to warm himself as he rocked back and forth from left foot to right foot.

"It's time for me to go," whispered a voice.

Gerrid turned to face what he thought was a look of sadness on Bryann's face. He glanced at the ground to gather his thoughts. "I understand. I'm surprised you stayed this long." Gerrid moved closer to her. "Where will you go?"

The two of them gazed briefly into each other's eyes until it became uncomfortable. Then Bryann looked away, not wanting to be drawn in by those same captivating eyes she once rescued. "I don't know. I'll figure that out after I get moving."

Gerrid felt deeply for Bryann, and yet he found himself pushing down his feelings for her. She was from a different world than him, and he knew so little about her. Bryann was both wild, yet also tender and still. After the time they had shared together, she was as much a mystery as the day he had met her. He had experienced both sides, and he was surprised how much that drew him to her. He felt the urge to convince her to stay, to fight for her, but he was of the mindset that people need to make up their own minds about love and life.

"There is hope for your heart," said the prophet, surprised he had spoken the words.

Bryann looked back at him with a confused expression, then responded, "If you knew the path I've followed, you would not say that." Then she looked at the ground and felt a great sadness in her heart.

"I know you have little interest in the One Faith that I follow, but I had hoped to have more time to tell you about it. The moment never seemed to come." Gerrid paused and took another step closer. "We all have traveled paths that bring us shame, and I can see the sorrow in your eyes from that journey. There is another path, a path you were made to follow. You just don't know it yet. I pray that some day you will find it. Because, if you do, you will not only find love, you will find the path your heart was made to follow." Even as Gerrid spoke the words, he knew he carried doubt about his own journey. Despite this, a deeper faith he hadn't known was there had pushed the words to the surface, and it stirred him as he spoke.

Bryann wanted to believe it, but all she could think about was running. Something about this was terrifying her. She could feel the pounding of her heart wanting to explode through her chest.

The unseen shadow fairies danced about the corners of her thoughts taunting her. *You are pathetic to think that someone like him would ever love you. If he knew of your past, it would be over. Walk away while you can and save yourself the embarrassment.*

"I have to go," Bryann turned to walk away.

Gerrid reached out, taking hold of her arms and pulled her

back to him. "First I need to say goodbye." Leaning forward he gently kissed her trembling lips. She felt the world begin to melt away. Softly at first and then with greater intensity the kiss filled with passion and his arms wrapped around her tightly. Slowly she started to surrender to something she had never felt before in her whole life, the feeling of being cared for and the indescribable passion of love without harmful intent.

Then the voices in her head started again, and she abruptly pulled away from Gerrid. He saw the fear in her eyes as she put her hand to her own lips as if to try to feel the kiss with her fingers. Then her countenance changed into a frown. "No, don't do that. Don't ever do that again." Then she turned and walked toward the path in the distance.

"She's not going to forget that," said Dallien, stepping from the shadows and sporting a wily grin.

Gerrid smiled at his friend, then turned to watch Bryann fade into the shadows of the early morning dawn. The ache in his heart was unbearable as a familiar feeling of loneliness encroached.

Lena had begged Jef not to fight on her behalf, but he insisted. "I am still a man of honor and a warrior," he had told her, "and I could never forgive myself if I did any less than stand for you."

She had wept throughout the night, travailing in prayer until the morning sun filtered through the bars in the holding pen. Her new friend Pamela had stayed awake with her until morning, trying her best to bring comfort.

"Rest now," urged Pamela. "You are growing weak. You must sleep."

"I cannot rest now, Pamela, and besides, I pray stronger when I am weak." Lena stood and walked to the bars separating her from the rest of the Remnant still sleeping. "Wake up," prodded Lena. "It's time to rise and battle the darkness."

Santor was the first to stir, then he began to rouse the

others from their slumber. Wiping the sleep from their eyes, the Remnant slowly gathered at the bars where Lena was waiting.

"Listen to me dear ones," whispered Lena as loud as she could. She scanned the area where the guards were standing near the door. "We know not what the day holds for us. Whether it is to be life or death, we must face it fiercely and on our knees."

Kevis pressed his way into Lena's view. "It is too late for prayer, Woman," scoffed the Remnant elder. "We have prayed, and for what? To end like this? It has accomplished us nothing." Kevis turned away, expecting the others to follow him.

"Go ahead and walk away, elder," chided Lena. "Do you know all there is of prayer that you would instruct us? Do not speak as if it is something you understand. You stopped praying long ago. That has brought your undoing. Do not impose it on the rest of us."

"What you say is true, Intercessor," seethed Kevis. "I stopped praying long ago when the well ran dry, when we lost our homes, and when we were sacrificed at the stake. Stop wasting our time with false hope that leads to nothing."

"They will come," squeaked a small voice. "I know it. The Gap Warriors will come." The voice belonged to little Barrand with eyes full of hope as he pressed his way into view.

Kevis scowled and walked away.

"If anyone else wants to leave, now is the time. There is no room here for doubt. Only faith is allowed," exhorted Lena, pausing to scan the crowd. The group was silent, and one by one they began bending down to a kneeling position.

"Well then, teach us to pray, Intercessor," said Pamela with delight as she too knelt next to Lena.

"Come to us, Spirit Wind," prayed Lena. "We await your leading."

The guards had moved outside to watch the beginning of the festivities. Inside the air grew still, and time seemed to halt. Even the children were silent. A gentle breeze wafted through the barred windows and flowed across the kneeling Remnant.

Santor the elder began to tremble slightly, and Pamela felt an indescribable wash of violence rising within her as tears flowed freely down her cheeks. The others in the group quivered as they sensed the rising tumult of a fierce emotion pressing upon them, and they began to fear.

"What do we do? We are afraid," said Pamela.

"Fear not, dear ones," comforted Lena as she looked above the kneeling Remnant. She beheld a vision that their eyes could not see. A realm filled with a host of Guardians and Gap Warriors stood poised to battle the dark spirits of the void. The shadowed ones faced them in defiance, ready to hold them back.

One of the Gap Warriors clothed in translucent armor holding a gossamer sword looked at her and smiled, then she nodded at Lena.

"It is time to sing." Lena gripped the bars in front her. "I will teach you." Then she began to sing,

> "We exalt the one who stands high
> above all else.
> Hope of all hopes. He holds the ages
> within His hands.
> Be exalted, oh Ancient of Days.
> Be exalted above the sphere of man."

The Remnant joined Lena in singing a song they thought they had forgotten long ago. As their voices penetrated the boundary between flesh and spirit, a wave of fear and trembling roared through the shadowed ranks of dark warriors. Some of the lesser ones took to flight. Repulsed by the cowardice of the fleeing ones, the stronger ones struck them down.

That moment was abruptly interrupted by the sound of a horn rending the darkness. A flood of light shot from among the company of the warriors of the Gap. Two familiar figures emerged from among their ranks to position themselves at the front. Lena smiled. It was the Gap Warriors, Tryska, the elf girl, and Bixby, the knight.

They charged into the fray. The others followed, igniting a clash of weapons that echoed through the void, sending shards of light spraying in all directions. The scene slowly faded from Lena's view and she was back, looking at the kneeling Remnant before her. They continued singing, yet they were oblivious to what was going on in the world of the spirit. "You have done well," smiled Lena.

Pamela said, "Teach us more, Intercessor."

And she did.

CHAPTER 32

Vanus, the king's son, stood in his father's position on the royal balcony looking out at the arena. The restless sounds of the throng vibrated through the stadium in anticipation of what was about to unfold. To the right of Vanus was Drok Relnik, and to his left stood Haggron, the leader of the Red Ravens. Behind Haggron three more Red Ravens stood statue-like, staring straight ahead, their faces covered by the leather battle masks. Vanus was dressed mostly in white with a dark blue sash emblazoned with the symbol of Abbodar, an eye with a star in the pupil. The king's son feigned an adoring smile to the stadium crowd and, as they chanted his name in unison, it echoed off of the stonewalls of the arena.

Vanus held up his right hand, and the crowd grew silent. "May the gods of Terashom have favor on us today."

More cheers erupted. As hands were lifted to the sky in praise, the king's son waited patiently for the multitude to still. "Good people of Abbodar, I have an announcement to make," Vanus paused for effect. "The king and our forces have conquered Boogara."

Applause filled the arena and thundered off the walls. When it subsided, Vanus continued, "The king will return to join us before the end of the games to celebrate his victory."

After the cheers faded, Vanus motioned in the direction of the holding pens. Two husky men pulled barred doors open, and four Kidiri warriors walked out to the center of the arena. The crowd was mostly non-responsive. Then from another entrance, two Black Ravens entered the arena carrying a long sword in each hand and short sword in the other. The crowd thundered in applause.

The two Ravens who were clothed in black leather with matching black metal armor covering their chest, legs and parts of their arms, moved to face the four Kidiri warriors. The Kidiri were mercenaries from a nomadic tribe, born and bred for battle from infancy. Their attire was that of animal furs made of rough hides. Two of them carried short swords in one hand and a trident spear in the other. The other two Kidiri held crescent-shaped swords.

Without any introduction, Vanus reached into a large vase of red flowers and pulled one to hold it briefly before him, then he tossed it into the arena.

The frenzied cheers of the crowd drowned out the clashing ring of blades from the arena. The Kidiri attacked with reckless abandon, driving into the two Black Ravens who held their ground in response. First blood had been spilled, bringing the crowd to their feet in a frenzy of screams and cheers. The battle intensified before the first Kidiri fell from a swipe to his midsection. The second Kidiri toppled moments later as his head rolled across the dirt, leaving a path of blood in its wake.

The games had begun, and the taste for blood was in the air. Three more bouts were waged, pitting warriors from other lands against each another in one-on-one combat. One of the fights lasted several minutes, while the other two ended after a few strikes. The crowds roared after each bout as the lifeless bodies of the fallen warriors were quickly removed from the field, some dragged on the ground and others carried on stretchers to the death rooms.

Suddenly Vanus stood from his chair and held up his hand to silence the crowd. More movement from the walls of the stadium as workers carried a stake and bundles of wood to the area in front of the king's balcony. Through the doors of the holding pens two warriors escorted Lena, whose hands were bound with cords behind her back. Once they reached the stake, they bound her to it facing Vanus.

"Behold the witch, Lena of Talinor! She practices magic without the blessing of Terashom," announced the king's son.

Jeers swept the crowd. Vanus held up his hand until they silenced, then he motioned to one of his servants near him. Soon Cyle, bound at the wrists, was standing next to him, accompanied by two guards.

Cyle looked toward the arena and saw his grandmother at the stake. Struggling to pull away from the guards holding him, Cyle shot a piercing glance in the warlock's direction.

Drok Relnik smiled wickedly at the young Gap Warrior before speaking, "I thought you might enjoy the opening ceremonies."

Rage swelled in Cyle. He looked to his grandmother, and their eyes met. It was hard to read her face from that distance, but he felt a desperation in her eyes he had never felt before. Tears threatened to fill the corners of his own eyes, and his body trembled. His thoughts flashed back to something Mellidar had said to him. "The way of the Gap Warrior is not always an easy one. If you choose to trust the fear in you, then that fear will be your master. If you choose to trust the Ancient of Days, then you will be mastered by the one who rules all."

Fear enveloped him, and there was nothing Cyle could do about it. Maybe if he had listened to the Guardian in the first place, he would not be in this situation. Maybe he could help his grandmother. He had let fear take charge, and now he was regretting it.

Drok Relnik leaned into Cyle and said, "When your friends show up, we will have you as leverage, but first you can watch your grandmother burn at the stake."

Rage swelled in the Gap Warrior, and he struggled against the bonds that held him. More movement below brought Cyle's attention back to the arena floor. A man in armor was being escorted to stand in front of king's balcony. He didn't know who he was at first, then Cyle recognized him. It was Jef, his grandmother's friend and a former Tal warrior.

"Who will champion the witches cause?" shouted the announcer standing near Vanus.

"I will." Jef raised his sword slightly as he spoke.

"Then let it be so," said the speaker. "According to the rules of our land, if you should win the battle, the witch will go free."

The speaker looked over to Vanus who nodded back, then he continued, "Who will stand in the name of the king and for Abbodar?"

Haggron the leader of the Ravens nodded and pointed to one of the doors in the side of the coliseum floor. A Raven dressed in black appeared and walked into battle position.

A black one, thought Cyle. So there is yet hope.

"Please Jef," pleaded Lena. "Don't do this."

Jef looked at Lena and said calmly, "It is our only chance, my lady. Please bless me as I have decided."

Tears filled the Intercessors eyes and her body shuddered. She bowed her head and then jerked it back up when the crowd roared at the sound of metal swords colliding. The black Raven pressed his attack. Jef defended each blow, but he felt clumsy and out of practice. The power of the black one's blade stung his wrists each time their swords connected. Jef could not see the warrior's face through his leather mask, making it difficult to see the expressions that often come right before an attacking thrust. This made it difficult to anticipate the coming strikes. It wasn't long before the former Tal warrior realized that unless something happened to give him an advantage, he would lose.

SWORD OF DELIVERANCE

With his strength draining rapidly, he knew that his skills would not be enough to make up for it. It had been a long time since he had practiced with a sword and guessed that the Raven was just toying with him. The crowd began to boo when they realized what the Raven was doing. Thumbs were pointed downward all over the stands. Calls for death could be heard through jumbled shouts.

The Raven landed a vicious kick to Jef's midsection sending him to the dirt.

"Please take me instead," pleaded Lena. "Leave him. Take me."

Cyle struggled helplessly to get free from his captors. A swift elbow to his side put a stop to his effort.

Jef heard Lena's pleading through the noise of the crowd. His heart faltered as he realized he could not save her. A clouded picture formed before his eyes. Three warriors of light carrying weapons and clothed in battle armor moved toward him.

The one standing in the middle held a flute, and she spoke to him. "We are here to take you home, dear warrior. Your time here is done. Fear not, you have served well."

The Raven warrior raised his sword and brought it down one final time with the full force of his might. Jef breathed his last breath and fell to the ground. Lena turned away and began to weep deep sobs that wretched from her stomach. Cyle fought back the tears, mostly for the pain that he knew his grandmother was feeling. Relnik smiled as he watched the grief unfold before him. Vanus showed no emotion, but inside he was deeply troubled by what he had just seen, and he did not know why.

"It is time," urged the warlock. "Burn her."

"Tomorrow," said Vanus in a troubled tone. "We do it tomorrow."

"The people want it now. Why wait?" challenged an irritated Relnik. This was the moment the warlock had been waiting for, the destruction of the Intercessor. But he knew once Vanus made a decision, he would not change his mind.

"Take her back to the pens," ordered the king's son. "Tomorrow she dies."

The crowd groaned. Vanus gave the order to bring out more fighters to compete and the stadium returned to cheering. They were easily satisfied. Blood was what they wanted, and they weren't that particular about whose was spilled on the ground.

Gafney and Gerrid stood near the back wall where the visiting warriors gathered to await their call to enter the arena.

"She lives another night," said Gafney to Gerrid.

"He was a good man," said Gerrid. "He once served in my command."

"His death was not in vain. He gave us another day." Gafney placed a firm hand on the prophet's shoulder. "Tomorrow, when they bring her out to the stake, all eyes will be on her. It will be the time to free the Remnant and take them to the tunnels. I would move on that tonight, but they have increased the guards on Lena and the Remnant."

"What about Lena?" asked the prophet. "We can't leave her to burn at the stake. She's the last of her kind."

"I'm still working on that. I'm just not sure there's a way…"

"I think there is. I'm going to see the king's son."

"That's madness," Gafney shot back. "We have a plan, and it doesn't include you confronting Vanus. Besides, I believe the king's son is being controlled by the warlock. Nothing good can come of your idea."

"I had a dream last night," said Gerrid softly as he scanned the room. "At least I think it was a dream. I might have been awake. It's hard to tell anymore."

"I know little of the dreams of prophets, only of Gap Warriors."

"Nor do I. But I am trying to find my way in all this. It wasn't something I asked for."

"Tell me of the dream."

"A glistening sword cutting through the heart of

darkness—I believe the heart belonged to Vanus, but I can't tell for sure. It seemed to me that there was light somewhere in that darkness. It is hard to imagine there is any light in him." Gerrid remembered the torture he suffered at his hands.

"Was it the sword you carry?" Asked Gafney.

"I don't know," answered Gerrid, looking down at the weapon at his side. "This sword is mostly a mystery to me. Even when it was given to me by Graybeard, he said little about its purpose. I have felt its power, but the ways of the spirit are sometimes hard to understand."

"You will learn what you need to know when the time is right," encouraged Gafney. "I traveled a similar path with the weapon I wield now." He tapped the handle of Demon Slayer, his axe, which was held secure in cloth casing strapped to his back. "At first I did not comprehend its power, and I carried it with me for a long time before I understood what it could do. There were times I could have used it and didn't. In the beginning, I paid a price for my ignorance. Thankfully, now I know better."

"I am weary of waiting."

"I don't like the idea of you going face-to-face with Relnik and Vanus, so I'm going with you."

"No. I'm going alone. I don't want to risk you being taken. Besides, you need to gather the others and tell them to prepare to take the Remnant out. I will bargain for their release. Hopefully it won't come to that."

"How do you know he will give you an audience?" asked the axe man.

"I have something he wants."

"And what is that?"

"The sword. He won't be able to resist the chance to see how it works."

"But you don't know how it works," said Gafney.

"That's okay. He doesn't know that."

"Your plan holds no sense. He'll not listen to you, and he will take the sword."

"I was sent here to bring the Remnant out. At some point we have to trust in that. I am a prophet. It's time for me to prophesy."

"What will you tell him, prophet?"

"Let them go."

Gafney scratched his head and looked thoughtfully at the ground. "You seem clear about this move, prophet, so I'm going to trust that for now. But if there's trouble, we're coming to get you."

"Fair enough."

Cyle huddled in the corner of the cell he shared with Blades. This had been the most difficult day of his life. Before his eyes, he had watched his grandmother lose her dearest friend. He could accept it now that he was wrong. How stupid could any one person be? Fear had ruled the day, and he was to blame for giving into its deception. Would he ever learn? he thought to himself. Blades sat silently across from him in a world of his own thoughts. He should have listened to Mellidar. If he had, he wouldn't be in this mess. By letting fear rule his heart, he had opened the door to ruin.

The young Gap Warrior laid his head down on the dank floor beneath him and closed his eyes. What have I done? What do I do now? These were his last thoughts before he passed into the world of sleep.

The misty image of a fork in the road formed before him. fear tugged at him as he looked to the left fork. It seemed to him a path well traveled, and for one brief moment, he almost went that way. Then he remembered the message of Lady Shariana to seek the other path. When he wasn't sure what to do, he should wait until the Spirit Wind brought him what he needed from the other path. It was an uncomfortable thought. Cyle felt the urge to formulate a plan, but he resisted. Instead, he sat down facing the path on the right and forced himself to wait. Time passed at a crawl, and he was about to give up when he saw someone in the distance walking toward him. He could not make out who it was at first, but soon it became clear. It was Lady Sharianna. At first he felt embarrassed, but he held steady as the queen of the Guardians approached.

"What is it that keeps your heart in such a restless state, young warrior?" asked the lady in a strong tone.

"I can't feel him," said Cyle softly.

"You speak of the Ancient of Days."

"Yes. Others seem to feel His presence, but I don't know that I have ever felt it. This emptiness makes me doubt. How do I know for sure that He is real? I've seen the work of magic and felt the power in my staff, but something is missing."

It had always bothered Cyle that he could not feel the presence of the Ancient of Days, while others spoke of the power of the Spirit Wind and a personal bond with Him in their lives. Beneath the surface of his thoughts, there had always been a nagging doubt that the Ancient of Days was real. When he tried to believe, he felt alone and hopeless.

"So you doubt that He is real because you do not feel Him," said the lady softly.

"He doesn't feel real to me," said Cyle in a whisper. "I know it sounds strange because I have seen the power of magic in this world. But it means little to me when I can't feel His presence. The power was exciting for a while, but I still feel alone."

"And why do you think you feel alone in this world?"

"I don't know. I have felt this way for as long as I can remember."

"Everything has a beginning point Cyle. Think and you will remember."

Vague images flashed through Cyle's mind of a time when he was very young. He remembered his grandmother sitting by the fire in their home sobbing deeply. It scared him, for he had never seen her this upset before. It reminded him of watching her cry when Jef died in the arena. Even in that moment he pushed back the sadness and fear, allowing only anger to surface.

"What are you seeing Cyle?"

"It's a memory. I'm not sure how old I was. Maybe four, I don't know, but I don't like it. My grandmother is crying. She is very upset."

"How does that feel?"

"I don't know. I don't want to know. I don't like feeling her pain. I don't see the point." Cyle could feel anger threatening to rise up.

"You made a decision in that moment," said the Lady. "Do you remember what it was?"

Cyle furrowed his brow, "No, I don't remember, and I don't like thinking about it. I don't like how this feels."

"You push down your feelings and lock them away in a vault somewhere in your heart, and yet you do not understand why you do not feel His presence."

"What do you mean?" said Cyle, confused by the question. "I don't like talking about what I'm feeling."

"If you push back the pain, you push back the joy at the same time. What did you decide that day, Cyle? The Spirit Wind wants to show you, if you will allow it."

Cyle looked at the image of his grandmother in his mind. She was sitting at the fire hearth, crying and saying something about the death of his parents. "I don't want to feel this. That's what I was thinking."

"So what did you decide to do at that point?" asked Shariana for the third time.

"I decided not to feel the pain anymore," answered Cyle. "I wanted to protect myself. It was too much for me to bear. Losing my parents and seeing the pain in my grandmother was unbearable. When I think about it, I get angry."

"The Spirit Wind wants to tell you something about this, Cyle. Are you willing to hear it?"

Tears filled the young Gap Warrior's eyes. He wiped them away with his sleeve. "Yes," he hesitated. "I want to hear it."

An Image formed in Cyle's mind. He saw the arms of

someone enfolding his grandmother, bringing her comfort. He heard words that seemed to be meant for her. I will be with you and Cyle. I will not leave you abandoned and alone. The words brought comfort to Cyle, and he knew they brought comfort to his grandmother. More tears flowed as a new thought came to him. He sensed that it was not from inside of his own head, but it came to him. You must trust me with your pain if you want to feel my presence.

Trust. The word unnerved him, and he wanted to pull back. He liked to be in control. That didn't sound good to him. New thoughts came accompanied by images. He saw a beautiful sunrise over the mountain peaks, and he heard a voice say, "Have you not felt me in the sunrise at the beginning of a new day?" Then he saw rain falling. "Have you not felt me when the summer rains bring freshness or when your grandmother bakes you a loaf of bread and kisses your brow?"

Cyle had to admit that he did feel those things deeply, and he found himself whispering, "Yes I felt you." He felt foolish for missing it, but it was true. He felt loved by his grandmother and his friends, especially Choppa. They had always been there for him, and he had taken that for granted.

"He wants me to trust Him," said Cyle, through a quivering voice. "He wants me to trust Him with my pain."

And will you?" asked the Lady.

"I will try."

"That is enough for now," said a familiar voice that startled Cyle. It was Mellidar standing next to Lady Shariana.

"I beg forgiveness for the disrespect I have shown you, Mellidar," said Cyle, looking at the ground.

"You are forgiven, Cyle. Now, are you ready to reunite your heart to this mission?"

"I am."

"Then it's time to train, Gap Warrior."

Gizshra, high commander of the shadow wraiths, almost

threw up when one of his charges reported to him the events of the day. He was pleased to hear of the demise of Jef, but that was short-lived when he was told that the Intercessor Lena had esecaped death for at least another day.

"How could this happen?" screamed the shadow wraith at the cowering spirit before him. "We have more control over this kingdom than any other, and somehow we can't gain control of it when we need it most."

The slinking wraith said nothing for fear of recrimination.

"Answer me, you pathetic…argh. What's gone wrong?"

"The light is breaking through, commander," the demon managed to squeak out a reply. "It's caused confusion among the ranks, but we are regrouping even now. We have planted a new plan in Drok Relnik. It is sure to turn the tide back in our favor."

Gizshra leaned over the cringing spirit and hissed, "You had better be right if you want to continue in the same form you now inhabit."

"We will overcome, master," assured the demon, trying to sound confident. "The tide is changing."

CHAPTER 33

Pamela held Lena in her arms as she sobbed uncontrollably. Her friend, Jef, was gone and for what? She would have gladly taken his place. He was younger and had so much life in front of him while she was nearing the end of her life due to her sickness. Who would carry on her legacy of intercession now that Jef was gone? She so wanted to leave it in his capable hands. The times of intercession they shared together would be greatly missed along with his friendship. He was kind and good-natured, always looking out for her best. The emptiness and confusion she was feeling seemed unbearable. Just as she felt she could stand no more, Lena heard Pamela praying over her. She looked up. There were others of the Remnant gathered around her doing the same.

By midmorning Gerrid stood in the king's court before Vanus, the man who had every intention of taking the sword from him once he discovered how to command its power. The king's son was surrounded by four of his own guard, and to his right side stood Drok Relnik flanked by four Red Ravens. Farther back was a second layer of protection with at least twenty Black Ravens holding position. Gerrid stood twenty paces away from Vanus with a guard standing on his right and left.

"So we meet again, my friend." Vanus eyed the sword in Gerrid's sheath strapped to his side. "I thought by now you would be long gone." He stood from the throne, put his hands on his hips and breathed deeply. "Why are you here? Surely it is not to show me the talisman you carry?"

"I admit that is not the main reason for coming to you, but I knew it would open the door for us to meet."

"So it has," said Vanus, taking three steps toward Gerrid.

"Careful," warned the warlock. "We don't know what it can do."

"No we don't," agreed the king's son, "but what I do know is that he will not harm me. It is not in him to do so." Vanus smiled, and then he boldly walked down the rise and stood right in front of the prophet. His guards started to move in closer, but he held up his hand to stop them. Then he continued, "Speak your mind, prisoner."

"I am here to ask you to let the Remnant go."

Vanus replied in a mocking tone, "Is that all?" Then he looked back at the warlock and the others standing in the chamber and said in the same tone, "He wants me to set the Remnant free." Vanus turned back to Gerrid. "And what makes you think I would do that?"

"The price of keeping them would be far greater than the

price of setting them free." Gerrid was stunned by his own words. He couldn't believe they came out of his mouth, but he knew it was true. He wasn't sure how, but he knew.

"Is that a threat, prisoner? Think carefully before you respond. Your life may depend on it."

"The message I give you is not a threat. It is a warning. And please understand that I share it because I am compelled to do so, not because I want harm to come to you or your kingdom."

"I spared your life, and this is how you repay me?" Vanus was irritated.

"As I said, I mean you no harm. But you should know that if you refuse to release the Remnant, there will be a price to pay. The decision is yours."

"You speak boldly for a man without an army," responded the king's son in anger, "or do you have an army hidden away somewhere that we don't know about? Perhaps it is these Gap Warriors that Drok Relnik is so afraid of. Maybe they are your army." Vanus was shaking, and his face was turning red. "No one comes into my court, threatens me and lives to tell about it."

Before Vanus could motion to the guards, the vision of metal cutting through a darkened heart reappeared before Gerrid's eyes and somehow he knew what to do next. In one fluid motion he drew the sword from its sheath and plunged it into the heart of Vanus and held it there briefly. Others in the room, including Gerrid, watched in shock at what was happening. Before anyone could respond, Gerrid withdrew the sword from the man's chest. Gerrid felt as though the room was spinning around him, and he wanted to fall down.

Vanus fell to his knees. With eyes wide, he grabbed at a gaping hole in his chest. Gerrid was shocked to see that there was no blood pouring out of the wound. Inside the hole he could see a vast darkness, an endless void. The others in the room had started toward the king's son to help him, but they had halted their approach when one of the guards yelled, "What manner of magic is this?" Then the guard stumbled backward, shaking in terror.

Vanus felt the world around him slipping away, and suddenly he was in another place. He heard shrieks of terror and cries of anguish, then pitiful weeping that made him cringe. His eyes could see only darkness that began to tear at him from the inside out. Images flashed through his mind. Memories of every pain and injustice he had caused others through his own dreadful deeds burned into him. He could hear his victims screaming in torturous pain. Then came a stripping away of any defenses he had used to hold back the shameful truth of his miserable life.

The anguish continued to flood him like a mighty wave. He could not push back the ruination of his own evil deeds. He was feeling the sum total of all the suffering he had caused, and before his eyes he saw them all: women, children, young men and old. But even worse, he had no defense to stop it. He realized that he could not stand up against it much longer. It was killing him. The suffering caused by his evil choices was now choking the life out of his soul. Fear penetrated every part of his being, his heart raced and his tongue felt like it was on fire. He was nearing the brink of insanity. Then something changed. Far away in a vast sea of darkness, he could see a tiny speck of light almost undetectable to him. He hoped it was real because it was the only thing at this point that was keeping him sane. Vanus began to weep—not in the world of man, but in the world of the darkness that he once loved and now hated. He loathed himself and the shame that consumed him.

I don't want to die. Vanus heard his own thoughts echo through the void.

A penetrating voice responded through the blackness. Then choose life, or you will surely die in this very hour.

Who are you? cried Vanus.

I am the beginning of all things and the author of all that is to come, said the voice.

Vanus wailed in anguish, I deserve to die! Take me.

That is true. You do deserve to die, but I offer you life this very day. Take it and you will live.

Gerrid and the others looked on as Vanus's body shook violently. They could hear him whimpering in pitiful tones as he writhed on the floor. His body shuddered and grew still, then he moved and slowly rose to his feet. A crimson scar appeared on his chest in place of the gaping hole caused by the sword. Vanus looked around the room as if he was looking through them to another place. His eyes eventually focused on Gerrid.

"What is this madness?" cried Drok Relnik. "Magic is forbidden unless sanctioned by the Terashom."

"This is no magic," said Vanus through labored breathing. He held his hand out to signal the warlock to stay back. "This transcends any magic I have ever known."

"You have been bewitched by this enchanter…"

"Hold your ground, warlock," commanded Vanus. "I see things more clearly than I have ever seen them." The king's son looked at Gerrid who appeared bewildered. "The Remnant shall go free as you have requested. Release anyone we are holding that is connected to them."

"This is lunacy," charged Drok Relnik. The warlock's plan to destroy the Remnant and the Gap Warriors was unraveling before his very eyes. Never had he been so close to such a victory, and now it was all slipping away because of the foolishness of Vanus.

"Silence," Vanus fired back. "It has been decided. I will hear no more of your protests, or I will have you thrown into the dungeons. The Remnant will be released on the morrow."

Drok Relnik seethed within. Holding his tongue took every bit of self-control he could muster. He glanced toward Haggron the leader of the Red Ravens who was standing motionless a few steps from him and offered a subtle nod. Haggron nodded in return and slipped out the side entrance of the chamber.

CHAPTER 34

When Gafney and Gerrid appeared the next day with two guards to release Cyle and Blades from their cell, Cyle could not believe his eyes. Gafney handed the two of them their weapons and offered his hand to Cyle. "It seems as though you prefer to do things the hard way, young Gap Warrior, and yet, somehow you end up back in the game." Gafney smiled. "This is Gerrid. You may remember him as the commander of the Tal military."

Gafney went on to explain what had happened. When he was finished, Cyle told them of his meeting with the street hounds and Blades.

When the four of them arrived at the holding pens, Cyle pushed through the doors to find most of the Remnant on their knees gathered around his grandmother who was kneeling in the middle of the group. He smiled and felt a small spark of joy for her, knowing that in spite of losing Jef, she was finding great comfort in the prayers of the Remnant.

Lena felt a stirring and looked toward Cyle. As soon as their eyes met, he ran to greet his grandmother, and threw his arms around her neck. "You are safe," whispered Lena in her grandson's ear, holding him tight. Pulling back from the embrace, she studied her grandson. "I see you have the mark." Lena gently touched the scar on Cyle's brow. "You always did like to learn things the hard way."

Cyle blushed. "I love you, Grandmother." He hesitated before continuing, "I am sorry about Jef."

Tears filled Lena's eyes. "I shall miss him greatly."

"Well, Prophet," said a voice from among the Remnant, "it seems you have followed your path after all." Pamela smiled and pressed to the edge of the crowd. "And what of my niece Bryann?"

"She has gone her own way."

"That is too bad," said Pamela. "I had hoped she would

stay with you."

Something tugged at Lena's garment, and she looked down to see little Barrand's eye's peering up at her. "Is this Cyle, the Gap Warrior you told us about?" asked Barrand with eyes wide open.

"It is," smiled Lena.

"And who is this?" asked Cyle.

"This is Barrand, and he has been praying that the Gap Warriors would come."

"Well then, it seems your prayers have been answered," said Cyle as he reached down and picked up the boy. "You must also meet Gafney. He too is a Gap warrior, but don't let his lumpy personality scare you."

Barrand giggled.

Dallien and Gerrid approached. "We must prepare to leave," said the prophet. "We have been granted our freedom by the king's son."

"How can this be?" said Kevis, almost sounding angry. "We are slated for the arena tomorrow."

"The arena will have to be left to the warriors," offered Dallien. "Thanks to Gerrid, Vanus has had a change of heart."

"Thanks to the Ancient of Days," said Gerrid.

Later that morning, as the sun sprayed its rays through the clouded sky, Vanus stood on his balcony and announced to the arena crowd that the Remnant was being set free. The crowd showed no reaction. They were more interested in seeing the competitive battles that were to come.

At the same moment the exit gates creaked open, and Gerrid appeared with the Remnant crowded about him. Drew, Choppa and Packer were there to receive them. After brief greetings, Cyle left with Blades and Packer to gather supplies for their group to make their journey back to Talinor. It would take at least a day just to walk the Remnant out of the city. This was the second time Gerrid had walked through these very doors to freedom, and he wondered what the odds were of something like this happening twice.

SWORD OF DELIVERANCE

Vanus did not attend the arena games for the first time in his life. They had become meaningless to him, but he knew they would continue with our without him. He had not seen Drok Relnik since the decision to set the Remnant free. Sitting in his chambers on the edge of tears, he stared out at the city through the big window and struggled to put words to what he was feeling. His thoughts reflected on his father who would return home near the end of the arena games and the celebration that would mark their military victory. But what did it matter? Vanus was devoid of any notions of celebration, and the thought of it repulsed him.

From his bedroom balcony he could make out a crowd of people moving down the street away from the arena. It was hard to tell for sure, but he thought it was the Remnant. He felt a small amount of relief knowing they would finally be free. "Go in peace," he whispered under his breath. Even though he had made the order to release them, he knew that a force, far more powerful than anything he had ever witnessed before, was at work in all of this. After all those years of searching to control the power of magic so that he could harness it for his own purposes, he now had allowed the opposite to happen. He had surrendered his own control to a different kind of power. He could have been killed instantly by that power, but he knew he had been spared. For that he felt grateful.

Several hours passed as Vanus sat starring out the window until the afternoon sun dipped behind the surrounding buildings and cast shadows over the empty streets. Cheers from the arena erupted several times during the day, and with each outburst came a feeling of nausea. Vanus struggled to keep from vomiting. This place and the whole idea of it sickened him now. It was a reminder of everything he had done wrong with his life and everything he had believed in. He tried to console himself with the thought that the Remnant was finally free. They had done nothing to deserve the treatment they had suffered.

The sound of footsteps in the hall startled him and brought him back from his thoughts. A knock rattled the frame at the door, and he bid his servant to open it. Drok Relnik pushed past without waiting for an invitation to enter and was followed by two Red Ravens.

Vanus felt the defiance of Relnik and said, "Do you not have other business to attend to or have the games bored you as well?"

"I bring you unfortunate news, Vanus." Relnik paused before continuing, and Vanus thought he caught the faintest hint of a smile at the corner of the warlock's lips. "It seems the assassin has finally caught up to your father."

"What are you saying?" pressed Vanus, tension rising in his chest. "Has something happened to my father?"

"Unfortunately, yes. Your father is dead."

"What? How can this be?" Vanus was yelling now. "He is supposed to be home in two or three days."

"I am so sorry, your majesty," Relnik feigned sympathy. "They think it was poison."

"Poison? My father was poisoned traveling home to Abbodar? This is madness. How can it be so?"

"We must take you to a safer place," warned the warlock. "You are now the king, and as rightful heir to the throne, surely you will be a target."

Vanus tried to grasp what had happened to his father, but the shock of it all was overwhelming. Drok Relnik and the two Red Ravens led Vanus to the safe room where the king goes in the event that the palace comes under attack. When they entered the room, it was musty and dimly lit. Haggron, the Raven commander, was waiting with two Black Ravens. Vanus suddenly felt uneasy about it all, but wasn't sure why. Drok Relnik turned to face him. When Vanus looked him in he eyes, he knew something was not right. He could feel his stomach begin to churn.

"Where are the guards?" asked Vanus as his eyes darted about the room. "And my assistants. Where are they?"

Drok Relnik did not respond to Vanus at first. He only stared at him through empty eyes. The Ravens in the room stood motionless, and Vanus could feel the darkness encroaching.

"You were a fool to let them go," seethed Relnik.

"Things have changed. I have changed."

"You are right about one thing," said the warlock. "Things have changed. Your father is now dead, and you are the only rightful heir to the throne." Drok Relnik paused and smiled before continuing, "Unless of course the enemy who killed your father was to get to you. Then they would rule instead of you. Isn't that how it works in or outside of the arena? The conqueror reigns."

"It would seem that you have been busy." Vanus felt strangely calm as he spoke the words.

"There are powers at work here that are far beyond your understanding. You have wasted my time and theirs with your foolish pursuit of a lesser magic."

Vanus thought to command the Ravens standing in the room to come to his aid, but he knew it was hopeless to do so. They were under the warlock's control now. "And what will you do with me, warlock? You've killed my father. Am I to be your next victim?"

"You are a fool, Vanus. You have no real qualities that would allow you to rule this kingdom," Drok Relnik seethed with disgust. "You piddled your time away playing with magic when there were greater paths to follow. I tried to tell you."

"That you did, warlock. Now you will kill me and take over in my place, will you not?"

"It is as you say."

"I am not afraid of death, warlock. I have understood more about life this day than ever before. But I ask you, what is your gain?"

"I will unite the army's of Boogara and our own along with the other lands we now rule, and we will conquer Talinor."

"I see," said Vanus. "They are the light you so desperately detest, and now you must put it out."

The warlock smiled. "Enough talk. Take him to the temple and prepare him to be sacrificed in the arena. A sacrificed king will bring great reward from the gods." Relnik turned to Haggron the Raven commander. "Send men to bring back the Dissenters. Their destiny will be found in the arena after all."

When Drok Relnik stood before the arena crowd and announced to them the death of their king, complete silence followed. He told them of his intentions to sacrifice the king's son, Vanus, and the crowd grew restless until he told them that he would be their new king. The crowd erupted in cheers. They understood without explanation that the warlock was the one who had killed the king. It was merely a matter of completion to sacrifice Vanus. Their applause reflected the high value a warring culture put on the conquering victor, even if it was their own king who had been conquered. It was not the first time a king had been slain in Abbodar and replaced with the one who had killed him. It was how most monarchs rose to power.

Gerrid could feel the weight of the past few days bearing down on him. He was relieved that the Remnant was free, but he was not sure yet how he would get them back to Talinor. Something made him uneasy, but he wasn't sure why. Maybe he would feel better once they were out of the city. They had traveled all day by cart and on foot until they reached the edge of the city. For now, they would rest, and tomorrow they would get an early start crossing through the valley that separated the city from the mountains. If they pushed hard enough, they would be at the foothills by day's end. With a little luck, they would make it to the old temple ruins by mid-afternoon the next day.

Blades appeared before Gerrid, out of breath. "Trouble is coming. My people have told me that the king has been slain and that his son will be sacrificed in the arena tomorrow. Drok Relnik will be the new king and he has ordered his men to find us and take us back to the arena. They'll be here before dark."

"Curse that warlock," spat Gafney. "I hate warlocks. Especially this one."

Cyle stepped forward. "We need to move now and make a run for the hills where we can find cover."

"We will be out in the open and vulnerable," warned Drew.

"Bernard and I can hold back to slow them down," roared Ginzer as he glanced over to Bernard who looked surprised at his cousin's offer. "We may be old, but we can cause some trouble."

"Too risky," countered Cyle. "Your offer is a brave one, but there's no point in putting the two of you at risk."

"And now the young ones are schooling us, cousin," laughed Ginzer.

"Aye," put in Gafney, "even I see the folly in the plan."

"It is time," said Cyle, staring at Blades. "We need your people to slow them down if they can. Will they help us?"

"They will do as I say," said Blades, looking back at the city through the dimming light of the day, "and I will do as you command." Blades motioned with his hand, and over twenty street hounds appeared from the shadows of the alleyways. Countless others appeared along the rooftops. One young girl who looked to be about sixteen years of age moved out from among them and approached Blades. He walked over to her, and after a brief conversation, she motioned to the hounds. Four of them came over to join them. Blades returned with the four, and the girl walked back to where the street hounds were standing. They disappeared back into the shadows, following her.

"They will do what they can, my friend," said Blades looking at Cyle, "but it will only be a delay. There is no way we can stop them."

"These four," Blades motioned to the hounds standing next to him, "and I will be going with you."

"I can't ask you to do that," Cyle pushed back. "Slowing them down is risky enough. If you go with us now, you may never be able to return."

"That is a risk I am willing to take. These four who stand with me are willing as well." Blades held up his swords, "By the laws and honor of our clan, my weapons and I are bound to you."

"All because I defeated you?" questioned Cyle as he pondered the similarities between the street hounds and the warring culture of Abbodar.

"It is our way for as long as I can remember. Even the four who are with me now I once defeated in street battle. They are bound by honor to me. It is all we know," said Blades as he nodded toward his followers. Most of them appeared older than he, except the one girl who looked younger than the rest. Each carried slings strapped to their waists and their own blades. The girl also carried a crossbow.

"Then they are with us," decreed Gafney who was getting more irritated by the delay. "Enough with the talk. It is time for us to take to the hills while it is still light."

Nights came slowly at this time of year, but that day seemed to be in a hurry to swallow them up. Gerrid wanted to get the Remnant through the valley before the stars came out. They were completely defenseless out in the open. Once they reached the trees in the foothills, they could find cover. He couldn't help but size up his situation tactically, but he knew there really wasn't any point to it. He had commanded an army once, but now among those he led there were only a handful capable of fighting—Gafney, Ginzer, Bernard, Cyle, Choppa, Drew, Blades and his four fighters. The prophet passed over each in his mind: Packer was just a boy who couldn't be counted on for much, but then again he was very resourceful. Kevis, the Remnant leader and his friend, Dallien, whom he knew could hold his own with a blade, along with eight hunters handy with a bow and fourteen other men capable of holding a sword who had reluctantly offered to take up arms.

Choppa and Packer, under the direction of Gafney, had gone into the marketplace earlier that day to purchase bows and a handful of swords with the money given to them by Vanus. Some of it was spent on food, pack animals and carts to carry the older ones. Gerrid had been given a note with the king's seal to provide safe passage. There would be enough to hire a ship to take them back to Talinor once they arrived at the coast. If not for Vanus's change of heart, they would not have made it this far, but now that was changing. Once again Gerrid found himself fighting against the impossible weight of their situation.

"We move then," ordered Gerrid loud enough so all could hear.

"There is one more thing before we go," said the familiar voice of Lena. "Barrand wants to say a prayer to the Ancient of Days."

The others moved close to hear the little voice of young Barrand as he began his prayer. "We need your help to take us away to a safe place. Please help us in our journey and please protect us."

Lena leaned over and whispered something in the little boy's ear.

"Darkness surrender to the light," said Barrand sheepishly.

Lena leaned in a second time and spoke to him again.

Barrand yelled, "In the name of the Ancient of Days, darkness give way to the power of the light!"

A wash of dread erupted throughout the void, causing the demons to shutter to their core. "What is this disturbance?" screamed Gizshra. "I can sense a new defiance rising."

There was no response from the demon horde surrounding the shadow wraith, for they did not know what was happening. The dumbfounded looks on their faces only incited their leader's rage to a higher level. "Find out what is happening," screamed Gizshra, "before I smite you all to dust."

The cringing throng scattered in all directions, leaving a mist of sulfur and sparks. Gizshra looked at the shadow wraith standing to his left. "Something is threatening to close the breach. I can feel it. These few Gap Warriors and a single Intercessor are not enough to cause this kind of disturbance. It must have something to do with the fool Vanus releasing the Remnant." Gizshra rubbed his scaled hands together, causing sparks to spring from his palms as he began to pace. "What do you think Belosh?

"Drok Relnik has ordered his men to bring the Remnant back to the arena for sacrifice. The Gap Warriors and the Remnant will not be able to withstand them. It will be over soon."

"Your confidence gives me little reassurance, but at least it is something. Go, Belosh. I want you to be there when they overtake them. Do all you can to see this through. I will manage things from here."

"As you command, my lord."

CHAPTER 35

The clatter of hooves thundered through the streets of Abbodar as one hundred warriors rode atop their steeds at full gallop toward the edge of the city in pursuit of the Remnant. Among them were eighty warriors, fifteen black Ravens and five red Ravens. In front of the warriors were twenty ravenous scavengers panting with lust for blood. Those on the streets ran for cover while others watched from their windows through a cloud of dust. One man didn't move fast enough to avoid the charge and was swallowed up in the trample of hooves.

Their commander, a Red Raven named Drishk, led the pack. His heart pounded at the thought of reaching the fleeing Remnant and overtaking them, but most of all, the demon within him stirred as an unquenchable yearning to destroy the Gap Warriors erupted inside of him. One of the greatest honors of a demon of the void goes to those who destroy a Gap Warrior. If it could succeed, it would be assured of a promotion to the status of shadow wraith and given its own charges to command.

"We are almost upon them," whispered the dark spirit to

the Raven he possessed. Drishk smiled. The demon continued, "You will kill them all."

Drishk pushed back at the demon's request. "I have my orders. I must bring back the Remnant."

"And I have mine," said the demon. "Kill them, and I will reward you."

Before Drishk could respond, the air filled with a whirring sound as stones rocketed down from the rooftops, pelting the riders' horses and causing them to stumble and rear as they pounded against each other. Another volley of rocks combined with arrows rent the air, spraying into the scavs. It had little effect on them physically, but it was enough to confuse them. Some turned and attacked each other in the confusion. The faltering steeds came to a complete halt.

Drishk shouted, "Keep moving forward. We don't have time for this." The commander kicked his mount and urged his horse forward. But stopping had been a mistake as more rocks and arrows reigned down, pelting several warriors and bringing at least six of them to the ground. Armor provided protection, but some were left momentarily stunned or wounded. The Ravens, struck by arrows in less vulnerable places, tore them from their shoulders and thighs and tossed them to the ground. "Onward," the commander bellowed once again, and the warriors responded by urging their mounts forward.

The shadow wraith, Belosh, stood with the dark warriors he commanded and watched from a safe distance within the void, waiting to crossover through the breach once it was advantageous. The barrier between the world of flesh and the void was weakest in Abbodar. The further they moved away from the dark influence of the city, the more difficult it became to pass through. Belosh despised the waiting. Even though there were other servants of the darkness living in the natural world, he hated that his kind, the warring spirits, could only enter when the breach was weak enough. With a weak breach, they often still had to battle through

Gap Warriors to cross over.

Something was there at the breach. He could feel it. There had been a shift in the last few days, a resistance that was holding them back, but he was not ready yet to challenge it. It had to be connected to the Intercessor that still lived. Disgust and rage swirled inside his anxious spirit at the thought of Lena alive and praying to hold them back, but it would be too little too late as far as he was concerned. They had managed to destroy the other Intercessor in the arena, leaving her to stand alone. One lone Intercessor would not be enough to stop them because he knew, as did all shadow wraiths, that Intercessors were the most powerful when they could make their petitions while in agreement with other Intercessors. Belosh smiled, relishing in the ignorance of the Remnant. They did not grasp the power they could unleash against his forces if they would just unite in agreement through Intercession. The deceiving spirits that lived in the world of flesh were succeeding at blinding them to the very power that could free them. For now, he would wait as more charges were being sent to join them. Soon they would have enough to mount an offense against whatever resistance lay before them.

In the world of flesh, the Remnant had made their way to the middle of the valley, but Gerrid knew it was not far enough. When he looked back toward the city, he saw a cloud of dust rising from the valley floor.

They were coming.

Does it end here? he questioned under his breath. Have we come this far for nothing? Anger threatened to overtake him.

He could feel the fear spreading through the Remnant, and children could be heard crying. One child caught sight of the dust cloud and screamed, causing the others to cry even louder. They were all looking to Gerrid for his next directive when Kevis moved out from among them.

Looking tired and defeated, he spoke, "So is this your plan, Prophet? Is this where it is to end?"

Dallien and Cyle were standing next to Gerrid. Dallien

pushed back at Kevis. "Stand back, Kevis. Your words only incite more fear that will bring us no good."

"What will do us good is to surrender and throw ourselves at their mercy." Kevis held his ground. "We don't have the weapons or the manpower to stand against them. You know that if we fight, we will be slaughtered."

Gerrid could hear voices of agreement rise up among the Remnant, and he could see the fear etched on their faces, except for three among of them—Lena, Pamela and little Barrand. He stared at them, his heart sinking, and time seemed to stand still. He waited for Lena to speak, but she did not.

"We have no choice but to stop here and make a stand." Gerrid pointed to one of the wind shelters in the distance. "We will put as many of the older women and children in the shelter as we can and the rest of us will fight."

Kevis started to object, but the Prophet fired back, "I have decided. Move them into the shelter."

Under whispered protests, they moved them to the stone shelter. Once huddled inside, Lena gathered them around her to pray. "You may think that we can do nothing but hide while those outside fight for us, but we too must fight." Lena noticed Pamela nodding in agreement, but she could see the fear in the rest of them. "Do not be afraid. Fear will only distract you from this battle. No matter what you hear outside, you must not falter in your prayers."

Lena heard the soft whimpers among the children in the room. The older women tried to comfort them. Lena pushed harder, "Children, now we need you to be strong. Stop crying and listen to my voice. I am going to teach you how to use the power you have been given by the Spirit Wind. Do not think that because you are young you have no power. Age has nothing to do with it. There will be an unseen battle that wages beyond the one you hear or see outside. That unseen battle will be critical to the outcome of the battle beyond these walls, so we must intercede and be in agreement in our prayers."

The Intercessor spent the next several minutes calming them, challenging them to stay focused. It proved difficult because every time they heard noises from outside the shelter someone would start crying. Gerrid and the others set up positions to ready themselves for the fight. After cramming over one hundred in the wind shelter, there were still another seventy-five left outside. Thirty of them were told to hide behind the shelter, and the other forty-five were given weapons to fight. Twenty could manage bows, and the rest were given axes and swords. Ginzer, Bernard, and Dallien split them into three fighting groups while Drew and Choppa took the archers and positioned them in a flanking position. Blades and his four comrades offered to take the point. The fear and tension was palatable. Some were just boys and girls, and most had never held a sword before.

Gafney and Cyle approached Gerrid. "We must leave you now, Gerrid," said Cyle as he looked over to the shelter where his grandmother was with the others.

"I understand, though I have dreaded this moment. I knew you could be called away."

"We'll be back, lad," said Gafney as he pulled his axe from the leather sheath on his back. "The breach is vulnerable, and the Guardians are restless."

The others watched the two Gap Warriors walk away until the air around them shifted, and then they were gone in a blaze of light and dust. Gerrid looked to the horizon and saw that the riders had cut the distance in half. His heart sank, and then he saw something that made his heart drop a little more. Scavs. He could see them running out in front of the horses. He had not factored them into the equation, and he knew they would arrive before the soldiers. Scanning his makeshift troops, he saw that the members of the Remnant were backing up. The look of terror on their faces betrayed what was in their hearts. Gerrid harbored no blame against them. How could he? His own heart was fighting the same battle.

"Steel your hearts," cried Bernard. "If we die today, we'll

SWORD OF DELIVERANCE

die fighting the good fight."

Drew called to the handfull of archers to notch their first arrow. He thought of Addie and wondered if he would ever see her again. Sadness washed over him as he glanced over to Choppa who was gripping his crossbow, and next to him stood packer with sling in hand. Fear was in their eyes as they glanced back and nodded a feeble look of encouragement.

The enemy was close enough now for them to hear the thundering hooves of their horses and the howls of the scavs. Wait, thought Gerrid, something isn't right. The sound is different. He had heard the cries of the beasts before, but this wasn't the same.

Then he saw it, and at once he understood. Before he could say anything, Dallien yelled out, "The howls. It isn't the beasts howling, it's the wind." Then he pointed. From every direction they could see dust rising to the sky and hear the sound of the howls rising with it.

Kevis called out to Gerrid, "What now, Prophet? We can't all fit in the shelter."

"Pull together," yelled Gerrid through the wind and dust that intensified about them. "Move next to the shelter and pull the wagons over to use as a wind block." Gerrid knew it was a desperate plan, but what else could they do at this point?

Drew and Dallien grabbed one of the wagons and dragged it next to the building while the others scrambled to do the same. The winds increased and the sound grew louder as the swirling dust pelted their eyes and skin, making visibility almost impossible. Inside the shelter, the children were crying and screaming in terror.

Pamela yelled as loud as she could, "Silence! Be still all of you. Listen to Lena and pray."

The charging Ravens and the warriors that accompanied them bolted toward one of the wind shelters nearby. Some were successful, but when there was no more room, those still outside turned their mounts and retreated back toward the city in a desperate attempt to escape the deadly howls. Most of them would not make it. The scavs pressed forward toward the Remnant, driven by primal instinct and a lust for blood. Several lost their footing and were swept away by the deadly gale.

At the Remnant shelter, those who could not fit inside clung to one another while huddling between the wagons and the brick walls. To their advantage, the wind was blowing from the direction of the other side of the shelter. Bernard and Ginzer quickly staked the wagons to the ground in an attempt to hold them secure. It would not last because they all knew the worst was still coming. A flash of fur erupted through the haze of dust, snarling as it charged at the Remnant near the wagons. Blades lashed out with his two crescent swords. Drew and Choppa loosed arrows simultaneously into the side of the beast. Another scav charged in with its gaping maw snapping at one of the men, missing by inches. With a second strike, razor sharp teeth fastened onto the shoulder of an elderly man, dragging him away. He screamed through the mist.

"We can't hold this position," cried Kevis. "All will be lost."

"For the homeland and the One Faith!" yelled Bernard, charging forward with axe ready. His blade lashed out in defense of the huddled Remnant.

"Not without me, cousin," shouted Ginzer, following close behind him.

Three scavs appeared before the two of them, and at the same time a vicious wind kicked up, ripping one of the wagons from its stakes and pushing the two scavs back several paces. After regaining their footing, the scavs lunged toward Bernard and Ginzer with jaws wide open. They struck at the two dwarves seeking death to fulfill their blood lust. The plan to bring them back alive was forgotten in the absence of the warriors. A new sound filled the air—another howl that sounded different than any they had heard up until now. A torrent of feral growls followed, and something slammed into the three scavs, driving them backwards. At first Bernard thought it was another confused scav attacking its own kind, then he realized it was Keesha, the silver wolf. She grabbed one of the scavs by the neck, snarling and clenching down at the same time. The scav screamed in pain. The silver wolf shook the creature like a rag doll and flung it aside. Then it charged after the other two, and they all disappeared into the swirls of dust.

Gerrid knew they would not last much longer with the wind growing stronger. "Hold on!" cried the prophet. But he knew it was pointless.

Another wagon tore loose, and two bodies lifted with it. Gerrid wiped his eyes to clear them of sand, and then he peered through the swirling dust and saw movement from the direction they had been headed. He thought his eyes were playing a trick on him, but he looked harder. He was sure something was moving toward them, something massive. What now? As if they didn't have enough to deal with, it looked like a mountain of dust was headed in their direction. His heart sank deeper into his chest.

"What is it?" cried Packer who was holding onto a faltering wagon.

"Demons," answered another.

The misty forms were almost upon them when Gerrid's heart calmed as he recognized what it was. "Stone giants," whispered the Prophet under his breath, and then he yelled and waved at them, "Here! Over here!"

The giants surrounded the Remnant to form a protective wall as others climbed on top to form a barrier that covered the huddling members of the group. The giants molded together almost seamlessly to form a block from the deadly howls that lashed furiously against their stone-like bodies. Some of their faces peered in at them through the protective shell. One of them spoke, "I am Boulder. Hutch sent us," said the stone giant in a comforting voice. "You are safe now."

Inside the shelter, Lena led the huddling Remnant in prayer, urging them to agree with her. "We stand united against the dark forces." She heard some of them whisper agreement. "Stronger. Speak it out," challenged the Intercessor. "We resist the weapons mounting against us, and we stand firm in the promise of agreement. Send your warring emissaries to do battle on our behalf. We loose them and their power to be unleashed against the darkness."

Belosh was a seasoned warrior and his instincts as a shadow wraith had served him well, but there was an uneasiness creeping in that he was tempted to ignore. His troops had swelled to sufficient numbers, and they were growing restless to cross over through the breach in the void. He could feel their bloodlust growing by the second, and he knew that regardless of what he was sensing, he had to obey the orders that had come down from his superiors. "It is time," commanded Belosh. Holding his sword above his head, he motioned his soldiers to attack.

Chilling screams filled the void as wraiths of all shapes and sizes surged toward the faltering breach. There were dark ones, large and powerful, mighty warriors, yet several others were short and squatty, pathetic and afraid. But all were ravenous to enter the world of man to take on any form of flesh they could inhabit and control. Some would enter confused hearts that were ignorant of their dark influence. While others would welcome the dark ones gladly because they had been deceived by their own greed and desire for power. Even creatures of lower intelligence like the scavs and bog beasts could be controlled. The shadow wraiths, the most powerful of all, would be allowed to maintain their own forms once they crossed over, but their time in the world of men was always limited. Eventually they would need to return to regain strength, but not before they could cause great harm and loss of life.

The dark horde swept past Belosh toward the weakening breach. As he watched from the rear, rage swelled as he envisioned the battle ahead. His charges began piling into each other, and they, along with their war cries, came to a sudden stop. Belosh moved forward and the wraiths parted until he could see the cause of the obstruction. Standing in the breach was a small band

SWORD OF DELIVERANCE

of Gap Warriors. Among them was Gafney clutching his axe, Demon Slayer. Cyle stood ready spinning his staff. Next to him stood Tryska with her flute strapped to her back and two short swords in each hand, glistening in the faltering light of the void.

Cyle looked at Tryska and asked, "Where did you get the swords, Gap girl? I thought your weapon was a flute."

Tryska smiled. "I don't question the gifts I am given. I just use them."

Belosh pressed to the front, taunting, "Is this all they could spare to defend the breach today?" He laughed, displaying a grin of razor sharp teeth.

Gafney shot back as he felt the power of the Spirit Wind pulsating between his palms and his axe, "Do you find humor in your death, Wraith?" The muscled Gap Warrior spun Demon Slayer in his loose grip. "My blade hungers for your scaly hide, and you will be the first it feasts upon today."

Cyle smiled. He enjoyed it when Gafney taunted the dark ones, and it was clear by the look of dread on Belosh's face that he was not enjoying it.

"Take them," cried the wraith commander. "Reward of advancement goes to the one who kills the axe man."

Gafney charged straight toward the shadow wraith commander with deadly intent as Demon Slayer sliced through three smaller wraiths who were attempting to obstruct his path to Belosh. The three screamed in pain as Gafney's blade sent plumes of ash and sulfur sparking in all directions. Simultaneously, Cyle and Tryska launched forward with reckless abandon, as his staff and her blades cut through attacking wraiths in a dance of deadly precision.

Gafney pressed toward Belosh, but each attempt was thwarted with a wave of fresh demons. Each time Gafney sent them back to the pit, he could hear Belosh laughing and taunting, "Come and get me, Gap Warrior, if you can."

A demon blade sliced toward Cyle's throat, but one of Tryska's swords was there to block the thrust, giving him the brief opening he needed to return with a deadly counter strike. Demons swarmed and pressed in from every side. Cyle yelled, "Too many. We need help."

Belosh wailed gleefully when he heard Cyle's words. Cyle glanced over his shoulder just in time to see Gafney's axe splintering through several demons, sending them spraying, but they were still quickly losing ground against the dark ones. Something moved to the left. Two more Gap Warriors joined in the fray. Cyle recognized one of them whose name was Sherrol. Arrows flew in rapid succession from her bow as exploding demons felt the tip of her arrows and evaporated into sulfurous dust clouds. Her golden hair sprayed outward as she spun in circles, loosing her shafts against the dark creatures of the void. The other newcomer he did not recognize, but Tryska did, calling out his name in delight. "Fender, you've come to rescue us."

Fender smiled in the elf girl's direction, then turned and sliced through an attacking wraith with his blade. But it did little to slow their advancement as they kept coming in waves. Several of the dark ones slipped past their defenses and escaped through the ever-widening breach into the world of flesh and blood. As each one passed, Cyle groaned in agony. For the first time in battle, he thought of his grandmother, hoping she was praying for them.

There were now five Gap Warriors with the addition of Sherrol and Fender, and they enjoyed a brief shift in the battle to their favor. Unfortunately, it did not last long before they lost ground again to the ever-encroaching swell of the dark ones. A cry of pain filled their ears. It was Fender. A demon blade had found its way past his defenses, slicing through his right shoulder. Blood was oozing from his right arm which now hung limp at his side. He switched to fighting with his left hand, and the other Gap Warriors reacted, forming a defensive shield around their comrade to protect him.

"He's going to die if we don't take him from here," warned Tryska while dispatching two more demons with her two blades.

When she sheathed them, Cyle yelled, "What are you doing? This is no time to stop fighting."

Tryska ignored the question. Instead, she drew forth her flute and began to play. The music filled the void, sending demons into writhing agony. Yet they pressed into the small band of warriors as some still got past them and escaped through the breach and beyond.

"We're leaking demons like an open wound," yelled Gafney as they went flying by him. At that same moment, what he saw confused him. A massive shape formed in the opening of the breach, almost blocking the passage. "What is it?" No one else saw what he saw or heard his question. The axe man said it again only louder, "What comes our way?"

An explosion sent the dark phantoms flying in all directions away from the huge form. It slowly materialized through the haze of sulfurous smoke.

"What is that thing?" shouted Cyle.

Shrieking demons began retreating in the opposite direction back toward the void.

Tryska recognized him first. "It's the one they call Stone Hutch."

Above his head the stone giant held a massive club in both hands. "One Faith." He roared the battle cry that echoed through the void sending terror into the hearts of the lesser demons. The club in his grip slashed out in a frenzy of swipes that bowled through several wraiths. Demons flew in every direction, screaming at the unfettered power of the giant warrior. As they fled his wrath, Belosh the wraith commander, was left unguarded. Gafney seized the opportunity to strike and quickly moved in. The look in the shadow wraith's eyes as Gafney approached betrayed his fear. The exchange was brief and Demon Slayer soon found its mark. Belosh wailed in pain, disappearing in a plume of smoke and sparks.

"He's a big one," said a relieved Cyle, sizing up the massive stone giant.

"Aye, that he is," replied the axe man.

"I had to carry his weapon to him," put in Tryska. "It was no easy task."

"Where's the wolf?" asked Gafney. "She's always with you."

"I don't know. I thought when I played the flute that she would come."

"She was needed elsewhere," answered Hutch. "They sent me instead."

CHAPTER 36

Once the howls had passed, Abbodar Commander Drishk discovered that most of his men had either retreated back in the direction of the city or been lost in the storm. He had no choice but to send for reinforcements. Only three Red and five of the Black Ravens were among the thirty soldiers who had survived the deadly winds. They would continue on until others joined them.

On the other side of the valley, the Remnant and the Stone Giants arrived at the base of the hills. Half of the wagons had been lost to the wind, and all of the horses that pulled them had perished with them. The Stone Giants had saved them from the howls, and now they took the place of the horses by pulling the wagons. Eight of the Remnant had been lost to the howls, and if not for the giants, almost half would have perished. Gafney and Cyle returned after their battle in the void, and little Barrand pestered them to tell him all about it until Gafney threatened to feed him to a scav. After that he picked him up and tossed him in the air a few times before sending him away on a mission to protect Lena.

The sun had fallen below the treetops, casting a soft glow of afternoon gold upon the dilapidated rock walls surrounding the ancient ruins. Sera came running from the entrance, skipping and shouting greetings before she stopped a few paces back and scanned the group. When she saw Packer, she screeched and ran toward him, almost colliding into him. She threw her arms around his neck and kissed his cheek. He turned red and started to wipe it off.

"Don't you dare," she warned. "It is bad luck to wipe off the kiss of an elf."

Packer turned a deeper shade of crimson.

Drew sprinted past Sera into the arms of Addie, kissing her and clinging to her as he swept her off her feet. Behind the two lovers stood the Gap Warriors Hutch and Tryska looking on. The other two who had battled next to them in the void.

The next morning Gerrid called a meeting to discuss their next move. He did not have a plan, and that caused him concern. He was a strategist, and he always tried to have a plan. But this situation was vastly different than anything he had encountered in the past. He knew that their time here was very limited, and that they would need to move out as soon as they could. The soldiers would not give up pursuit and thinking otherwise was foolish. Dallien and Blades, along with the other four street hounds, went to stand watch over the valley. They were only gone for an hour before returning to report the bad news. Ravens were setting up a perimeter to block their exit, and more were on their way. Dallien estimated that there were about thirty in their company.

The ruins of the old temple were built against steep cliff walls, which meant the only way out was the way they had come in. That would be certain death. Even though the Raven numbers had dwindled, they would still be too much for the Remnant to handle. Holing up in the old temple ruins seemed to be their best bet, until a new plan was established.

Until then, Gerrid and Gafney formed a temporary plan to remain in the ruins. They called upon the Stone Giants to rebuild the outer walls of the temple, using the rocks lying at their base. It was a desperate plan, but it was all they could come up with given the circumstances.

With the aid of several of the younger Remnant members, the giants worked in perfect harmony throughout the day, piling the fallen stones on top of the lower sections until they were almost as high as the rest of the barricade, while the others worked below. Portions of the wall still had walkways left that were solid enough to allow them to place sentries there.

Cyle and Dallien had all the weapons brought to the courtyard to take an inventory. They had food stores to last them for at least a week, maybe longer.

Adding to their odds of survival was the addition of the powerful Stone Giants who would be standing with them against their enemy. Their tribe still honored Hutch's position as the king's son and would follow him as their leader. The Stone Giants had a very superstitious culture, so they had several questions for him about the mysterious new path he had chosen to follow. The day Hutch had asked the Stone Giants to rescue the Remnant from the howls was the first time they saw signs of the supernatural powers working in him through the weapon he had been given. When they saw him walk into the temple and disappear in a flash of light, they knew something had changed. Hutch was still trying to understand it all himself. He struggled to find words to explain to them the transformation that had happened in his life.

"The forces of nature and spirit are different than we have been taught by our tribe," he told them. "The light holds power over the darkness, but we must fight to overcome it in the name of the one who created the light. He is known as the Ancient of Days."

The younger giants were captivated by Hutch's explanation and wanted to know more, but the older ones were cautious and continued to press him with more questions. Hutch assured them that he would tell them more, and that they did not need to fear the power of the curse as long as they were willing to honor the light.

As the day drew to an end, the Ravens made no attempts

SWORD OF DELIVERANCE

to attack. Gerrid and Dallien strolled into the main courtyard to survey the reformed walls of the temple. Sections of the ramparts that still stood held those who were armed and willing to defend. With the exception of a few who had known battle in the past, most had the look of fear in their eyes. Some of the Remnant were too young, in Gerrid's opinion, to fight in this battle, but they had insisted. He eventually relented. He knew he would have done the same thing when he was their age.

"The street hounds will give a good fight," encouraged Dallien.

"Agreed, my friend," said Gerrid. "I wish there were more. Please tell me if there is another way because this seems a hopeless cause."

"Hope is never lost to those who stand with the light," said Lena as she approached with Pamela and a handful of the Remnant. "There may be losses, but we fight on in honor of those who have made the sacrifice of their own life," said Lena, thinking of Jef.

Then Kevis walked from the shadows with a small band of supporters accompanying him. "This is beyond hopeless. It is insanity." Kevis pointed to the walls. "Look at them. The walls can barely support those who stand upon them. They will crumble at the first attack."

"And what would you have us do, Kevis?" shouted Dallien. "Your words are laced with defeat, and your heart reeks of cowardice."

"You are a fool, Dallien, if you think there is any chance of living beyond the first battle."

Those on the walls had turned to listen, and others came, filling the outer court to see what was happening. Hutch and Gafney walked over to stand behind Gerrid. Then came Choppa, Ginzer and Bernard. Cyle moved next to his grandmother, as did Drew with Addie who stood next to the hunters. Still others came to gather and stand behind the Prophet, Gerrid. Finally, all of the Stone Giants lumbered over to stand with him. Sera and Packer watched from the ramparts.

"It seems you are a voice of one, Kevis," challenged Lena as she stepped toward him.

"We have heard enough of your thoughts, Intercessor. Each time we end up in a worse place."

Lena continued, "We escaped the arena, then we survived the howls. Now we will survive this." Lena pressed even closer until she was right in front of Kevis. "At some point you gave your life to follow the One Faith. Darkness has clouded your heart, and it sickens me to see it."

A slight smile creased the corner of Cyle's mouth. He liked his Grandmother's passion, although when he was younger, it did scare him. He knew she was still grieving over Jef's death, and that was part of what was driving her in this moment. She had lived through enough wars and death to last a lifetime. He could feel her pain, and it was the first time he had felt it this deeply. To his surprise, it helped him to understand her better. He was realizing that nothing was a guarantee in this life. There would always be enough heartache to go around, but it wasn't the pain that was his enemy. It was his fear of the pain and lack of faith that robbed him of the courage he needed to be the man she had raised him to be.

Kevis was speechless, but his face betrayed the shame inside his heart. He mumbled something, turned and walked away, followed by his supporters.

The sound of flute music lifted into the air. It was Tryska standing upon the highest tower of the temple as the afternoon sun dipped behind her, silhouetting her form against the sky. The music reached down from the high place where the elf girl stood playing. Its melody penetrated the thoughts of each one below, evoking something deep and primal. It was not an unfamiliar stirring to the Gap Warriors among them or the others who had fought with them in the past. But to the people of the Remnant, it came to them as a new revelation of courage mixed with righteous defiance. A new identity of hope began to fill each mind, breaking away their old identities and the chains of thinking that had beaten them down in the evil land. For so long they had seen themselves as victims, slaves and paupers. Now it was time to think like warriors and many of them were eager to embrace the new identity, others resisted.

"The place where we are standing was once a holy place that belonged to the followers of the One Faith," said the Prophet, looking back at the ancient temple. "I do not know much of its history, but what I do know, is that it was desecrated by the followers of Terashom and forgotten. Look around you and know that at one time, your faith thrived here. Our people once worshipped here freely with unfettered hearts, and for some unknown reason, the Ancient of Days has brought us back to this place." Gerrid looked at the surrounding ruins and wondered what it was like when the people of the One Faith had been free to worship here.

"Remember when you fight today that this is the home of your ancestors. Defend it with honor." Gerrid looked at the Stone Giants. "And it has been your home and a place of refuge. So together we will stand, and we will call upon the Ancient of Days to strengthen us. He has brought us this far. He will not abandon us now."

When the prophet finished speaking, there were no cheers, only silence accompanied by tentative nods of agreement and thoughtful stares. A picture formed in his mind of an upper room filled with members of the Remnant interceding with Lena leading them. The image stirred his emotions with both courage and hope.

Gerrid looked at Lena. "Dear Lady, you are being summoned. Take those who are willing and able to the upper room in the highest tower." He pointed. "Train them to fight with the weapon of intercession. If we are to have a hope in this conflict, we need to regain the high ground on all fronts."

Lena did not say a word. She just looked at Pamela and nodded, and the two of them turned and walked toward the tower. Others joined until there was at least thirty following.

"And now for the rest of us." Gerrid paused and looked at those who were left standing before him. "It is time to choose a weapon," said the Prophet, pointing to the weapons pile.

They stood frozen, staring at the weapons. Most of them had never handled one before now. The silence was broken as little Barrand shuffled over to the pile, grabbed on to a large axe and began tugging at it, barely able to pull it free from the pile. He tried desperately to lift it in his hands.

A young man stepped forward and took hold of the axe in Barrand's hands. "It is our duty, young Barrand. Someday it will be yours."

Barrand released his grip. Slowly the others followed his lead with their heads downcast.

"Help them choose a weapon that suits them and give them as much training as you can while there is still time, but be on the ready. They will come for us," warned Gerrid.

"Someone approaches," came the call from the makeshift rampart on the wall near the gate. Packer and Sera appeared in the opening of the dilapidated gates near the temple courts. Sera smiled, shouting, "They are here!"

Fear coursed through the refugees in the courtyard. Some grabbed the closest to them for support. Then another person appeared through the opening behind Packer and Sera, and still others followed until close to fifty men, women and children stood behind them. "They have come to join us," announced Packer. "They have heard stories in the outlying villages of a Prophet with a sword of great power who travels with a band of magic warriors."

Gerrid paused and surveyed the new arrivals as even more continued to pass through the entrance behind them. "Let me be clear," the prophet's voice grew stern. "The weapon I carry is not a weapon of magic. It is a weapon of light driven by faith in the Ancient of Days. To stand with us is to stand with the One Faith of Talinor. If you are to join us today, then you must choose to whom you will swear allegiance." Gerrid looked to the Stone Giants clustered together near a pile of rocks and then to those positioned on the walls. "Choose the creator of the light and follow the One Faith and you can remain. Choose to remain with the dark magic and you must leave now and go back to the faith that rules this land. The choice is yours. If others come, tell them the same before they are allowed to enter this place."

The flute music began a second time as Gerrid finished his discourse. Everyone felt its gentle touch. A rush of wind, born of Spirit, blew through the courts below and then rose up to where Tryska stood in the tower. From her vantage point, she could see its impact on those gathered in the courtyard. Some fell to their knees and began to weep, their bodies shaking. Some resisted and turned to leave and disappear through the temple gateway.

Boulder of the Stone Giants stood and spoke through a graveled voice, "For too long we have followed a path of fear and hopelessness. We left our own people to escape the curses of our tribe, but now we see that the greatest curse was in what we believed. As for me and my people, we will stand with you, and like our brother, Stone Hutch, we too will follow the One Faith."

The giants locked arms in agreement with their brother. Sera squealed in approval.

"For those who have chosen the way of the One Faith, you can stay as long as you are willing to support us in this fight," said Gerrid.

A young man carrying a bow stepped forward. "We will fight at the risk of losing our lives as long as we can go with you to your homeland when you leave this place."

"If you survive what comes next, you are welcome to go with us," said Gerrid.

"Others will follow us," said the young man. "We are not the last."

"Then let them come," said Cyle, "as long as they understand and accept what we stand for and the way of our Faith."

"There is one more thing," said Packer. "They say that

Vanus will be sacrificed in the arena for high crimes against the kingdom."

"A new day is dawning," announced Drok Relnik to a cheering arena crowd. He had been planning this for almost two years. Scheming to turn the tide of popularity to his favor. First he won the trust of the king and his son while secretly turning the small army of Ravens and the Terashom priests against the king. The priests had always had great influence and political power in Abbodar, and the Ravens were the ruling class. Now that the king was out of the way, the only thing left to do was to kill his son. "Today we offer the ultimate sacrifice, Vanus, son of Vandross, the former king of Abbodar."

Relnik's announcement was met with a mixed response of cheers and a faint murmur. The side gates of the arena opened, and two Red Ravens entered, escorting Vanus with his hands bound behind his back.

The warlock proclaimed, "Vanus has defiled the rule of Terashom. He has released those who have practiced magic without sanction by our priests. The penalty is death."

Vanus now stood before the stake and the pyre of wood that surrounded it. Relnik continued, "If there is anyone who would champion this man's right to live, let him do so now and face the two Red Ravens that stand with him."

In Abbodar there had only been one time before this that a king was executed for violating Terashom. That was over sixty years ago when one of the former kings of Abbodar had shown favor to a Prophet named Graybeard. The Prophet had been sentenced to death for preaching a different form of magic. It was later believed that it was his message that gave rise to the cult of the Dissenters. The king's wife was fascinated by the Prophet and decided to visit him during his imprisonment. She continued to see him on several occasions and became enamored with his teachings. Some say he bewitched her with his seductive magic. She convinced her husband, the king, to let him go. When

Graybeard was set free, he fled the country.

The priests of Terashom had always carried the weight of power in Abbodar and, to the surprise of many, they put the king and his wife to death for allowing a practitioner of unsanctioned magic to go free. No one had volunteered to champion them, so they burned at the stake for their crime.

Drok Relnik believed that the same would happen now, and that no one would be foolish enough to challenge one Raven, let alone two. He smiled knowing that he was only moments away from having complete control over Abbodar. The warlock could see the look of indifference on the face of Vanus, and it caused a slight unease in him. Relnik had seen the change in the king's son, and it disgusted him to the core that Vanus had been seduced by the other side. Yet, it was the very thing that had opened the door for this moment.

Movement came from the left side of the arena at the warrior's entrance. Guards near the entrance separated as two figures walked between their parting ranks. One was the arena captain and the other a helmeted man dressed in light battle armor. Relnik could not recognize him through the helmet guard he wore, and the uniform was unfamiliar to him. An unsettling feeling crept in, but it was quickly interrupted by the frenetic cheers of the crowd who were elated with the rare chance of seeing a battle with the two deadly Red Ravens.

Relnik studied the warrior, and again he felt his gut churning inside. The arena captain and the man stood quietly before the king's balcony, waiting to be addressed.

"And who are you that you should defend this man?" asked Relnik.

"The laws do not require that I tell you who I am," said the warrior, "only that I offer a challenge."

Relnik grimaced, knowing the man was right. The laws of Terashom ruled this kingdom, and even the king was subject to those laws. That was also why Vanus was standing before him tied to a stake. If this champion somehow managed to win this battle,

Vanus would be allowed to walk out of the arena. Even though he would gain his freedom, he would be banished from Abbodar forever. Relnik weighed the situation carefully, searching any options that might allow him to increase the advantage the Red Ravens already had.

One voice yelled from the crowd, "Let them fight." Then the crowd joined in chanting, "Let them fight! Let them fight!"

The warlock raised his hand to silence the crowd. "As you wish, challenger. You may remain a mystery to us." The arena erupted again, and Relnik gave the signal to begin the fight. Vanus looked on, not knowing who had come to defend him, but he harbored little hope of success. The Red Ravens had a marked advantage. He thought, with deep regret, of all he had done to contribute to the evil powers dwelling within the Red Ravens and how Relnik had earned his trust only to take advantage of his own lust for the dark magic. He had resigned himself to die this day. But now the fire of hope for life was rekindled even though the flame was a dim one.

The mystery warrior stood with sword in hand to face the two Red Ravens. The Ravens bowed toward the warlock and then faced their single foe. The two held swords, one was jagged and curved, the other a medium-sized battle sword. Haggron, their leader, nodded to the two, and they charged. The lone warrior responded by advancing directly toward them, deflecting their swift striking blades, sending sparks outward as he shifted and passed between them untouched. He turned to face them again and prepared for a second advance. This time he ran at their center. Then at the last minute, he shifted to the left. He sliced his blade hard at the one nearest him, but no blood was drawn.

"His weapon has power," said Haggron to the warlock.

"It matters not. He cannot win against these two."

The dark spirits inside the Ravens hissed in unison to the hosts they inhabited, "Careful, fool. This one wields power from the other side."

Red blades shot out at the lone warrior, and with cat-like

speed, he avoided them by rolling to his left. He came up again to parry the oncoming strikes. Until now, the warrior had not marshaled a significant offensive strike with his own sword. The two Ravens pressed hard, pushing the warrior backward with their swift strikes. The dark spirits inside of them were screaming, "Finish him! Finish him now!"

The warrior sensed their bloodlust rising, and he felt the dark power in their strikes giving them a force stronger than human strength. This time he stepped to the right and counter-thrusted at the one nearest him, but again, he was met with a strong defense. The fighting continued for several minutes. Each time the Ravens attacked, they were met with a successful counter defense. Drok Relnik was unsettled. He had never seen anyone last this long against two Red Ravens. Then something caught his eye that he had not noticed until now. Small prisms of light emanated beneath the palms of the warrior. The warlock stood and walked closer to the railing to confirm if he was seeing correctly. Maybe his mind was playing tricks on him, or maybe Haggron was right. He wields magic in his blade. There was no rule against it in the arena.

The mystery warrior appeared to be tiring. His movements were slowing down and his strikes were lacking the precision he had at the beginning. He stumbled and fell back, landing on his knees with his chest heaving. He gasped to fill his lungs with air. The dark spirits within his attackers screamed the command to finish him. In response to the inner voices, the two charged with deadly ambition, but the warrior was ready for them. He rolled to his right. His blade lashed out, and the edge of his sword sliced through the left shoulder of the one closest to him. Sparks erupted from his blade, and the demon inside the Red one screamed in a voice only his host could hear, "Kill him, fool! He is of the light. He is a Gap Warrior."

The Red warrior clutched his shoulder and shuddered, but only briefly, for he had been trained to ignore pain. The other Raven advanced, only to be met with two deadly strikes to his midsection. He faltered, and as he fell for the last time to the ground, the dark spirit left his body. The last thing he heard leaving this life was the voice of the demon howling obscenities at him as it returned to the void from which it came.

The other Raven was thrown by the unexpected turn, and it was enough to give the opposing warrior an opening. He took advantage of it by driving his blade in a deadly strike that sent the Red one to his knees where he froze staring in disbelief. He toppled lifelessly to the blood-soaked dust. The dark spirit inside of the fallen Raven cursed as it exited his body.

The arena crowed went silent, but only briefly before it exploded into cheers. Relnik had put his trust in the Red Ravens, and it was the first time that two of them had been defeated by a single combatant in the arena. The warlock constrained his rage. The crowd noise died and now he would have to speak. But before he could say a word the arena captain cut the bonds holding Vanus then decreed, "In keeping with the laws of Terashom and the arena games, the death sentence on Vanus, son of Vandross, has been lifted."

"What is your name, warrior?" demanded Relnik. "Remove your helmet, and tell us who you are."

The warrior reached up and removed the helmet to reveal a man who appeared to be about thirty-five to forty years of age with sand-colored hair that reached to his shoulders. "I am Bixby."

Relnik clinched down on the rail in front of him. As he peered down at the warrior, he searched his memory, trying to recall why this man looked familiar to him, but he could not find what he was looking for. "And where do you come from, warrior?"

Bixby paused weighing carefully what he would say next, fearing that the warlock might remember him as one of the Gap Warriors who fought against him at the battle for Talinor. "It has been so long since I have had a place to lay my head and call my home that. It is difficult to say, but my place of birth was right here in this kingdom in the city of Karn."

Drok Relnik leaned over and whispered to Haggron, the Raven commander, "Wait until they have left the city and destroy them."

Haggron nodded and signaled to one of his men to approach him, then passed on the order to his charge. The man turned and disappeared through the nearest door.

CHAPTER 37

Cyle stood on the makeshift rampart for the better part of a day and waited for the first attack, but nothing happened except for those who kept coming in through the narrow opening into the ruins. It didn't take long for the young Gap Warrior to realize that the reputation of the Prophet was spreading throughout the realm. A man with a magic sword was here to deliver those from the captivity of Abbodar. The ones who came carried their own supplies and weapons although most of the weapons were crude and in poor shape. By the end of the first day, they had grown in number to over fifteen hundred. Gerrid put them into military training as soon as they arrived. Some of the older ones had served at one time in the Abbodar military.

As dusk approached, there was movement coming from the ridge below. Three men on horses led, and one of them carried the banner of the realm. Another twelve followed on horses. Their mounts stopped about a hundred paces from the wall. One man who was small in stature and dressed as one of their priests, dismounted and stepped forward. "We want to talk to the one they call 'Prophet.'"

Gerrid appeared through the opening in the wall with Gafney, Cyle, Tryska and Stone Hutch in his company. The Prophet had insisted on bringing Hutch. He hoped the giant would intimidate them.

"Do you trust them?" said Cyle to Gerrid as they approached.

"I trust no one who serves the darkness, but our archers are at the ready on the wall and in the trees to our left."

"Well then, no doubt you have thought this through," whispered Cyle.

The priest was a portly man, short and balding. He was nervous, and that only served to make Gerrid uneasy. "Speak your mind, Priest." The prophet's tone sounded impatient and brash.

"I come in service to Abbodar to ask for your surrender." The priest's voice trembled.

Cyle wondered what he was afraid of.

The priest continued, "If you return with us, we will not harm you. You will be given your freedom."

"We are free now, Priest. Why would we risk such a foolish arrangement?"

"Please, I am only here as a messenger. Please consider that you cannot win in this campaign. There are several warriors that will ascend upon this place at dawn if you do not agree to these terms."

Gerrid looked at the Red Raven and the other warriors in his company. "Tell your commander that if he does not allow us to leave peacefully we will destroy all those who oppose our exodus."

The Raven laughed. "You are a fool if you think you can stand against us for more than a glimmer of time. Surely those who follow you know this is futile." The Red Raven said it loud enough so that those on the wall could hear him.

"Do you know who it is that stands with me now?" Gerrid looked at his comrades. "This is the legendary warrior, Gafney of the axe, also known as the Demon Slayer of Talinor, and this is Cyle of the staff and Tryska the wolf girl, Defenders of the Breach and terrors of the void." Gerrid paused, and as if on signal, a chilling howl shattered the air. A giant wolf materialized at the treeline to their right, causing their horses to rear. "Oh, yes, and the wolf. I almost forgot. She hates to be left out of the introductions. Tryska smiled. "And lest I forget further," Gerrid nodded toward the giant, "Stone Hutch, commander of the Stone Warriors and destroyer of the Gehemish, the most powerful demon of the void."

"Enough of your empty threats, Prophet," the Raven pushed back. "Come to think of it, my Ravens have never battled Gap Warriors or Stone Giants before. They will welcome the challenge." The commander pulled back on his mount and kicked it into a gallop. The priest stumbled to his horse and barely made his way to the saddle before almost falling off the other side. He turned his mount and disappeared into a cloud of dust.

"Gehemish?" said Hutch. "What's a Gehemish?"

"I don't know," said the Prophet, grinning. "It sounded good at the time."

"Defenders of the Breach," put in Cyle. "I always liked how that sounded."

Gerrid looked at Gafney, "We should double the night watch and keep some of the archers on the wall, just in case."

Gafney nodded as they walked back toward the courtyard. "You gave an excellent speech, Commander," said Gafney. "You made us sound good."

"You are more than good. They will soon discover that for themselves."

"The Stone Giants will watch through the night," said Hutch. "They will not miss the sleep."

"I too will stay the night," added Tryska.

The five of them stopped before passing back into the temple area and looked back across the field and down into the hill where they could see the enemy campfires burning. Cyle asked, "What chance do we have?"

"Last night I had a vision," said Gerrid. "The enemy attacked and though lives were lost, something unfolded in the heavens above. There was a great invisible battle in the sky over the battlefield." Gerrid paused and looked up. "We will not be fighting this fight alone. We must take care not to allow what we see before us to determine the course of our faith."

The Prophet's comment was followed with an awkward silence until Hutch broke its grip. "I know little of visions, but what I do know is that something powerful is inside me. It flows from me through my weapon. I have known nothing like it ever before in my life. I believe in it, and even more, I believe in the one who gives it."

"Well put, my friend," said Gafney. "Nothing like the faith of a new believer to stir our courage."

"Tomorrow when they storm the walls," said Gerrid looking up at Hutch, "I would ask that some of the giants hold the opening at the gates. I also want them staggered along the wall among the others. Their presence will give the rest of us courage."

"They will be there as I will command them."

"Thank you, my friend," said the Prophet. "We would not make it past the first light of midmorning without you."

"For the One Faith," said Hutch, and then he turned to walk back toward the temple buildings where the Stone Giants were waiting for him.

Others seeking to follow the prophet came during the night, and by first light, their numbers had swelled to over two thousand. They were quickly organized and given the duties that come in time of battle. Some would bring supplies to the wall for those stationed there, and others would tend to the wounded. Those who were too young would hide in the inner temple.

Drok Relnik was now in charge, and he wanted the Remnant returned to the arena and destroyed. Relnik's obsession with the Remnant didn't make sense to Gerrid. The warlock had risen to control of the most powerful kingdom in the known world. With the recent conquering of Boogara, it seemed Abbodar would have enough to manage. Gerrid understood why the warlock wanted the Gap Warriors eliminated. They had always been a threat to his power, but the Remnant—that was a mystery to him. The followers of the One Faith had not been a significance force since the days when they began growing in numbers. That began after Gerrid arrived in Abbodar, but it all fell apart when he went to prison.

Once the Boogaran's were defeated in the battle against Talinor, the warlock fled and made his way to Abbodar to plot his schemes to gain power. Boogara became vulnerable after falling to Talinor. Their military had been depleted significantly, and their king had died during the campaign. King Vandross of Abbodar had already been planning to invade Boogara, so when Drok Relnik appeared at his doorstep, he saw it as a gift. The warlock's time with the Boogarans had given him knowledge of the very kingdom that the king wished to conquer. It didn't take long for Relnik to gain the king's trust and his son, Vanus, was drawn to the warlock's magic.

Gerrid's mission to return the Remnant to Talinor had turned into a driving passion. He knew that he would stop at nothing to see them to their new home even though he was still not clear why it was so important to get the Remnant back to his homeland.

Startled from his thoughts, the prophet turned to see Packer and Sera approaching. "What brings the singing elf girl and the street hound out tonight?"

"We have lobbers," said the elf girl cheerfully.

"Quiet," scowled Packer, holding his finger to his lips. "They could hear you."

"What are lobbers?"

"It was Packer's idea," Sera smiled. "We stacked piles of smaller rocks at the bottom of the ramparts."

"Rocks. Okay." Gerrid was confused.

"The stone giants can hurl them at the attackers," added Packer.

"That's an excellent idea," Gerrid smiled. "I'll tell the giants right away." The prophet started toward the wall.

"You don't have to do that," said Sera. "We already have."

She smiled.

"Okay, anything else you want to tell me?"

The two of them looked at each other and smiled, then looked back at the Prophet. "Yes, we are running low on food," said Packer. "The arriving refugees are bringing food with them, but it's not enough to feed everyone."

Drew appeared just as suddenly as Sera and Packer. "I can take some men to hunt for game. It's dark and we can slip out easily enough without being seen. With any luck we can be back by tomorrow night."

Gerrid thought for a minute, then responded, "Good call, hunter. Take one of the stone giants with you to help carry what you harvest."

Drew nodded.

Gerrid turned toward the stairs that led to one of the high towers and started toward the top. He wanted to see beyond the walls to the open area beyond. Lena and Pamela approached from the shadows. When he saw them, he turned and came back down.

"How are you holding up, Gerrid?" Lena said, concerned.

"I am trying to hold on to the things that give me strength, and one of them is knowing that you will be interceding for us tomorrow."

"We have not stopped interceding since the meeting this morning, and we will continue to do so through the night."

"Thank you. I know that without the force of intercession, we would not last the morning." Gerrid paused and surveyed his surroundings as if he was looking for his next words. "Much of this is new to me. The visions, the impressions and dreams come to me like partial glimpses of a greater story. I don't always know what they mean."

"It is important for you to understand," urged Lena, "that not all prophetic messages are to be interpreted by the Prophet alone. Sometimes you will know clearly the meaning, and other times you will need to seek the council of others you trust. And yet at times, you will not know the meaning until the occurrence unfolds before you."

"That is very difficult for me. I will admit it. I like to know as much as possible when my life is being threatened, and so much is on the line. Especially when the dark forces are at work. In the past I have left that up to the Intercessors and the Gap Warriors."

"It takes time to learn to battle the dark magic," said Lena. "Sooner or later, we must all learn to fight against it. Some believe it can be avoided, but it is a force we must reckon with. Think of our own Talinor and what happened there when they ignored the spiritual forces that were bringing down their own kingdom. In their foolishness, they ended up embracing the dark magic in the name of religion. They ignored the ancient teachings that warned of the power of darkness and refused to see it as their enemy. Instead they sought after it to bring it under their control. I know I spent many nights walking the streets, praying for them."

"I know," admitted Gerrid. "I myself fell into the same trap. There was much shame in those days for anyone who wanted to remain faithful to the One Faith."

"We are glad that you came back to us, Gerrid. In the providence of the Ancient of Days, there is always a plan unfolding, and it is in our seeking Him that we will discover how the pieces of that plan fit together." Lena reached out and took Gerrid's hand in hers. "Do not forsake the knowledge and skills you have gained in leading others into battle. In many ways they will parallel what is happening here, but now you will learn to add to that new knowledge that comes from the leading of the Spirit Wind." Lena paused and fixed her gaze on Gerrid and then squeezed his hand before she continued, "And remember, you are not alone. The Gap Warriors, the Intercessors and those who fight on the front, we are all Defenders of the Breach fighting to overcome the darkness to bring forth the light of the One Faith."

Lena's words helped Gerrid feel less alone. It should have been obvious to him that the others had been right by his side fighting the same battle only in different ways, but the one thing that still bothered him was the arrival of those looking to him and his sword for their deliverance from this place. This made him very uncomfortable. "Look at them." Gerrid gave a surveying glance over the hundreds who lay sleeping on the ground in the open air. "They are here because of me. They see me as the answer. It makes me very uncomfortable."

"Today you are the answer. Tomorrow it will be someone or something else. Sometimes the faith of the desperate can be fickle. The heart longs to be free of its captivity, so when hope is perceived, the heart chases after it—often ignoring other provisions that have been given. Look at little Barrand. He thinks it's the Gap Warriors. At one time, we Intercessors were in abundance, and we enjoyed a great amount of respect. We were the answer to everything, and you see what that came to. We are now but a few struggling to do our part." Lena looked at the mass of sleeping bodies. "Now they think you are the answer because of the exploits you have done, so they have come looking for miracles of magic to deliver them. There will be miracles and deliverance, but it will not be a result of one gift or one person. It will take all of us to overcome the oppression we face. Even those who sleep before us will play a part. The Remnant, the refugees and the Stone Giants—they are all important. You are one piece of the puzzle, but that does not diminish the importance of your role. You cannot be replaced, and neither can any of the rest of us. This doesn't work if we don't all do our part."

"Maybe you are the real prophet here, Lena," Gerrid smiled. "Your words are born of the Spirit Wind. So it seems the Prophet has received a prophetic message."

"The endowments of the Spirit Wind are not limited to any one person. As you can see, some carry them in greater measure." Lena reached for Pamela's hand. "Now, Pamela is going to pray for you."

Pamela looked surprised by her comment. "Me? You want me to pray?"

"Yes. Why do you look so surprised, dear Pamela? Weren't you listening? You too must do your part." Lena took both of Pamela's hands in hers and placed them on Gerrid's shoulders. Then she commanded Pamela, "Pray, Intercessor."

Pamela felt the Spirit Wind cascade over her, causing her to shake slightly. "Help Gerrid be strong. Help him to know that we are with him." Pamela paused briefly and felt an inner stirring she did not understand, and then words came to her that she knew were not her own. "Increase the vision you have given Gerrid so that when the enemy rises before him, he will see beyond his own ability. Reveal to him what is transpiring around us that is beyond our natural sight, so that what is happening before him does not confuse him." Pamela paused, and she saw something she had never seen before in her whole life. In the distance there was a horde of dark beings wielding weapons that she knew were created to destroy the followers of the One Faith. She trembled at the sight, and a deep sense of dread began to seize her as the shadow fairies shot their arrows of doubt into her thoughts.

"Pamela." Pamela almost didn't hear Lena's voice urging her on. "Ignore them and keep praying. You are not yet finished."

Pamela regained her focus and continued, "The weapons of the dark will falter against the weapons of our faith as long as we do not bow to fear." The words coming out of her mouth surprised her. She found herself listening intently to what she was praying as if it was for her more than anyone else.

"Rise us up above the fear and restore to us the heart we have lost as a people, the heart of a warrior. For too long, we have walked as victims and slaves bowing down to fear, causing us to cower and lose sight of who we really are."

Another voice added, "The weapons we fight with are many, given to us by the Spirit Wind," prayed Varina, a young Remnant girl of about seventeen years. Then, embarrassed, she grew silent.

"Go ahead, child," prompted Lena.

The girl continued, "Give us courage and the faith to follow it. Help us to see beyond what is before us to what surrounds us and protects us."

"Thank you for the Gap Warriors," prayed little Barrand from atop one of the Stone Giant's shoulders with closed eyes. "And thank you for sending the Stone Giants to help us."

Gerrid jerked opened his eyes and was filled with awe at what he saw. Several of the Remnant had gathered, and many of the refugees had joined them. Among them were the massive Stone Giants. The only ones missing were those standing watch on the wall. The rest had gathered to join in the praying while his head was bowed. What happened next surprised the Prophet.

Santor reached out and laid his hands on one of the elder stone giants and began to pray. "These are not a cursed people. Though they have been called cursed and have lived as the cursed of their own tribe, we say that this curse is not their destiny."

Santor paused, and Gerrid filled in, knowing that the words he was about to speak to the Stone Giants came from the prophetic gifting within him. "There is nobility in you, and you have been chosen for a noble cause. You thought you had fled to this desolate place to live out your lives in exile and shame, hidden away from the rest of the world and your tribe. But there was a greater purpose to it all." Gerrid could already see the power of his words taking hold of the Stone Giants. By the looks on their stoic faces as they stood in silence, appearing as rock pillars with the light from the fires flickering off of their stony skin, their eyes reflected the deepest of longing and hope. These are a noble people, thought Gerrid. He continued, "Do not be confused, for you have been brought here for a time such as this—a time to fight the dark curse that hangs over this realm, for your own freedom and for the freedom of those who stand about you." Gerrid looked to the crowd. "We must stand together, for apart we will surely fall—Stone Giant with dwarf, elf, the children of men and anyone else that would stand with us against the darkness."

Tryska of the flute began to play a melody that the Remnant

recognized. The dark ones that watched from the shadows began to shudder and wince as they recoiled against the music. Sera began to sing first.

> Let all the people lift high the
> Ancient of Days.
> His Glory will not be forgotten.
> Let us exalt and honor his
> majestic ways.
> His might will not fail us.

"Hold your ground," hissed one of their dark commanders to his charges who were writhing in pain.

The song of freedom and praise rose up into the sky above them as the volume intensified and the Stone Giants joined in the singing. The enemy encamped at the bottom of the hill could hear them, and they cursed against it.

"Let us go, Master," pleaded one of the dark warriors hidden in the shadows. "We can bear it no longer."

The wraith commander was clearly in pain too and doing all he could to hold his ground. The music washed over him like acid penetrating into every pore of his leathery hide. "Pull back to a safer distance. Do not retreat, pull back and hold position."

Sera saw them grimacing and fighting to stay close, then they faltered and began pulling back, slowly disappearing behind the walls of the temple. She smiled and giggled under her breath.

"Why are you laughing?" whispered an exasperated Packer.

"They are gone." Sera smiled staring off in the distance.

"Who's gone?"

"The dark ones."

CHAPTER 38

Gerrid slept fitfully in the top of one of the towers, causing the night to go on endlessly. Each time he woke up, he would walk to the open window and look out at the enemy fires in the distance. The room he had taken for his own suited him even though it needed cleaning. Some of the refugees had volunteered to make it habitable by cleaning and airing it out. There was a bed in the room and a fireplace in the corner along with a table and some chairs. He guessed that it was once the lodging for one of the priests that had lived here.

The gathering earlier had been meaningful to him. Clearly the newly formed community of fugitives were counting on him and were willing to fight under his command. The unity of this new coalition was paramount if there was any hope of survival, and yet he knew that lives would be lost. He wondered how that unity would hold when blood began to spill. So very few among them were battle-tested. He shuddered at the thought. They would be the first to die. In war the strong survived. That was the way it had always been. He turned and attempted once again to sleep and escape this world and what was to come next.

"The swords were given to you for times such as this," said the Guardian, Veneda, as she ended her training session with Tryska. "Do not allow them to distract you from your flute." The Guardian's words were stern and decisive. The battle was close at hand and the intensity was always palatable right before the fight. "Always begin with the flute before drawing the swords. As you know the flute, when played to glorify the Ancient of Days, will create confusion in the ranks of the enemy. It is a necessary advantage not be forgotten."

Tryska looked down at the two blades held firmly in each palm, knowing that Veneda was talking about the Ravens who had been infested with the shadow spirits.

SWORD OF DELIVERANCE

"They are physically stronger than you are, so you will need to use your speed and quickness to escape their blades. Of course, the wolf will help you. She is never far."

"You look more troubled than I am used to, Veneda. What is the matter?"

"You and most of the Gap Warriors have had your battle experience from fighting in the void. This time will be different. I have done all I can to prepare you. Just remember, human strengths can be as deadly as the dark magic, especially when the two are merged into one. Keep an eye on your comrades, you will need each other."

"I will do all I can."

"I know you will, Tryska. The elfin blood in your veins runs deep with courage. I have never doubted you. Now I must go. The Guardians are gathering, and as you know, we too will be fighting behind the veil, doing our best to hold the breach in check."

"God's speed be with you, Veneda."

"And with you, child."

The sun crested the cliffs behind the temple, slowly chasing the shadows from the surrounding landscape. Red Raven Commander Drishk called his captains to his side to instruct them. "We are over two hundred strong." He paused to look over his charges. "That should be more than enough to finish this before midday."

"Yes, sir," agreed the captain closest to him.

"Send the warriors first, then if need be, the Ravens. Though I doubt we will have much left to do once the soldiers are done."

"As you wish, Commander."

It was happening now. All the talk and all the prayers would have to be enough to sustain them. In the second tower, some fifty members of the Remnant prayed under Lena's direction, and the rest who could fight stood with the others on the walls and near the front gate. Two thousand was their total now, including the refugees, but only eight hundred were of age or strength to enter the battle. The rest would help to mend the wounded and deliver supplies.

Gerrid, with Dallien next to him, stood on the wall nearest the main entrance which had been narrowed in size. Stone giants had placed boulders there in an attempt to limit the enemy from flooding through. Ten giants stood blocking the entrance ready to defend, and behind them were several armed refugees and Remnant members. Gerrid signaled Drew on the south wall and Choppa on the north wall, and they in turn gave the order for the archers to ready their bows. The Abbodar warriors came as a flood over the rise, howling and screaming. Their battle cries sent waves of terror through the refugees. Drew released the first arrow of the campaign, sending it skyward, parting the air until it found its mark in the chest of a charging warrior in front of the approaching wave. He stumbled to his knees and was immediately trampled under by his charging comrades. The skies filled with a swirling sound as some fifty arrows followed, renting the sky. Only a few found flesh.

"Stand ready," yelled Gerrid, then he pointed at the giants on the walls and gave a signal. They responded by hurling rocks down upon the warriors who were now within reach. The stones rocketed into the warriors, smashing them to the ground. Some rose back up in a daze and continued their advance while others lay silent on the ground. Another hail of arrows flew downward, and with the warriors now closer, more of the flying shafts found their marks.

The attackers charged the wall of Stone Giants who were protecting the gate. Hutch stood in the middle of them, giving orders. "Hold strong, Brothers and Sisters of the rock. We are the only thing standing between our friends and the enemy."

Hutch's charge empowered the giants who struck back at the charging wave with their powerful clubs, pounding and

SWORD OF DELIVERANCE

smashing against their assailants, and in some cases, sending two or three flying backward with one swing. Arrows and rocks continued to assail the warriors while the Stone Giants held their own for several moments. In that time, many of the attackers were vanquished. Then there was an opening, and the first of them broke through the giant's defense into the area where Gafney and Cyle stood ready. Soon Tryska, Ginzer, Bernard and Blades joined them, along with the street hounds that formed the second line of defense. Behind them were the rest of the refugees and the Remnant.

Bernard bellowed the battle cry of the dwarves. "For love, light and country." He was the first to charge, Gafney and Ginzer responded, and the three led the assault with their axes.

One of the warriors slammed into Cyle, sending him reeling backward into the dirt. The ground around him was spinning out of control as he tried to shake away the dizziness. His attacker wasted no time. Seeing the opportunity, he bore down upon Cyle with blade ready to deliver the death strike. An arrow pierced attacker's neck, and the man fell on top of Cyle, knocking the breath from his lungs. Gafney dragged the fallen warrior off of the young Gap Warrior and flung him aside. Then he pointed to the wall, and Cyle saw Choppa waving with his crossbow in hand.

Drishk raged at what he was seeing. They were losing the contest, and it was the first time he realized his own misjudgment by underestimating the power of the giants. In addition, with the added refugees who had joined them, they could not prevail in this contest without a better plan and greater numbers. Their blades had little effect on the stone-like skin of the giants. It would take a force more powerful than a blade to bring them down. Drishk hated to ask for help. It would be seen as a sign of weakness, and it would mean a demotion in rank. But he felt he had no other option. He gave the command to his rider to return to Abbodar and bring back reinforcements. When he gave the order to withdraw the troops, he had agonized over the decision especially when only thirty of the two hundred sent out had returned. He had considered sending in the few Ravens that were in his charge, but then he realized that it would be better to hold them back until he had the troops and resources he needed to make a successful assault.

Cheers erupted along the ramparts and throughout the temple yard when the enemy took to flight. It was their moment, and they had won the first round. Gerrid looked down from the wall in amazement at their victory. Miraculously, all had survived in the skirmish, thanks to the giants. But some had been wounded and they would need the attention of the healers.

"Take the wounded for care and stand ready," ordered Gerrid. "They will be back, and we must be ready." Something stirred inside the Prophet as he paused to look over his troops. He saw men and women who had lived their whole lives cowering under the tyranny of an oppressive yoke of slavery and poverty. They had in every way come to think of themselves as powerless victims. By coming to this place, they had risked everything with little hope of surviving, and they had done more than survive today's battle. They had overcome.

Gerrid knew that the worst was yet to come, and that they would most likely not withstand the next assault, but that did not repress the vision that was unfolding before his eyes. Looking out at the refugees below him in the courtyard, they began to transform from lowly victims to powerful warriors outfitted in glistening armor, standing fearless in the face of battle. He spoke the words filling his mind and heart. "Listen to me and hear well my words, for I have seen who you are today." The prophet paused until he had everyone's attention. "You came here as victims of a dark and oppressive power in hopes of escaping its tyranny. Today you fought to survive, and you did survive. For that, we are grateful, but today is a new beginning. It is not enough just to survive. We must overcome. You are no longer victims. You are overcomers. You are no longer refugees fleeing for your life. You are warriors, and you must fight to conquer, not just to survive."

All eyes were on Gerrid now, and there was complete silence following his words. They had heard him. Now they were soaking up the meaning of what he was saying. Some were struggling to fully comprehend the full impact of it all, but most of them felt the power of the Prophet's words taking hold and capturing their hearts.

Gerrid spoke into the silence, "You are no longer slaves you are conquerors. The next time you fight, fight to conquer and send the enemy to flight."

The prophet looked skyward, and everyone else did the same. High above, an eagle carried by the thermal winds soared against the morning sky. The sound of flute music filled the air.

By late morning, all was quiet, and there had been no sign of retaliation from the enemy. Another one hundred refugees entered the camp. With the enemy's numbers depleted, it was not difficult for them to sneak past and gain a clear path to the temple gate.

When Patti entered the main gate with a small group of new arrivals, Bernard recognized her from the night they had spent at Bittles Tavern. The old dwarf approached her from across the yard and greeted her. "Hello, Patti. What brings you to our little fortress?"

"Well, I was hungry, and I heard ye had a giant among ye that cooks a wonderful spit of game."

"Ho, Princess, you don't need to worry. I'll not be cooking any meals in the near future, but we could use some help in the kitchen. The food has been horrendous."

"I'll help as long as ye promise not to come in and offer assistance with the meal."

"I can't make any promises, but I don't expect I will have the time to prepare any meals as long as I'm needed out here. Someone needs to protect you."

Patti grew silent and gazed up at Bernard as a tear formed in the corner of her eye. Bernard froze. He wasn't sure how to respond to her show of emotion, and then she hugged the dwarf and buried her head in his chest. He could feel the warmth of her tears against his chest.

"It's okay, Patti. You are here now, and we will give a strong fight to protect you and the others. We will find a way."

Patti just squeezed the dwarf tighter while he awkwardly rubbed her back to offer comfort.

Midafternoon arrived without incident. Dallien, along with Blades and his men, had been out scouting the enemy camp and had returned with the report that reinforcements from Abbodar were arriving to join the enemy encampment. The scouts were almost certain that there would not be another attack before their depleted numbers had time to be replenished, and that could be as late as tomorrow or the next day. By nightfall everyone had eaten, and many had gone to sleep, having been exhausted from the day's battle. Gerrid climbed the stairs to the top of the tower, weary from the events of recent days. He wanted to be completely at peace and trust that his God was leading him, that a way of deliverance would open up to him, but he could not see it no matter how hard he tried. The waiting was draining his energy and faith. Lena had told him to put his trust in the Ancient of Days. She seemed strong in her ability to trust what she was suggesting, but the enemy was increasing in number beyond their walls. Winning the battle earlier simply meant a greater force to be reckoned with the next time around.

"Please," whispered Gerrid, gazing up at the stars, "show me how it will be done. What do you want me to do? I need a plan or some kind of direction."

Silence.

The Prophet sighed, aware of the exhaustion bearing down on him. As his eyes grew heavy, he could no longer hold them open. Making his way to the bed, he plopped his tired frame down and lay back to stare at the ceiling. Darkness closed in, and the peace he yearned for found him in sleep.

Something in the darkness of his mind stirred and shifted. Gerrid thought he might have been sleeping for several hours, but he didn't know for sure. He knew he was in that half-state between sleep and waking and was not ready to awaken. His body was still spent, and the aching in his muscles seeped through the wall of unconscious sleep. He moaned, an unsettling feeling washed through him, and the thought hit him. Get up. His senses sharpened, and he opened his eyes and saw the moonlight shining through the big stone window.

Raising his head slightly, he felt a rush of fear over take him. His body froze as his eyes began to dart around the dimly-lit room. Someone or something was in there with him. No, he told himself. It was just his imagination, but he continued to scan the room, unconvinced it was nothing more than shadows playing tricks on him. The uneasiness intensified when he noticed a slight movement beyond the light across the room. Maybe it was his eyes playing ticks. No, there was something lurking in the shadows watching him. His heart pounded faster, remembering that both his swords were several steps away leaning against the wall. There was a lot of ground to cover to lay hold on one of them. The shadowed form moved again, removing any remaining doubt that something was there.

Again, Gerrid measured the distance between him and his two swords—the one given by Graybeard and his battle sword. He feared he could not reach them in time. But he felt he had no other option, so he took a measured breath and sprang from his bed to gain purchase on one of the blades. Imagining a rush from behind closing in on him, Gerrid made an instinctual move that came from years of battle experience. Right before reaching his weapons, he pivoted and rolled to the right, then came to his feet to face his assailant. Standing before him was a figure holding two short swords clothed in a black assassin's robe with a headscarf covering the face. The eyes were shrouded by shadows, peering out between two slits.

Graybeard's sword was closest to him, and his battle sword

was on the other side of the room even farther out of reach. The assassin saw him looking and stepped between him and the nearest sword to block his path. He considered yelling for help, but his instincts urged him to wait. Both of them stood frozen in time, peering at one another through darkness. The hesitation on his killer's part struck the Prophet as odd, but he had no time to analyze only to react. Grabbing the water jug on the floor, he threw it at his assailant who ducked as it soared out the window. This gave Gerrid the flicker of time he needed to grab a blanket from his bedding and spray it outward, striking the assassin in the head hard enough to dislodge the scarf that concealed his identity.

Gerrid's heart sank when he saw who it was beneath the disguise.

Bryann.

She had been sent to kill him, and he realized that it was she who had been sent to assassinate the king the night he first met her after his release from prison. Now he knew why she was out on the streets that night in Abbodar.

The look in Gerrid's eyes disclosed the deep sadness held within his heart. Bryann averted her gaze in an attempt to avoid that unmistakable look on his face. She blinked to clear her watery eyes, and Gerrid could hear the anger in her voice when she whispered, "This is who I am. I know no other way."

The moment was gone. She struck out, lighting fast, but he surprised her and rolled beneath her blades, crashing into her knees and sending her to the floor. Close enough now, he grabbed the sword of Kem Felnar while Bryann sprang from the ground into an attack stance. She was upon him instantly, slashing death strikes with her two blades.

The Prophet defended himself by deflecting each blow, but he felt his heart weakening. How could this be happening? He knew he cared for her, and he thought her feelings for him were genuine. Had he misjudged the whole thing? Gerrid drove at Bryann with aggressive strikes, and she retreated backward, feeling the skill and power within his attack.

"This will not be as easy as you thought now that I am awake." To his surprise, Gerrid felt anger rising inside. "I will be a little harder to kill now that I am not sleeping helplessly," said the Prophet through gritted teeth. Then he unleashed a flurry of fresh strikes, driving her farther backward. A look of fear and surprise registered in her eyes.

He halted his attack long enough for Bryann to catch her composure. She replied, "What kind of a person do you think I am? Do you really think that I would have killed you while you slept?"

"Asleep or awake, it's all the same to me. At least if I had been sleeping, it would have spared me the heartache that bears upon me now. I have never known a person who would kill someone who loves them."

Shock registered in her eyes as she fought to reply, but the words were stuck in her throat. No matter how hard she tried, she could not find them to speak. A merging of grief and rage threatened to consume her, and she felt the overwhelming urge to throw up. "I am unlovable." The words barely escaped her lips. "I tried to tell you that once." The second part sounded angry.

"Believing a lie does not make it true. It only feels true."

"I have taken life without just cause and without remorse. Even you must agree that there is no absolution for one who has committed such atrocities as I have. Now I am certain that you are a fool because only a fool would fall in love with an accursed person like me."

"You are the fool, Bryann, because I forgive you. Even if your blade takes my life tonight, I want you to know that I forgive you for that too." Gerrid paused and looked her in the eyes, and she quickly averted her gaze. She would not make that mistake again. "Look at me," insisted the Prophet.

"No. I will not."

"If I die at your hand, I will die loving you still."

Bryann screamed, clenching her swords as she launched herself at Gerrid with her deadly blades, desperately striking out as if she could kill the love he had for her. Gerrid swayed backward, took two retreating steps, and blocked the blows as they came. Then he did something he was not expecting to do. He reacted the way he had in countless battles before this one, and without thought or reason, his blade deflected and sliced out, reflexively slashing through Bryann's chest. It was then that she finally looked him in the eyes, and he saw it for the first time. She loved him too. He dropped his sword and rushed to hold her one last time in his arms.

Her lifeless form fell limply into his grasp.

"My love," he whispered in her ear, and with tears flowing, he felt his heart exploding with unspeakable pain.

"What have I done?"

CHAPTER 39

Gerrid saw something move in the doorway, Sera and Packer standing side by side, and he noticed that the little elf girl had tears flowing down her face. Packer stood next to her, staring blankly. The prophet looked back at Bryann's lifeless form and saw that her breathing had stopped. Reaching out, he touched her cold cheek as his tears dropped onto her face, causing rivulets of water to run down her cheeks. He could not bear to look down to see the death wound he had left in her chest.

There was more commotion at the door as others gathered. Lena pressed through with Pamela close behind her. She was the first to speak. "Stand back," she ordered. "It is her time of reckoning. Do not touch her."

Gerrid froze, not wanting to let go of her.

"Let go of her," warned Lena. "There is nothing more you can do now except leave her to her fate." She gently but firmly pulled Gerrid back, and he began to sob.

The past came flooding in without any defense holding it back, and the truth that came with it brought a torrent of agonizing shame. For the first time in her life, the wall of denial was shattered, and every evil act, no matter how heinous or seemingly insignificant, flooded her mind. She could not turn it away no matter how hard she tried. She lost all sense of who she was or why she was in this place, and that was terrifying. It took every ounce of strength to hold onto her sanity. Kill me. End this. I deserve to die. She pleaded in her mind.

There is a choice before you, said a voice beyond description.

Don't listen to that, said a second shaming voice. You don't deserve hope. You have done nothing but rob others of it.

More images flowed before Bryann's mind; each filled with reminders of a life lived in ruin. All that she had shoved aside could no longer be pushed back. The darkness of her heart was terrifying her. She trembled.

You can't have her.

Listen to me, said the voice beyond description. You get to choose, not shame.

He can't be trusted, said the shaming voice.

How can I have life? How can you offer it to me?

It has always been offered to you. This is the last time you will be offered the gift of freedom.

Nothing's free, hissed Shame.

Ignore it, and it will continue to condemn you. Send it away, and you will understand what you have been blind to all your life.

How do I send it away?

No. Don't send me away. Who will you be without me?

Who would I be without shame? The thought had never occurred to her before now. The idea that she could die never knowing who she truly was, both frightened and captivated her at the same time.

How do I send it away?

No! screamed Shame. You will be lost without me.

Tell it to leave, and it will go away. Once you have done that, you will not only be able to hear my words, you will be able to understand them.

Bryann drew in a deep breath and exhaled words barely above a whisper, Leave me now, and do not return to me.

Howling screams of tortured souls echoed off of the darkness swirling around her. Slowly they faded away as a soft light glowed far off in the distance.

What do you want from me? asked Bryann, feeling vulnerable.

What do you want from me? asked the indescribable voice.

I don't know. I don't even know who you are.

I am the one who has always been and always will be. Some call me the Ancient of Days, but I am known by many other names.

I know about you. From my aunt and the others who follow you.

It is not enough just to know about me. You must trust me to know me, then you will be free.

How can I trust you? You left me alone when I needed you most.

A memory unfolded before Bryann. She was a little girl playing in the house, and her father had come home drunk. He beat her mother until she was unconscious. She tried to stop him, and he grabbed her and hauled her outside, threw her in the dirt and told her he hated her and her mother. He left and never returned. Bryann had become that little girl again with all the pain and shame piling up on her.

You come to me now, cried Bryann, but I needed you then. Where were you?

A torrent of tears flooded her eyes, and the darkness began to slowly melt away as if the answer to her question was trying to break through. She looked down and all about her was a field of daisies, bright and yellow as far as the eye could see.

I hate them, she screamed, and I hate you too.

The daisies began wilting from the farthest away to the ones nearest to where she stood. Bryann knew that she was watching her own death unfold before her eyes, and the darkness closed in around her along with a vast emptiness. She held back the urge to vomit at the wretched smell of decay brought on by the death of the flowers. Soon the whole field was brown and lifeless. She looked down at her feet, and there on the ground was one last daisy. Still alive and as bright as the midday sun, the daisy had a sweet fragrance, and it was the smell that triggered the memory she had not thought of since she was a child. It was a few days after her father had left for the last time. Still feeling the pain of her loss, she had taken a walk to the meadow and found that it was full of the yellow daisies she had grown to love so much. While sitting in the middle of the field crying with tears of abandonment and struggling to breathe her next breath, she thought, I'm on my own. I will always be on my own. Now it's up to me to take care of myself. The memory still held unspeakable heartache.

A thought emerged as a warmth and presence closed in around her. Your deepest heartache will become your greatest strength. Drops of moisture fell over her skin, washing away the pain. Somehow she knew they were tears, but they were not her own. They belonged to someone else, someone who loved her deeply—the Ancient of Days. Then she remembered something Gerrid had told her the day she left him at the tavern. There is a path you were made to follow. You just don't know it yet. I pray that someday you will find it. Because if you do, you will not only find love, you will find the path your heart has been longing for and was made to follow.

This must be the love Gerrid had spoken of. Even though it was completely alien to anything she had felt or experienced before, she knew it was real, and it was healing her ravaged heart. Glancing toward her feet, she saw one last daisy still alive, and she knelt down to pick it from the ground. She hesitated to pull it from the life-giving soil that held it firmly. Her tears, still flowing, began to wash the soil at its base, and instantly it grew to twice its size.

You see, child, the sorrow of your past can bring life instead of death, whispered a gentle voice that sounded like that of a lady, but she couldn't be sure.

Before now, she would not have believed it was possible that life could come from death, but now she understood that death would produce death when you feared it and when you allowed the fear to control you. No one in this world could have ever loved her the way she was experiencing love at this moment, not even her father or her mother. The rage she had carried for herself and everyone else and all she had ever known was melting away as something brand new filled her heart. A desire to love and bring life to others mysteriously surged and swelled up from somewhere deep inside.

What is this? she wondered. So different and so new was the feeling that it confused her at first, and her impulse was to resist it. But that resistance quickly turned to longing, and she knew she had to surrender her heart to its summoning if she was ever to be free. She let go and trusted for the first time in her life, and when she did, she knew she would never be the same again.

When she regained consciousness, the first thing she saw was Gerrid's tear-filled eyes gazing down at her with an unmistakable look of shock on his face. Without hesitation she reached out and wrapped her arms around his neck, and he returned the embrace. She was the first to speak. "You were right. There is another path. Can you ever forgive me?"

Gerrid gathered Bryann deeply into his embrace, and with his own tears flowed, he felt the warmth of her tears on his chest. "You were forgiven before you asked," he said, smiling. Then he pulled away and looked down at her, noticing the wound on her chest was gone. He then glanced at the sword on the ground beside him. *What kind of weapon is this that delivers men and women from the darkness?*

CHAPTER 40

"What if we are summoned to the void to defend against a breach?" asked Cyle. "Who will fight the demon-infested ones?"

"We won't be," answered Gafney. "It is too late for that. The void has come to us through the Ravens, and it is up to us to send them back there."

"There are too many of them and not enough of us," said Cyle nervously.

"Don't forget your grandmother," said Tryska. "She has been leading the Remnant in intercession all night and will continue throughout the day."

Hutch sat quietly, twisting his club into the dirt while he listened intently to Gafney, Cyle and Tryska discuss the coming day's battle as they stood near the entrance of the temple yard. Next to the giant stood Ginzer, Bernard and Choppa.

"When the Ravens attack, we need to stay close to each other," warned Gafney. "We will be outnumbered, and they will seek to destroy us first. If we fall, it is over."

Dallien said, "We can have some of the archers give protective cover from the wall. The Ravens may be infested, but they are still of flesh and blood, and flesh still bleeds."

"A good call," said Gafney.

"It is how we hunt the larger wild boars. One group goes into the canyon while the other takes the higher ground to protect in case of attack."

"The Ravens will be well armored," said Cyle. "The aim of the archers will need to be straight and sure. We will be close to your shots."

"We have men who can make those shots. I will warn them to use caution."

"They gather to advance," Choppa yelled from the wall.

The Stone Giants readied themselves near the front gate. Lena and several of the Remnant huddled in the top of the south tower where they could see the battle as they interceded. Archers readied their bows on the wall, and the rest of the refugees stood armed in the yard, waiting to defend against those who breached the giants at the entrance. Earlier that day Packer, Sera and several of the refugees collected the scattered stones from the previous day and brought them back into the yard for the next battle. Bernard and Ginzer took five stone giants, five archers and thirty fighters each and divided into two groups to set up flanking positions outside the walls in the cover of the trees adjacent to the battlefield.

The first column of marching warriors appeared on the rise at the base of the hill below. They looked to be around five hundred. Behind them were more hidden by the treeline, so it was difficult to get a good count. Every heart upon the wall pounded at the sight of the advancing soldiers as they came to an abrupt halt a thousand paces from the temple. The banners of Abbodar bristled in the morning wind as a lone soldier stepped out from the column a few paces and stopped. "It is your last chance to surrender to the will of the new king. If you resist his authority, this place will become your graveyard," announced the lone warrior.

All was silent except for the sound of the wind flapping the banners and the dust swirling across the ground that separated the opposing forces. "Tell the king we reject his authority and all that he stands for," shouted the Prophet from atop the wall. Bryann was standing next to him, and she grabbed hold of his hand as her heart stirred with fear and excitement. As she looked up at him, the thought occurred to her that her newfound life and love for this man could be short-lived in light of the overwhelming odds they were facing. That's okay, she thought. It will be the best day of my life, and I will live it protecting life instead of taking it.

"As you wish," responded the soldier. Then he nodded to his left.

Another man in the middle of the column signaled by waving a black banner emblazoned with a gold sword upon it, and then a primal roar of howls and screams erupted skyward from the troops, sending shivers through the defending refugees. Many wondered if they had made the right decision in joining the Remnant. The first row bolted toward the wall and the entryway. Three stone giants stood blocking their route through the gates with five more right behind them. Arrows and rocks shot into the air, spraying down upon the advancing forces and bringing several staggering to the ground. Packer's insistence of having the Stone Giants fashion heavier arrowheads to penetrate the enemy's armor was proving effective. Ladders were hoisted and slammed against the walls with warriors ascending them as more arrows sprayed down at them. Those that reached the top were met with the deadly edges of swords, spears and axes. Gafney moved in a raw and unfettered display of quickness and power, striking with Demon Slayer and sending the climbing attackers back to the ground below. Next to him was Cyle with his staff spinning and hammering the enemy as they crested the ramparts, and Tryska fought next to him with her two short swords spinning in a rhythmic dance of death, blocking and striking out at her attackers.

Dallien, with Blades and the street hounds, fought on the other side of the entryway, joined by several refugees and the Remnant. They were struggling to hold the wall from a breach. When Hutch saw them faltering, he climbed the rampart and slammed into the surging tide, pounding back with his club before they could press through into the courtyard below. With each of Hutch's sweeping blows, they grunted painfully as his club sent their bodies flying back several feet into the air before falling to the earth below. At the front entrance, the Stone Giants were holding strong, pushing back each wave with their powerful strikes. Enemy blades sporadically penetrated their defenses, causing only superficial damage to their stone-like skin.

From atop the wall, Gerrid anxiously scanned the battlefield for the Ravens. He knew at some point they would appear, but for some unknown reason, they had chosen to remain missing from the campaign. With still no sign of the Black or Red ones, he anxiously wondered why. Even with the aid of the Gap Warriors, who were greatly outnumbered by the Ravens, the warriors were primarily here to face the Ravens because of the dark power that infested them, and he wished there were more of the defenders. He glanced up at the window in the tower where Lena gathered with a small number of the Remnant who were interceding on their behalf. Everywhere the Prophet looked, there were walls of impossibility closing in, but something new was rising in Gerrid's heart, a kind of defiance that ignored the logic of the overwhelming odds mounted against them. He recalled the time he commanded the Talinor army and they overcame the massive forces of the Boogaran horde. At that battle he had little to no hope of victory until the very end, but they still overcame.

This time he was different. This time he had found the faith to put his trust in the Ancient of Days. The pain and resentment for the two years of suffering he had endured in prison had faded and had been replaced by a deeper knowledge and understanding of his own suffering. This caused him to gain a depth of compassion for the Remnant and the refugees who had suffered under the savage reign of this evil kingdom. He had realized that the compassion he had for these people had been reignited in a place that had been meant to break him. What was intended for his destruction had made him stronger. Not only had his suffering given him a greater capacity for compassion, it was that same compassion that was driving his intense defiance against this enemy that would seek to enslave innocent lives.

"Send the others," yelled Gafney, drawing Gerrid back to the moment.

He nodded and gave the signal to Bernard and Ginzer to attack from the flank. When the two dwarves broke into the open with the Stone Giants in their company and several refugees charging with them, it sent a wave of confusion into the Abbodar ranks. Bernard and Ginzer saw what was happening and hastened their charges into the fray to take advantage of the confusion. The attackers on the field below appeared to be faltering, and once again, it looked as if the refugees would turn them back. Something stirred at the back of the faltering ranks, a muffled howling sound. It could not be the deadly wind of the howls because they were too high above the lowlands.

Scavs.

Their growls grew clearer now, and Gerrid could see the black four-legged monsters, maybe twenty of them, knocking aside the Abbodar warriors in a frenzied rush to the gate.

Gerrid turned to Bryann. "Stay here and watch the wall. I'm going down."

Bryann nodded, and Gerrid disappeared over the edge.

Gafney, Cyle and Tryska arrived before Gerrid to meet the charge. The scavs reached some of the refugee fighters first and clamped onto them, ripping at them with their razor sharp jaws, then tossing them aside. Arrows flew into them with no effect. Gafney yelled up at the archers, "Save your arrows." Then he turned and sliced through one of the beasts, sending a shower of sparks and flame outward.

More sparks and flames erupted as the Gap Warriors attacked the demonic creatures. Cyle's staff and Tryska's blades delivered deadly strikes as the power of the ages flowed through their weapons. Hutch joined them with his club, pounding the creatures into the air and causing some to explode before their carcasses fell to the earth. Gerrid fought nearby, desperately trying to protect the refugees, but it was a losing battle. The scavs were pressing them backward toward the opening. The stone giants struggled to hold the gate, but the scavs kept coming. Gerrid lost count of their number, and for the first time in the conflict, it seemed the tide was turning against them.

Cyle glanced to his left where scavs surrounded Dallien and Blades. He ran in their direction, knowing they would not make it without the help of the power he wielded in his staff. A warrior crashed into him, knocking him to the ground. Slightly dazed, he shuffled back to his feet. The time he lost may have cost the two lives he sought to protect. Focusing on their desperate plight, he ran toward them. His stomach churned when he realized he would be too late. From the other side of the two, Gerrid was running with the same purpose of saving his friend, Dallien, but he too would not make it in time. Despair raged in Cyle as he knocked aside another warrior with his staff. Four scavs dove toward the two, and in the same moment, Cyle heard the music of the Tyrska's flute. The hovering scavs erupted and jolted backward, the air suddenly rippling with heat and light. A giant creature of fur and fangs materialized in the midst of the scavs. Cyle recognized Keesha instantly as she lifted her muzzle to the sky and rent the air with her war howl. At first sight, Dallien and Blades thought she was there to kill them until she grabbed the nearest scav by the neck with her massive jaws. The creature screamed in terror as she shook it and flung it through the air. The body bowled over two of the enemy warriors, then she seized a second with the same result. Cyle and Gerrid brought their weapons to bear on the other two scavs, and with Keesha's help, dispatched them in short order.

"Thank you, my friend," yelled Blades.

"Where are your men?" asked Cyle.

"Two have fallen, and I was separated from the others at the beginning of the charge."

Gerrid observed a slowing in their enemy's advance. Some of them had come to a complete halt and were looking back behind them in the direction they had come.

It could only mean one thing, thought Gerrid. Another wave of warriors or something even worse...

CHAPTER 41

"It would be foolish to send in the Ravens now," hissed the warlock as he paced back and forth in his war tent.

Haggron had never seen his master so visibly anxious. "The Ravens hunger to fight, and they grow tired of waiting to avenge the humiliation by the warrior who killed the two Ravens in the arena," said Haggron. "Even they have a limit to their patience."

"These Stone Giants have proven to be a bigger problem than I had anticipated, and I am not convinced that the Ravens will be able to overcome them without some help." Relnik paused, put his hands on his hips and stared out the opening in the war tent. "I need you to be patient with the plan we discussed and hold your men back until I give the order. Your men will have their chance, but they must be patient a little while longer. Once the Stone Giants have been dealt with, you can unleash them."

Things had come to a standstill in the fighting with most of the Abbodar Warriors pulling back toward the edge of the battlefield. The refugees and the giants showed signs of fatigue, and many were fighting wounded. Several refugees had fallen in the last wave, and one of the Stone Giants had fallen while three others were unable to fight on because of their wounds. Gerrid knew his fighters were spent, and the thought of fighting through the rest of the day brought a wave of exhaustion down upon his shoulders. It was quickly swept aside when he saw Bryann on the wall. That one glance of her brought a fresh spark of hope, but that was quickly dashed when he saw the others on the wall pointing and yelling. A rumbling sound lifted from the distance. At first he thought it sounded like the howls, but the winds did not reach this far up into the hills.

Gerrid ran to the wall, and by the time he had reached Bryann's side, he could see clearly what they were looking at. His heart sank into his stomach. He glanced at Bryann, and she could see the pain in his eyes. She reached out and took his hand into hers and squeezed it tightly.

"Gargenmalls," whispered Gerrid.

He saw at least twenty, maybe more of the massive monsters cresting the rise as dust stirred beneath their pounding feet. The enemy lines quickly parted before them to give them passage through their ranks. The rumble they heard was the pounding of drums sounding a cadence that the creatures marched in step with.

As they drew closer, Gerrid saw something else that they could not have expected. The giant beasts were wearing armor of roughly hewn metal that covered their chests and helmets protecting their heads. This was why Drok Relnik had held the Ravens back. He knew that the Gargenmalls would be powerful enough to stop the Stone Giants, especially now that they were exhausted from battle.

Gerrid looked down at Hutch who was standing near the opening in the wall. He called down to him, "Too many."

Hutch looked toward the approaching Gargenmalls, then he looked back up at Gerrid on the wall. He could feel the power beneath his club vibrating in response to the advance of the hideous creatures forged of the dark magic. The giant knew that the Stone Giants alone would be no match for them. Then he noticed them at his side—Tryska, Cyle, Gafney and Keesha stood with weapons blazing in their palms.

Boulder pressed in close to Hutch. "I am with you, friend."

"I fear the malls will be too much for the clan," said Hutch. "You have done enough already, and your wounds are many. Stay here with the others and defend the gate."

"It has already been decided," said Boulder with the giants already gathering around Hutch. "We'll be fighting with you against the giant demons."

Hutch put his hand on Boulder's shoulder. "Together then."

"Don't you know, Brother," said Boulder, "we are no longer cursed. Let the blessing carry us into battle."

Hutch embraced Boulder, two stones grating together.

Gerrid called down from the wall, pointing toward the enemy line. "The Ravens are advancing behind the Gargenmalls. If the Stone Giants falter, they will rush in like a death flood." Then he climbed down from the wall with Bryann following, but before they could reach the Gap Warriors, Lena stepped into his path.

"I must go with them," said Gerrid as if he knew why Lena was there.

"Your place is here with the Remnant," said Lena. "You are their deliverer and protector."

"She's right," agreed Bryann. "They are going to need you back here."

Gerrid knew they were right when they said it, but it didn't make things any easier. He had always gone to the front with his men, and staying back at the wall was almost unbearable.

The Prophet felt someone grab his hand. It was Sera, and Packer was standing with her. She was looking up at him, and for the first time he saw fear in her eyes.

"We're going with you," charged Bernard, lifting his axe to the ready.

"Aye, we are," put in Ginzer, doing the same.

Gafney pressed back at them, "We need you two to stay back and hold the gate against those who break through."

Bernard proceeded to object.

"Come now, Cousin," said Ginzer. "Who else can hold this gate except us? Without the giants, they would not have a chance."

"Well then," Bernard nodded reluctantly.

"Pray for us, Grandmother," said Cyle as he moved to hug Lena.

The Intercessor responded, "May the power of the ages carried by the Spirit Wind deliver victory into your hands."

Gerrid surveyed their dwindling company of fighters.

Even with new refugees joining them every day, their numbers had been greatly depleted, and he guessed that almost half of their numbers had fallen, while another two hundred lie inside, too wounded to return to battle. He decided to send three hundred with the Gap Warriors to help hold off the enemy while the Gap Warriors and Stone Giants battled the Gargenmalls.

Dallien would not leave his friend, Gerrid, but Choppa would follow Cyle and Blades with the few men he had left to join him.

"Gentlemen," said Gafney as he addressed those going with him, "it's time to take the battle to them." Gafney paused, looking to the distant troops and trying to gather his next words. He wasn't one for giving speeches anymore than he was one for hearing them, but he knew by the look in their eyes that they were afraid. He needed to say something to take them onto the field. "Don't let the fear you feel shame you into retreat. We all feel some measure of fear; that is to be expected in moments like this. You have nothing more to prove here. You have already proven your mettle as warriors. If any of you wish to stay back and defend, no one would shame you for it. But if you go forward from here to this day's field of battle, do not second-guess your decision. Now is the time to conquer the fear inside. It will do you no favors once we enter the fray. If you are with us, then so be it. Stay if you wish, but no wavering from here on."

Gafney turned and began a slow run toward the approaching enemy. The others slowly fell in behind him. The ground between them and the Gargenmalls grew narrower. The closer they got to them they could see the claws protruding from their massive hands. Some of them carried crude clubs and hammers. With the aid of the dark magic, the creatures had evolved. Now they were able to use weapons.

Cyle looked beyond the monsters where the Black and Red Ravens took up the rear, and his stomach grew queasy. He thought he was going to throw up. What cowards that they should send the beasts first to do their dirty work. As he thought of the last time he battled one of them, he shuddered. He tried desperately to recall the lessons Mellidar had given him to prepare him for this battle, then he felt the scar on his head throb. Maybe that lesson was enough to remember for this day.

The ground vibrated with the bounding of the Gargenmalls as they marched in sync to the beating drums. By the time they reached the monsters, the sound was deafening. There was no hesitation between the two sides as Stone Giants collided with the massive creatures. It sounded like an earthquake splitting the mountains. The Stone Giants pounded against their armor with clubs and spears, and it proved difficult to get pass their defenses. One of the larger beasts grabbed a Stone Giant and sent her hurling through the air, bowling down two others. She rolled back to her feet and ran back at the beast in an attempt to find an opening for her spear. Cyle gave aid by running behind the beast and hammering his staff into its calf. Flames erupted and the creature howled in pain.

The Gargenmalls were pushing them back, pounding them relentlessly with their claws and weapons. The giants were quicker, but the Gargenmalls were stronger and, by sheer force, they were gaining ground. Gerrid could see from his vantage point that it wouldn't take long for them to push them back to the temple wall. Relnik's plan was working. The Stone Giants and the Gap Warriors could not stop their advance. Foot soldiers were breaking past the defenses and attacking the gate. Ginzer, Bernard and Dallien, along with a handful of refugees, desperately fought to hold them back.

"Take the children and elderly deep into the temple," yelled the Prophet to Packer and Sera.

They both climbed down the wall and began gathering the refugees.

An oppressive air hung over the room where Lena was interceding. More than fifty of the Remnant surrounded her, and she kept urging them to intercede. She could hear little Barrand crying next to her. The room was filled with the blue light of the shadow fairies dancing and flitting about, dropping thoughts of poison in their hearts.

"Why are you crying, little Barrand?" asked Lena.

"The lights are scaring me," said Barrand. "The blue lights are flashing and talking bad thoughts at me."

Then Lena could see the fairies and the distraction their lies were causing in the Remnant. They had almost completely stopped praying. Their whispers floated about the room like a poisonous chorus of voices. "You cannot win. All is lost. Prayer is not working. It will change nothing."

Lena looked through the window to the battlefield. The refugees were being pushed back at an alarming rate. If it continued, they would be here within the hour. She looked at the Remnant and challenged, "Listen to me, Intercessors." When Lena spoke those words a rush of chills cascaded over her body. Everything became clear in an instant. These were Intercessors before her. This was the reason Gerrid had been sent to deliver them back to Talinor, and that was why Drok Relnik was not going to give up until they were all destroyed. Next to the Gap Warriors, they were his greatest threat. Now she just had to convince them of their true identities.

"Listen to me, all of you," Lena's voice grew stern as she glanced from face to fear-filled face staring up at her. "There is a reason that you have tarried with me here today. Your hearts have led you well to this moment, to stand by my side and intercede with me. It is in the heat of the enemy's attack that we have the opportunity to discover our true identities." Lena waited until all eyes were upon her before she continued. "It is time to send the lying thoughts away. They only mean to rob you of your true purpose today."

"I am afraid," whimpered Barrand.

Pamela gathered the boy into her arms and comforted him. "She's right. Listen to her. We are afraid because we have submitted our hearts to the lies in our heads," Pamela challenged

SWORD OF DELIVERANCE

the group. "If we die today, we should not die cowering in fear. We should die fulfilling our destinies, defiantly battling as Intercessors."

"For too long you have listened to the lies of doubt. In doing so, you have lost your way and lived as slaves to fear, "warned Lena. "It is time to renounce the dark thoughts that enslave you and embrace your true identities as Intercessors."

"Go away," shouted Barrand as if he could see the shadow fairies. Instantly, something shifted in the atmosphere of the room.

"Leave us now," commanded Pamela.

"Yes. Leave us," said another as more joined in until all were in agreement against the dark lies.

Lena was the next to speak. "Now it is time to stand in agreement and renounce the evil that shrouds this battle and send it to flight." Lena looked at Pamela, "Lead us Intercessor." Pamela hesitated. "It's okay. I will guide you, and we will agree with you. Be bold, dear one."

Pamela felt warmth flowing over her and washing through every part of her being. Anger stirred from somewhere deep inside. At first it frightened her.

"What is this anger?" she asked Lena through quivering lips.

The Intercessor smiled. "It is the spirit of defiance rising up in you. Do not fear it. Let it flow."

Pamela took a deep breath and began her entreaty. "Today we say 'yes' to the Ancient of Days. We say 'yes' to the one who gives us life." The Remnant voiced agreement as Pamela continued. "We say 'yes' to victory over this present darkness, and we say 'no' to all who do not bow to the light." She could feel defiance rising from deep within, like a primal fire threatening to break out of control. "We stand together today and say 'no' to the weapons formed against us. Deliver us from the hand of the enemy who would seek to destroy us."

The void exploded with the energy of light colliding into darkness. A gathering of Guardians and Gap Warriors attacked a horde of shadow wraiths, driving them back into the void where their cries of anguish could be heard echoing throughout the dark abyss. As the warriors of light sealed the breach they set guard over the portal they had sent them into.

The Gap Warriors and the Stone Giants were losing ground against the armored Gargenmalls. Their size and numbers were taking a toll on the giants and draining them of what little energy they had left. Two of the monsters attacked Hutch, pounding at him, seeking to destroy him with their massive claws. Keesha appeared, biting and clamping onto the leg of one, trying to pull it away from Hutch, but the stone giant's energy was quickly waning. The larger of the two slammed into Hutch, knocking him backward, causing his head to hit the ground. Lights flashed above his eyes, and the world around him spun out of control. Gafney and Cyle leapt to his aid just in time to deflect the onslaught of blows and razor sharp talons aimed at Hutch's midsection.

"We can't hold any longer," said Cyle to Gafney.

"We can't retreat either," replied the burly Gap Warrior.

"In case you haven't noticed," yelled Cyle, "we have been retreating almost from the beginning."

But Gafney did not hear Cyle's words over the sound of swirling wind filling his ears as a hail of arrows parted the air, striking the enemy warriors and cutting into the Gargenmalls They pierced their thick hides, igniting a wave of painful screams from their massive maws.

"Who is it?" asked Gafney, trying to determine the direction the arrows were coming from. Then he saw treeline nearest the mountains shaking, and the sound of war cries filled the air.

"Buntoc," said Cyle.

The mountain warriors came flooding out of the trees, shouting their war cries. Clothed in colorful feathers and face paint, they ran straight at the Gargenmalls. Out in front were

SWORD OF DELIVERANCE

Drew and his small band of hunters with Nolan and Bayson at his side. They were firing wave after wave of arrows at the beasts and the enemy warriors. The Buntoc warriors poured over the ground like an army of ants attacking an intruder. Ropes with weights attached to the end of them flew and wrapped around the monster's feet until they brought them crashing to ground. The Buntoc flung nets at the giant monsters while they were still on the ground and began spearing them.

Drew waved at Cyle after releasing another shaft. "It seems your God has a plan after all."

A surge of energy flowed through the Stone Giants and Gap Warriors with the arrival of the Buntoc. The Stone Giants and Gap Warriors worked in harmony to dispatch the remaining gargenmalls while several more enemy warriors were struck down in the process. Cyle watched in amazement at the unfolding drama, and he could see that just down the hill at least one hundred, maybe more, Red and Black Ravens were set to bring another wave. The Stone Giants were spent, and a number of them were wounded, but it was hard to tell from where he stood.

"I'm going down there," said Gerrid to Dallien. "Take my place, I'm going to call them back to the temple."

Bryann grabbed his hand, "I'm going with you."

Gerrid started to push back.

"No," Bryann put her hand over his mouth. "Your battle has become my battle. From now on, I will be by your side."

The young Prophet looked her in the eyes, and he knew instantly that she was not going to back down. He leaned in and kissed her on the forehead and said, "Everything in me wants to tie you up and leave you here, except for one small voice inside telling me that you are right."

By the time Gerrid and Bryann arrived at the battleground, the Gap Warriors and the Stone Giants were clustered in a group encircled by the Buntoc warriors who were poised to protect them.

"Who are they that they would risk their very lives for us?" asked the Prophet.

Drew pressed closer. "They are Buntoc, and I am one of them. They are here for me and for you."

Gerrid looked again at the sight of the tribe of warriors who stood surrounding them with weapons drawn ready to defend. "Me? Why me?"

"Because you are the one who the prophecies spoke of long ago," said Cyle. "It seems that many years ago, the prophet Graybeard visited these people and foretold of a warrior who would come bearing a weapon of deliverance that would bring them to freedom."

"It is as the eagle warrior has spoken," said Bayson, one of the Buntoc warriors. He and his brother Nolan stepped forward.

Nolan was the first to ask, pointing at Gerrid's sword strapped to his back, "Is this the weapon the prophet spoke of?"

"I believe it is," said Gerrid.

"How can one weapon deliver us from that?" Nolan pointed down the hill to the gathering of ravens. "We do not have the power or the numbers to stand against the Red and Black ones, and the Stone Giants are battered and have little fight left in them."

"But we will stand with you, if you need us," put in Bayson. "We are Buntoc, and we will honor the prophecy."

"You honor the One Faith by your words, but I cannot ask you to fight the Ravens. That is my fight and the Gap Warrior's fight, or as you call them, the Eagle Warriors. This is our time. We will make this stand."

"There are too many of them," countered Bayson, "and so few of you."

"True enough, my friend." Gerrid looked down the hill toward the enemy camp. Their time for talk was running out. "Even when the darkness gathers in overwhelming force, it cannot easily overcome even the smallest amount of light. It may appear that we fight alone, but I assure you, there are other unseen forces at work engaging in this conflict." Gerrid paused and looked at the wounded Stone Giants and the Buntoc warriors. Among them stood the remaining refugees who had survived to this point. "You have all done your part. We live today because of your valor, but now I need you to return to the temple and prepare our people for an exodus. Pack up supplies. We are going to leave this place soon."

"This is a hard order to follow," said Drew. "But we have come this far by trusting you, so we will do as you have commanded."

"And now it's time." Gerrid looked at Bayson and Nolan. "Gather all your people, the women and children hidden in the trees, and bring them to the temple to wait for us." Then he commanded the refugees and the Stone Giants to go with them.

After the others had departed, Gerrid, with Bryann by his side, gathered the Gap Warriors who remained with him—Gafney, Cyle, Hutch, Tryska and the silver wolf. "The Ravens will come alone to face us. They are a proud warrior race, and they hunger to fight you, to conquer you. They have heard the stories of your exploits by now, and it seems that one of your kind killed two of them in the arena. Then there were the others you killed days ago, all the more fueling their lust for revenge. They will wait no longer." The prophet glanced over their shoulders, and they looked back. "You see, even now they draw near. My only wish is that there were more of you."

"One more is better than none."

They all turned to see two men walk out from behind a fallen Gargenmall.

"Bixby," Tryska ran to greet the Gap Warrior with an embrace. Keesha followed the elf girl, wagging her tail and licking the warrior's face.

"Where have you been?" grumbled Gafney, showing a look of disgust on his face. "We could have used your sword."

"I accept your warm greeting, old friend," said Bixby, offering his hand to Gafney who brushed it aside. Instead, Gafney embraced his friend in a bear hug, lifting his feet off the ground before setting him firmly back to the earth. "It's good to see you too, old man." Bixby smiled and patted Gafney on the shoulder. "We would have been here sooner, but it's been slow going. After killing the two in the arena, they released us, but they never planned to let us get clear of the city. Relnik's assassins have been tracking us, so we had to move cautiously."

"So it was you we heard about who killed the two Ravens," said Cyle who was excited to see the Gap Warrior. "It's been a long time, and I can't think of anyone I am more glad to see right now." Cyle offered a hand followed by a hug.

"You've grown, young Gap Warrior."

Cyle smiled.

Bixby looked at the huge Stone Giant, Hutch. "I hope he's with us."

"He is," answered Cyle, "and he is also one of us."

"Good, very good." Bixby smiled.

"Why is he here?" asked Gafney, pointing at Vanus.

"He's okay," said Gerrid. "If he hadn't given the order to let us go, none of us would be here."

"And I was sent to defend him in the arena," said Bixby.

"I will do as you command," said Vanus, looking at Gerrid.

The prophet nodded, musing at the turn of events. He had never feared Vanus, but he didn't fully trust him yet either.

"Is there anything you can tell us that will help us to face the infested ones?" asked Tryska.

"There is something I discovered when I faced the two in the arena," put in Bixby. "There seemed to be fleeting moments of confusion whenever my blade struck theirs. I think the dark ones that infest them sense the presence of the power in our weapons, and it confuses them."

"I saw it as well when Cyle and I faced them," said Gafney. "I didn't know what to make of it, but it makes sense that the collision of the two forces would disorient them."

"Watch for it, and take advantage of it," said Bixby. "It

comes and goes, and it is brief, but it can be leveraged to our advantage."

Cyle felt a slight relief at the news. He was grateful for anything that would help give him an edge.

"They're here," warned Gafney as he looked down at his axe. "I can feel the vibration in my blade. Demon Slayer grows hungry."

CHAPTER 42

Every one of the Gap Warriors—Bixby, Tryska, Cyle, and Hutch—felt the power pulsing under the weapons they held in their palms, even Gerrid.

The Ravens walked past the dead carcasses of the fallen Gargenmalls and slowly formed a semicircle around the Defenders. The Red Raven leader took one step out and faced them. It was Haggron. Gerrid recognized him. He didn't seem to be in a hurry as he briefly stared at them before speaking. "You," he pointed at Bixby, "you are the one who fought in the arena defeating the Ravens."

Bixby said nothing and gave no sign of a response to the charge.

"It will be my personal pleasure to kill you myself," hissed Haggron. Then he shifted his gaze back to Gerrid. "I had considered unleashing all my charges on you at once, but that would be a shameful thing for a Raven. There would be no real contest in such an action on our part. I want the people of Abbodar to know that you were defeated by our skill, not our numbers. There would be no honor in such a victory and no stories to tell."

As Haggron spoke his intentions, he could hear the dark spirit within him raging against his words. *Kill them all now, you fool. Stop playing games!* hissed the demon inside. Haggron's pride would not allow him to surrender to the will of the dark voice. It was that same pride that had initially drawn the Red Raven into an alliance with the demon that was now prodding him to ignore its wishes. Haggron pressed on with his plan. Holding up his right hand, he motioned to attack, and twenty Ravens responded by stepping forward. Ten Black on one side of Haggron and ten Red stood on the opposite side, pulling their weapons to the ready. They had been waiting for a long time for this moment of vengeance and a chance to face the legendary Gap Warriors.

Keesha growled deep in her throat as the fur on her back bristled and shimmered in the afternoon sunlight. The silver wolf snarled, baring her teeth. She appeared to be growing in size, and then she disappeared in a glimmer of light, followed by a vicious growl. In a flash, one of the Black Ravens flew backward, slamming into the ground. As if on signal, both sides struck out at one another.

Haggron wanted to charge Gerrid himself, but he would wait and let his men wear the Prophet down before putting himself in harm's way. The Red Raven commander motioned to the twenty who instantly responded with a charge of deadly intent, only to be intersected by Bixby and Tryska slicing out at the Ravens with several lightning-fast strikes that briefly put them on the defensive. The other Gap Warriors spread out to take the charge of the twenty. *Too many at once,* thought Cyle, trying to focus on the Red Raven that was attacking him. *Watch for the moment of disorientation.* He could not focus on one too closely when there were so many blades coming his way. Finally, after several defensive blocks, one of his strikes penetrated through a brief opening. When his staff hit the Raven's helmet, it exploded with sparks, sending him stumbling backward, only to have two more Ravens rush in to take his place. All this time he feared fighting one of them, and now he was fighting several at once. Two more pressed in on Cyle, and he could feel the presence of another behind him. In an explosion of power and light, the two in front of him disappeared in a cloud of dust. When it cleared, he saw Hutch holding his club, alive and dancing with sparks. The giant smiled, and then he turned and dealt a vicious blow at the nearest Raven.

Tryska spun into the air in a twirling death dance, deflecting the blades meant to destroy her. Each time one of her two swords connected, sparks ignited. She had killed one of them already and Gafney had killed a Red one and a Black one. Tryska noticed it first, and it sent a chill up her spine. As soon as one was destroyed, Haggron would send another from the outlying group of Ravens to replace them. The number would never drop below twenty, and the elf girl wondered if she would ever see her homeland again.

Ginzer and Bernard watched from the gate. "They won't last much longer," growled Bernard. "I say we join them."

"No, Cousin, don't go chasing after foolishness now. By the time we get there, we would be the only ones left to fight. We'll hold our position here with the others as ordered. We'll get our chance soon enough."

"I'm not a watcher, and I'm no good at waiting. But I'll do as you say, Cousin," huffed Bernard.

Drew appeared first from beneath the canopy of trees followed by the Buntoc warriors who had been sent back with him to join those at the temple.

"By Shadazar," yelled Bernard when he saw the Buntoc with Drew. "Look what the hunter has brought with him."

Then Bernard sensed movement behind him. Lena was leading the Remnant to the temple entrance, and next to her was Packer and Sera.

"My lady, shouldn't you be in the tower where it is safe?" cautioned Bernard.

"We've come to sing the song of the Prophet." Lena paused and looked at Sera's smiling face. She continued, "It is time, and we need you to get us close enough to be heard."

Bernard was going to push back at the request, then he paused and looked at Ginzer who shrugged his shoulders and whispered, "I think we should do as she says, Cousin. I don't see backing down in her eyes. Besides, it looks like you are going to get your wish after all."

Bernard found no peace in the notion of bringing the Remnant closer to the battlefield, and he found himself resisting.

"With or without you, brave dwarf?" said Lena calmly.

"We will escort you, my lady." Bernard looked reluctantly at Drew and the Buntoc. They were a strange sight to the two dwarves who had never seen anything like them before. "Bring twenty of your friends for protection, hunter. We may need their help."

Drew nodded toward Nolan and Bayson, the Buntoc chiefs who turned and began separating out twenty of their best warriors.

"I'll be going too," said a voice from the wall. It was Dallien.

"Well then, will anyone else be joining us?" huffed Bernard. "I wouldn't want anyone to feel left out."

"We will sing as we walk out," said Lena.

Sera started first and the rest followed her.

>"A weapon forged within the fires of
>faith long ago,
>And when he holds it in his hands,
>he will surely know…"

The Sword of Deliverance vibrated in Gerrid's palms as he struck out in a horizontal arc attempting to gain purchase of any one of the Ravens that surrounded him. Pictures flashed through his mind of the day Graybeard had given him the sword and the prophetic mantle that he could feel hanging from his shoulders. It seemed heavier to him now. Flashing blades assaulted him from every direction, and all he could do was offer a defense against the relentless wall of steel, which was closing in on him. He knew that his defense would not be enough. The Gap Warriors appeared briefly to push them back, giving him a brief respite, but then they would disappear again into the storm of battle.

To his left, he saw Gafney slammed into the dirt, dust sprayed outward, and the thought of losing the axe man sent a wave of dread washing over him. As quickly as he had fallen, Bixby and Cyle were next to him to protect, desperately trying to push back the blades of the Ravens. To his right was Hutch down on one knee, lashing out with his club, but his energy waning.

At first, when he heard the muffled sound above the clashing metal, he thought he was imagining it. But as it grew louder and clearer, he began to make out that it was someone singing. But how could that be out here on the battlefield? Singing? It made no sense. Some of the words to the song broke through to him, and he did not know if it was coming from inside his head or from beyond the clash of battle.

> "A weapon forged…" metal clashing…
> "long ago."
> "Freedom reigns within the light.
> There is no other way.
> Freedom reigns within the light,
> where he will lead the way."

The singing was clearly discernible now, and as the words of the song entered his ears, a flood of power gushed forth from the sword in his hands, flooding into his body in waves. For a brief moment, he was lost to the world around as he was engulfed in the presence of the Spirit Wind that filled him with peace and power.

Driven by the surge of fresh energy, Gerrid launched forward a renewed attack. The blade in his hands led him, and at the same time, he moved with a speed and grace unlike anything he had ever experienced before. Within seconds, three Black Ravens and two Red ones lay at his feet. The other Ravens were not phased by the deaths of their comrades. They saw it as an opportunity to move in and kill the Prophet with their own blades. The one whose blade brought the Prophet down would become the warrior of legend and fame a status to which few could ever even aspire.

Another Black one fell, then two Red ones faltered under the lighting-fast strikes of the sword of deliverance. The Prophet and blade had become one. Haggron looked on in amazement as the Prophet attacked with supernatural speed, slicing through his best fighters and sending them to the ground. The fallen Ravens writhed on the ground, and wailed through chilling screams of death as demons were released from their dead bodies.

"Enough toying with them," yelled the Raven commander as he turned to signal the remaining Ravens to unleash the full force of their might upon the Prophet and the Gap Warriors.

The Ravens responded with Haggron leading them. They rushed to close the distance between them and the small band of warriors that defied them. The Raven commander was almost upon them when he halted just steps away from Gerrid. The Prophet and the Gap Warriors saw the look of shock on the commander's face and turned to see what he was looking at.

The once fallen Ravens were slowly rising to their feet, while others remained crumpled and lifeless on the ground. The rising Black and Red Ravens were taking up their swords and attacking their own.

Both sides paused briefly, stunned by what they were seeing. A fresh surge of power pulsed through Gerrid's body as he realized what was happening. The Sword of Deliverance and the Prophet became one again as he flew forward into a fresh attack. With the Gap Warriors still battling at his side, he felt the blade leading him, almost taking over. He blocked oncoming strikes and countered with cuts that sent the enemy Ravens to the ground where they lay writhing. Demons screamed as they flew from their bodies, and for a brief time, they lay still. Some remained that way lifeless and lost to the darkness, but the ones who chose the light rose up and joined arms with the Defenders and the Prophet. Twenty Black and Red Ravens now fought with the Defenders in the battle for freedom, and their numbers were increasing as they continued to fall under the power of the blade in Gerrid's hands.

When the delivered Ravens reached thirty strong with mostly Red Ravens among them, the surge led by Haggron wavered. He would deny it later, but he feared the power of the swordsman who had been transformed before his eyes by a mysterious force of magic. Haggron ordered his men to move back and wait for reinforcements. His men offered no objections to his command.

Gerrid looked about and realized that in the heat of battle, they had been pushed back to the temple gates. Just beyond the walls the Remnant was still singing within the courtyard. He turned in the other direction where reinforcements gathered to advance from down the hill. He drew in a long breath and slowly exhaled. He was out of ideas, and he knew that Relnik was not going to give up until he had destroyed the Remnant. Deep down, the warlock knew that the Remnant were Intercessors. It explained why he was so determined to kill them.

"There is a way." Gerrid recognized the voice. Vanus stood before him. "Deep within the temple lies the mouth of a cave. It is a portal built by the original inhabitants of this place. I believe it was designed as a way of escape in the event of an attack. It is said that when the temple fell in day's past that some of the believers escaped by way of the portal. I believe the stories to be true, but I do not know where the passage will take you."

"I have seen the cave you speak of. It is guarded by a demon and his charges, and he has forbidden us to pass."

Vanus paused to look toward the battlefield and then back to Gerrid. "It has to be better odds than what awaits you here."

"We will never make it to the entrance," argued Gerrid. "They will catch us and cut us down before we reach the portal." Gerrid pointed toward the approaching warriors. "They and the remaining Ravens will be upon us before we can make it through to safety."

The delivered Ravens that had joined them in the battle moved in behind Vanus. Thirty of them, mostly Red ones, stood at his back.

"They want to stay behind and hold the entry. It will give you the time you need to escape."

"They will perish against such odds," protested Gerrid.

"They know that," said Vanus.

Gerrid looked confused. "Why would they surrender their own lives for us?"

"Because they have finally found life, and they know that their destiny is to die here today, so that you can go free."

"And what of you, Vanus? What will you do?"

"I will stay with them."

In a flash, so many things finally made sense to Gerrid. The time in prison, the connection to Vanus and even the torture that he had endured all had meaning. If it had not happened, this moment could not have happened. Vanus and the delivered Ravens would not be here to ensure their final exodus to freedom. Gerrid knew that Vanus was right. This was their destiny, and they would all die for the freedom of the Remnant and the others.

"What lies within the portal?" asked Gerrid.

"I do not know," answered Vanus, "but it is your only way out now. I suggest you take it and move quickly."

Gerrid looked at Dallien who was standing next to him, "We're going home, my friend." Dallien smiled and hugged his friend. "Did you hear that?" Gerrid lifted his voice to those standing in the courtyard. "We are going home."

The refugees cheered, and Dallien shouted, "Quickly then. Gather nothing and follow the Gap Warriors."

The courtyard began to empty. Gerrid turned to his former

enemy to face him one last time. He wanted to say something, but his heart failed to give him the words he thought he should speak.

"I spent much of my life seeking the power of magic, thinking I would be able to control it. Little did I know that when I met you, what I was looking for was right in front of me." Vanus smiled.

Gerrid looked down, feeling a mix of shame and humility.

"I have come to realize that the greatest magic in this life is the power that delivered me from the darkness in my own heart. Now there is a compassion for others that I do not understand, but I can't imagine life without it." Vanus paused and looked at the Ravens that had been transformed just as he had by the Sword of Deliverance. "There is only one thing left for us to do. We have decided to spend what life we have left in the hope of saving you and the Remnant."

Gerrid felt the tears forming at the corners of his eyes and noticed the same in the eyes of the king's son. "I will never forget you," whispered Gerrid.

"Nor I you, Prophet." Vanus reached out, and the two grasped arms in the traditional military handshake. "Now you must go, for they will soon be upon us."

Gerrid nodded and slowly turned toward the temple entrance where he saw Bryann waiting. Vanus and the remaining Ravens gathered one last time at the temple entrance to prepare for the assault. By the time Gerrid entered the temple door, the ringing sound of metal upon metal filled the air behind him. He grabbed Bryann's hand and pulled her behind him into the darkness of the Temple.

CHAPTER 43

The Gap Warriors had led the eight hundred surviving refugees, which included Stone Giants, Buntoc and the Remnant into the meeting room of the temple. Several of them were huddled down the passageway leading to the main hall. Gerrid and Bryann had to press their way through the crowded halls in order to reach the main room. When they entered the meeting hall, they found them all anxiously waiting in fear of the massive creature that guarded the cave opening.

Gerrid and Bryann made their way to the front where the Gap Warriors were waiting. The giant gatekeeper at the entrance stood clothed in dark armor that covered his whole body. In his right hand he held a mace, and in his other he held a cobalt sword. A helmet of silver and black covered his head where shadowed eyes peered through two dark slits.

"We need to move now if we are going to get out in time," warned Gerrid, anxiously looking toward the back of the hall. "The Ravens won't last long against the odds."

"Look! There are others." Cyle pointed toward the cavern opening. They could see dark figures standing in the shadows behind the gatekeeper.

"I say we charge them and open a way," said Gafney, pulling Demon Slayer from the sheath on his back. A look of confusion crossed his face as he peered at the axe in his hand.

The other Gap Warriors offered the same confused look at their own weapons. Tryska spoke first while she looked at her two blades, "I don't feel the power beneath my hands."

"What's happening here?" asked Bixby, equally bewildered.

"They are not here to keep us from passing," said Lena as she approached. "They are here to keep others from passing."

"How do you know this, Grandmother?" asked Cyle.

"Your weapons know it. Believe me. If the gatekeepers meant you harm, your weapons would sense the threat." Lena looked back at the giant warriors standing in the shadows of the cavern. "They know who you are and what power your weapons carry. They will let us pass, and they will stand against anyone who tries to follow."

"I've never heard of such a thing," said Gafney, twisting his axe nervously in his palms. "Still, they look like creatures of the dark to me. How do we know we can trust them?"

"Long ago, Kem Felnar passed this way carrying the Sword of Deliverance. This was the passage he took," assured Lena. "I have read the histories and it tells of such a journey. I did not realize this was the place until now."

Gafney was still battling doubt when he caught sight of movement near the entrance. It was Sera walking toward the opening in the portal, humming a tune and dragging Packer by the hand behind her. The two of them entered the cavern opening and disappeared into the shadows without incident.

"Well, my friend," Bixby looked at the burly Gap Warrior, "it seems the child will lead us."

Gafney grumbled something under his breath and then said, "I'm right behind you then."

It wasn't easy, but Gerrid was able to convince the eight hundred to follow him into the portal. Many faltered and wanted to turn back, but there was no retreat. The refugees huddled together, looking straight ahead as they passed by the giant warriors standing within the shadows. They could feel the giants peering down at them and hear their breathing as they caught glimpses of them moving out of the corners of their eyes. Once they had all passed deeper into the portal, a swirl of wind enveloped the whole party, and with it a new wave of fear. The place was dark and difficult to see ahead, but the ground they walked on was well-suited for travel. Children whimpered as they clung to the nearest legs.

"When will it end?" said a fearful voice.

"Ahead," someone cried out from the front of the

procession. "Look, there's a light."

Hope rose among their ranks as the light ahead grew brighter with each step they took until it filled the cavern about them. The eight hundred walked even faster as they drew near the opening. It had only been three days of travel since they had entered the portal, but they were weary beyond words. It had been a long ordeal from the time they were captured in the woods and taken back to the arena, then released by Vanus only to have to fight for their lives at the temple ruins. Precious loved ones had been lost. Many were left scarred with life long wounds, but they had made it.

The refugees shielded their eyes as they poured out into the light of day. Giant pine trees blanketed majestic mountains that surrounded a beautiful valley filled with lakes and streams that spread out before them. At the far end of the valley stood the walled city of Talinor. Gerrid could not believe his tear-filled eyes. He was home. He did not understand how the journey through the portal could have happened so quickly.

Cyle found his grandmother and hugged her close. "Talinor, Grandmother. It has never looked so beautiful."

"I have to agree with you, Grandson." Lena drew a deep breath of air into her lungs to capture the moment. "That's the breath of hope. Take it in and let it fill you."

Gerrid smiled at Bryann. She smiled back and pulled in closer as he drew her into his embrace. "This is your new home. What do you think?"

"It's beautiful," said Bryann, laying her head on his shoulder and sighing deeply. "Home is not a feeling I am familiar with. So far I like how it feels."

"All I know is that today we've come home, and I can think of nowhere I would rather be than here with you."

The End…

EPILOGUE

Gerrid and Bryann stood arm in arm looking out of the main tower of the walled city of Talinor to the hills and fields beyond. The shadows of the setting sun stretched slowly across the streets below. Singing voices were heard coming from a temple somewhere in the distance.

"You look nervous," said Bryann softly, then kissed Gerrid's cheek. "Are you?"

"About what?" asked Gerrid, smiling.

"You know what." She smiled back. "Just one more week, and we will be married."

"Oh, that. You have no need to worry. Marrying you only brings me joy."

"Then why are you so distant lately?" Bryann pulled Gerrid to face her. "You seem so far away?"

"Something is not right. I keep having dreams and visions that I do not understand." Gerrid scratched his beard. "They are trying to tell me something, but all I can tell you is that it is not good." The door to the chamber rattled with a knock, then opened to reveal Tryska, Cyle and Lena staring through fearful eyes. Lena was the first to speak. "We have received news from the homeland of the elves in the Crystal Mountains. The armies of Drok Relnik are marching that way as we speak. They have sent messengers to ask for our help."

"That explains the dreams I have been having," said the Prophet. "I keep seeing a bright light surrounded by darkness that is pressing in to overcome the light. I was confused because the darkness was pushing back the light." Gerrid paused, "Darkness isn't supposed to overcome light."

"My people are in trouble," said Tryska. "We must help them. Talinor must help them."

Gerrid knew the minute Tryska said the words that she was right, and it was his place as the Prophet to speak with the king regarding these matters. He looked at Bryann, took her hand in his and saw within her eyes the same dread he felt in his own heart. "I don't know what to say. We've only been home a few months. And what about our wedding."

Bryann put her hand on Gerrid's lips to quiet his next words. "Our wedding can wait. The elves cannot."

"Lena, can you meet with the intercessors and have them pray over this matter?" asked Gerrid.

"They already are," Lena answered.

"Then let us go and see what King Shandon has to say regarding this matter," offered Cyle.

"There is one more thing," said Lena, "Shandon has fallen ill, and the healers have no hope for him to live beyond the end of the week."

"Then let us make haste while we still can," urged Gerrid. "If I cannot convince the king to make a decree to help the elves before he passes, we will lose our best chance."

They turned to exit the chamber when suddenly bells started ringing from all over the city. "No," cried Tryska.

"It's too late," said Lena. "The king is gone."

Tryska backed slowly away from the rest of them until she was near the stairwell. "I must go now." The elf girl paused and stared at them with tears streaming down her face. "My people need me. I can wait no longer." Tryska turned and disappeared down the stairwell.

ABOUT THE AUTHOR

Doug grew up in the Central Valley of California where he discovered true adventure at the age of 16 when he found a living faith in God. His mother, Lena (the intercessor), and stepfather, Allan, nurtured the spirit of risk in their four children through tough love and spontaneous adventures. His interests include photography, love of the outdoors, traveling the world and hanging out with the characters in his books (most of whom he based on some of the amazing friends and family members in his life). Doug lives in Northern California with his wife and best friend, Shari, and his faithful German shepherd, Jasmine. He is an associate pastor as well as the director of the LifeBridge, an organization that combines counseling and inner-healing prayer to bring freedom to individuals struggling to find their destiny.

Douglas J. Tawlks

To inquire about inviting Doug to speak or train for your organization you can reach him at dtawlks@thelifebridge.org

For Information on the Life Bridge Mission you can visit them on the web at www.thelifebridge.org.

Don't forget to visit www.defendersofthebreach.com to share your own reflections on this book.

CPSIA information can be obtained
at www.ICGtesting.com
Printed in the USA
FSOW02n0700030916
24534FS